Monogamy

Monogamy

A Novel

Sue Miller

HARPER

An Imprint of HarperCollins*Publishers*

MONOGAMY. Copyright © 2020 by Sue Miller. All rights reserved. Printed in the United States of America. No part of this book may be used or reproduced in any manner whatsoever without written permission except in the case of brief quotations embodied in critical articles and reviews. For information, address HarperCollins Publishers, 195 Broadway, New York, NY 10007.

HarperCollins books may be purchased for educational, business, or sales promotional use. For information, please email the Special Markets Department at SPsales@harpercollins.com.

FIRST EDITION

Designed by Leah Carlson-Stanisic

Library of Congress Cataloging-in-Publication Data has been applied for.

ISBN 978-0-06-296965-1

20 21 22 23 24   LSC   10 9 8 7 6 5 4 3 2 1

For Doug,

mainstay

Acknowledgments

This book was, to my regret, a drawn-out project—it took six years to write. There were people who helped me through those years in one way or another, and I want to say thanks:

to Ben and Zoe Miller, for lifting my spirits without even knowing they were doing it,

to Shellburne Thurber, photographer extraordinaire, for telling me everything I needed to know—and about a twentieth of what she knows—about her art,

to Jill Kneerim and Maxine Groffsky, who had to tell me—and did it gently and generously—that I'd made a long false start to this material,

to my Walker Street friends—Laura Zigman, who knows a lot about How Things Work and was happy to share that,

and Joan Wickersham, for our talks over many afternoons made warm by the fire and her rare company,

to the Walshies, my second family,

to Michelle Huneven and Michele Souda and Lynne O'Hara, dear friends,

to Doug, who read it again and again as it grew and changed, without complaining, to Graham and Annie, who kept me interested for all those years,

to Suzanne Gluck, who took me on and changed everything,

and to HarperCollins and Terry Karten, my warm and judicious editor, who have welcomed me home.

Thank you all, for everything.

Monogamy

I

ANNIE HAD BEEN single for seven years when she met Graham. Whenever she thought about her first marriage, even long after it had ended, her primary emotion was a kind of shame. Shame that she could have been attracted to someone she felt so little for in the end. That she could have lived with him for so long.

She had excuses, if she'd wished to use them. Alan had been remarkably handsome in a preppy kind of way—tall, with a thatch of blond hair that flopped elegantly across his forehead. And she'd been young, so young and ignorant that she'd regarded him at first as a superior sort of person—he knew where he was going, he knew what he wanted. Annie was shakier on those issues. She had just graduated from college with not much sense of what came next.

Then there was the fact that *he* felt he was a superior person too. He had an easy contempt for the people around him—even for their friends. For a while, Annie had enjoyed sharing that careless contempt, unsure of herself socially as she was. How much fun! to come home from a party and sit around bad-mouthing all the people who'd been there. How sophisticated, how competent, it had made her feel. How adult—she was twenty-three.

Soon enough, though, as she might have foreseen, Alan's disdain turned to her. To her life, to her useless preoccupations—she was taking course after course in photography at the Museum School then. To her pitiful income (she did portraits of dogs for their owners, she photographed family reunions and graduations and birthday parties). To her self-delusions (she kept sending off photographs of local events to *The Phoenix*, to *The Boston Globe*, in hopes that she could get work as a stringer). It seemed to her a failure of character that she hadn't known this would be coming, that she should have imagined she'd be exempt from his general critique of the world.

It was when she was driving home with him from a party, a party he was speaking of in that familiar, slightly irritated tone, that it occurred to her that she simply didn't like him. Over the next few days she came, almost literally, to see him differently. Everything that had seemed admirable about him seemed just the opposite now. Small. Defensive. How could she ever have thought she loved him?

She didn't love him. She felt she never had.

Had she? Had she ever loved anyone? She felt herself to be without love—it seemed a kind of incapacity, a hollowness within her. This was the first time she had this thought so clearly, and also the first time she connected it—slowly, over some months of self-examination—to her photography. In her work, she felt, she was like him, like Alan. Cold, removed. Was it possible that this was why she'd chosen it?

In any case, she withdrew from Alan. He noticed this, finally. He wanted to talk about it, but she felt she had nothing she could say to him. How could you say, "I don't like you anymore"? "I don't think I ever loved you"?

She suggested they separate. He was surprised by this, which surprised her. She had assumed, as critical of her as he was, that he must have wanted out too. They had some weeks, then, of anguished back-and-forth. He pleaded. Annie felt awful. But even in the midst of his pleading, he couldn't resist offering more of his general critique of her, and that made it easier for her, the ending.

She left. She took none of the things that they'd accumulated together—the expensive wedding gifts from his kind, moneyed parents and their moneyed friends. The silver vegetable servers with covers, the napkin rings, the fish knives, the linen tablecloth and napkins—she left all of it behind, thinking of it as the price she was paying for her freedom. At the time, she thought there ought to be a price, she felt so guilty, so ashamed of this failure.

But she kept the camera his parents had given her when she'd begun to be interested in photography, an expensive Rolleiflex that she'd only slowly learned how to use. That, and her books, many of them purchased for courses in college, filled with markings and notes she'd taken in a neat, careful handwriting she could barely recognize as her own.

So she was free, at twenty-nine. Which should have made her feel liberated, expansive. And she did, in some ways. Except that for a long while after the divorce, she was uncomfortable around men. For at least a year, maybe longer, she read almost every gesture, every remark, as controlling, as dangerous for her.

But all of that was behind her by the time she met Graham. By then she had shed that sense of danger, she could enjoy men again. And some of that enjoyment was the pleasure of casual sex, something that wouldn't have been possible for her when she emerged from college, when she married at twenty-three. But postdivorce, in a world that had itself changed, Annie learned to sleep around. Happily. Enthusiastically. Fairly indiscriminately too, so that later she couldn't call up the names of some of the men she'd had sex with.

Sometimes, though, at the end of one of these casual relationships, she experienced a kind of melancholy that lingered for days or longer, a sense that, free as she felt she was, pleasurable as she felt that freedom to be, there was part of her that might be hoping for something else. Some deeper connection.

Even, perhaps, monogamy again.

She met Graham at a party he was throwing, a party to celebrate the opening of his bookstore.

He had been lucky in the weather the night of this party. After several rainy, gray weeks that had darkened the brick sidewalks of Cambridge and depressed everyone, the sky had brightened through the day, and at five o'clock it was a lovely late-spring evening. People were suddenly out everywhere on the streets, walking, enjoying the benign touch of the air, air that still carried the scent of the various trees budding and blooming and dropping their pale confetti all over town—hawthorns, crabapples, lilacs.

Annie had ambled slowly over from her attic apartment on Raymond Street with Jeff, someone she slept with from time to time. They'd spent several naked, sweaty hours before this in her bed.

The bookstore party had been an afterthought. He'd been invited—did she feel like going?

Why not? she said.

Why not was the way she had come to navigate the world then. The way she'd come to understand it in the years since the end of her marriage. There was always the next thing, the next possibility. The man, yes. Sex, yes. But also perhaps just something interesting. Something to look at. Something to do.

They'd showered together, she and Jeff, before they started their stroll down to the bookstore. Annie's long, dark hair was still damp when they left her apartment, though it had dried by the time they arrived.

She stepped inside ahead of Jeff, stepped into the store's heat and hubbub, into the heady odor of women's perfume and cigarette smoke and here and there the whiff of pot. There must have been sixty or seventy people already there, milling around, talking loudly to be heard over some barely audible music playing in the background. The crowd was mostly her age—thirties, forties.

From the moment she entered the room, Annie was excited. She felt sexed, maybe a bit predatory, intensely aware of her body in all its parts, of her thighs moving against each other, slick and slippery in spite of the shower.

When Jeff brought her over to Graham to introduce her, Annie recognized him. She'd seen him often around the square, sitting with an espresso at one of the little tables at Pamplona, or ducking into a bookstore, or drinking at Casablanca or The Blue Parrot or Cronin's—a large man, bearded, visibly energetic, even from a distance, with a mop of curly hair. He was almost always with other people—talking, laughing, gesturing expansively. One of those habitués, then, of whom there were perhaps three or four familiar to her. She had felt envious sometimes when she saw him—envious of his liveliness, of what looked like his easy sociability, of the active pleasure he seemed to take in the people around him.

He took her hand in both of his as she reached out to shake. "*What* is it?" he asked, leaning down to hear her over the noise.

"Annie," she shouted, looking up into his light eyes.

"Ah, Annie," he said. He smiled, and the eyes almost disappeared. "I'm glad you came." After perhaps a few seconds too long, he let go of her and turned a little so he could gesture at a long table set in the middle of the room, a table covered with wine bottles, with three or four towers of clear plastic cups, with multiple ashtrays, some half full, with baskets of bread and two huge wheels of Brie, one of them already ravaged. He said something—she thought maybe, "Have at it"—before he turned to greet someone else and she and Jeff moved away, obediently, to get some wine.

After the first few conversations they tried to have as a couple—leaning forward, shouting at people one or the other of them barely knew—they drifted apart. Annie looked at the spines of the books on the shelves, at the people standing in groups near her. She found herself talking briefly to someone she'd known years before in a photography class, but even as they were speaking, she could watch his eyes moving around the crowd, trying to spot someone perhaps more promising. She talked to several people she didn't know— quick, shouted exchanges. *How do you know Graham? Yes, what a perfect night for a party. Did we really need another bookstore in Harvard Square? Thank God the rain stopped, I thought I'd go mad.*

She went back over to the big table a few times to get more wine, one time lingering to eavesdrop on a long conversation between a man and a woman who clearly didn't know each other very well. She was asking him many, many questions about a trip he'd taken recently, and listening with what seemed like great interest to his account of how strange the people were, "sort of innocently *open*," he said. Annie was trying to figure out what country he was talking about, and then she realized it was not a country at all—it was Chicago, the city she'd grown up in. She laughed out loud, and a man standing near her stared at her for a moment. She looked back at him and smiled before she turned away.

And through all of this, she kept seeing Graham as he moved around the room, as he embraced people, men as well as women, as he threw his head back to laugh. His shirt was visibly damp with sweat by now, his skin slightly pinked from the heat. Or perhaps, she thought, just from excitement. When passersby stopped to look in the open doorway, trying to figure out what was happening in here, he would call out "Come in! come in!" He seemed so ingenuously happy and enthusiastic that she couldn't help smiling as she watched him. At one point he caught her glance and looked steadily, quizzically, at her for a moment before smiling back. As if he were really registering her, Annie thought. Maybe he'd noticed her too, here and there in the square, though that seemed unlikely, she was so much less noticeable a person—a *personage*—than he was, in his size, his ebullience.

Several times she spotted Jeff somewhere in the room too, once leaned over a woman, listening attentively. She recognized this posture. He'd assumed it with her too when he was picking her up at the party where they'd met. She watched him now for a few moments. It seemed to be working in this instance too—the woman gazed up at him, apparently dazzled. He was good at it.

At some point she went outside to cool off, standing among a small group of people gathered there. She fell into a conversation with a tall, middle-aged man who vaguely resembled Al Pacino. She couldn't place his accent. New York? He was a friend of Graham's, he said. His partner, in fact.

"Partner?" she asked. Was he gay then, Graham? She felt a quick jolt of disappointment.

"Yeah, you know, the guy who owns the bookstore with him."

"Oh!" she said.

Peter, he said his name was. Peter Aiello. They talked for a while, easily, a bit flirtatiously, and then he saw someone inside the store he needed to speak with and moved away.

Annie stayed outside, by herself. The air was fresh and cool, the first stars visible in the deepening blue of the sky. She found herself wishing she could just leave—leave, and walk home alone. It wouldn't bother Jeff for more than a few seconds at the most.

Or maybe it would.

This was the trouble with these ruleless relationships, she thought. You couldn't really know anything for certain about what the other person might be feeling. Might be entitled to feel.

She went back in and made her way slowly through the press of people to the table, to get herself another glass of wine. Just as she turned to face the room again, wine in hand, she bumped into someone. It was Graham. He was holding a glass of wine too. White wine, she was happy to note, as she felt it slosh abundantly across the front of her shirt, cool and shocking.

"Oh, shit!" he cried. He grabbed napkins from the table and began dabbing at her awkwardly, mostly at her bosom, such as it was, which was where the wine had landed. "Oh, I'm so fucking sorry."

"It's all right, really," Annie said. She was as much embarrassed by his response as by having caused him to spill the wine.

"It isn't," he said. "How could it be? Look at you!" He dabbed away, talking all the while, lost in apology. "What a klutz I am! I'm just so sorry!"

"Really, it was my fault," Annie kept saying, trying to stop him, trying to slow the hand that wielded the napkins.

"No, no. How could it be? It was me. Oh, God, I'm so sorry."

"Don't be. Please." But now he was insisting on his idiocy, saying what a clod he was, an asshole. Until, just to make him shut up, Annie raised her glass—red wine, unfortunately—and tossed it at him, at his shirt. A blue shirt, as it happened, a beautiful soft shirt, now with a dark stain blooming on its front.

His hands froze, he paused for a visible intake of breath, and then he burst into laughter. A *guffaw*, Annie thought. Of course Graham would guffaw.

"Off the hook!" he cried. "Thank God!" He started to use the dampened napkins now to wipe at himself. "Free at last!" He looked at her. "Thank you. Thank you so much!"

He was grinning at Annie now, and she was smiling at him. They were standing close, people pressing in at their backs.

After a moment that began to seem too long, he said, "Here, we both need more wine, don't we?"

"Well, I don't *need* it, but sure."

He reached over to the table, now a mess of empty and half-empty bottles, crumbs, plates daubed with partially eaten food, here and there cigarettes stubbed out on them. He turned back to Annie with two opened bottles—red, white, one in each hand. He poured, first for her, then for himself. When he'd set the bottles back down, they raised their glasses vaguely toward each other and each had a sip.

Graham was looming above Annie—though what she felt was that he loomed *around* her, that she had somehow entered a space he owned. Heat radiated from him.

His face had become serious as he bent to her. He said, "What are you doing with Jeff?" His voice, she noted, was deep, resonant.

"Why do you ask?"

"I don't know. It seems an odd pairing, somehow." He was speaking very near Annie's ear, and she could feel his winey breath warm on her cheek, the rumble of his voice in her spine.

She pulled her head back to see him. "We're hardly paired," she said, looking into his eyes.

His face changed. "Ah! Good news." He smiled down at her, and they relaxed into the noise. Annie wanted him to touch her, she realized. She was waiting for it, her body was waiting.

Then, leaning forward again, he asked, "May I walk you home?"

"Now?" Annie pulled back again, laughing. She raised an open hand to indicate the people pressed in against them. The party was at full tilt, louder, bigger, more lubricated than it had been all evening.

He looked around, as if only now taking in all the people. "Oh!" he said. "Yeah. Later, I suppose, would be better."

"But see, the thing is, I'm leaving with the one what brought me." Though she was feeling some regret about that.

They looked at each other. It struck Annie that they were commiserating. Graham was nodding, over and over, as if taking in terrible news. "Well, I like to hear that," he said at last. "It speaks well of you, I suppose. But also . . ."—he made a rueful face—"also I *don't* like to hear it."

When she left a while later, with Jeff, Annie turned at the door to look for Graham. She found him—he was so tall, so prepossessing, that he was easy to spot. She waved, and he seemed to take a step in her direction, but then someone in the group standing with him must have said something to him, and he turned back, away from her.

She lay awake that night. She kept thinking about Graham—his apparent joyfulness, his ease, the feeling of his rumbling voice in her ear. Even his size. How tall was he? she wondered. Six-three? Six-four? More than a foot taller than she was, certainly. Ridiculous, really.

And he was so big. She'd never been attracted to a fat man before.

But no, she thought. He wasn't really fat. He was barrel-chested, large, yes. But somehow the way he carried himself—and of course, also his quick appreciation of her—had canceled out that notion for her. She remembered mostly wanting to touch him, wanting him to touch her. She'd been aware again, in the moments they stood so close to each other, of the wetness between her legs.

Alone in her bed under the skylight, Annie felt it all merge, the by now free-floating sexual alertness that had lingered from her afternoon with Jeff, and her happy encounter with Graham. She might have felt bad about using the sensations she'd had with Jeff to feed her response to another man, but she didn't. It didn't seem complicated at all to her—just the necessary way she'd stumbled onto Graham.

He *interested* her, she thought.

And then: C'mon, how could you even begin to know that? You exchanged about two words.

But he had seemed so open, so without caution or defenses. So sweet, really. So eager—for her, certainly, but also somehow for *life*, she would have said. In the dark, thinking of him, she was smiling.

The next evening she stopped in at the bookstore. It was miraculously clean. The shelves that had been pushed against the walls the night before were back in place, filling the room. There were comfortable chairs set here and there, floor lamps next to them. Graham was busy behind the long checkout counter in front of the plate-glass window, talking, answering questions, manning the cash register. Annie chose a book almost at random from the fiction section—something by John Gardner—and got in line.

When it was her turn, he looked up and his face changed. "Ah, it's Annie!" he said, grinning. Then a moment of doubt. He looked worried, suddenly. "Isn't that it? Annie?" he asked. She nodded, and he smiled again, more slowly. "What are you doing here?"

"This." She held her book up, and he took it. While he was ringing her up, Annie said, "Also I thought maybe I could walk *you* home."

His hands stopped. He looked at her. His face lifted in a way she would become familiar with, a way that meant he was purely happy, a way that would come to mean that she was happy too.

"Well, you'd have to wait," he said. "I don't get off till ten."

"I can wait," she said.

"Music to my ears," he said.

And so it began, with Graham.

Annie misunderstood it at first, probably partly because the sex worked so well between them from the start. Happy sex. Seemingly uncomplicated. As soon as they began to sleep together, her worries about it vanished. In bed he moved above her, below her, inside her, as if in an element made for him. Swimming in sex—easily, slowly. More of the same in Annie's life, but better.

For a while it didn't occur to her that it would ever be anything more than this. In her dizziness about how well things were going, she didn't notice the changes in him. In herself. She thought of herself as still sliding through the world in the same way—loose, free, wild. *Why not?*

It was true that she felt overwhelmed sometimes—by Graham's size, by his energy, his appetite for people, for music, for food. By his appetite for her. It made her uncomfortable, occasionally. She actually slept with Jeff once again after she'd started with Graham. And with one other man, someone friends introduced her to, a bass player, who made her laugh in bed by remembering for her an early Chekhov story about a double bass and a naked woman. She thought of these adventures, she even explained them to Graham, as the result of a generalized excitement created by her affair with him. It was only looking back on them later that she understood she'd also been using them, using them as a way to resist Graham.

But Graham was persistent, a joyous lover, an enthusiast, and finally Annie gave over to him. How could she not? She'd been waylaid, really—by happiness, by his love for her, and then, more slowly, hers for him. By the end of the fifth month she'd known him, she'd moved into his place on Ware Street, a quick walk for him to the bookstore, for her a short drive to her studio in Somerville.

What she told people at first was that she'd moved because her very informal lease was coming up for renewal and the couple who owned the house that contained her attic apartment were going to raise her rent. But she knew, even before she and Graham spoke openly about it with each other, that a life together had begun. Within the year—actually on the anniversary of the store's opening ("The two happiest days of my life," he always said)—they were married.

Annie was happy too. But occasionally through their years together, and in spite of everything that was pleasurable and loving between them, she would feel it again, the sense of his having overtaken her somehow, overwhelmed her.

2

HERE'S GRAHAM, AWAKE even earlier than usual this morning, sitting alone in the kitchen in the clean, grayish predawn light. He's wearing an old cotton bathrobe, faded blue—a *nothing* color in this light. It's frayed at the collar and cuffs. Under it, a T-shirt. His bare feet, crossed at the ankle under the table, are unusually slender and high-arched for someone so big. His hands, too, holding his mug, are shapely, the fingers long and tapered, reminders of his life as a thinner young man. Normally his expression is alert, ready to be amused at whatever might happen next. Now, in repose, he looks tired. The air is full of the smell of coffee.

He's at the expansive table where everyone sits during the dinner parties he and Annie like to throw. Facing him on the other side of the table is a row of tall windows that open out over the backyard, still in shadow at this hour—the leaves of the lilac bushes that line one side of the patio are an almost blackish green.

The newspaper, most likely containing the report of what the newly anointed Democratic presidential candidate Barack Obama has said or done the day before, is laid out in front of him, but he's not reading it as he usually does. Instead, he's remembering his first wife, Frieda. Remembering the day she left him: the chilly morning, homely Frieda in her old tweed coat, trying to hold back her tears as she carried Lucas out to the car. Just thinking of it makes him almost physically uncomfortable, even after all these years. He takes an audible, openmouthed breath and shifts his weight in the chair.

Their apartment then, his and Frieda's, was on the second floor of a sagging frame house on Windsor Street in Cambridge. He was standing on the brick sidewalk in front of it with nothing to do at this point but watch her, having already hauled down the last of the things she had wanted to take—a carton of her books, a carton of toys for Lucas. The trunk of the car, an old blue Ford Fiesta pocked with rust, was held almost shut with the bungee cords he had stretched over the many other boxes and suitcases she was taking. As she bent to settle Lucas into the back seat, Graham could see the tears glistening on her cheeks.

"Mumma's owie?" he heard the little boy ask. His small, pretty face, looking up at her, was frightened.

"A tiny one," Frieda said, trying to smile. "Just tiny." She pushed at her cheeks with her palms. "I'll be okay in . . . three minutes."

She'd turned then, and come to stand in front of Graham. "I'm sorry," she said. Her eyes behind her glasses were swollen, the wet lashes spiked darkly together.

"No," he answered.

No, because it was he who had wrecked things. No. Because it was he who was sorry.

Sorry in every sense of the word, he thinks now, in his comfortable kitchen. A sorry bastard. My fault.

Mea culpa.

An open marriage. They'd agreed on it at first. It had been that era—the world was shifting and changing rapidly around them, and Graham had stepped forward into this altered universe eagerly, along with what seemed like half of Cambridge, compelled by all the things it seemed to promise—among them a different meaning for marriage, for sex.

The problem was that Graham had been happy in this new world, and Frieda hadn't. She tried, she dutifully had a few lovers in the first year or so. But then she got pregnant with Lucas and realized that she'd never really wanted any of it.

But Graham did want it, he still wanted all of it, it was part of his excited sense of everything that was newly possible for him. And because Frieda didn't ask him to stop—wouldn't have been able then to ask him to stop—he went on doing it, obliviously, happily.

Frieda, private uncomplaining Frieda, kept her suffering about this to herself until she was too angry, too wounded, to continue. It was over, she told him. It hurt, it hurt all the time.

Afterward he sometimes thought that, as much as anything, she was angry at his physical transformation. When he looks at photos of himself from college or from the early days of their marriage, he barely recognizes the tall, gawky boy captured in them. In one image he remembers with pain, he had on a shirt that could have passed for a pajama top, it was so shapeless, so hopeless, so *plaid*. And always those thick, dark-framed glasses. The idea that they're now chic, that beautiful women willingly wear them, this amazes him.

The beard had been the first change. And when he grew his curly hair longer, as men were doing then, he looked like another person entirely. People responded to him differently, women especially. And in an answering response partly to that, and partly, he supposes, to all the other changes that were opening out to him in those heady days, he slowly more or less *became* another person— buoyant, outgoing, confident.

Frieda doesn't look like another person, even now. She's still the suitable mate for that old version of Graham—a tall, big-boned woman with a wide plain face and her own pair of thick, perpetually smudged glasses. He can't see her without the tug of all those old feelings—guilt, sorrow, love.

They're friends now, he and Frieda. They've had to be, for Lucas, but they both would have tried anyway, because in some sense they still love each other. Though part of what they're loving is the sweet, serious people that they once were. That Frieda still is.

Not him. Not sweet. Certainly not serious. A joke, really.

He sips his coffee. Even this coffee makes him remorseful, this amazing cappuccino with its thick, creamy foam. He made it on the expensive espresso machine that Annie gave him last year for Christmas. Her generosity, along with the machine's sleek perfection sitting over there on the counter—these both seem a chastisement to Graham.

He's been much more careful in his marriage to Annie. More careful and more faithful.

Yet not entirely faithful.

Which is partly what's making him remember the end with Frieda. Because he's done it again.

A light thing, that's what he'd thought at first. A fling. He'd had one other short affair much earlier on in his marriage to Annie, in a period when things were suddenly difficult between them, for reasons he didn't feel he really understood. The earlier affair was with a woman he'd known for a while, a married woman, Linda Parkman. A friend, in their large circle of friends. He hadn't seen it as any kind of threat to his marriage, and neither had Linda. It was a tonic, actually—and it had turned him eagerly back to Annie when it was finished. She had asked him once about his suddenly increased ardor, and he'd made some kind of joke about it.

He remembers now coming into a party in someone else's house at around that time, looking across the room and seeing her, seeing Linda. By then, things were easily over between them. Well, relatively easily—just a mild bump or two. And she had ended it, for which Graham was grateful—it was the kind of thing it would have been difficult for him to do.

Whose party? Whose house? That was lost to history. There was always a party then, and the houses, the apartments, with their worn sofas, their secondhand chairs and lamps, their straw rugs, were pretty much all the same anyway.

So he saw her on somebody's couch in somebody's living room. Her face is what he recalls clearly, frowning in concentration as she listened to the woman who was speaking to the little group settled near her. Her chin was resting on her hand, one finger set sideways across her upper lip. When she looked up and saw Graham, her eyes rounded, her lips pursed, and the finger straightened out, rose vertically across her lips to touch the tip of her nose: *Shhhhh.*

He had felt a quick pulse of relief, of pleasure. He'd smiled at her then, and turned away.

He hadn't gotten off scot-free, though. He'd made the mistake of talking to Frieda about it. He'd let himself think it wouldn't matter to her, that they'd moved so far away from the grief of pulling apart that he could treat her like a confidante, a friend.

Not about this, he couldn't. She wept. She called him a fool. She said he might as well attach reins to his penis and gallop around after it. She asked what the point of all her pain back then was, if he was still at it in his marriage to Annie. Was it all a perfect waste?

There was something about Frieda that had always made him feel protective, even though he'd been so bad at protecting her. Her awkwardness. Her earnestness.

No, he'd said to her then. No, of course not.

"What did you learn, then?" she asked shrilly. "What is it that you learned from all my suffering?"

They were sitting across from each other at the kitchen table in her shotgun apartment on Whittier Street. He'd just returned Lucas after a weekend. He reached out to touch her hand across the scarred tabletop, but she pulled it back and turned sharply away, to the side. He could watch her mouth pulling into a bitter shape as she tried to keep herself from crying.

"I did, Frieda," he said. "I learned."

"Not enough," she said. And for weeks, she wouldn't talk to him.

Now he sees that she was right. This time it isn't working the way it did before, and he feels he may have put things with Annie at risk, something he never intended.

Things with Annie: your marriage, you asshole!

The problem is that Rosemary—Rosemary Gregory, the woman he's slept with maybe four, maybe five times—has started to behave as if there's some kind of commitment between them, as though she has a claim on him. Twice she's called him at work at the bookstore in the morning, a time when he's almost always sitting in the office, surrounded by other people. Her tone in these calls is too intimate, and this scares him. He needs to end it, but that's something he's never been good at—at disappointing people. At being, as he sees it, *unkind*.

Rosemary is sort of an old friend too—more a friend of friends, actually. But he and Annie have liked her well enough—her and Charlie, her husband. In fact, they've probably liked Charlie better. He's smart, affable, well-read. He designs interactive museum exhibits.

But they're divorced now, Charlie and Rosemary. Newly divorced. Graham should have remembered the rule: you don't fool around with the newly divorced.

They were seated next to each other at a large dinner party. He was flirting with her. Graham likes to flirt with women. He likes being courtly, flattering people, making people feel good; but especially making women feel good. Everyone knows this about him. Rosemary should have known it too. People, including Annie, make fun of him for this behavior.

He can't even remember what he was saying, but he was, as usual, joking around. *The merry grass widow. How men were going to be lined up to receive her favors.*

She had looked levelly at him. She was gorgeous, he'd always thought so, but in a dramatic, almost stylized way that didn't much interest him. Careful makeup, careful hair, lots of expensive-looking ethnic jewelry. "Well, why don't you just jump in at the head of that line?" she said.

Thinking she was simply being flirty too, he said, "Damn straight. I'll just push all those other guys aside."

"Thursdays are usually best for me," she said. "Late afternoon. I'll expect you."

She would?

Or was it an answering joke on her part?

He had no idea, he realized. And she turned away just after she'd said it, turned to talk to the man on her right, so he didn't have the chance to make it part of his game, to let her know he wasn't taking it seriously.

He let one Thursday pass, but then he thought that perhaps it might be awkward socially to see her again if she hadn't intended it as a joke, if she'd actually been inviting him. Maybe he should go, then. Go, and explain himself. Explain that he'd just been horsing around. *Not that he wouldn't love to, et cetera, et cetera.* He didn't let himself think until later that to ponder going there at all was further horsing around on his part, horsing around with the itch of what had begun to feel like a real possibility. And by then it was too late.

Outside, the shadows have lifted and the birds are launched into the frenzied call-and-response that starts their day. He gets up and comes around the table to the windows. Someone—Annie—has left a sweater on one of the old chairs that sit on the mossy brick patio. Its white is startling against the other, muted tones.

He had misunderstood Rosemary, he knows that now. With the

quick turn she'd made on his playful tone, she had seemed to him worldly-wise, sexually sophisticated. After the first time they had sex, he tried to make a light remark about this, about how they had stumbled into bed with each other by accident, each of them joking, neither of them getting the other's joke.

"I don't see it that way," she said.

Suddenly he felt a little short of breath. "Oh," he said. Her face after sex was pinkish—almost chapped-looking. They were still in bed, in her grand bedroom. Even up here there was an expensive-looking kilim on the floor.

"I don't see it as an accident at all," she said.

"You don't."

"No, I think it was inevitable."

He didn't know what to say to this, or even how to take it; but slowly, over the next few times they were together, he began to understand her, to see that she was, if anything, absurdly romantic. Certainly not jaded, or even sophisticated. She was lonely. In need. This made him feel sorry for her, but it also frightened him.

Ah!—his attention is drawn now by the appearance on her back porch of his elderly neighbor, Karen. She pauses there for a moment, her head tilted back, maybe to smell the morning air. Then she laboriously descends the stairs and begins to survey her garden. She's dressed in one of what Graham thinks of as her "outfits"—in this case a wide-brimmed straw hat, a knee-length white night-gown, and tube socks. She has bright blue sneakers on her feet. There's something jagged-looking and silvery on these sneakers—maybe lightning bolts? They glint every now and then as she moves around.

He watches her stand for a few moments in front of various plants, her hands on her hips, as though she were chastising them. Occasionally she bends over to painfully, slowly, pull a weed. Her old cat trails her. Sam, orange with white patches. He twines around her legs when she stands still, his tail lightly whipping her mottled shins.

Graham and Annie are worried about Karen. What were once charming eccentricities have *ripened*, he would say, into more troubling behavior. She seems addled sometimes. Only a few days earlier he found her in the house when he came home from work, standing irresolutely, frowning, in the middle of his living room.

"What are *you* doing here?" she'd said sharply to him.

"I might ask you the same question," he said. "But I won't." She laughed then—gaily, it seemed to him—and headed toward the back door.

He thinks now of how strange it is that she should be so much in their lives. More than their own parents ever were—certainly more than his, anyway. And this purely the result of the accident of buying the house next door to hers all those years ago.

Standing at the window, he remembers walking with Annie behind the real estate agent through the dim rooms of the house. Annie, small and slender ahead of him, her dark hair still long then, a thick ribbon down her back, her carriage elegant. The graceful accommodating dancer's turn to whatever the agent was pointing out.

They'd been house-hunting for a while, feeling more and more discouraged as they slowly discovered how limited their choices were going to be. This, the house they were looking at—the house they ended up buying—was a converted coach house. You walked up a long driveway at the side of the much larger, *real* house, as he thought of it, to get there.

It had been divided then into what were essentially dark cells, tiny rooms that had depressed him on that walk-through. But what Annie said afterward as they talked about it was that those walls would be as easy to take down as they'd been to put up. That when the towering old pine that leaned over the roof was removed, the light would pour in. That the house was essentially surrounded by open land—all those other people's backyards. In that era before gardening was chic, most of these yards were overgrown with thick, tall grasses gone to seed—a kind of prairie encircling the house. A prairie, except for Karen's yard, shockingly lush with the perennials, the roses, the shrubs, that the others would slowly acquire as gentrification took hold.

On the day they moved in, Karen, then middle-aged, a handsome, tall, prematurely white-haired woman with a Brahmin accent, had welcomed them with a jug of the cheap wine they all drank at that time—Almaden or Mateus, something like that—and a strange-tasting pasta casserole she said she'd made herself. When Graham returned the empty dish to her, he asked her what it was, exactly. She told him she'd invented the recipe. "I think what really makes it work, though," she said in her toney voice, "are the canned plums I always add to it."

Annie sometimes used this line when she was complimented on a meal. Thinking of this, of her excellent imitation of Karen's voice and patrician accent, he smiles.

As if on cue, above him, footfalls, and then, a minute later, the rush of water through the pipes: she's awake. He goes to the coffee machine and with the push of a few buttons, the turn of a valve, makes a cappuccino for her and a second cup for himself.

All this is part of their routine. He gets up first, usually around five. He goes downstairs, he makes his coffee and sits alone with it while he reads the paper—the headlines and maybe an article or two. In the summer, he can watch the sun rising slowly over the houses that back up to his and Annie's, rising until the tops of the trees in his neighbors' yards look as if they've burst into flame. Usually he enjoys every ritualized part of all this.

Not today.

He brings both cups of coffee up the steep back stairs to their bedroom. When he leans against the bedroom door, it swings open to the dazzling morning light up here. In this light, propped against the pillows on their bed, Annie, in her blue-green kimono.

Maybe because of the light, maybe because of his guilt, maybe because he's been thinking of Frieda—Frieda, homely and in pain—

he sees Annie afresh. Annie, this graceful, delicate woman he's married to, her wide mouth moving now with pleasure into the smile that transforms her, that thrills him now as much as when he first saw her, thirty years before, at the opening party for the bookstore he still owns.

"My sweet husband," she says, reaching up with both hands to take the cup he holds out to her.

The bookstore. It had been another part of Graham's transformation. For years after he quit graduate school—all but dissertation on a doctoral degree in English literature—he taught as an adjunct here and there in the Boston area, finally mostly adult education classes, all the while trying to write his novel. He was slow to give that up, but at some point he saw that he wasn't going to be able to write a book he'd want to read, or, more important, that he'd want anyone else to read. It had felt liberating to acknowledge this to himself and others, to shed his painful sense of the obligation to be somehow *remarkable*; but it left him with the unanswered question of what to do with his life, and simultaneously the realization that working on the novel endlessly had been a way to avoid facing that question.

As he took stock of himself, he remembered the time when he had worked a part-time job for a year or so in a small bookstore in Harvard Square—gone now—and it seemed to him that he was most happy then, living among books, talking about books. He began to nurture the notion of a bookstore of his own.

So when an uncle of his—the lone success in his mother's family—died and left him what he described to friends as "a little chunk of change," he and an older friend, Peter Aiello, who always seemed to have many of those chunks more or less just lying around, bought a storefront on Mount Auburn Street, the plan being that Graham would run the store, with Peter as a silent partner.

On the opening night—*of all the gin joints in all the towns in all the world*—Annie walked in with a guy, a guy he'd sent an invitation to for reasons he couldn't later recall. And in spite of everything that seemed ladylike and elegant about her—her slender dancer's body, her grave, sober face—she also carried a kind of charge that he felt instantly. He understood it as sexual, yes, and it turned out that was apt—she told him later that she'd been fucking Jeff all that afternoon. But in the moment he imagined it as directed at him, connected to all the changes he'd made and wanted to make in his life, to who he wanted to be; and his impulse was to try to be sure she didn't somehow slip away.

Now Graham sits down in his chair by the bedroom window and lifts his feet, sets them on the end of the bed.

"What news?" she asks, after she's had a sip or two of her coffee.

"I don't know." He lifts his empty hand. "I didn't read the paper."

"What?" Her eyebrows rise in theatrical surprise. "You're supposed to be my conduit to the wider world."

"I know, I know. Falling down on the job. But . . ." He shrugs. The sun is warm on his feet. Only now does he realize how cold they were downstairs.

They are quiet awhile. He's aware again of the racket of the birds. They both drink their coffee. He has a mug with his store's name on it. Annie has a wide white bowl that was an enormous cup before the handle broke off. She has to raise it to her lips with both hands now.

She lowers it to the worn quilt that covers her lap and looks at him, frowning. She says, "Are you worried about something?"

"No, everything's fine in my little world."

"Hmm," she says, looking steadily at him. "Because you seem a bit . . . preoccupied."

He can hardly stand it, this solicitude toward him, a solicitude that only compounds his guilt. She knows something is bothering him, which makes him ever more evasive. Which worries her the more.

Don't, he wants to say. Don't be concerned. Don't care about me.

"Just, store stuff," he says. "Nothing important."

"Well, what? What store stuff? If I can help . . ."

"No. No, everything's fine."

She makes a face—eyebrows lifted skeptically, mouth drawn down. "I guess I have to believe you," she says. "Thousands wouldn't."

He smiles at her. Then, to change the subject, he says, "Karen's out and about."

"*Is* she. Gardening?"

"So to speak. In not exactly gardening togs."

"Oh dear."

He nods, first up and down, then—what to do?—side to side. "All that's missing, really, is the boa."

She laughs quickly and says, "Shit. Well, I'll talk to her on my way out, for all the good it'll do."

They sit in what he hopes is a comfortable silence. In the early days of their marriage, Graham sometimes climbed back into bed with her after they'd drunk their coffee and they made love, but they've mostly given that up in recent years. And on those rare occasions when they start in, as often as not, absent the magic blue pill, Graham winds up "underperforming," as he calls it. Still, it brings them close again each time, the warm touching, flesh on flesh.

He's thinking of this when she says, "What are you up to today?"

He smiles at her. "More of same, of course. Ever more of same. But I think I'll stay home this morning. Work at my desk here." Then he remembers. "Oh, and I'm having lunch with John." His oldest friend, from college.

"John *Norris?*" Her voice has a surprised pleasure in it, her smile changes her sober face.

"Yeah. Didn't I mention it?" She shakes her head. "He's in town for some conference, I think at MIT, so he's making time for me today."

"But how nice. Maybe *he* can cheer you up." He doesn't answer her. After a moment, she says, "How long will he be around?"

"I'm not sure. He might have told me, but I don't remember."

"Why don't you ask him for dinner tomorrow, then? If he can. One extra person would be nice. Balance out the boy-girl thing. And I'd love to see him."

This is the dinner party they're having the next night—Friday—to celebrate Jamie Slattery's reading at the bookstore from her new book, an apocalyptic novel set in a fictional New Orleans after a flood more devastating than Katrina.

Jamie is an old friend, but old friend or not, they often have parties for the writers who read at the store. He and Annie are known for these parties—for the meals Annie cooks, for the free-flowing wine, for the talk. In the old days, for the dancing too. It was only a few years ago that Graham finally threw out the stack of 45s he'd held on to for years, most of them so scratched or spilled on that they were unplayable anyway. He still misses them. At odd times he'll think of one of them—Shirley and Lee doing "Let the Good Times Roll" or James Carr singing "Pouring Water on a Drowning Man"—and he'll feel a pang of regret—yes, for the loss of the music, but more for those gone-by times. They mostly don't dance anymore either.

He and Annie talk now about the various people who are coming tomorrow, they exchange what each knows about what's been happening recently in one or the other of their friends' lives, and for these moments, everything seems the same to Graham, he can almost forget his anxiety, his sense that he deserves to lose all of this.

Then she says, "You're staying home more than usual these mornings."

"Well, I can get more done here, really. And then I've been doing that late-afternoon, early-evening shift at the store."

"I know," she says. After a moment, "You like that better?"

"I do. I do in some ways. It's a big rush right after everybody gets out of work, but then it quiets down and you can actually talk to people." This is all true, but also there's the problem of Rosemary calling him at the store in the morning.

"Ah, the house specialty," Annie says. "Talk. And more talk."

"I suppose," he says.

"I miss you here when I get home, though. The house feels lonely."

"Mmm."

"You're not avoiding me, are you?"

He reaches over to touch the tented shape of her feet under the quilt. "Hardly." Though that may be part of it too, he supposes. He looks over at her. She's lifted the cup to drink, and he can see only her dark brown eyes, steady on him above its rim.

"What are *you* up to?" he asks.

She groans and rests the cup again on her outstretched legs. "Packing up," she says. "Getting ready to take the stuff over to Danielle's. My bubble-wrap day."

Annie is a photographer, and she has a show coming up at a gallery in the South End. It's a big deal for her. She hasn't had a solo show in almost five years.

And he forgot. Fucker that he is. He forgot all about it. He feels a sudden deeper remorse: he was so lost in his own shit that he forgot her life, going on around his. Her life, having to do with what she makes and then puts out into the world, with all that's fraught about that for her—even more so now because of the long pause that's preceded this show.

"Ah," he says. "Well, if you need help, you know where I am."

"*Most* of the time I do," she says, and smiles.

He knows that she's teasing, but it startles him anyway. He hopes that doesn't show in his face.

———

He can hear Annie's voice rising and falling softly while she's taking her shower: she often talks to herself. As he passes the old bathroom door on the way to his office, she distinctly says, "Yikes!" and then something else he can't hear.

It seems to him that these private conversations must be a bit like dreaming for her, but a kind of dreaming more closely based on the concerns of her daily life than would occur at night. Once he heard her say, "I should just *shoot* the guy," and thought for a moment that she was talking about him, about something he'd done that had made her angry. But then it occurred to him that she was probably thinking about someone she wanted to take a picture of, and he laughed.

His office is at the front of the house. It's a small room with a single window that looks out over the long driveway belonging to their neighbors in the real house—the driveway that is also essentially the walkway from the street to their own front door. He starts to neaten up his desk, which is, as always, heaped with books and papers and spreadsheets, printouts of reviews, schedules of upcoming readings at his store and others'. He has two of Jamie's earlier books stacked next to his computer. He's reread them quickly in preparation for writing her introduction—he always introduces the writers who come to the store, unless there's a special reason for someone else to do it. Several drafts of that introduction are lying on top of everything else. When he's made what seems to him like orderly piles of most of the stuff, he looks over the last version he's done of the intro and starts to tinker with it—partly because it needs work, but partly also to look busy when Annie comes to say goodbye.

And here she is, standing in the doorway in jeans and sandals and a white linen shirt, her wet hair pinned up at the back of her head. "I'm off," she says.

"You look ravishing."

"Mmm. Thanks. Maybe you could ravish me sometime." She comes into the room and bends over him, tugging lightly at his beard. His secret weapon, she calls it. She's told him often how much she loves its soft touch on her thighs, her cunt.

He's enveloped in her smell—soap, perfume, something clean and bleachy from her clothes. "I'll ponder it," he says.

"Ahh! Nothing like ponderous sex, is there?" she says, and laughs. She kisses him lightly and turns to leave the room. He hears her pause partway down the stairs. She calls back, "Late dinner tonight, then?"

"Yes," he says.

The front door slams, and he's alone again. He's relieved to be alone, he realizes. Pathetic.

As he edits the introduction, he's also intermittently thinking of Annie, of their earliest lovemaking. Of her body, of what they did with each other, of where they did it—her apartment, sunstruck and hot in the attic of a huge house on Avon Hill, the scudding clouds visible above her in the skylight as she rode him slowly. In his car at night in the dark parking lot behind some long-gone jazz club in Central Square, stopping, holding still when someone passed close by. Images like this have come to him often in the last few weeks, mostly, he thinks, as a way to make a distance between himself and Rosemary—reminding himself of those days when everything about Annie, too, was new, when everything they did with each other seemed a way they were claiming each other. For him, that he was *owning* this part of her, and this, and now this.

Sitting here at his desk, he suddenly remembers that in the midst of all that, when he was most besotted, she told him that she'd slept again with an old lover—Jeff, it was. Jeff, the guy who'd brought her to the bookstore party. Jeff, and then, unbelievably, another guy too, someone she'd been fixed up with by friends, friends who didn't yet know about Graham's presence in her life. How astonished he'd been that she wasn't, like him, feeling the overwhelming sense of a beginning—a beginning that would have made even the idea of sex with someone else impossible.

He remembers now that she said the impulse was born, in fact, exactly from being with him—the sense she had because of that of being wildly fuckable. Of wanting everything. "Really, almost everyone," she said. She laughed then, before she saw his face.

He's stopped by this memory.

And then he understands what he's up to. *Oh, blameless, blameless Graham—because she did it too.* That's what this is, he thinks.

But she did it before we were a couple.

For a while, this checks him. He types in the changes he's made to the introduction to Jamie, and reads it through, speaking it aloud once more. He looks over the monthly figures from the store.

Then it begins to nag at him again: isn't it possible, might she not have *amused herself* with someone else, maybe even after they were a couple? After they were married?

Amused herself, he thinks. *A little amuse-bouche.* He thinks of going down on her, his own amuse-bouche. How he loves it. A time back then when he felt he wanted to enter her, swim into her, headfirst, mouthfirst.

These images, these thoughts, arrive and disappear as he finishes at the desk. He gets up finally and goes into the bathroom, into the lingering scent of her shampoo, of her soap—but something else too, something elemental to her.

The sun from the skylight above the shower warms him even before he turns the water on, and he stands gratefully under it and the spray. When he's finished and steps out, the air is cool on his wet body. He dries off, inspecting himself as he works the towel—the diminishing number of white hairs at the top of his chest, the sling of his belly, the fattish penis below it, his burden, apparently. He sighs and goes to the bedroom to get dressed.

Standing in front of the closet, he slides the hangers along. The light brown linen suit, he thinks. An off-white shirt. The soft leather shoes just a shade darker than the suit.

All this—these expensive clothes and his love for them—was a later element in his transformation. It happened at about the time he bought the bookstore, just before he met Annie. He had wanted to mark the end of his catch-as-catch-can life—the blue jeans, the secondhand tweed jackets, the thick Frye boots. He wanted, he supposed, to look more like a man of substance. A burgher. The spring the bookstore opened, he'd bought two suits, one seersucker, one a pale gray linen. Then, in the fall, two more suits, light wool ones.

He'd actually talked to his shrink about these choices, these decisions.

The shrink was part of his old life. An éminence grise, Graham was given to understand later, who didn't seem to feel the need to play by what Graham had always understood to be the rules for shrinks. He talked freely about himself to Graham, he shared anecdotes from his own life. He did have a couch in his office, but he and Graham sat opposite each other at a wide desk—like colleagues, Graham thought, working on some shared project. Sometimes his flatulent old dog scratched at the door, and Dr. Fielding got up and let him in. Their conversations on those days were punctuated by Boogan's occasional prolonged farts.

He had started seeing Dr. Fielding after he and Frieda split up. First about his guilt over that—over Frieda and Lucas—and later about everything else: his family background, his sexual life, the store and how it was changing everything for him. And then, after she'd entered his world, Annie.

But from the beginning they had also talked every now and then about clothing, talked about it as an expression of Graham's wish to be changed, somehow. To be a better person. Or at least a different person.

He'd stopped seeing the shrink by the time his interest intensified, by the time he began to really know about the quality of the clothes, to care about it—the fabric, the leather, the cut, the stitching. By the time he became, as Annie calls him occasionally, "something of a fop."

Those early clothes are all gone now. Even the clothes he's putting on today are old enough to be a bit worn, but he finds them the more beautiful because of this.

He looks at himself in the full-length mirror before he leaves for lunch. He's thinking of how much it would amuse his friend John if he were here, watching Graham costume himself.

Rather like Karen, he thinks.

Only different.

He laughs, quickly. "Enough," he says aloud, and heads down the narrow, tilting staircase and out the door into the perfect early-summer day—the sky the blue of a child's bright crayon. The humid air a kiss.

3

AS SHE STEPPED out of the house, her hair still damp from her shower, Annie paused to look over at Karen's yard, thinking that she would speak to the old woman if she was still outside, that she'd comment somehow on the possibility—yea, the desirability—of getting dressed before going out to meet the world. But Karen was back in her house, apparently. Sam, her fat orange cat, sat alone and imperturbable at the opened gate between her yard and theirs, looking back at Annie in his bored, slightly contemptuous way. She gave him the finger and continued down the driveway past the Caldwells' dark dining room windows and to the curb, where her car sat waiting.

Her car. Annie loved this car. It was an old green Citroën van that she'd kept alive at great expense. She could have bought several newer cars for the money she'd spent over the years getting it ready to pass inspection—always a dicey call. She even loved the guys who'd repaired it for her over and over, who groaned dramatically whenever she called to make an appointment. At one point they'd had to replace its entire underside—it was so laced with rust that when you drove through a puddle, water splashed up under your feet.

As she got in and started the engine, she was swept anew by her sense of deep friendship for it—a pleasure in its smells, in its improvised elements: the radio that turned on and off via a doorbell installed on the dashboard, the seat covers she'd made out of a bright-orange-and-pink-striped Sunbrella fabric when the old plastic covers had cracked and worn through.

It had served them so well through the years, in so many ways. She had a sheet of plywood and a mattress she could install in it, and in their impoverished early life together, she and Graham had driven up and down the East Coast several times, sleeping at state parks and the occasional rest stop, pulling the curtains across the windows when they wanted to have sex. When the children were young, in the days before mandatory car seats and seat belts, Lucas or Sarah and sometimes a friend or two had sat in folding chairs in the open back space, chairs that occasionally slid sideways, to their delight, if she or Graham took too sharp a turn.

And if she took the seats out of the back entirely, the space was more than ample to transport her equipment when she traveled to take pictures. Or to haul framed work here or there, which would be her task today.

It couldn't last much longer, the van, but she didn't want to imagine living with another car, a newer one, this one spoke so eloquently to her of the past, of her happiness then, of her hopes for herself. Of her youth.

In her youth—relative youth: her mid- to late thirties—Annie had seemed on the path to a notable career. She'd had a New York gallery then, and the two solo shows they mounted early on in her professional life were both well received, which had perhaps misled her about how the rest of that life was going to go.

The first show, called *Emergency*, consisted of shots she'd taken over about a year and a half in the ER at Boston City Hospital. Closeups of the hands of doctors as they worked, shots of their faces in concentration, alone with whatever they were doing. Shots of nurses, one standing exhausted at the station between patients, clutching some kind of stained linens, her eyes half shut, another mysteriously running down a long, empty hallway. A picture of a cluster of doctors and nurses working over a patient with an open, bleeding abdominal wound, their bodies forming a kind of human triangle around him, the apex an IV bag held aloft by a nurse kneeling on the bed. A doctor in the hallway, laughing with someone, his scrubs sprinkled lightly with blood. These photographs had resulted in her only book, beautifully produced by a small press in Boston.

The second New York show was a series of photographs Annie had taken of her mother over several years, beginning even before the first show was up, photographs that recorded the shifts in her face and carriage as she descended into Alzheimer's disease: the slow withdrawal of alertness, the visible draining of physical energy, the seeping away from her eyes of some sense of vitality and focus, so that in the last few pictures her body seemed stilled, her face devoid of personality or intelligence—a mask. For one of the last shots Annie had set her own infant daughter, Sarah, across her mother's lap. She lay there, unsupported, frowning in what looked like surprise as she stared up at the old woman, whose hands were set uselessly at her sides, whose eyes showed no sign that she even registered the baby's presence.

There were fine reviews of this show, though several, while praising the pictures themselves, were disapproving of the enterprise— "voyeuristic," one critic called it. The Museum of Fine Arts had purchased one of the photographs for its permanent collection, and it was this material that won Annie grants from the National Endowment for the Arts, from the Massachusetts Cultural Council.

But her oldest sister got wind of it at some point, and there was a stink in the family, a taking of sides that ended in what seemed a permanent estrangement for Annie from everyone but the younger of her two brothers. It wasn't a great loss for her—she hadn't been close to any of them, even in childhood—but she did feel some of the shame her sister called down on her. In the last painful telephone call they had, she had said Annie was "cold." It was as though no time at all had passed since their adolescence together, Audrey's voice was so full of assured and easy contempt. "You always thought you were so much better than anyone else," she said. "But you're not. What you are is cold. You're a cold little bitch."

Annie was proud afterward to have managed some of that coldness in her response: "It's so good to have your diagnosis, Audrey."

But in fact it had been hard to hear Audrey's judgment, partly because it was so close to what she often thought about herself—the coldness part, anyway. Not, she thought, the bitch part—whatever that really meant. The coldness, though, that cut deeper. But it was something she'd learned over the years to make excuses about to herself. She'd connected it to her being a photographer, to the distance required to do that work, to the need to develop a certain way of looking at people for what could be *used*, what would be good in a picture, even if it was rooted in a moment of pain, or in what should have been a private joy.

Her sister's comment made her begin to wonder: maybe instead of her work fostering in her a certain tendency toward remoteness— or even creating that sense of remoteness—maybe she'd been remote from the start. Maybe she'd become a photographer to find a way of living with that. She recalled that at various times in her life she'd felt she married Graham because he was warm, because her life with him made her more generous than she actually was, connected her to people in a way that would have been impossible if she'd still been on her own.

All of this pushed at her, and it slowly brought her to what she understood afterward was a kind of failure of nerve. Sarah was a toddler by then, and Annie took that as reason enough to slow down for six or seven years, grateful for the permission that being a mother seemed to give her.

"But this is just the moment when you *don't* slow down," Frieda had counseled earnestly—Frieda, Graham's first wife.

Annie hadn't paid attention to that. What did Frieda know about Annie's world? She was, after all, a schoolteacher, a safe job if ever there was one.

She should have listened. By the time she started to try to come back, things seemed to have changed in the world of photography, and her work wasn't as hot, as transgressive, as the work getting noticed then, the work of newer artists—Goldin, Mapplethorpe, Mann. The New York gallery that had done her first shows wasn't interested in what she offered them now, a series of shots of friends—artists, writers, photographers—in their work spaces. This made her doubt herself in a way she hadn't earlier. When she looked at these photographs after they'd been turned down, they seemed to her banal, they had no reason to exist. Why had she even taken them?

It made her feel, as she said to Graham one night after dinner, "Just done. Done in. Done for. Done over. Fucked." She made her voice tough, she didn't cry, and he poured her another glass of wine in commiseration.

In response to all this, she had turned to a different kind of project, an easy book Graham suggested to her. A book that would make use of images she and a photographer friend, Natalie Schumer, had taken over the years of parties at the house and events at the bookstore. They supplemented these with new pictures, mostly by Annie. Graham did the text around the images. He'd called it *Memoir with Bookshop*.

Mike Hodges, who'd published Annie's *Emergency* book, published this one too—mostly, Annie thought, out of friendship. It sold some copies at the store, but never took off beyond that. But she got a local solo show out of some of the pictures at a small museum in Framingham, a show called *Friends*—and many of them were included in group shows here and there.

It went like this for a decade or so. Annie kept at it—that was the way she felt about her work during this period. She had about a show a year, most of them group exhibitions in small, mostly local venues—she had stopped even trying the New York galleries.

But she had tried again with a show she called *Couples*—shots of odd pairings that intrigued her. One of two old ladies—sisters, Annie guessed, though not twins: one was taller and larger than the other. But they looked very like, and they were wearing matching shapeless old-fashioned raincoats and wide-brimmed rain hats tied neatly under their chins. She caught them on a stormy day just as they stepped, arm in arm, off a curb on Linnaean Street into the rain-slicked street, each looking for traffic in the opposite direction from the other, as synchronous as dancers—as Rockettes! Annie had thought, loving the sense of incongruity.

Another, of Natalie Schumer's parents playing cards—something they did every evening, Natalie had told her—had turned out to be one of Annie's favorites: Natalie's parents, dressed as if going out somewhere, he in a brown tweed suit, she in a sweater set and pearls, her hair a rigid halo around her head. Both wore puffy slippers on their feet, which Annie was sorry not to have been able to get into the picture.

In the photo Annie finally chose, Natalie's mother—Hannah was her name—was just looking up from her cards. They partially blocked her face, but you could see her eyes, the steady murderous gaze at her husband over her hand. He was oblivious, fussily rearranging his own cards. It had made Annie think of a snake one of her brothers had for a while as a pet. He would drop a mouse into its cage every few weeks or so, a mouse that would obliviously putter, putter, putter around for days while the snake slept, occasionally eyeing it, waiting for the hungry moment to strike.

Again the New York galleries weren't interested. So Annie made the rounds of several Boston galleries, and the Hughes Gallery, owned by Danielle Obermann, took her on. The show did fairly well, Danielle was pleased with the result, and from that point on,

Annie was able to count on Danielle for a show of her own every three or four years, in addition to the odd group show.

In between these shows, just to make money, she sometimes "rented herself out," as she thought of it—something she'd done in the early days of her work life too. Weddings, family portraits, graduations, bar mitzvahs, some of which, of course, yielded images she could use—that she *did* use—at smaller shows. This time she found she welcomed it. The simplicity. The freedom from any kind of expectation. She found herself thinking maybe she should just settle for this—wasn't it enough?

But then a commission had dropped into her lap—a commission from a New England magazine to shoot a series of family farms in Maine, in New Hampshire and Vermont.

She took it because she was desperate to work, because she needed the money, but it turned out that she loved it, driving around back roads by herself, stopping at farm stands, at old houses that overlooked apple orchards or grazing cows. Knocking on doors, talking to people and then shooting their lives. She'd begun to use color some time before this, and she loved working with it in this project, playing digitally with tones and light in the shots of people in their worn clothes standing in front of the deep red barns, or in the lush early green of hayfields.

And for her own composing pleasure, she shot a series of photographs with no one in them—empty fields edged by the outlines of trees, the light falling across them in different ways over the course of several days. She shot the sagging outbuildings, the worn wooden fences, the tumbled stone fences running through the woods that had grown up around them. She took some pictures of the interior spaces she'd looked at too. She found herself focusing a lot of attention on these images, on the hard-used homes, the old-fashioned kitchens, the tired furniture.

Of course, she sent only the peopled shots to the magazine. They paid her the modest fee, and the article came out some months later, a kind of Norman Rockwell presentation of the sturdy folk who still lived off the land in rural New England. It seemed entirely trite to Annie, though she had liked the people in the photos, and the photos themselves, she knew, were fine for their purpose.

Left over were the shots she had taken of the barns, the collapsed sheds, the houses, outside and in, everything worn and tired looking, slightly begrimed in some cases. Occasionally a figure was almost visible, usually just at the edge of the frame—someone glimpsed passing by an open doorway, someone turned to do something at a stove, someone leaving a room, having completed a chore—the back of a pants leg, the sole of a shoe, a hand, a blur. But just as often, there was no sign of anyone.

Annie found she liked them, these odd pictures. More than liked them. Even in the completely unpeopled shots, she felt the sense of a presence in the absence, the sense of someone having just departed.

And taking them had been a relief, she realized. The relief of not thinking about herself at all while she shot them. Of not thinking about how the people she was looking at would also be looking at her. Of not thinking about how she would need to explain herself to them. About what it was she wanted from them.

It made her remember the pictures she had taken of her mother. The *use* she'd made of her. The power she'd had over her. The power you always had, you always exerted, when you photographed someone. Even if they had consented to it.

The innocence of consent! she thought. And the way it was so often wrong to ask it, in one way or another.

At a party at their house, she had taken a picture of a friend of hers, Edith Hodges, standing with her husband Mike—Mike, the publisher who had done her first book and Graham's memoir; Mike, who had moved only months before out of the large house on Avon

Hill he'd shared with Edith and their four children to live with the man he'd fallen in love with.

She'd invited both of them, Mike and Edith, to a party she and Graham were throwing, after checking with each of them ahead of time to be sure this would be all right.

She had spent a part of that evening moving around, taking pictures, as she often did at these gatherings. She'd spotted the two of them standing together in the wide opening between the living room and the kitchen area, so concentrated on each other, so yearning toward each other, that they canceled out everything around them. Edith's eyes were glittery with unspilled tears. Her hand was on Mike's sleeve, gripping it so tightly that the fabric was pulled into a kind of knot under her fingers; and he was leaning slightly toward her, as if to shelter her from view.

As she was developing it, Annie could see the power of what she'd captured: the anguished impossibility of their deeply felt bond made visible.

"Of course, if you think it belongs," Edith had said when Annie showed it to her and asked if she could include it in the *Couples* show.

Then, because she suddenly understood how wrong she was to have asked this, Annie said, "You don't have to."

Edith had tilted her head and smiled tolerantly at Annie, as if to say, *Once you've asked, of course I have to.*

In that moment, Annie had known that she wouldn't—that she couldn't—use it. Not without regret, of course.

What she wanted now, she realized, was to give up on people. Or more accurately, to see them differently, to imagine them differently through their absence. To make images that said something about the people who weren't there. She thought of some of the paintings of Vuillard, or Bonnard—the figures half seen, the rooms themselves often more the subject than the people in them. But rooms suffused with the feeling of a liminal presence. Or with the feeling of an absence—but an absence full of implication, of mystery.

Images that worked like memory, she thought. The way memory is triggered by objects. The way objects, spaces, the arrangements of *things*, can call up those who aren't there, can give life to them again. Of course, not the literal life that direct images give, but the sense of the living presence. She thought of the Danish painter Hammershoi—she'd seen several of his paintings in a museum show in New York. She'd liked best the ones that had no people at all in them, gray and clean and infinitely suggestive.

So she started up once more, started up with the feeling she had thought she might have lost forever. The feeling that she knew what she was looking for, what she wanted to make.

And these were the photographs she'd be packing up today, the selection from the hundreds she'd taken. The selection that would be made public, as of Sunday.

Driving through the crowded, sun-dazed streets of triple-deckers to her studio, she was thinking now of Sunday: of the party at the gallery, the wine, the friends and possible collectors she would move around among, make nice with. The exciting pleasure of being at the center of attention in the crowd. The pleasant nervousness as people bent to look closely at what she'd seen, at what she'd made of what she'd seen. The wait after that for sales, for reviews. And then, if the show was a success, maybe the other kind of pleasure, the deeper, rarer kind.

Between now and then, though, she had a few hurdles to leap. Self-constructed hurdles, she reminded herself, but still, hurdles. Hurdles that she'd chosen to distract herself from all her fears around the show.

First, of course, she had to schlep the chosen photographs over to the gallery. And then on Friday—tomorrow!—there was the dinner at the house after Jamie's reading, the dinner for eleven. Twelve if John Norris could come.

When she'd woken this morning to the light in the bedroom, it had seemed, momentarily, like too much.

"But you're used to that," she told herself, speaking aloud now in the car.

And of course she was. Over the years, Graham had come to rely on her to provide for the many gatherings he liked to have in connection with events at the bookstore. The gatherings that she liked to have too. She enjoyed it, almost all of it. The preparation, the cooking itself, the old friends who sat around the big kitchen table in the candlelight, the long, meandering conversations, the comfort, the pleasure of it all.

And always, Graham would stand up at some point in the meal and offer a toast to her. Always he—and sometimes friends who'd stayed on late—helped with the cleanup. And often in the old days— less now—if they hadn't drunk too much, if she wasn't too exhausted, she and Graham made love after everyone had gone home.

If she had to pick a central element to their marriage, it might be this. More than their general compatibility, more than their child or their shared sense of humor—this. This nexus, this web: the parties, the bookstore, the food, the friends. Occasionally still, the sex. As she pulled into her parking space in the lot behind the studio building, she was thinking of all this, hoping that tomorrow it would work its usual magic—that Graham would come back to her from wherever it was he'd been.

4

GRAHAM AND JOHN NORRIS met each other in their freshman year
of college at the University of Massachusetts, after a drunken party.
They had stayed on together in the trashed common room after all
the others left. Almost all: one guy remained, snoring steadily on
a couch as John and Graham earnestly offered their stories to each
other. And discovered that they shared a history: both of their fathers had abandoned them when they were young. Vanished, gone,
with no forwarding address and no way to trace them.

John's father at least had a reason. He'd embezzled some money
from the office he worked in. He *needed* to disappear. He'd left a
note for John's mother, a note "which she didn't care to share with
us," John said, bitterness in his voice. And it seemed that from time
to time in John's growing up, his father must have sent some money
to her, because the family lived in relative comfort, and when he
and his sister started college, both of them inexplicably had enough
dough for tuition.

Graham's story was shabbier, but he offered it up. His father
hadn't come home one night for dinner. Graham had three younger
brothers, and they were all clamoring for food, so the meal was
served without him. In the chaos of eating and cleaning up and

doing homework and watching television, no one, not even Graham's mother, really worried about his father's absence. He'd often stayed out drinking with friends after work—he was a roofer—not coming home until all of them were in bed, asleep. One of Graham's clearest childhood memories was of waking to the sound of his father stumbling up the stairs in the dark, talking loudly, angrily, to himself. This was where Graham first learned all the swear words that became so unremarkable to hear later, in the 1960s and '70s—*fuck, shit, asshole, cunt, prick*—but which shocked him then because of the suggestion of violence in his father's voice, of the darkness and fearfulness of sex.

But this time his father wasn't there in the morning when they got up either.

Graham's mother called the Springfield police. Apparently they weren't concerned. His mother slammed the phone down after the call and turned to her sons, who were waiting for whatever the news would be. "'Probably off on a toot,' they said." She snorted. "Assholes."

A few days later, after the police finally did a cursory investigation of the disappearance, that's what they concluded. A toot.

It turned out to be a long toot. A toot that never ended. A toot that left Graham's mother in a state of free-floating rage, which she directed mostly at her children.

And it stayed directed at them for as long as Graham was living at home. As he put it that first night to John, it was as if he and his brothers were the ones to blame, as if *they* were the ones who'd left—which was very convenient for her, Graham noted, because as a matter of fact, they were still right there and available to take the brunt of her anger.

"She *hit* you?" John asked, incredulous. Graham had laughed at his surprise. She had, of course she had, but mostly in a way that made Graham feel sorry for her—quick slaps at one or another of their faces, a wild swing at the back of someone's head or his butt as he walked past. Laughable, really. And ineffectual. So sometimes he was able to tell himself it wasn't really so bad.

But then he'd remember some incident. Once, his mother sitting on one of his younger brothers in the front hallway, screaming, lifting his shoulders up repeatedly so that his head banged the floor over and over.

Graham had been watching afternoon television in the living room. The laugh track rose loudly enough over his mother's voice to allow him to pretend to ignore her. He remembered that he'd actually tried to justify her rage to himself, thinking that after all, his brother had stolen money from her purse—what did he expect? And maybe his brother was thinking that too, because he wasn't resisting their mother, though he was of an age and a size that if he'd wanted to, he could have.

Once, drunk, she'd really come at Graham, but he was able to pin her arms down against her sides. Trapped in this odd embrace, she had leaned her head against his chest. She started to cry, as though he really was holding her, as though he were comforting her.

This had repulsed him. He'd let go of her and turned quickly to leave, to flee. At the door he'd looked back. She was standing there, wailing, as helpless as a child, and all he could feel in that moment was a perverse joy. He was *glad* she'd hit him, glad she seemed to dislike him so. It meant he didn't have to feel sorry for her. He could leave without guilt now, and when the time came to really leave, to leave forever, he would be able to escape without guilt too.

He did escape, as soon as he finished high school. He saw her twice again in his life. Once when one of his brothers got out of prison, a seven-year sentence for trafficking heroin. There was a party for him, and he wanted Graham to be there. And when his next oldest brother died of cancer at thirty-two, Graham went to his funeral. He was married to Frieda by then, and Lucas was a baby, so he brought them along, a kind of shield.

He's late for his lunch with John—he can see him as he enters the dining room at Harvest, a small man, bald, bent over the table reading something in the light that's falling in from the patio. It's crowded and noisy out there under the spreading tree, where everyone wants to sit in this weather. The rumble of conversation and the clinking of implements drift in through the opened doors. It's quieter here, inside. Dimmer. More elegant. Just a sprinkling of people, couples mostly.

Graham remembers abruptly the funkier way the restaurant had looked years earlier, with the big central bar taking up about half of this room. One night, in that version of things, he'd seen Marianne Faithfull, middle-aged then, sitting unnoticed and alone at a small table, drinking, smoking. This is one of the things Graham loves about having lived in the same place for so long—the layers of time you're always moving through.

John's concentration is so intense that he doesn't notice Graham until he is standing next to John's table. A technical article of some kind, Graham can see by the charts and footnotes, even as John feels his presence and looks up. He rises, smiling broadly. He hugs Graham, arms reaching up to pat him on the back.

"Apologies," Graham says as they both sit down.

John is still smiling. He has a boy's unlined, open face, though it always looks slightly worried in repose. "It was ever thus," he says.

This isn't quite true, Graham thinks. Not the *ever* part anyway. *Occasionally thus* would be more accurate. But John's words were spoken in a tone of wry affection, and it was the affection that Graham heard most clearly. "I know, I know," he says.

They compliment each other on the health of their appearances. As they're looking over the menu, talking about what to order, John asks about the bookstore and Graham talks about how much better they're doing, about the possible resurgence of the independent. John mentions Annie, and Graham tells him about her show, for a moment feeling the pang again of his forgetting it. "It's being mounted as we speak. How long are you staying? Maybe you can get to the opening. Sunday afternoon."

John shakes his head. "That won't work. I have stuff right through the afternoon, and then as soon as I'm done, I have to leave. I have permission to attend this conference on the condition that I get my ass back up to Maine the second it's over."

"What a taskmaster."

They are talking about Betsy, whom John married as soon as he graduated from college—at about the same time Graham married Frieda. The difference being that John and Betsy are still married and have three children.

The waiter comes, and they order their food—fish for John, a salad for Graham. They talk about their kids—John's three are all in math or tech stuff, are all doing well. He speaks with pride about each of them.

It's a blur for Graham. He doesn't understand their work any more than he understands John's, and he's distracted anyway. He'd like to talk to John about the situation he's in with Rosemary. He wants help. He wants advice. Or perhaps not advice. Perhaps just sympathy.

"And Sarah?" John says now. "Lucas?"

So Graham takes his turn with this instead—his kids, two of them, one from his marriage with Frieda, one with Annie. Lucas, doing well in publishing in New York, Sarah working for an NPR talk show in California. "I'm not sure exactly what it is she does. Kind of research, I guess. She's happy though. I think. Maybe a bit afloat."

He doesn't speak of his ongoing sadness for her—he isn't sure he has a right to it. She *is* happy, he thinks, but she seems to him to live mostly for her work and for the long hikes she takes in the Sierras each summer with a group of people she knows from college.

"Yeah," John says. "Probably not much of a career path there."

Graham smiles. "She'd be so full of contempt if she heard you say that. 'How fucking bourgeois can you be?'"

"Yeah, well, watch me," John says.

They grin at each other. After a moment, Graham says, frowning, "It's just I don't think she has a dating life at all."

"Maybe she's gay," John offers cheerfully.

"She could still have a *dating* life."

"Yes. Of course." John waves his hand, as if dismissing his own stupidity. "Of course she could." After a moment, his face thoughtful, he says, "But it might be a reason she wouldn't talk to you about it."

They speculate about this—if Sarah were gay, would she feel comfortable telling Annie and Graham? Would one of John's boys, telling him and Betsy such a thing? They assess their readiness for this, their openness to it. They agree Graham would be easier about it. They wonder about it: Is this because Graham is more relaxed about his kids than John is about his? Because Graham is more relaxed, period? Or is it because Sarah is a girl, and somehow, because they're both straight men, lesbianism would be easier for either of them to accept than homosexuality?

They think so, they think that's right. "You just can't escape it, can you?" John says. "Straightness."

"*Maleness*," Graham says, feeling his sense of shame descending again. Or maybe, he thinks, just self-pity.

The food comes and they start to eat, reporting to each other on how things taste. Graham is a foodie, mostly because Annie is a good cook. He always finds the food here only adequate, though also seemingly ambitious to be better than that. Today, as usual, he's slightly disappointed, and John makes fun of him for his impossible standards. "It's a *salad*, Graham. Cut it some slack."

After a few moments Graham sets his fork down and says, "I'm in a bit of trouble, my old friend."

"Uh-oh." John's gaze up at him is quick. "The usual?"

"What do you mean?"

"Well, women."

"That's not usual."

"No? Wasn't that what ended things with Frieda?"

"That was decades ago, John. A different world. Different times."

"Okay, but wasn't there something earlier with Annie too?"

"God, one thing."

"Okay," John says. He has another bite of fish. He looks at Graham again. He's frowning, serious—his almost smooth face that of a troubled child. "Still, I remember it."

Graham is silent for a long moment. Finally he says, "This is different. This is the first time in a long, long time."

"Okay. I take you at your word," John says. "So. What was the draw?"

Graham explains the history of the thing, how he'd more or less backed into it. John's face has shifted, become faintly amused, but he's listening.

"I went a couple of times more," Graham says. "It was kind of like drinking too much. I'd tell myself I really should stop, and then I'd tell myself, well, just this once more and then I will."

"The sex was great." This is a question.

"Sure." Then, because this seems tepid, "Yes. It was good." His tone is dismissive, but he's thinking of the shock of Rosemary's soft, lush flesh, so different from Annie's. The amazement of entering her. The unqualified, undrugged hard-on he had that first time.

"And you don't need to tell me, because I know, I know it was because it was new, it was different. And then"—he will think later in the day with chagrin of saying this—"amongst other things, she had shaved her pussy. Or, I suppose, waxed it."

Why is he telling John this? Why isn't he telling him also how it reminded him instantly of Sarah as a little girl, the deep, naked cleft? How alarmed he was at first? How he wasn't sure, for a moment, that he would be able to go on?

"Ah." John nods his head knowingly.

Graham sits back. He's surprised at John's response. "Well, what's *that* about?"

"What do you mean?"

"I mean, I guess it's . . . Well, I have been led to believe that it's the norm now."

"It is."

"But why? When did this *happen*?"

"While you and I were sound asleep, my friend," John says, and a smile changes his worried-looking face. He adds, "It's from porn."

"Yeah?"

John makes a small noise, a kind of uncomfortable laugh. Then he sets his fork down and says, "The thing is, in most porn now, women are bare. I mean, no pubic hair at all. It's, you know, it's useful, in porn. It's so everyone can *see* everything. And I guess that's more or less where kids—men in particular—learn about sex now. From porn. So that's their expectation, they're accustomed to it. That's what they want. At home too, as it were. It's sexier to them." He shrugs, making a face. "So slowly it becomes the norm. It probably ends up feeling sexier to the women, too."

"But this is a woman who's my age. Maybe five years younger."

"What can I tell you? Maybe she celebrated getting divorced by getting a wax job."

The waiter appears at the table to ask them if everything's all right. Yes, they say. Yes. They smile. Delicious. He nods, approvingly, and leaves.

After a long moment, Graham laughs. He leans forward and says, "How do you *know* all this crap?"

"Three boys, my friend. I know so much more than I ever wanted to about how sex works today."

Graham laughs again. John smiles ruefully across at him. "It seems to me it's a little . . . sad, in some ways."

"It is, I think."

They both pick up their forks and knives and return to the food.

Graham says, "I can't believe we're talking about this. Over lunch."

"I know. I know. We should be more high-minded."

"It's me," Graham says, feeling it: John is high-minded. "My bad. My fault."

"If it's any comfort, I think of you as fairly high-minded. It's just this thing, this thing you have with women."

"C'mon, John, I don't have a thing. It's been a long time anyway. And then this . . . mess." They are quiet for a few moments, eating.

"Have you ever cheated?" Graham says. "On Betsy?"

John shakes his head. "I haven't." He shrugs. "I just feel so . . . bound to her. It's unthinkable, really." He smiles. "On the other hand, I have *thought* about it every now and then. Maybe more than that." He grins at Graham. "So, actually I guess it is. Thinkable."

Graham returns the smile. He has finished eating. He sits back, watching his friend.

John says, "If I didn't feel I'd be doing it *to* her, in some sense—Bets, I mean—maybe then I could. But that's what it would feel like." He frowns. "Maybe this is part of my response to the missing-father thing. Just, I always have to be there." His face changes. He grins. "*Uxorious.* Remember you called me that once?"

Graham shakes his head. "I don't."

"Well, you did. I had to look it up. And I suppose I am."

After a moment, Graham says, "I feel that bond to Annie, too. That need to be there. I do."

John frowns. "So why this other person? Why isn't it enough, with Annie?"

That isn't the point, Graham thinks. It isn't the point. "It *is* enough, with Annie," he says. "It was something else I wanted with Rosemary."

"What?" John's hands open on the table.

Graham shrugs. "Excitement, I suppose." Maybe even this very anguish, he thinks. "And it could be that if she'd been more interesting at that level, I'd actually want more now, instead of just wanting out." He is trying not to think about that, wanting more. He is, after all, right to want out. Right for all the reasons he didn't let himself think of when he wanted in.

Or didn't *want in* so much as *allow himself to respond to her.* He suddenly sees this clearly. It startles him. God. So even in this, he hasn't been an adventurer, a seeker, so much as a schlump. No, a schlemiel. He slowly shakes his head. He made nothing happen.

It happened *to* him. Because he let it.

John's face has sobered. He says, gently, "So, you plan to end it."

"Well, I've tried." He clears his throat. "I have. But it seems apparent to me that she . . . she would prefer not to."

"Ah," John says.

"It's because of the divorce, I know it. Her divorce, which is less than a year old. And I understand it. I understand it. I did it too after the divorce from Frieda. That's just what divorced people *do*, at first. I wanted to be with someone, and for a while I grabbed at whoever happened along. I honestly thought I loved them all. Seriatim, of course. I would have sworn I did. And I think that's what Rosemary—her name is Rosemary—I think that's what she's feeling. It doesn't have much to do with me, I don't think. I was just the one who happened to be there."

"But also the one who went along with it."

"Yes," Graham says. "As is my wont, as you so kindly point out."

They sit in silence for a few minutes, looking out to the patio, which has slowly emptied out, only two couples left.

"I'm sorry," John says. "I just . . ."

Graham sighs. "Okay. I mean, you're right. I did go along with it. I did. But we were coming from different . . . well, with different expectations, I guess."

"Okay." John leans forward, his face earnest again. "So let her know that. That she misunderstood you. That you misunderstood her."

"I've tried. I've tried to be honest."

John smiles.

"I know. I know." Graham does know. He's not honest. He wants too much for everyone to like him to be honest.

Annie is honest. She tells the truth. She's told him, honestly, about things she's done that she regrets. People she's hurt. About how she struggles with her feelings of reserve. Of "chilliness," she's called it more than once. And she told him, after all, about the lovers she had after they met. Even about someone later in their marriage that she never slept with, but was attracted to.

But Graham is trying, anyway, to be honest now with John. Trying not to excuse himself.

The waiter comes over and clears their plates away. He asks if they need anything else. Coffee, John says, and Graham asks for some too.

"You have to talk to her," John says, when the waiter has left.

"But I have."

"More. You have to be mean." He shakes his fist and then smiles again at Graham. "A little tiny bit mean. I know that's hard for you, but you're going to have to. Tell her Annie is your first love and your last love, and that's not going to change."

"She is. She is. Well, not the first, of course. But yes, the last. She's . . . I love her. I love her still. I'm not interested in a life with anyone else. At this point I'm not even interested in sex with anyone else. I just feel . . ."

John waits for a moment, and then he says gently, "That's it, then. That's all you have to say."

"Yeah." They sit in a silence that feels warm and enveloping to Graham. On the walk back to the bookstore, he will think of the word *eased*. He's feeling it now, that ease, and it makes him understand how anxious he's been for these weeks.

"So what's the conference?" he asks.

It's on artificial intelligence, and John talks about it for a while—it seems, to Graham, with the same eager tone he was using himself when he was telling John about Rosemary earlier. But this is just so much *better* than his own tired tale. He feels an increasing sense of shame as John goes on. He thinks again of the cheesiness of telling him about Rosemary's bare pussy.

The coffee comes, and then after that, the check. Graham picks it up quickly. They argue for a moment, but Graham succeeds in holding on to it and setting down his credit card. While they wait for its return, they talk in a more desultory way about the health of friends, illnesses. People they both know who've died. How impossible it is to believe in, death. That it's striking so close.

John describes a funeral he thought was "wonderful." His word. He'd like something like that when he dies, he says.

Graham looks at his friend, so boyish, so . . . *unmarked*, he thinks. "You're crazy even to be thinking about it," he says.

As they are standing on the street saying goodbye, Graham remembers to ask John about the dinner party the next night, whether he can come.

He'd love to, John says. He might be a little late—there's a cocktail hour after the lectures are over, and he feels obliged to make an appearance—but he'd love to. They embrace, and turn away from each other.

Graham walks slowly through the gentle air down Mount Auburn Street, aware of a sense of relief. (It's now that the word *eased* comes to him.) It doesn't matter, it never does, exactly what he and John say to each other, it doesn't matter what advice John gives him—in this case it is, after all, the same advice he's been giving himself for weeks now. What matters is their history together, the way they understand each other. John can say anything to him, really, and Graham will hear in it the affection, the loyalty, that comes along with the words.

But there was that one time, he remembers now, when this

wasn't so. How much it wounded him! A dinner years earlier, a dinner with John at his and Annie's house. They'd had champagne to celebrate their being together, they toasted one another, they talked about their lives, their work.

Eventually, as usual, he and John came back to the central topic between them: their lost fathers, and how it affected them to be abandoned, how it stayed with them. About the various ways they acted out as young men. Annie was mostly quiet at this point, listening, watching them. As the evening passed, the wax from the candles had made odd shapes on the table, and she was idly picking at some of these shapes.

They talked about their relationships to their mothers. Graham's, of course, was by now a nonrelationship. John's was one of resentment. He'd always felt that his mother might have known where his father was, at least some of the time. But she'd died, and if she did know, that information had died with her.

After a long, silent moment, John had said, "It's so odd, isn't it, that with these useless jerks for fathers, it's our mothers we're so pissed off at."

Graham offered his theory: the problem was that they both felt their mothers should have been better at being *women*. At being wives. "They should have held on to our fathers for us," he said. "It was all their fault."

They were quiet for a moment. Then Graham said, "Lost boys, lost boys." He smiled. "It excuses everything we've ever done wrong, of course. We wuz *done to* first."

"Oh, everyone was *done to*," John had said.

"I suppose," Graham said. "You know the Larkin poem. 'They fuck you up, your Mum and Dad.'"

"God, that's in a *poem*?" John said.

Graham stood up, his chair sliding back making a harsh sound on the floor, and recited it from memory.

"The English scholar, strutting his stuff," John said.

"But it's the only stuff I have," Graham said. "And there are so few opportunities in life to strut it."

He sat back down. They were all silent a moment. Graham could see that Annie was stifling a yawn. Her neck corded, her eyes silvered with tears.

John said, "It doesn't save you from being an asshole, though—having been fucked up."

"You talkin' to me?" Graham said in what he thought of as a tough-guy voice.

"I'm talking to—or maybe I'm talking about—all of us. Just, it's an old tired story, that's all, the damaged person who can't be held responsible for the damage *he* causes."

Graham felt shamed. He felt John had misunderstood him. "You know I wasn't serious, right?"

"I don't know," John said. "You ask too much of other people, I think sometimes."

"Like what?"

John had paused then. It was as though he knew he was about to hurt Graham. He looked at him across the table in the flickering light, and then he shrugged. "Forbearance, I guess. If not forgiveness."

Graham had felt Annie's eyes on him. He looked at her. She was watching. They were all solemn for a moment.

Then John had changed the subject, and they were on to something else—the kids, or politics, or the Red Sox—and Annie got up to make some coffee, which it turned out no one wanted. Graham opened another bottle of wine, and Annie excused herself, went up to bed.

They sat for a long time after that, he and John, talking. They talked while they did the dishes too, their voices pitched loud over the clatter of it—talking, laughing together.

A while after Graham had come to bed, Annie spoke to him,

almost a whisper in the dark. "What did John mean, do you think, when he said you ask so much of everyone? Their forbearance."

Graham was startled. He'd assumed she was asleep when he lay down next to her. He had been on his side, curved toward her, but now he flopped onto his back and looked at the ceiling, at the faint light from Karen's back porch slanting across it. He was glad Annie couldn't see his face. Finally he said, "Just, I think, that I'm a loud fat man who spends more of his time away from home, glad-handing everyone I see, than I should. I drink too much. I have to have everyone's love. So, yes, forbearance is called for. Maybe forgiveness too."

That's it, isn't it? he thinks now, walking along Mount Auburn Street. A greedy, fat, entitled baby. Everything born of some unsatisfied need on his part.

He thinks of the forgivable entitlement of babies, of their great need. He remembers the perfect faces of his own children in infancy, their fragile heads moving with a desperate snuffling motion as they sought the breast. Little animals. He thinks of Frieda with Lucas, Annie with Sarah, both of them seemingly so lost when the children were little. "I don't even have a mind anymore," Annie said once, picking up Sarah to nurse her.

Annie, with fat full breasts! He had been so surprised by that, the newness of it. Remembering this, his joy in it, he feels again the downward pull of the task awaiting him—the job of making it right again.

He passes the glass front of the store and turns into its doorway.

The bookstore. He loves it. He loves walking through the door. He loves the tables where the fiction and nonfiction books that the staff like best are set out. He loves the deep, comfortable chairs scattered around, and the pleasure of seeing people in them, reading under the floor lamps. He loves the low-ceilinged room upstairs where the art books, the books on photography and travel, are kept.

He loves the wooden counter running in front of the big plate-glass windows that look out on Mount Auburn Street, he loves the office in the back with its long single desk where they all sit in a row, facing their computers. He loves the kinds of conversations they have—about writers, about wonderful passages that must be read aloud, about fictional characters. Conversations often broken off midstream by something someone has to do, but always, he feels, important. He loves unboxing the books, pulling them out, looking at the typeface, the cover, the author photo, the acknowledgments.

He waves at Bill behind the counter, then goes to the office to tell Georgie and Emily and Erica he's here. Georgie passes him a message slip. "A woman," she says. "She didn't give her name. She said you'd know." He pockets it without looking at it. He talks to Emily about the numbers to order from Knopf, he talks to Erica about arrangements for Jamie's reading.

He goes out to the floor to make himself useful by calling the people whose special orders have come in. In between a couple of these calls, he takes out the message slip Georgie gave him and reads it. "It's Thursday," it says, in Georgie's neat handwriting. She's put quotes around the words, and there are three question marks on the line where the caller's name should go.

He makes his next call to Rosemary. When she answers, he says, "I'm not going to make it today."

"Oh," she says. "I'll miss you."

He doesn't answer.

"Is it hard to talk right now?"

"It's always hard at the store." Though at the moment, everyone out here is busy. He could say whatever he wanted and no one would hear. "But we do need to talk."

"Good," she says. "When?"

"I'll let you know."

"When?" she says.

"I'll call you tomorrow. There's a lot to discuss."

She's quiet for a long moment. Then she says, "That sounds ominous."

He doesn't know what to say. Finally he offers, "Well, maybe it is. A little."

"What's that supposed to mean?" she says. And after a moment: "Graham?"

"I'll call tomorrow, " he says. "We'll make a time."

There's another long silence. "Fine," she says, and hangs up.

Graham stands there for a few minutes. Outside the window, an elderly man wearing a black beret—a Harvard type, Graham thinks—is talking to a woman his own age. Their polite white heads bob over and over, while the large black dog at the end of the leash the man holds is shitting in the dirt around the tree Graham considers his own. Graham doesn't move, though. He doesn't bang on the glass as he might otherwise do. His heart is pounding, but he feels sure now that he can do it, he can end things with Rosemary. He was rude, a bit, though he hadn't really intended it. Perhaps, yes, unkind. But he had put something in motion. He had said they would talk. Now that would have to happen.

5

ANNIE'S STUDIO WAS in Somerville, in an old red-brick industrial building near Union Square, an area full of other old industrial buildings, almost all of them converted into condominiums by now—you could tell which by the curtains or the treelike plants visible inside some of the old steel window frames. The artists in Annie's building knew the days were numbered until this happened to their building, and Annie had actually begun to look around for another studio. She understood, though, that it would be hard to replace this one, she'd had it for so long and it was so perfect for her. Graham had helped her build it out, making it into a two-room space. Both rooms, the darkroom and the open area, were just the right size—the working area large and light, the darkroom smaller and windowless.

She used the darkroom only occasionally now—almost all of her work was in color and digital at this point, and she paid a lab to have the printing done. Slowly the little space had filled up with boxes and files and camera equipment. She felt almost apologetic every time she opened the door.

In the middle of the larger room she had a big square worktable set up. She moved around it now, getting ready to wrap things, setting out the equipment she'd need—the bubble wrap, the tape, the box-cutter.

The pictures she and Danielle had agreed on were leaning against the walls all around the room. It had been a difficult process, choosing which ones to include. Annie had unthinkingly left up some of the photos she'd taken at the start of the farming article, the ones that still had people in them. When Danielle saw them, she'd assumed they would be among the images they'd hang in the show. She couldn't believe that Annie didn't want to use any of them. As a result, the tone between them was strained from the start.

Then Danielle didn't want several of the pictures that Annie liked best. One the grimy kitchen of a farmhouse, everything *embrowned*, as Annie thought of it, but with a solitary, pristine bottle of milk set out, a pure, almost overwhelming white against the worn maroon linoleum of the counter. Another, the unoccupied living room of an elderly couple Annie had grown fond of. The television was on, turned to a morning talk show, and the furniture was clustered around it, as though the blurry talking heads were honored guests. The fireplace was visible behind the television—the fireplace that might have been central in some earlier life. Instead it was overflowing with sloppily stacked-up old newspapers and magazines.

"God, these are incredibly depressing," Danielle said. She preferred the photos of more civilized, orderly interiors. She liked one of Frieda's bedroom, spare and neat and chaste-looking, the bed carefully made. She found it "Dickinsonian."

Danielle was hard to argue with, and part of that was how impeccable she was personally. Small—about Annie's size—delicate, her hair cut just so, in a sort of Louise Brooks bob. She had perfect skin, she wore clothes that were unusual and yet also elegant—Issey Miyake kind of clothes. Clothes that reeked of money. You couldn't stand in front of her in blue jeans and insist on anything. "Really?" she'd say. It was never a question.

"Really?" she'd said to another shot Annie liked—a picture she'd taken of her own empty bed, the sheets tangled after she and Graham had made love, books scattered on the floor on either side of it. "A little too cluttered for me. And we've seen this kind of thing before, don't you think?"

Well, Annie knew what she meant, but she had thought of the image as an evocation of the intimate, sexual heart of a marriage. She had wanted it to be the first thing people saw at the show.

They'd agreed on several other shots of farmhouse interiors, tidier, cleaner, but in their own way just as arresting—maybe even disturbing. One had dozens of gnomelike figures set everywhere, as though they were observing or supervising the life of the absent inhabitants—or taking over, which was how Annie liked to think of it. Another was of a kitchen saturated with color and busy with pattern, every shelf covered with flowered paper, the walls with cheerful or kitschy mottoes. The chairs at the table were cushioned in gingham, and hanging on the wall over all of this was the picture of a gorgeous, Aryan Jesus Christ, looking down with forgiving pale-blue eyes while he held open the bosom of his white robe to reveal, through a tidy opening, his valentine-shaped heart, a vibrant orange-red. After they'd agreed on several more like these, Danielle had yielded to Annie on three or four of her favorites.

Once she'd finished wrapping the framed photographs, it took Annie a long time to load the car—one picture at a time, up and down the three dark flights of sloping stairs over and over, once nearly tripping on one of the loose aluminum strips nailed along the outer edge of each step. When she turned to shut her studio door for the last time, carrying the last photograph, she was startled at how barren the room looked, how emptied out.

It was after two by now, and she was tired and hungry. She drove to the South End, and then through its streets of bow-fronted brick town houses, most of them renovated—the outward signs of that being the polished brass of the door hardware, the fresh black of the wrought-iron fences and ornate railings, the chic plantings in the tiny front yards.

She bought a sandwich to go at a shop she liked on the ground floor of one of the old town houses. She sat on a bench in the nearby park to eat, watching the Chinese boys playing pickup basketball on the asphalt court and the dog owners standing around talking to each other in the enclosure while their pets dashed wildly back and forth in barking waves.

She was thinking of this morning, of Graham. It was clear to her that he'd forgotten completely about the show: *What are you up to today?* She shook her head now—it had been so surprising.

Was she angry at him about that, then?

Not really, she thought. More puzzled. Puzzled because it loomed so large in her own thinking. And because it was so unlike him to forget what was happening in her life, even momentarily.

But something was going on with him. And she didn't know what.

Well, there it was, wasn't it? He had his life, his worries, and she had hers. Was that what was happening between them? The thought made her sad.

When she was finished eating, she went across the street to the chic wine shop there and bought a dozen bottles, half red, half white, for the dinner party tomorrow night. For dinner tonight, too.

She drove the few blocks to the gallery and parked in the vast empty lot next to it, encircled by the old factories, almost all of them full of offices and galleries and restaurants now. She carried the first framed photograph in. She could see Danielle in the office, busy on the phone. Her assistant, Valerie, was seated at the desk in the open gallery space, and she got up to help Annie, going back and forth with her, hauling the pictures in. Together they set them down, leaning them against the white walls below the paintings that were coming down the next day.

Before she left, Annie stopped in the office doorway to talk to Danielle. She was, as usual, a bit cool, a bit distant, but cordial. Just before Annie left, she said, pointing her finger at Annie, "This show is going to be good. It's going to get you going again."

"Well, I'm glad to hear that you think that." Annie couldn't keep the surprise out of her voice.

"Of course I do," Danielle said. She sounded surprised at Annie's surprise. "I wouldn't be interested in putting it up unless I felt strongly that way."

"Yes, of course," Annie said awkwardly. "Well, good!" She patted the doorframe for emphasis. "Great. I'll see you Saturday, then."

She drove distractedly back to Cambridge, the sun in her eyes as she headed west on Memorial Drive. She saw without truly noting them the tilted sailboats crowding the glimmering river, the half-naked joggers on the sidewalks that traced its banks, the Canada geese moving in slow waddling groups on the grass, their long necks arched to peck at the ground, their goslings strung out unevenly behind them, disorderly and confused-looking.

She was pondering the surprise of Danielle's vote of confidence. One of those mysterious people, so reserved as to seem critical when nothing like that was intended, apparently. How did she manage to have a life? She was married, she had grown children. What would it be like to have such an unreadable wife? Or mother, for that matter?

Then she was remembering that Sarah had accused her of something similar once when she was twelve or thirteen. Something like unreadability. It was after a dinner during which Sarah had loaded her plate with second helpings of everything. They had been to the doctor not long before, weight had been discussed, and Annie couldn't help herself, she made some comment. She couldn't now remember her exact wording, but it didn't matter. Sarah had burst into tears and fled the room. Her feet were thunderous as she mounted the back stairs.

"Oh, Christ," Annie had said wearily. She and Graham pushed their chairs back at the same time. "I'll do it," Annie said. "I started it."

She found Sarah lying on her bed, turned away from the doorway. The light from the hall fell on her rounded shape and on the poster on the wall behind her: Suzanne Farrell, *en pointe.* It had always made Annie sad, looking at it. Sarah had been five when she picked it out to decorate her room. She was taking classes at the Boston Ballet School. Already at that age she towered over the other students, those little fragile-looking girls. And it wasn't just her height that had made Annie ache for Sarah. It was her solidity, her unpretty thick legs, her loud voice, her big hands.

Annie asked if she could sit down.

"No," Sarah said, without turning over. "I don't want you here, and I don't want to talk to you. I don't want to hear any of the *understanding* things you're going to say. Because I know what you think."

"And what do I think?"

"You think I'm a fat pig."

"Oh, Sarah, that's not what I said."

"It's what you meant. You think I'm fat, and you hate me." She had readjusted herself slightly on the bed, and her voice was muffled now, smaller.

The problem for Annie was that she didn't feel loving toward Sarah at this time. Sarah was always angry at her. Annie felt it was because she was angry at life, and perhaps at herself, for the hand she'd been dealt. The big, smart, nondescript girl, too shy even to have friends. "I couldn't possibly hate you, Sarah. How could you think that?"

There was a long silence. Then the little voice said, "Well, you sure don't love me."

"That's not true. I do love you."

Sarah lifted her head and looked back over her shoulder at Annie. "How am I supposed to know that?" she said clearly. "You never show anything that you feel."

That was it, wasn't it? How Sarah thought of her. Annie couldn't remember what else they had said. Maybe not much more. She did remember going back downstairs and talking about it with Graham. Graham, whose relationship with Sarah at that stage—at every stage really—was so much easier than Annie's. They had conferred over the leftover dinner wine. They didn't often talk about it together—Sarah's size, her isolation—but now they did, keeping their voices low. How could they help her? Was there anything they could do to make her feel better?

Perhaps we should ask *her* that question, Graham said.

So he went up. When he came back down, he reported that Sarah had let him sit on the edge of her bed and rub her back, briefly. But when he asked her their question, whether there was anything he and Annie could do, she said no. She said they should just stop trying, that it made everything worse for her to know how much they worried about her.

Now Annie remembered that later that night, just as she was finally dropping off to sleep, Graham had spoken to her out of the dark in his gravelly voice: "Are you allowed to say that your own child makes you almost unbearably sad?"

They lay side by side without speaking for a minute. Annie felt swamped by her own sorrow about Sarah, by her inability to feel loving toward her at that period in their lives, by her awareness of Sarah's understanding of that, at whatever level she was experiencing it. "No," she had said then in the dark. "I don't think we want to begin that conversation."

* * *

SHE HAD ALREADY prepared the white beans with thyme and olive oil for tomorrow's dinner, and the plan was to put the lamb in a marinade tonight. But she still had some shopping to do—last-minute things.

Back in Cambridge, she stopped at Formaggio, the fancy neighborhood shop, for cheeses—cheeses and crackers and several kinds of olives. They had cherry tomatoes that looked nice in the produce section, so she got those too, and a few other things for a light dinner tonight.

Standing in line to check out, she was mindlessly looking over at the flowers displayed in the corner of the shop. There were tulips, lilacs, peonies, irises. Gorgeous, she thought. Hopeful, as spring flowers always are. She'd get some. For the party, of course. But for Graham, too. A pick-me-up against whatever it was that was bothering him.

She stepped out of the long line, sacrificing her place, and went over to the flower stand. As she was waiting for the person manning that counter to trim the bunches of things she'd chosen, to wrap them in the clear crackling cellophane they used here, she thought she saw Rosemary Gregory by the produce section. She couldn't quite tell, the woman turned away so quickly.

But when she went back over to rejoin the line to pay for the cheeses, yes, there she was. Annie stepped in line behind her. She was in gym clothes, her hair pulled back, enormous running shoes on her feet. "How are you?" Annie asked, thinking of Rosemary's divorce from their friend Charlie, of something Graham had said about her after a party they'd all been at a month or two earlier. That she seemed a bit . . . what was it? Desperate, maybe.

"Oh, I'm fine," Rosemary said.

"You shame me, exercising," Annie said. "I haven't been in weeks." This was almost so. Maybe ten days anyway. She'd been feeling vaguely guilty about it.

"I try to go every other day," Rosemary said.

There was a little silence that was just beginning to feel awkward when Rosemary spoke again. "Some bouquet! What's the occasion?"

"Well, we're having some people over after a reading at the store." And then, because she remembered at that moment that, of course, Rosemary hadn't been invited, she said, "The same party you've been to a dozen times." This wasn't true. They'd had Rosemary and Charlie over maybe three times, total.

Trying to change the subject, she said, "Really, though, they're for Graham."

"Oh?"

"Just that he's been a little blue lately, and I want to cheer him up. Plus, of course, it's a way of telling him what a nice husband he is."

"Oh," Rosemary said, her voice suddenly less friendly. "Well, good. Good for him. Good for you." And she stepped forward to pay for whatever she'd bought.

Leaving Annie feeling awkward and chagrined: the party Rosemary hadn't been invited to. The mention of a nice husband to someone just divorced. Why did she have to open her big mouth? She'd probably offended Rosemary. Worse maybe: wounded her.

But her sense of discomfort about this fell quickly away as she drove home through the warm green of the tree-lined streets. Inside, the house was lit with the rays of late-afternoon sun. She loved this time of day, the thick slantwise yellow light. She went back through it to the kitchen area and put away the food and wine she'd bought. She had just finished arranging the flowers in an old white slop pitcher when she saw Karen standing in their backyard. She was dressed now, but barefoot. The cat sat by the old lilacs between their properties, apparently waiting to see what she would do next.

Annie set the big pitcher down on the table. She opened the back door and went down the steps to where Karen was standing. She greeted the older woman, but Karen didn't answer her. She was looking at the boxwood that circled Annie's brick terrace.

Without lifting her eyes, she said in a soft, puzzled tone, as if to herself, "I've no idea why I planted these horrid box shrubs, when I detest them so. They'd better come out, I think."

"Oh, I think not," Annie said, perfectly cordial.

Karen looked up at Annie. "But they're so . . . unimaginative!" she said. "I've always hated them."

"That may be true," Annie said. "But since this is our yard, that just doesn't matter."

Karen's mouth opened. She was frowning, about to speak, but Annie spoke first. "Why don't you come inside, Karen? Come in, and I'll fix us a drink of some sort."

Karen looked at her. She seemed to be pondering this.

"Then we could sit out here, on my patio, to drink them."

The old woman's face shifted somehow. For the first time she looked as though she knew who Annie was. "Now that sounds lovely," she said. She smiled her chilly New England smile. "I've always liked your patio."

"Let's go get that drink, then," Annie said.

They went in, and Annie fixed Karen a shandy, always her drink of choice. She'd put two bottles of the good white wine in the refrigerator earlier, and now she opened one with the nearly hydraulic fancy corkscrew Graham had insisted on. ("When we want wine, we want it now!") She carried both of their glasses outside, leading the way. They sat on the terrace in the wicker chairs there, surrounded by the boxwoods, by birdsong. Her wine was a little too warm. In the distance somewhere, someone was playing the piano. Chopin, Annie thought. Nice rubato.

She looked over at Karen. "I love that dress you're wearing," she began.

6

AT FIVE THIRTY Graham takes over the second register, next to Bill. There's a steady flow of customers. Never a line, he never has to call for backup, but he has barely a moment to stop and think. And then it slows, and there are once again browsers moving slowly around the store or sitting in the chairs, reading. This is the time of day when he and Bill usually lean back against the top of the low wooden bookshelves that run under the windows behind the counter, lean back and talk to each other between customers.

Today that's not going to happen, though, because Graham realizes he's made a decision while he was so busy. Maybe it has to do with what he remembered John saying about him all those years ago, that he asked too much of people, that he needed forbearance. Maybe it has to do with Annie this morning, Annie in the sunlight, lifting her hands to him and saying "My sweet husband." Or John— John at lunch, saying about Rosemary, "Be mean to her, a bit. That's what you have to do."

So the next time he and Bill are standing idle next to each other, Graham asks him if he thinks he can manage alone until Sasha arrives—the part-timer who comes late and helps with the closing up.

"No problem," Bill says.

Graham fetches his suit jacket from the office. He locks that door behind him and says his good-night to Bill.

Outside the sun is lowering in the sky. In its syrupy yellow light, Graham walks fast. He turns right on Ash Street and walks up to Garden, then past the old brick hotel, past the intersection by the music school where you always have to wait for the walk signal. When he gets to Shepard, he turns right. He passes what used to be the Radcliffe Quad when he was young. Left on Avon, right on Martin, and there, almost at the corner of Gray and Martin, is the big house Rosemary lives in, a house she's going to have to put on the market, she's told Graham.

He's startled by her appearance as she opens the door. As she clearly is by his. Her mouth opens and her hand rises to her hair, which usually falls in long, carefully curled-under sweeps around her face. Now it's pulled tight and held in some kind of clip at the back of her head. Her face is scrubbed clean of makeup, pale and washed-out in a way he finds prettier, actually, than her usual careful presentation. This is not a presentation at all, and he's somehow touched by it. By her.

"I didn't expect you," she says, stepping back into the hallway, holding the door open for him.

"I know. Am I intruding?" He smiles at her. "Or really, I guess, *may I intrude?*" He bows slightly, a joke.

"Well, of course, now that you're here. I just wish . . ." And her hands rise again, a vague gesture. "I just got out of the shower." She shuts the door and they stand awkwardly in the wide hallway for a silent moment. Then she gestures behind her at the stairs, which rise up to a landing with a multipaned window. "Shall we?" she asks, smiling.

"Let's just sit for a while," he says, taking a few steps toward the open archway to the living room.

"Oh!" She hesitates. "Okay," she says, and follows him into the room.

He sits down on one of the two small matching couches facing each other on either side of the fireplace. The word comes: *settees*, they are. She remains standing, though she moves to the fireplace and rests her elbow on the wooden mantel above it. She's in khaki pants, and her feet are bare. Her toenails are painted a rich emerald green, another surprise for him the first time they made love.

He looks around. It's an old-fashioned room. Formal furniture, worn oriental carpets on the floor. Bookshelves on either side of the fireplace. He's been in this room only once, the first time he came over, but he didn't really take it in then. They'd had a drink, sitting on one of the couches together, but once they began touching each other, kissing, she suggested they go upstairs. After that, they went directly up to her bedroom each time he arrived, up to the king-size bed she'd shared until recently with her husband.

"You're making me a little nervous," she says now. Her smile looks forced. Anxious.

He feels suddenly overwhelmed by pity for her. He should have warned her, he should have let her fix herself up. His mother used to call it "war paint" when she got ready to go out. Lipstick, rouge— nothing as complicated as Rosemary's stylized eye makeup, or the skin makeup, whatever it was, that let her look unblemished. Today she's pale and freckled, and her eyes are unshadowed. They look exposed, smaller.

"Why don't you sit down too?" he says. He pats the settee next to him.

She does, she comes over and sits down, but at the opposite end of the settee. She swings her legs up, tucks her feet under her buttocks.

"Tell me why you've come, when you said earlier that you wouldn't." Her voice is flat, without the teasing, seductive tone she usually uses with him.

He's conscious of trying to make his own voice gentle. "I've come to say I can't come anymore."

He watches as her face changes, several times. At first, briefly, it's as if he'd struck her. She sits up taller. Then she almost smiles. Somehow, within a few seconds, she's achieved a kind of pained dignity. "Why not?" she asks. Her voice is polite enough, but still expressionless.

"It's too dangerous. For my marriage."

She looks levelly at him. Then she smiles in an unfriendly way and says in mock surprise, "Oh, you're *married!*"

He waits a moment before he answers her. "As it turns out, I am. Or really, as it turns out, I always was." He takes a deep breath. "I always felt . . . bad, about this. About us. Even when I felt most good."

She is silent. Then she says, "When was that?" her voice empty again.

"When I felt most good?"

"Yes."

"When we made love, of course. When all of that fell away for a few moments."

He's become aware of her hands in motion on her lap, her fingers scratching at her thumbs. "And then it came back?" she says. *"All of that?"*

"Yes."

After a moment, she speaks again. Her voice is almost hoarse. "And what, exactly, was all of that?"

He takes a deep breath. "It was Annie. The way I feel about Annie. The way I always feel about Annie."

"Except for those few moments when that *fell away.*"

"Yes."

Her hands still. "Well, you must have wanted it to fall away."

"I suppose I must have in some way, or I wouldn't have come. But that's not what I'm aware of feeling."

There have been pauses between everything they've been saying to each other. Now, after another pause—as though it's taking her a long time to form the correct question—she says, "What are you aware of feeling?"

He can't tell if she's mocking him, but he doesn't want to think about that now. "Mostly that I love Annie. That I want to guard my love for her."

A bitter little smile reshapes her lips.

"That I want to protect her. That I don't want to hurt her."

"How nice that must be for her. To be protected."

Now it's his turn to pause. "I'm sorry. I'm sorry that I can't protect you, Rosemary. That you're, more or less, out here on your own. I'm sorry."

Her face goes rubbery, unpretty. Tears rise in her eyes. He can hear her breathing slowly, trying to stay in control of herself.

"It's no consolation, I know," he says. Yet he wants to console her. He wants to protect her too. "I know a little, I think, of how it feels to be newly alone. To want someone. Anyone, really. To be . . . unready to see how unlikely it is for some particular person to work out."

"A person such as you." An accusation, as she says it.

"Such as me." He bows his head slightly: *okay*.

Her breathing slows, her face sags. It seems she won't cry, after all.

"I'd be a bad bet even if there was no Annie, Rosemary. I would have been. I'm just not good at saying no. I want—I always want to say yes. And I *want* to want to say yes. To everything. I'm a greedy person. More or less bottomlessly hungry." He thinks of babies again. "What I've tried to be, with Annie, is less hungry. In general, less hungry. More hungry just for her."

"No luck there, it would seem."

"Well. You interrupted a long string of luck."

She looks away, out the big curved window in the bay behind the couch. The settee. "Just *my* luck, I guess."

He reaches out. He puts his hand on her knee, the part of her closest to him. "It *is* your luck. Your luck that I'm getting out of your life. As a lover."

She looks back at him, sharply. "Oh, you'll be my *friend*," she says, with heavy sarcasm.

"I am your friend. I wasn't your friend when we started this. But I am. I am being your friend now."

"Sure. A friend I won't see again. Or talk to alone again. Or touch again."

Without planning to, he lifts his hand from her knee.

She looks down and laughs, a quick bitter noise. "Yes, indeed," she says.

After a moment he says, "Do you remember what I was saying to you when all this started? At dinner that night?"

"No."

"I said how many people were going to be lined up to be your lover. How many men. And I meant that. It's just that I shouldn't have been the first in line. I should have been smart enough to treat it as a kind of joke when you suggested it—that I get in line. But it's true. There will be others. Better others. In the sense that I've been a crappy other. Chock-full of my own torment and guilt. And useless to you."

She looks out the window again. It's open a few inches. The air stirs outside, the leaves rustle. She looks back at him, her face unguarded. "But what if I love you?" she says softly.

"You don't." He shakes his head. "You wouldn't ask it that way if you did."

Her voice instantly hardens. "Oh, you know better. You know better than I do what I feel."

"And if I say yes, that I do?" They sit, each looking at the other, as quickly as that, enemies.

She smiles. "Do you know what you sound like, Graham?"

"No."

"You sound exactly like a parent, talking to an adolescent."

Suddenly he's remembering talking to Sarah in her adolescence, telling her it would end—her loneliness, her pain. Her weight problem.

How little he's done for anyone he loves, really.

"I'm sorry," he says. "I don't mean to. It's the last thing I mean to sound like. Or to be."

She's looking down now. "I think you should go," she says tonelessly.

"Fair enough." He stands.

Rosemary doesn't move. She's still not looking at him.

He waits for a moment. Should he touch her? Kiss her goodbye? He'd imagined something like that, he realizes. Yes. A fond goodbye. Forgiveness.

Stupid, stupid.

All he can see of her from this angle, standing above her—her face turned down—is the top of her head, the pinned-up damp hair drooping against the curve of her cheek.

He crosses to the archway at the foyer and stops. "I'm sorry," he says.

"Sure," she says, softly.

Without looking back again, he goes to the door, opens it onto the evening air, and steps outside.

For the first few blocks, he carries his remorse with him. And then it begins to lift—though there's shame in that, isn't there? In that lifting?

Yes. And remorse, for that quick reversal.

But he can also feel a kind of joy rising in him, a release. His pace over the bumpy bricks quickens. On the sidewalk outside the convenience store a few blocks from home, he sees a white plastic five-gallon bucket with a few only-slightly-tired bouquets left in it. Daisies and some other purplish flower. Annie, he thinks. An offering for Annie. He pulls a bunch out of the water, the stems dripping, and takes it inside to pay for it.

Carrying his bouquet as he walks, he begins to feel somehow *aimed* at her. An arrow making its way directly to her. He actually tries running for a few steps, but that's not going to work. He slows down, panting. Amused at himself, at his absurd idea of himself—the heavy bear, as arrow—he laughs out loud. He'll make a silly story of this for Annie. Another offering. He takes his jacket off and slings it over his shoulder, dangling it from one finger.

At home, Graham shuts the front door behind him and turns to the shadowed house to call Annie's name. But he can tell, even before he does, that she isn't home. That there is no one home. He was so ready to be received back into his own life that his disappointment feels like a kind of grief. He's suddenly tired. He goes slowly through the living room to the big kitchen to find a vase for Annie's flowers.

But then he hears her, outside, her voice steady and gentle. The back door and the windows are open, and she's sitting with Karen in the old chairs on the patio. Graham stops, motionless, the flowers in his hand. He stands within the kitchen's shadows, looking out at her, feeling a wash of relief, feeling how close he has come today to the nothingness of a moment ago, when there was no one here to welcome him.

Karen says something, her voice querulous, and Annie answers her.

He watches her face, the play of amusement and concern as Karen talks now at some length about something. Her eyebrows register her response. Graham loves her eyebrows, her dark eyebrows, and the way they give her away, even when her face is most still.

He notices then that there's another—a much better—bouquet set on the kitchen table in the old white pitcher. It's enormous and droopy and lush, giving off an intense lilac odor.

Ah! *These* are the flowers that he should have bought for Annie, the ones he would have bought if he could, the ones that would have spoken to her of everything—his sorrow about himself. His love for her.

He steps forward and bends over them to breathe in the rich, erotic perfume. Something funny happens for a moment in his chest, and then it seems to him that the world shifts and is full of an almost painful joy. Just as he lifts his head to look at Annie again, she looks up too, she sees him there in the dark, and her face opens to him in a kind of answer.

7

ANNIE AND KAREN had been talking for a while when she looked up at a motion she'd caught in the kitchen and saw Graham there. He was in shadow, but she could see his face—he was looking back at her—and, as happened every now and then between them, she felt such a welling of love for him that her body seemed to *soften*, somehow. She turned back to Karen in a state of intense awareness, awareness of waiting for him, of feeling everything attendant on this moment.

He came outside a few minutes later, carrying a glass of wine, wearing one of his beautiful old shirts, his amazing shoes. "My two favorite women," he said.

He stepped toward Karen. Annie was watching the old woman as he bent over her. Her toes, with their thickened, untrimmed nails, actually turned up in pleasure when he kissed her on the top of her head.

He came over to Annie then and lightly touched his lips to hers, his soft beard brushing her chin, her cheek.

Stepping back, raising his glass, he said, "Here's to beauty. By which I mean both of you." He drank in a dramatic gesture, swinging his arm wide before bringing the glass to his mouth.

"And you," Karen said, raising her glass too, and then drinking. Her lips made a light smacking noise. She lowered her glass and said, "You arrived in the *nick* of time—I've just gotten back from my trip."

"What trip?" Annie asked.

She frowned at Annie, annoyed. "Paris!" she said. Her voice was impatient. "Paris, of course."

Graham and Annie looked at each other. She raised her eyebrows for him. After a few seconds, Graham turned to Karen and said, "Someplace I've always wanted to go."

"Well, you *should*!" Karen said. "It's lovely. Fully as elegant as they say it is."

He laughed.

After a moment, Annie said, "Karen and I have been having a drink in our unimaginative backyard."

"What a thing to say!" Karen cried.

"Well," Annie answered, "that's what you said about it."

"I never did," Karen said.

"You hinted at it, I think. A bit broadly, I would say."

"Well, I didn't mean it then. Don't be so quick to take offense."

"I don't think I am," Annie said.

"How did your packing up go?" Graham asked Annie. He had sat down by now too, and had watched their exchange, amusement lighting his face.

Annie looked over at him. He seemed relaxed in himself, in a way he hadn't in a while. A couple of weeks, maybe. "The point there is that it's done."

"You're not moving!" Karen said, her face alert now, full of concern.

"No, no, no," Annie said.

As Graham started to explain things to Karen—the photographs, the show—Annie stood and went up the stairs into the shadowy kitchen to get the lamb into its marinade and pull together a quick, simple dinner for Graham and herself. When she set her glass down on the table, she saw that next to her dramatic spring bouquet was a cluster of bedraggled off-season flowers, stuck in the small earthenware pitcher. Graham. It made her laugh, but then she took the big bouquet and set it on the kitchen island. She moved Graham's bouquet to the corner of the table where they always sat to eat.

When he came inside, she was just assembling the salad—a Niçoise, using the cherry tomatoes she'd bought earlier. She thanked him for the flowers.

"Just a token, I'm afraid," he said.

He set the table while she made a dressing and then poured them each another glass of wine.

It was still light enough as they ate that they didn't have candles on the table, though the room turned dark fairly rapidly. But there was something pleasant, Annie thought, about sitting here in the indoor twilight with the back door open; and Graham continued to seem, in some way she couldn't have described exactly, himself again. His easy self. She assumed it had something to do with seeing John, with the pleasure that always brought him—someone he could talk to about anything.

So she asked about lunch, and Graham told her about John's conference, about his kids. "Oh! And he said he'd be able to make it to dinner tomorrow, by the way."

They talked about Karen, about her increasing ditziness.

Then he asked her, and she told him, about her day—about how long the packing up took, about lunch in the park in the South End. About the oddness of Danielle. "Plus—oh God!—I ran into Rosemary Gregory at Formaggio and completely blew it."

He looked startled. "What do you mean, you blew it?"

"Oh, just that I kept stepping into one awkwardness after another. I had the flowers, you know"—she gestured at the bouquet—"and first I said they were for the party, which, of course, I hadn't invited her to. And then, because I was trying to scramble out of that one, I said they were for you, for you for being, as I so gracefully put it to a recent divorcée, a good husband."

After a moment, he said, "I'm sure she didn't notice. Or mind."

"Actually, she sort of walked off, so I think she did. Mind."

"Well, it may have had to do with any number of other things, too. You don't know."

She shrugged.

"I wouldn't worry about it," he said.

Just before they rose from the table to turn on the lights and begin their cleanup, Annie said, "You *are* a good husband, you know."

He didn't say anything for a moment. Then, "It means everything to me. For you to say that."

She couldn't see his face, but his voice was even deeper than usual, a soft rumble.

She reached the light switch first and flicked it on, and they stood for a moment in the sudden light, surprised by each other.

8

SOMETHING WAS OFF, Annie felt it even as she opened her eyes. The light leaking into the room at the bottom of the window shades was all wrong—too bright—and the house was utterly silent around her. What time was it? She turned to look at the clock, the glowing green digits: 6:21. She turned slightly and saw that Graham, who usually woke her well before this, was still there next to her in bed, still sound asleep.

Then, before she moved again, before she touched him, she knew. Much later, when she was talking about it with Frieda, she said she knew on account of his color—because he had no color. (He was gray, really. An odd, almost yellowish gray.) But what she felt in the instant before she really noticed that, though she never spoke of this to Frieda or to anyone else, was that his soul was gone. *That* was what she knew the moment she looked at him, even from her odd vantage point, with her pillow partially blocking her view. That his soul had vanished and his empty body had been left behind with her.

But not his soul, no. Annie didn't believe in the soul. It was just that something essential to Graham, to everything Graham was, wasn't there any longer. She could see it. She knew it.

She turned her body then, and stretched her hand out to touch him. His arm first, the arm lying nearest to her, its inner white flesh exposed, the hand turned up, palm open and relaxed.

His skin was cool under her fingertips.

She slid toward him, rising up on her elbow to look at him—at his face, at his gray face. It looked sunken under the thick beard. It seemed to her that it had lost its meaning somehow. After a few moments, she reached over and ran her fingers across his forehead, his nose. They felt cool too. Cool and waxy.

Annie rose up in the bed then, and knelt next to him. Her breath was coming fast, she could feel her heart, each thud seemed to shake her whole body. She put her hands on his arms, his chest. He'd pushed the sheet down nearly to his waist, and his right hand rested on the white cloth. She touched that hand and then that arm, cool too under the soft fur that covered it. She sat back on her heels and closed her eyes, trying to calm herself.

When she looked at him again, she saw that his eyes were slightly open. Open, but empty. After a few moments, she reached up to close his lids, aware even as she did it of the number of times she'd read of this act, or seen it, in films, on television. The ritual gesture, the acknowledgment of death.

But Annie was doing it mostly because she didn't want to look at his eyes, so strangely blank and unfocused. The flesh of his eyelids, that usually thin and vulnerable-seeming flesh, felt oddly thick when she pushed it down over his eyes. She sat back again.

She stayed there, just looking at him for a few minutes more. For a moment it struck her as strange that his eyes stayed shut. She started to cry, but felt instantly that that wasn't going to help her. And of course, nothing could help him. She stopped, she made herself stop.

She got up and came around the bed and sat down next to him. His body tilted slightly toward her weight on the mattress. She felt for a pulse in his cool arm. Useless, of course.

His mouth was open, and she reached under his jaw and pushed it up. When she took her hand away, it dropped open again.

The eyes stay shut, but not the mouth, she thought. It must be the heavy bone of the jaw.

She felt a quick wave of self-reproach for being even slightly interested in this, interested in anything else besides the fact of Graham's death. Though she understood too that this interest wasn't real, in some sense—that it was a way of not considering what was real. She felt it intensely then, the sensation of living for these moments on two levels—the one that seemed to be trying to disengage from what was happening, the one that was trying to realize it, to know it.

She leaned forward and put her hands on his cheeks, holding his face between her palms. There was something that she should be doing, or feeling. Surely this would come to her, the answer. Nothing she was doing now, nothing she could think of doing, felt right. She took her hands away from him. She stayed there, her hands in her lap.

She lost track of time. Perhaps twenty minutes passed, perhaps only a few. She wept, finally, she remembered that later, but she knew even as she did that she was weeping mostly for herself, for the life that she could already feel stretching out in front of her, without him. How would she live? How on earth would she pass the days? He had been so much at the center of her life, of their life together. It was, so much, one life.

She got up and took a tissue from the box on his side of the bed. She wiped her face, she blew her nose.

When she looked at Graham again, she noticed that he was wearing one of his old T-shirts, grayed with age, pinholed here and there. He had nothing else on, she knew this. This was his bedtime uniform in warm weather, it was all he ever wore. She sat next to him again and pulled the covers down. There: his long, shapely white thighs, the darker penis curled over one of them, the grayish, abundant pubic hair. His belly had relaxed and flattened out slightly.

She had the thought that she should put some clothes on him. Someone would have to come, someone who would see him like this. She couldn't think who that might be at the moment—the doctor, some ambulance guys?—but she'd have to call someone at some point, and she didn't want anyone looking at Graham naked.

But then she couldn't imagine dressing him. The work of it seemed impossible: lifting his heavy body, turning him.

It was crazy to think about it anyway, she told herself. Nobody cared. Nobody cared but her. And she didn't care, not really. She pulled the sheet and the light blanket up to his chest, as though he were a child she was tucking in. She leaned forward and kissed him, and was conscious even as she did it of how false this was. She didn't feel anything for him, for this body. He was gone.

And finally she wept for that, for how hopeless it was, anything she could do for him now, any gesture she could make. For how empty his body could be.

She couldn't have imagined it. Graham *was* his body—big, energetic, alive. Stilled, he was more absent than anyone else would have been.

They had trouble getting him down the stairs, he was so heavy and unwieldy, and the twisting, uncarpeted stairs were so narrow and steep. Plus one of the EMTs was a small woman, as small as Annie—though her arms, in her short-sleeved shirt, were ropy with tanned muscle.

Annie wasn't looking. She never looked, even when it was just furniture being moved up or down the stairs. There was something about it that was reasonlessly terrifying to her. She could never stop imagining everything that could go wrong, all the horrible possibilities—things dropping, breaking, people falling backward under their heavy loads, getting crushed. And now, with Graham, her fear was more intense than ever. While the EMTs struggled, Annie was in the bedroom, sitting in Graham's chair, trying not to think of what was going on out in the stairwell.

The rumpled bedclothes still held the suggestion of his shape, his body. Through the open window drifted the pleasant smell of the nighttime damp burning off. She heard birdsong and the quiet stir of air in the trees. Somewhere in the distance there was the sudden clash and clatter of an extension ladder being raised. Life, going on.

From the hall came a bump. "Jesus Christ!" the woman said softly, but not softly enough. The man whispered urgently, "I know, I know," and it sounded as if they had stopped for a moment.

Then, muffled laughter.

Laughter!

Well, okay. After all, there was something comical about it, wasn't there? The ridiculously perilous stairs, the big man, the little woman trying to carry him. Laurel and Hardy. All you'd need were the bowler hats.

Suddenly she found herself starting to laugh too. She went quickly into the bathroom and shut the door. Sitting hunched over on the edge of the tub, Annie let it come, the laughter, snorting and sniggering in her effort to be quiet, not to shame herself. It quickly began to feel dangerous, something she couldn't control. It went on and on. She couldn't stop herself.

Finally, thinking it would help, she went to the mirror over the sink and looked at her reflection. Her face was wet with tears, but she was still laughing. Laughing and crying at the same time. It was grotesque. She was grotesque, a mask of tragedy with strange, humorless laughter coming out of its downturned maw. She turned the faucet on and bent over the sink, lifting the cold water to her face again and again. She tried not to look at herself when she wiped her face off with the towel. Her breathing had grown regular, but she felt exhausted.

She opened the door and heard nothing. They were gone, then. She stepped into the hallway and stood there, looking across it into Graham's study. She'd left his yellow filing cabinet drawer open when she went looking for his living will, the brightly colored metal drawer stuffed with information important to him. On his desk were his piled papers, his books, his computer. Above it, on the wall, a framed photo of her, staring out of a window, the cold light falling on her dramatically. Her photographer friend Natalie had taken it when she was pregnant with Sarah.

The telephone sat there too, a landline only Graham used anymore.

Annie had to start calling people, she knew this, but she hated the thought of it—the necessarily dramatic announcement, the inevitable reaction, the need to give herself over to other people's responses: to their shock, their pain. She wasn't ready.

She thought of Sarah. She would call her first.

But what time was it there, in California. Fiveish?

No, she should wait a bit longer.

Then: Lucas.

But Frieda, Frieda should be the one to call him.

And she couldn't call Frieda first, before Sarah. She'd wait. Wait to call Sarah first, and then Frieda.

She went down the stairs herself then, the painted narrow stairs. She crossed the living room into the open kitchen. It was a little after 8:15, she saw on the stove clock. The sunlight was pouring into the room—weekend light, as she thought of it. On weekdays she would be getting ready to go to her studio by now.

She turned on the coffee machine she'd bought for Graham and did the minimal pushing of buttons that resulted in two shots of espresso and a pitcher of steamed, frothed milk. She sat at the table in the kitchen. The bouquet Graham had bought her had wilted a bit more in the night, she noticed. She drank her coffee slowly, falling again into the almost tranced state she'd been in earlier. She was conscious of time passing, but she couldn't have said how much, how long. She heard Graham's phone ring and then a distant voice leaving a message. Her cell might have rung too, but she wouldn't have heard it—she'd turned the sound off last night before they'd gone to bed. Even after she'd called the doctor and the funeral home this morning, she hadn't turned it back on.

Abruptly, she remembered the motion she'd felt in the bed in the night. She'd woken partway—it came to her now—with Graham's stirring. She'd thought he might be about to get up, to go to the bathroom, and she'd turned over to try to go back to sleep. Was it then, she wondered? Then that his heart was stopping? Was he aware of it? Did he know he was dying? Was he in pain?

She'd started to rock herself back and forth, thinking of that moment for him. His aloneness in it seemed so pitiable, so awful.

And then the thought: Could she have saved him, could she have helped him, if she hadn't turned away because she wanted sleep, more sleep?

She stopped. She put her hands down flat on the table. There was no point to this. It wouldn't have made a difference, in all likelihood. And perhaps she was wrong anyway. Wrong about the moment of death, wrong about the motion she'd felt, or thought she'd felt, whatever it was.

It made no difference. He was gone, either way. He was dead. She made herself think the word, and then she said it out loud. "Dead."

She'd used it earlier with the policeman, too, the young policeman, a boy really, who'd asked her how long she thought Graham might have been *gone* when she woke.

"You mean dead?" she had said.

He blushed, oddly, and looked down quickly at the pad he was writing on. "Yes," he said.

"I don't know," Annie told him. "He was cold though. Or cool, I guess you'd say."

He'd seemed to be writing this down, and then he went on to ask her other questions: how old Graham was. Sixty-four, she said. "No, sixty-five." (The birthday in April, the gifts, the party with Graham happy at its center, all the friends at the long table, the row of candles down the middle, and in their gentle light, everyone's face so young.) He asked whether Graham had had a heart condition, whether they'd gone to bed at the same time, what time that was, whether she'd heard anything in the night. Annie hadn't remembered it then, Graham's stirring, so she was telling the truth, more or less, when she said no to the policeman.

(The police would have to come, Graham's doctor had said when she called him. An unexpected death at home, they had to be sure. "You understand." Annie had said yes, though she didn't understand at all, not until the policeman, so young, so polite, a freckled redhead, began to ask his questions.

"And you need to find his living will, too," the doctor had said. "He had one, right?" Annie had liked this doctor the one time that she'd met him, at a reading Sherwin Nuland gave at the store.

"Yes," she said.

"Be ready to show it to the EMTs, okay? We don't want them doing CPR on him."

"God, no! He's dead!"

"Well, they're required to try, otherwise."

He would meet the ambulance at the ER, the doctor told her, and sign a death certificate, a necessary step. What she would need to do meantime was to choose a funeral home. Somewhere they could send Graham. His body.

The funeral home, then, was the one clear decision she'd made this morning, and that had been imposed on her. Actually, it was hardly a decision. She'd phoned the only funeral home she knew of, a brick building with an enormous sign on Mass Ave that she'd driven by every time she went to her studio. The woman who answered the phone there said they would arrange everything. Annie didn't care, she didn't ask what the *everything* was, she just wanted to get off the phone.)

Finally she made herself get up and wash out her coffee cup. She emptied the dishwasher. She started to reload it with the leftover dishes that had been sitting, rinsed, in the sink, the dishes from last night's dinner—their plates, their silverware.

She was remembering last night's dinner with Graham as she worked, calling up the details. Sitting at the table, they'd laughed together about Karen, her trip to Paris. Then agreed that really, it wasn't funny. And laughed again. It had made Annie think of her mother's long, slow decline, and they'd spoken of that briefly.

She'd talked about her day, getting the photographs over to the gallery. She told him what Danielle had said, and how surprised she'd been. She told him then what she had remembered Sarah saying all those years earlier about her—that she was unreadable too.

"Not so," he'd said, and reached over to cover her hand with his. "You're an open book. Open to me, anyway." And she had felt it again, the loosening, yes, the opening, of her body.

"Nice metaphor," she'd said. "Especially for a bookstore guy."

He had put an apron on, as he usually did, to help her clear the table, to rinse the dishes, a sight which always amused her with its incongruity—the big man, the old-fashioned full apron, sprigged with dainty flowers, given to her years before by her kind first mother-in-law, and beginning now to fall apart.

Suddenly she was recalling a time when she and Sarah, then a little girl, were still at the table, and Graham in the same fancy apron was cleaning up. They were in the old version of the kitchen, the version whose walls they would knock out a year or so later to make the one large open room on the first floor, the room where the parties happened—the room they joked about, the joke being that if they put a bed in it, they'd never have to use any other part of the house.

On that particular evening, though, Sarah and Annie were sitting at a small square table in the corner of the old room, some of the leftover dinner dishes still around them.

She was talking with Sarah about something odd. What?

"Inappropriate touching," that was it, following up on the ideas in a handout Sarah's day-care center had given the parents, the handout with the rules that would keep the children safe from sexual predators. This was in the era when there was a general panic about this issue, when there were trials in which very young children were witnesses against their caregivers.

As she put the plates into the dishwasher, she was remembering that it had been dark out. So maybe it had been a wintry night. But the room was full of warm light, candlelight. She and Graham often lit candles for dinner then, in part because it harkened back sweetly to their days alone together, before Sarah; but in part too because Sarah took such pleasure in blowing them out when it was time to go up to get ready for bed.

Annie had had a cup of tea sitting on the table before her, Sarah hot chocolate. Graham had set his glass of wine on the counter while he cleaned up. They'd already played the requisite postprandial three or four rounds of I Spy.

Now Annie was asking Sarah, "What if someone wanted to touch your body, the private parts of your body? What would you tell them?"

Sitting in her booster chair, Sarah waited a moment before she answered—gravely, a bit hesitantly. "I would tell them no." She was looking at Annie: Was this correct?

"That's right!" Annie said. "Let's say it together. Ready?" Annie inhaled loudly, drawing herself up, mouth open, eyebrows raised, and Sarah did too, watching her mother, trying to do exactly what she was doing. "No!" they said, almost at the same time.

Sarah had liked that. She had sat back, smiling at Annie with her mouth open, her neat, scalloped baby teeth showing. Then, watching Annie's face for approval, she said, more loudly, "No! no! no! no!"

"NO!" Annie shouted back at her, and Sarah laughed. This was right up her alley. Sarah loved being loud. She *was* loud, occasionally embarrassingly so.

Now she yelled at her mother, "NO! NO! NO!" rocking her whole body with each word.

"Nosirree BOB!" Annie yelled back. She was enjoying herself; it gave her almost as much pleasure as it gave Sarah, yelling no, scaring away some imaginary bad guy.

From behind Sarah and Annie, Graham said, "No way, José!" and Sarah instantly echoed him, only much louder.

Annie had turned to look at him then, this is what she was remembering now. He was standing by the dishwasher in his apron, a dripping plate in his hand, watching them. Annie could see that he was taken with what Sarah had made of this exercise, an exercise he'd excused himself from, he'd seen it as so ridiculous. Now his eyes were steady on her, alive, amused.

Oh, Graham.

Together then, all three of them had done "Nuh-uh!" They did "No dice!" They did "No ma'am!" and "No sir!" They did "Nix!" and "Ixnay!"

Then Sarah wanted to do it all over again.

So they had, they did, Sarah and Graham and Annie, all those years ago.

Annie stood motionless at the sink, the warm water still running over her hands, lost in this memory.

After a minute, she started to work again. Rinsing Graham's

wineglass, the last one he would use, setting it into the dishwasher—this seemed ceremonial to her. Final.

Unbearable.

At about nine thirty, she called Sarah—waking her, Annie could tell by her scratchy voice. She had rehearsed the words, and she spoke them just as she'd said them to herself.

"I have terrible news, Sarah." And without pausing, "Daddy has died, in the night."

There was a long silence. I forgot to say my name, Annie thought. I forgot to tell her who was calling.

"No!" Sarah breathed. "Not . . . Mom!"

"In his sleep."

"Oh, my God, Mother. I can't believe it. I'm . . ." Her voice grew small. "Just, I can't believe it."

Annie explained it, waking to find him dead, how fine he was last night.

Sarah asked a few questions, and then, within a minute, said, "Well, I'm coming back there. I'll be there probably sometime tonight. I'll let you know."

Annie felt ashamed of the impulse she had to say "Don't. Please don't." She didn't, of course, but she had a sense of the way it would be for the next days, her own powerlessness, her inability to control anything.

Frieda cried out violently, like someone struck. She cried out twice, actually. Then, after a long silence on both ends of the line, she asked, "Are you sure?" as though it were possible that Annie might have made a mistake about this. A question so absurd, so absurdly desperate, that Annie was able to feel for her. To understand, really, deeply, maybe for the first time, how much Frieda had loved him. Had gone on loving him.

They talked for a few more minutes. Frieda wanted more details than Annie wanted to offer, but finally she asked whether Annie had told Lucas yet. When Annie said no, no, of course she hadn't, Frieda was audibly relieved. "Well, I'll do that, then. I'm sure he'll want to come up."

At about ten thirty, when she knew that everyone at the bookstore would be long settled into various routines, Annie called the office there. She was imagining it as she listened to the phone ringing—the small, narrow room at the back of the store, windowless, the walls covered with autographed posters advertising many of the readings they'd had over the years. There was a long desk against one of these walls where they all sat in a row facing their computers—Erica, the events person, who arranged the readings and all the attendant publicity; fiftyish, hippie-ish Georgie, still lovely in a girlish way—she was the secretary and general factotum; and Emily, small, quick, efficient, who did the books and the ordering. And then, of course, Graham.

Who owned the store. Or was owned by the store.

Or who *was* the store, she thought.

Emily answered, and in response to Annie's news said her version of how impossible it was, how unbelievable. Already this felt familiar to Annie, this response, and she did her part. When it seemed that had gone on long enough, she said, "Right now, though, here's the thing: Could you just get the dinner party canceled? Let everyone know?"

"Oh!" Emily said. "Oh, of course . . ." There was a long pause. "But, should we, shouldn't I, cancel the reading too?"

"No, no, the reading has to happen. Graham would never have wanted that. Just. I can't do the dinner."

"Of course not. Of course, no one would expect that. God!"

"And Jamie, too. Just tell her how sorry we are. I am. And, you'll have to find someone else to introduce her." Graham's job, always. "So, if you could just, let the others know . . . the ones who were coming to dinner? . . . Do you have a pen?"

"Yes, right here. I'll get paper, just a sec."

So Annie listed the dinner guests for Emily; the old friends, the two writers, the other photographer, the painter, wives and husbands and lovers. Emily would call them and they would know about Graham, and Annie wouldn't have to go over it and over it. At least with those friends. There would be others, too many to think of, but now the word would start to spread, wider and wider, and she wouldn't be in charge of the news. Now it was no longer hers. Graham, his death, were no longer hers.

After she hung up, she sat for a few moments, considering what came next in this long, empty day. She was about to go upstairs to begin to get ready to face it, when it occurred to her that she should let Danielle know that she wasn't going to be able to come to the opening on Sunday—even the thought of it seemed impossible. She pushed the numbers in, and after a few rings Danielle came on. Annie wasn't sure what she said, maybe just, "I'm not going to be able to make it on Sunday." Something like that.

There was a long silence, and then Danielle said, "This better be good."

9

THE MOMENT SARAH clicked off her phone, Thomas, who'd been lying next to her, watching her face as it changed and then changed again, said, "What is it, Sarah?" His voice was urgent with concern.

Sarah turned to him. The early June sunlight through the venetian blinds made stripes across his smooth, tan skin. "It's my father," she said in a small voice that sounded unfamiliar even to her. "My father died."

He sat up. "Oh Jesus, Sarah!" he said. His hand on her back was warm. "I'm so sorry. I'm so sorry." When she didn't turn to him, he let his hand fall.

"Yeah." She nodded. "Thank you." Her voice was still strange to her own ears. She cleared her throat. "I just don't feel it yet. I don't *feel* anything."

"Of course not. I mean, how . . ."

"Yes." She gave a great sigh, as if trying to order her breathing. They sat together, both awkwardly upright in the bed, both naked except for the sheet still covering the lower part of their bodies.

"Was he . . ." Thomas faltered. "Had he been . . . ill?"

Now Sarah looked at him, at this perfect man in her bed, at his face so full of real concern. "No," she said. "No. He had a heart attack.

In the night. So . . ." She lifted her shoulders. "He just didn't wake up, I guess."

"So. Not a hard death, anyway."

"No, there's that."

"But a shock, it sounds like."

"Yes," she said.

The complexity for Sarah of this moment with Thomas was that she didn't know him very well. She wasn't ready to be grief-stricken with him. To share her father's death—her father's death!—with this gentle man she'd now been to bed with three times. It made the death seem even more unreal, even more impossible, having to find a reasonable way to speak of it with Thomas. It wasn't reasonable. It shouldn't be spoken of reasonably.

Her father! He was so alive for her. There was some part of her that almost literally did not believe it was real—his dying. She sat very still, waiting to feel something. Thomas sat behind her, watching her breathe, feeling helpless.

They'd met when he called her at the radio station to ask her out. Before then they'd talked on the phone twice, but that was work, that was when she was calling him, when she was getting him ready for his interview.

This was her job. To do the reading, or listen to the music, or watch the movie—all things the radio host, Shelley, wouldn't have time to do for every single guest. To mark the passages in the book, to gather the quotes, to make excerpts of the dialogue in the film, to summarize reviews—criticism, praise. To frame the questions, to work out a plan for the discussion and run it by Shelley and Mary, the producer; and then to talk with the guest, to be sure he would be easy to work with. To ask some of the questions Shelley might be asking. To make it possible for both people—guest, host—to sound at least knowledgeable, and perhaps—this was the goal, anyway—much better than that.

Thomas had just published a book on what he called "The Silent Minority"—Asian Americans—and after reading an enthusiastic review of it, Sarah had proposed it at the group meeting at which they planned out the programs for the following week. Thomas was funny on the phone, relaxed with her and seemingly at ease with himself. By the end of their conversation, she was sure everything would go well, he was so articulate, so comfortable with what he knew. So confident in his opinions. And more, she'd liked talking to him so much. This was always a good sign.

They didn't speak when he came in—she was in the booth, and then she had to leave to take a call before his segment was over. But when he phoned her at the station the next day, he said he was disappointed not to have met her. Perhaps they could have coffee? A drink?

Watching him cross the room to her, the only woman sitting alone in the café, the only woman waving at him, Sarah could tell he was disappointed again. She was used to this, this disappointment, but also used to the interest that preceded it—the interest based on her voice, which made the disappointment almost inevitable.

She was, as a high school acquaintance had once said to her, meaning it kindly at the time, *okay-looking*, and she'd learned, slowly, to make the best of that. She'd lost weight in her sophomore year of high school, the same year she'd made herself try out for any school play that came up. She got character parts—Ursula in *Bye Bye Birdie*, Mrs. Gibbs in *Our Town*. She'd had to work then to get her voice, so loud, so braying in childhood, under her control, so as not to overpower the other actors in their scenes with her. And backstage, she'd watched what makeup could do, though what she wore for her own roles emphasized what was least attractive about her. She made friends, of a sort. People who would at least say hello as they passed in the halls, or talk with her when they worked together.

It was better in college, where she'd worked at the student radio station among a bunch of eccentrics, running the eleven o'clock jazz show. At first she knew so little about what she was doing that she had to consult regularly with Graham. For a while, then, she was playing the music she'd heard in childhood as it had floated upstairs to her bedroom from the parties her parents were always throwing. But slowly she came into her own tastes. Diana Krall, Joshua Redman, Irvin Mayfield Jr., Jane Monheit.

In the talking she did between the musical segments, she tried to make her voice perfect for that hour—deep, restful, knowledgeable. That show, and maybe the voice she created for it, led to an internship and then a job at the radio station in San Francisco.

So when she talked to Thomas on the phone, she sounded confident, and she was. Her voice sounded like the voice of someone wise and sophisticated and curious and perhaps, sexy.

She had spent more than an hour getting ready the night they were to meet. She dressed carefully—a soft silk shirt, checked, a pencil skirt. Her jeans jacket over that. Dangly earrings, though at the last minute she'd taken those off and substituted the pearl studs her father had given her for Christmas the year before.

She didn't imagine that much would come from their evening together, though she was interested in Thomas. But then, as it lasted longer than she'd expected, and then even longer than that, she understood that he was interested, too, interested in her.

She liked him. Oh! she liked him. She liked looking at him, his black hair and almost-black eyes, the pretty light brown of his skin.

He wore a pressed white shirt, open at the neck, the sleeves rolled up. She liked looking at the shifting muscles in his forearms as he gestured.

She liked him because he asked her as many questions as she'd asked him on the phone when she was getting him ready for the interview. Because they talked so easily.

They talked about their lives, where they'd grown up, how they'd ended up here. He was from New York. He'd been born in Korea, but came to the States when he was two—his father had gotten a job teaching at Columbia.

"This is such a California conversation," he said. "That assumption that pretty much everyone is from somewhere else. Or that discovery, anyway."

They talked about radio, how special it was—listening without seeing, being required to imagine so much. They talked about old radio shows. He'd liked listening to the rebroadcasts of The Firesign Theater as a kid. "Good training for Monty Python," he said. They talked about Monty Python. Then John Cleese. Then John Cleese in *A Fish Called Wanda*. He said he'd seen it twice on a hot Saturday afternoon when it came out.

He must be around Lucas's age, she thought.

They talked about the pleasure, the illicit pleasure really, of spending a beautiful summer afternoon in a cool, dark theater, of coming out to a still-hot, still-light evening.

"But you feel guilty too, don't you?" Sarah had asked.

"Why?"

"Because you've wasted the beautiful day. Because you should have been doing something more . . . I don't know." She lifted her shoulders. "*Worthy*, I guess."

He looked across the table at her for a moment, amusement in his face. "I think I can be of help to you with that," he said. His eyes reminded her of her father's, the deep wrinkles when he smiled.

She laughed. "Do I need help?"

"Apparently you do."

He asked her about herself, about how she got into the work she was doing, about what came next for someone with her job.

"More of same, I think," she had said. The restaurant had emptied out. There was one other couple still there, and the waitress was setting tables up for the next day.

"You wouldn't like your own show?" he asked.

"God, no!" Only as she said it did she realize how deeply she felt this. "I'd like to *run* a show, though," she said after a moment. "Be a producer. I guess that's where I'm headed, finally."

"Why not be the host? You've got that wonderful voice, you ask such . . . *welcoming* questions." He was leaning toward her now, his elbows on the table.

"Well, thanks," she said.

"I was, just right away, completely comfortable talking to you."

She shrugged. "That's my job, of course."

"Ah, so it wasn't especially me."

He was smiling at her, flirting with her. And here it came, the question that often arose for Sarah with men. Was it the kind of flirting other guys had sometimes done with her, the kind of flirting based on the assumption that she would see it for what it was—essentially a joke? The kind of flirting made possible because of the mutual, but tacit, understanding that it wasn't intended to go anywhere—the way men were sometimes flirtatious and courtly to old ladies?

Or was it real?

She looked across the table at him, at his dark eyes steady on her, the smile playing on his lips as he waited for her answer. Why not take the risk? Why not?

"It was," she said in a soft voice. "It was especially you."

———

"So that was your mother?" he asked now. "On the phone?"

"Yes." Something funny must have happened to her face, because he said, "Oh, Sarah," and reached for her again.

"No, it's okay. I'm okay," she said, breathing deeply, making herself stop. "It's just . . . not real."

And now, exhaling loudly, she lay back down. After a moment, he did too.

It was almost funny, she thought, lying next to him, both of them looking up at the ceiling—like two people who've known each other forever. Like an old married couple. Outside, on the street, the noise of traffic had picked up. She could hear her upstairs neighbor now, thumping around, getting ready for work.

She felt him turn toward her. "How is she doing?" he asked. "Your mother."

"My mother." She made a little noise, an attempt at a laugh. "My mother is always okay. *That* is the division of labor in my family. Or that *was* the division of labor. My mother holds it all in, my father lets it out."

"Were you close to your parents? To him?"

"Oh, I adored him." Now she turned to look at Thomas, grateful to him, he was trying so hard. "She did too. My mother. I can't imagine her life now. Without him." She pictured her mother, she saw her sitting alone at the big table by the windows, and felt an unaccustomed pull of pity for her.

"What . . . was he like?"

"Oh." She smiled. "You could say . . . Rabelaisian. I think, in fact, it has been said of him. Certainly he was *big*, in every way. A lover of life. And *kind*. God, I would never have survived my adolescence without him. Without his kindness."

"Tell me," he said.

"My father." She thought of him, she saw him at the same big table, talking, laughing. Making her mother laugh, too. "Well, he was just *there*. You know, I think he had such a terrible growing up himself that he was just grateful in the aftermath of that. Just *glad*. A glad person. But also he understood, he understood how some things are just . . . insolubly painful. You can't make them better, you can't make them turn out differently. And what he was good at, in the face of that, was offering a kind of . . . joyous sympathy. Or is it empathy? Anyway, he was just there, steady and warm. He made people happy, without even trying."

He reached over, and stroked her hair. "I love the way you talk about him."

"You would have loved *him*," she said, fiercely now.

His hand stilled on her hair for a moment, and began again. "What was so terrible about his growing up?" he asked.

She smiled. "Most everything, I would say. Plus, I suppose, most of the things that were terrible—that are terrible—about anyone's growing up."

"Loneliness," he said.

"Maybe," she said. "Maybe loneliness."

"Sexual desperation."

She smiled, and he smiled back.

"Acne," he offered.

"There could have been acne."

"Unrequited love, probably," he said after a moment.

"Sure."

"But what about him in particular?"

Sarah moved closer to him and rested her head against his shoulder and chest. The sun had warmed his flesh. "Where to begin?" she said.

"I can wait," he said.

She lay there for a moment. "Well, there was the father who ran away, abandoned the family. And was never seen again. And they already had no money, even before he left." She sighed. "Then the mother who drank. And hit, apparently."

"Ah."

After a minute, he said, "And what about your mother? What's she like? Not *un*kind, I'm sure." He pulled his head back to look at her, and she smiled at him, at how beautiful she felt he was.

"Oh no, she is, very kind. But her kindness . . . it takes a different form. My mother . . . she wants to *solve* your problems. Or she wants *you* to solve your problems. She can't . . . *sit* with you. In your misery. It's too hard for her." She changed her voice, made it brusque. "'Let's. Make. This. Better!'" She slapped her hand on the sheet covering her thighs with each word.

They lay still for a long moment.

"Good luck with this one," she said in a small, pinched voice, and started to cry.

10

WHEN ANNIE CALLED, Frieda was playing the piano, an old upright someone had painted white at one time, now scratched and chipped here and there, the dark wood showing through. She had started to take lessons when she turned fifty-five, a birthday present to herself, as was the piano. By now she was working on pieces she actually enjoyed listening to. When the phone rang, she was practicing the left hand of a Mozart sonata, because, as her teacher said, she needed to make herself hear its music. It wasn't just *trailing around* after the right hand, he said. It was singing its own song, too.

She was thinking of this teacher as she got up to go to the phone. He was elderly now, white-haired and slightly stooped, but at a younger age he'd played for years in a moderately distinguished local quartet. Once, when she didn't understand what he wanted from her, he'd made an irritated noise and gestured for her to move, in his impatience actually pushing her farther down the bench with his body. He'd played the passage she was having difficulty with; and then, as if he couldn't stop himself, he went on, playing the piece through until the end. When he was finished, he sat for a moment with his head tilted back as if still hearing the music, his hands lifted in their beautiful arc above the keys.

Then he looked at her and dropped his hands into his lap. "More or less like that," he'd said, breaking the spell.

And though tears had been sitting in Frieda's eyes before he spoke, she burst out laughing at the preposterousness of his suggestion, and after a second or two of what seemed like confusion on his part, he had laughed along with her.

So she was smiling as she picked up the phone and heard Annie's small, exhausted voice announcing the impossible.

Of course, Frieda and Lucas had been invited to Graham's wedding to Annie, held in Peter Aiello's grand living room on Beacon Street. While they said their vows, you could see a light rain falling slantwise over the green of the Common. Frieda had wept through most of the ceremony, which she explained to Lucas as just a silly thing she was doing and to anyone else as pure sentimentality. "I can't help it. It's just what I do at weddings." And while that was true— she did always weep at weddings, at the innocent hopefulness of weddings—she knew that these tears were more complicated than that, that she was weeping for the sense of a door shutting forever against her.

She and Graham had stayed close after their divorce. This was partly because of Lucas, but it was also because of the deep, unresolved attachment between them. A few times in the first year or so after she moved out, Graham had tried to talk about this with her, but she knew that what he really wanted was to discuss their perhaps getting back together, and that was not a possibility for Frieda. She felt it would be psychologically suicidal. She deflected these attempts on his part, then. Sometimes she even made a joke of them.

But once he started to have lovers again, he stopped trying to bring it up. This made things easier between them, but it also made Frieda sad.

Frieda did not have lovers in this period of her life, or for a long time afterward. She had a child to take care of, she had a part-time job, and she'd gone back to graduate school, in history. She couldn't imagine, in those years, making the time for even a casual affair, her life felt so crazy to her.

But then along came Annie anyway, and that was that. There was no longer even the possibility of talk about her coming back together with Graham—though their affection for each other continued anyway, running under everything else that happened between them.

And one of the things that happened between them was Frieda's increasing closeness with Annie, a surprise to all of them.

Frieda had met her, at Graham's insistence, only a few months after he and Annie started living together. He wanted them all to be friends. Frieda could tell that Annie hadn't liked this idea. She was awkward with Frieda at first, stiff. Later, when they were, in fact, friends, she talked about it with Frieda. "It just seemed too New Agey to me," Annie said. "I suppose I thought it was . . . *undignified* in some way." She had laughed then, almost apologetically.

Annie *was* dignified, Frieda could see that from the start. The perfectly oval, serious face. The dancer's posture. Dark eyes. Dark hair, dark definitive eyebrows that registered her responses to everything. She pondered things, she took things seriously. And then, quickly, she would come to life, animated, delighted—at just seeing you, at a joke, at Graham's arrival home. Frieda had liked that unexpected combination of elements in her, it was one of the things that impelled her forward, into their friendship.

But there were others. Both of their mothers descended slowly into Alzheimer's disease at the same time, and over coffee, over glasses of wine, they exchanged horrible stories or hilarious ones about them—sometimes stories with both aspects intermingled, which seemed to Frieda the nature of that illness.

They told each other about their past lives. Annie talked about her first marriage, her chagrin over it. And Frieda discussed honestly her own marriage to Graham.

He had already told Annie about his infidelities—told her and taken the blame on himself for all of it.

"As well he *might*," Annie had said to Frieda.

"Oh, well," Frieda said. "It was the times too, of course." They were sitting late one afternoon having beers in Frieda's small apartment on Whittier Street—this was long before the neighborhood was gentrified, at a period when this corner of Cambridge was still full of graduate students and impoverished divorced women with children. Frieda had been surprised to find that she loved her life in this world.

"That's no excuse," Annie said.

"It sort of is, I think," Frieda said. It was hot outside, and the fan behind Frieda blew her hair forward in an unattractive way each time it swung in her direction. "This was Cambridge, after all, and in those years it was essentially a sexual playground for grown-ups. Or people who thought they were grown-ups." She laughed. "Like us. With some completely predictable results. What happened to our relationship—to our marriage—really being but one example." She had rolled her eyes then, and Annie laughed. Then Frieda had sobered, frowned. "The thing is, I just wasn't *made* that way. I tried to say that to Graham, many times over, but honestly, I don't think he believed me, he was having such a very fine time himself." She sat for a moment looking down at her hands. Remembering it, so clearly, she made a little noise, and then looked up at Annie, who was watching her intently. "In the end, I was just exhausted by it. I loved him, but I was so jealous all the time that I couldn't stand it. I couldn't stand myself, mostly. I was a weepy mess, for years. So I left. Took Lucas. Shoved everything I owned into the car and drove away." She shrugged. "And then *he* was a weepy mess. But in his case, it lasted for about two seconds."

She made a rueful face. "In fact, I went on being a weepy mess, mourning him. After I'd left him, for god's sake. For months. Maybe a year. Longer. God! Utter craziness. Because by that time, of course, he'd recovered and was a happy single guy at last, sampling from that big tray of female goodies passing themselves around." She didn't say—she probably didn't need to: she saw Annie blush—that at first she'd seen Annie as just someone else on that tray.

The result of the closeness that had developed and deepened over the years between Annie and Frieda was that when Lucas went through a hateful period in early adolescence, when, for more than a year, Annie was the only person he would talk to reasonably, the relief that Frieda felt about this—that he had a resource in his suffering, and a resource she trusted—was immense.

This was probably also the reason that, when the time came, Annie in turn shared with Frieda her concerns about Sarah, about Sarah's loneliness, about her size, about Annie's own inability to help or comfort her; and Frieda, who understood something about the kind of pain Sarah was feeling from her own difficult growing up, was able to talk to Sarah about it. About some of it, anyway. More important, maybe, was able to befriend her.

For years they went together every Wednesday evening to a program at the Museum of Fine Arts called "Drawing in the Galleries." Paper and pencils of every size were available, and charcoal. There was usually a live model, dressed or draped, or sometimes they were instructed to choose a sculpture or a painting to work from. This was something Frieda had done with Lucas for a while, but he'd grown tired of it. Sarah didn't. Oh, eventually, when she began to have real homework, she could no longer manage the evenings; but until then she and Frieda would work quietly side by side. "This is tricky, isn't it," Frieda would say. "The way his fingers curve."

"And he keeps *moving* them!" Sarah would whisper back.

"I love the way you shadowed her skirt," Frieda would tell her. "Yours is better," Sarah would say.

Afterward they always stopped in the café, where Frieda would have a glass of wine and Sarah was allowed to choose a dessert for herself. They spoke of school, or Sarah's dancing, or her parents; and Frieda listened and thought how odd it was, the trade that she and Annie seemed to have made during these years. Lucas for Sarah, Sarah for Lucas. It comforted her, and if she were honest, it eased some of the jealousy she felt.

But through all this, even after the bond between Annie and Frieda was a settled, predictable part of their lives, what Frieda couldn't help feeling was that Annie didn't know—couldn't know—the real Graham. And that she, Frieda, did. That she understood him in ways Annie would never be able to. After all, she had met him, fallen in love with him when he was homely, unbearded. She was a geeky girl, he a geeky boy, when they first went out together, when they married.

They were *suited* to each other. She did love him, and he loved her too, but she also felt he was as good as she would have. They were in the same *league*, was what she thought. What Annie didn't know—couldn't have known—what Frieda did know, was how the 1960s, the '70s, had made Graham who he was now. Had made him sexy.

Oh, he'd always been passionate—about life, women, food, books, music, booze. But when he was homely, people didn't find that as charming as they did later. *Later*, when all the changes in the rules came around. And for Graham, the beard, the full head of hair, the contact lenses, the sudden interest in elegant clothes. And the way all of those choices seemed to color everything he did or said. Seemed to change its meaning. Seemed to make him attractive.

Did make him attractive, Frieda understood that. Made him magnetic, even.

Which must have been what made Annie think that she and Graham were in the same league, that he deserved her. Only Frieda—Frieda and maybe some of his old friends—knew that if the beard came off, if the slight overbite were revealed, if you put him in his old clothes, then everything he did, everything he said, would be tonally altered.

No, without the transformation—what Frieda sometimes thought of as Graham's *disguise*—Annie wouldn't have been interested, Frieda was sure of it.

She thought that Graham understood this at some level too. That his worship of Annie was born of this, his sense of his extraordinary good fortune. His undeserved good luck.

And when, early on in his marriage to Annie, he confessed to Frieda that he'd been unfaithful to her with Linda Parkman, Frieda felt confirmed in this. She had a quick frisson of vengeful pleasure she could barely acknowledge to herself. Of course, for the infidelity itself; but then more deeply, more clearly, for the fact that he *hadn't told Annie* about it.

And the reason he hadn't told her? He couldn't *risk* telling her. What Frieda knew was that there was this difference for him between her and Annie—that he'd always been honest with her, with Frieda, more deeply so than he could afford to be with Annie.

But she was Annie's friend too. She was also angry with him on Annie's behalf for that early infidelity; and maybe even more deeply angry with him on her own behalf once again for everything she'd lost all those years earlier. Sitting opposite him in her kitchen, full of the pain she thought she'd relinquished long ago, she wept. He'd reached his hand out to her then, but she turned away from his touch. He'd sat there uselessly for a few minutes, watching her slowly pull herself together.

After she'd stopped crying, he asked her if she thought he should tell Annie.

"No!" she had said, too loudly. "You'd relieve yourself at the price of her suffering. Why should *she* suffer? *You* suffer for a change."

But oddly, or maybe not so oddly, the news of this—his infidelity with Linda Parkman—increased her pleasure in her friendship with Annie. She knew the shift had to do with her vague sense of having won something—what, she couldn't have said. But whatever it was, it somehow evened the balance between her and Annie, it made everything easier.

Sometimes Frieda wondered how it would all play out over time, this complicated web of love and something else among the three of them—the five of them, if you counted Lucas and Sarah. She occasionally indulged the fantasy that Graham and Annie would take her in in her old age. Or perhaps, she thought, if Graham died first, she and Annie would live together, two old ladies, caring for each other. She could imagine this, the dinners together in the evenings, the visits from the children, the grandchildren.

And then there was the thought she rarely allowed herself, the one that came by itself, unbidden, from time to time, the one she pushed away as quickly as she could: What if Annie died first, and Frieda and Graham were the ones left behind? Would they come to live together again? Surely by then he would be changed. Surely by then—maybe even by now—it would be safe, he would be less libidinous. Maybe the passing of time had made a monogamous man of Graham.

When she hung up the phone, Frieda stood for perhaps a minute, sightless, deaf. Then she crossed the room and sank onto the piano bench, her back to the keys, to the possibility of music, to the possibility of anything further. After a moment she opened her mouth to shout, to scream, but nothing at all came out.

II

FRIEDA TRIED TO call Lucas at his office a little after eleven, but he was in a meeting at the time with the editor in chief and the publisher, trying to persuade them to raise the amount he could offer for a first novel he was bidding on competitively. When the meeting was over, when he stopped in his office, he saw the note from his assistant on his desk: "Your mother called; wants you to call her back." But he was worried about being late for lunch with Ian Pedersen, one of his newest authors. New to him, but probably in terms of age, oldest. Seventy at the least, Lucas thought. He was in town and probably needed some encouragement. He'd been divorced recently, for the third time, and it had "knocked him for a loop," he'd told Lucas on the phone. He'd be longer than he'd thought getting this novel in.

In his hurry not to be late for Ian, Lucas left the office without calling Frieda.

He wasn't late, though Ian, who was always early, was there ahead of him, sitting in a booth facing the door, his glass of wine already half gone.

He *was* late getting back from that lunch, and late, therefore, getting to the meeting about next year's spring list. He wasn't able to call Frieda back until after three. He didn't worry about this, although it was a bit unusual for Frieda to call him at work. But she had, a few times. Once when she sprained her ankle, once when she was upset because someone had broken into the Whittier Street apartment in her absence and, among some other junk, stolen an old guitar of his, one he didn't even remember owning.

"Oh, thank God it's you!" she said. "Oh, God, Lucas."

He was suddenly alert. An accident, he thought. Cancer. "What is it? What's wrong?"

"It's Graham," she said. "He had a heart attack."

"And?" he asked, already irritated, irritated at the way she dramatized things, withheld the important information, buried the lead. "How is he?"

"He died!" she said, sounding surprised herself at this news.

Lucas was standing, looking out the window at the deep valley below him that was Broadway. He could hear the honking as it floated up to him. He had a momentary sense of absence from his own body, as if he were suspended in the air above what he was looking at. Later he couldn't remember what questions he asked or how his mother had answered them. Somehow he learned that his father had died in the night, that Annie had called his mother to tell her the news this morning, that Frieda didn't know whether there was a service planned or if so, when. He was aware of thinking, as he listened to her, as he slowly came back to the present, that this was very much a secondhand version.

He asked about Annie, how she was doing, and his mother said, "Badly, I imagine. But it's hard to tell."

Then—too late, too late—he thought to ask her how she was doing.

"Oh, I'm a complete mess," she said, her voice suddenly wobbly.

"Would you like me to come? Now, I mean?"

"Wouldn't that be difficult? To get away?"

"I could come for a day or two, certainly. Part of the weekend, anyway."

"And what about Jeanne?"

What about Jeanne? His wife, an actress, French. Mostly, at this point in her career, doing voiceover work and commercials. She had a cordial but not close relationship with Frieda, whose emotional valence was incomprehensible to her. And though he had made the case for his mother to Jeanne many times—talked about the hard things she'd been through—Lucas was comforted, too, by Jeanne's retroactive defending of him, of the childhood he'd had, living with Frieda, yearning for Graham.

"Jeanne wouldn't be able to come. It'd just be me."

"Well, I know Annie would be pleased if you came."

"We're not talking about Annie, Mom. We're talking about you."

She was silent a moment. Then she said, "Well then, I'd like it very much."

"Good. I'll take an early train in the morning. Be there well before noon, I would think."

After he'd hung up, he stood for a long time at the window in his office. In his mind he saw his father, that big, happy man, as he had looked when Lucas turned up at the bookstore after school on the days his father had him.

How had he gotten there? He supposed early on someone had picked him up at school and dropped him off. Someone—Annie?

Not likely Frieda. She was teaching by then, out in the suburbs.

But what he remembered best was later, when he was allowed to walk down to the store by himself after school, a walk that seemed endless, and bitterly cold in winter. But he had loved it: the sight of the old yellow overhead lights in the store, entering its warmth, everyone greeting him. His father coming out from the office or behind the counter, calling his name. "Lucas! Here he is, at last. My arctic explorer. My brave young man." Swooping him up, asking him questions, making jokes. Later, he'd settle Lucas in one of the big chairs with a book, or his homework, and every time he passed, he'd set his hand on Lucas's head.

How could he be gone? He was at the center of everyone's life. Frieda's, Sarah's, Annie's.

Then he was trying to imagine it, the way Frieda had said it happened: Annie, waking up, finding Graham lifeless in the bed next to her. He couldn't. He couldn't get beyond that point, that image.

Someone knocked on the doorframe. His assistant, Caroline. She was tall, blond, soft-spoken. She wore her hair in long braids that she pinned up in a bun at the back of her head, like some Scandinavian princess. She had printed out the manuscripts that two of his authors had emailed in—manuscripts he supposed now he'd be taking with him to Boston on the train.

He told her about his father.

Why? She hadn't even known he had a living father. But sympathy leapt to her face, transformed it. Tears stood in her eyes.

She put her hand on his arm. "I'm so sorry," she said.

And how odd that now, with this simple gesture, he was so stricken with his sense of loss that he had to turn away from her. "Thank you," he said, in an unsteady voice. When she left, he closed the door and sat down at his desk.

He was thinking about this on the subway ride home, standing close to the door, hemmed in, gripping the overhead rail and not seeing anything, anyone, around him. Why did Caroline's sympathetic but essentially rote response reach him, when the news from his mother hadn't?

Because his mother had her own sorrow, he supposed, and needed him. That was the impediment, wasn't it, to feeling his own grief? He had a quick flash of the resentment he'd felt for his mother as a teenager, a young man.

———

Frieda was good, she was honorable. She'd sacrificed so much for him. Even the job she'd taken, teaching history at the Canfield School, was work she did for him, so that he could attend high school there tuition-free when the time came, since none of the parental figures in his life had, as his father put it, two dimes to rub together.

He'd minded it, he'd minded it all. Minded being alone with her as a child, exiled from Graham, minded the sense that she needed him, minded driving out to the high school with her, minded her cheerful greeting when they ran into each other on the campus there. Minded the guilt he felt about resenting all this.

But here it was: there was a sadness at his mother's core that he had felt the wish to lift as a child, the impossible wish to lift. And because he could never achieve that, what he wanted as he grew older was to be free of it. To separate himself from it, and therefore from her. He'd tried boarding one year at Canfield, and he'd spent much of his adolescence hanging around at Annie and Graham's house.

He remembered abruptly a winter afternoon, sitting at the table in the big room talking to Annie, trying to explain his feelings about Frieda to her. Snow was falling steadily outside, thick, heavy flakes. The bare branches of the lilac bushes in the backyard were outlined in white. He was saying that he wished that Graham had never left his mother. "I mean, not that I don't like you as a stepmother, but it's like she's never going to get over it." He'd gone on for a while, listing his complaints, slowly becoming aware of Annie's silence, of the sense that she was just waiting, waiting for him to stop so she could talk.

So he stopped; and Annie told him that it was more complicated than that. That he should try to understand, now that he was a little older, how complicated it was. That it was Frieda who had left Graham, not the other way around. That Graham had been unfaithful to Frieda. Did he understand what that meant?

Yeah, he had said irritably. Of course.

She went on, explaining the way the world was then, the great experiment of the 1960s that Frieda had turned against, that had made her feel she needed to end her marriage to Lucas's father.

After that, his father had spoken about it with him too—because of course Annie had talked to him about her conversation with Lucas. What he said to his son was that Frieda was "blameless."

Lucas never forgot the word. Blameless.

It only made things worse for him, to be told that he had no right to his anger at his mother—which was how he heard all this. It wasn't until he went away to college—went away legitimately, as he thought of it—that he had the sense of shedding it all, Frieda's sadness and his responding anger at her.

But today, he realized, he was feeling it again. He saw that somehow his father's death would have to be, for him, first about his mother. That her sorrow would have precedence over his, would once again get in the way of what he wanted to feel, cleanly, selfishly: grief. Grief for the father he had loved so unequivocally, the one he held, always, blameless.

12

ANNIE WASN'T SURE how the afternoon passed. Mostly, she stayed in the house. At one point, for no particular reason, she went outside and weeded in the backyard, but then didn't have the energy or willpower to pick up the little heaps of wilting green she'd left everywhere on the bricks.

The funeral home called and asked her to come in and fill out some forms, so she drove over and signed her name several times. The young man in the office there offered her an array of containers for Graham's ashes, and, confused—who cared, really?—she chose one.

Her friend Edith came over late in the afternoon with takeout food from Formaggio and a bottle of wine. "In case you feel like eating," she said. "Or maybe just drinking."

Annie was glad to see her, glad to be held, to have to talk; but also glad when she left, relieved to let herself sag back down into silence, into the nothingness she felt, which she knew was just the holding off of a grief that promised to be, as it threatened every now and then, overwhelming.

Around seven, she was still sitting at the table with a glass of Edith's wine. She had set out the cartons of food and eaten a few bites of each one. Without bothering to put the food away, she had poured herself a second glass and had sat down again to drink it slowly.

Shadows had started to gather in the backyard when she heard the footsteps on the front porch.

Graham! Her breath seemed to stop.

For the three or four seconds that followed, she understood that everything that had happened wasn't real, that it had been a dream, a dream she'd had of his death. And now—of course!—he was coming home to her in life, just as he always did. Her breath seemed to stop.

But then the doorbell rang.

She thought of not answering, of just sitting there in the empty room, her heart still pounding, waiting for the footsteps to retreat.

But some sense of duty or obligation moved in her, and after those few seconds more, she got up and went to the front of the house.

When she opened the door, John Norris stood on the other side of the screen, beaming at her. He raised his arms and waggled the flowers he had in one hand and the bottle of wine in the other.

She was confused for a moment, and then remembered: of course, he'd been invited to dinner—*yesterday, when Graham was alive*—and because she'd forgotten that this morning, he hadn't ever been uninvited.

By the time she reached out to push open the screen door, his smile had dropped. He clearly knew, by how she looked and was dressed, by the deep silence in the house, that something was very wrong.

"Come in, John," she said.

"Did I get the day wrong?" he asked. "What is it?" He came into the hall. "What's happening?"

"Graham died, John. He had a heart attack."

"Christ! Annie!" He looked stupid, Annie thought. Almost funny, standing there with his mouth open, his hands, still full of his useless gifts, dropped down by his sides.

"Here," she said, wanting to help him, reaching for the flowers, the wine. He mistook her meaning, he stepped forward and embraced her. She felt the wine bottle cold on her back. After a moment, she stepped away, out of his arms, and he stepped back too.

This time when Annie reached for his gifts, he ceded them to her, his face blank. Then he lifted his empty hands. "But when did this happen? I just saw him." He looks like a confused little boy, she thought.

"I know," she said. "Come on. Come on back and sit with me." She started back toward the kitchen, and he followed her.

"I was having wine," she said. "Would you like some?"

"Sure." He sat down at the big table. "Sure. That's fine."

"I'm sorry I don't have dinner for you. Are you hungry?" She set John's bouquet and the bottle of wine down on the counter. She pulled her already opened bottle from the refrigerator. "I have some takeout stuff," she said, gesturing at the open white cartons. "A friend brought them by."

No, no, he wasn't hungry, John was saying. "But what happened? When did he die?"

She put a glass down in front of him, and as she poured wine into it, she said, "Last night. Last night, in his sleep." She noted with a kind of distant curiosity that her hand was shaking, her breath was still coming unevenly. She set the bottle down and sat kitty-corner from John, who was at the head of the table, in Graham's chair. His face was still a mixture of perplexity and shock.

She told him a few of the details, aware of a sense of practice in this—she was getting numb to these words, these words that had been so unbearable to speak the first few times.

"It's just unbelievable," he said. He still hadn't touched his glass.

Annie leaned forward and gently pushed it toward him. "I'm sorry I didn't remember to let you know when I canceled the rest of them."

"What?" He leaned forward, squinting at her.

"When I canceled the dinner party. I forgot you were coming. That Graham had asked you."

He sat back and nodded. After a long moment, he said, "God, we just had lunch."

"I know," Annie said. After a few seconds, she thought to say, "I'm really glad you saw him."

"Yeah." His voice was still full of a kind of puzzlement. Then he looked sharply at her, as if really seeing her for the first time. "Did he tell you about it?"

"He did. Not much. He's always just so happy to see you. He's always so . . . buoyant afterward." She shook her head. "Listen to me, talking about him in the present tense."

"Well. Of course. It's just impossible to think of him gone."

She smiled at John. "As if he were more or less too alive to die."

"I suppose," John said.

"If only it were so," she said. And then, because she didn't want to weep in front of John, she said, "No. It's just not . . . believable, is it?" They sat quietly for a moment. "I almost thought you were him. When I heard you."

John frowned, confused.

"Just now, coming onto the front porch," she clarified.

"Oh!" he said. "I'm sorry."

"No, no. I don't mean . . . It's just that I keep expecting him, I suppose."

John nodded slowly. "To walk in," he said.

"To walk in and start talking." She laughed, awkwardly.

"Yes," he said. He sipped the wine. They sat, not saying anything for a long moment. John looked over at her. "He was happy, you said."

"He was. He really was."

"Hmm." He swallowed again.

"And you know," Annie said, "he'd been a little . . . distracted, I guess you'd say, recently. So I was pleased that he seemed . . . back to normal. We had a lovely dinner. For which I have you to thank, I suspect. Whatever it was you talked about, it did the proverbial trick."

"Oh, it was nothing much. You know."

"Yes." She nodded. "That feeling of important things being said, and then you can't really remember any of it. Just that it felt that way. Important, I mean."

"Yes, kind of like that." Then, after a long moment, "He hadn't been . . . sick or anything. No warning."

"No. I mean, he was overweight, of course. He was on statins, so . . ." She lifted her shoulders. "But nothing that would make you think . . ."

"Yeah." They sat in silence. John seemed to be watching his own hand turn his wineglass slowly.

Because she didn't know what else to do, to say, she asked about his family then, how they were, and heard the same report—with fewer details—that Graham had heard at lunch and passed on to her. He said Graham had told him about her show, and he wished her well with it. He was sorry, he said, that he wouldn't have time to get over there. The silence fell again, a silence that felt awkward to Annie, but she didn't have the energy to break it.

After a moment, John asked about a service—he said he'd like to come if there was one, and she said she didn't know yet, it was one of the things she needed to talk about with Sarah and Lucas. "They're coming, tomorrow." (Frieda had called just before Edith came over, called to say Lucas would be up from New York. And Sarah had called a bit after that to tell Annie that she couldn't get on a plane until late in the evening, that she wouldn't get there until morning.)

"Oh," John said. "That's good then. So you won't be alone."

"No. Well, I think Lucas is coming just for the day. And he'll . . . be mostly with Frieda, I suspect. But Sarah will stay over until Monday. With me."

"Well, good." He nodded, many times. Then, in a rush, "One of the things we talked about was you, Annie. Was how much he loved you."

Annie smiled back at him.

"No, I mean it. He did. He said you were his first and last love." John dipped his head then, and almost smiled himself. "And then he corrected himself and said maybe actually *not* the first, but yes, the last."

"A stickler for accuracy. Upon occasion."

John nodded again. He pushed his chair back. "I'm going to go now, Annie." He stood up.

"You don't have to. Honestly."

"No, but you don't need to . . . entertain me, either. I'm sure you'd planned on having this evening to yourself."

"I had, actually. And I am tired."

"Of course you are."

She walked behind him to the front door. After they'd said good night, after she said she'd let him know about a service, either way, he paused for a moment. Then he said, "He really did say that about you. And I know that's how he felt." His eyes were steady on her. "So remember that, no matter what."

"Of course I will. Thank you. Thank you, John."

As she shut the door behind him and locked it, Annie was thinking, What a funny thing to say, really. "No matter what." How could anything more happen, beyond what had? Still, he was kind to have told her. And she could imagine Graham saying it, saying it in his wonderful, rumbling voice.

She went back through the house, back to the kitchen. She sat again for a while at the table. She was calling up those seconds when she had thought the footsteps on the porch were Graham, when she thought she'd been mistaken somehow about his death. When he was alive for her for just those suspended seconds more. Then the knowledge—again!—that he wasn't. That he was gone. That there was no way to reach across to him.

She had the thought that this would surely happen again, more than once. That she'd wake up some mornings, having forgotten he was dead, or having dreamed him alive, and have to face that loss again. She moaned, a soft sound.

She picked up her wineglass and went outside. It was fully dark. She sat in one of the old chairs on the brick patio, which was ringed by the small piles of weeds she hadn't picked up this afternoon—little dark blobs just visible in the light coming from Karen's house.

She turned to look over there. The lights were all still on, though that didn't mean a thing. Sometimes they blazed all night in every room because she'd forgotten to turn them off.

Would this be her fate? Annie wondered. Alone, drinking too much, the messy backyard, the dishes left on the table or sitting in the sink, the lights left on all night?

A wave of such bottomless self-pity took her that her throat hurt, as though something sharp were stuck in it. She stood up. She went inside. She turned the lights on and started to pick up the wine-glasses, the bottle, the cartons of food, the plates. The flowers John had brought for the party were still lying on the counter in their paper, tied with a pretty green satin bow. She went to the cupboard by the door to the back hall and got out a clear glass vase for the bouquet. When she'd settled the flowers in it, she set it on the big table, next to Graham's flowers.

That was how she'd seen him, she realized. When she heard John's footsteps, when she thought Graham was alive again, she'd seen him coming up the steps onto the porch, carrying the bouquet that he'd bought for her.

13

ANNIE HAD A white scar just above her forehead, hidden by the way she parted her hair. It dated from a time when Sarah was about two and a half, a time when Sarah had hit her, possibly with a kind of intent to kill.

They had been in a toy store, shopping, the three of them—Annie, Graham, and Sarah. Sarah was picking up one thing after another, wanting them all, whining. They'd negotiated and finally bought a small stuffed mouse for her, brown with little black beads for eyes and short, stiff whiskers. They'd paid for it and were ready to go, but on the way to the door, Sarah spotted an antique doll's house at child's-eye level and reached in to grab something from one of its rooms. Annie, who was directly behind her, squatted down next to the little girl and spoke to her. "I want you to put that back, Sarah." Annie saw that it was a stove from the doll's-house kitchen, a little cast-iron stove, an almost exact replica of the kind of stove Annie's mother had had in their kitchen in Chicago until late in Annie's childhood.

Sarah looked steadily at her mother. Annie could watch the idea alter Sarah's face, though she didn't know what the idea was until Sarah raised her hand with the stove and brought it down quickly, as hard as she was able to, hitting Annie's head.

Annie cried out, and almost simultaneously felt the warm blood start down her forehead.

In a swift motion, Graham, who had been standing behind Sarah, grabbed her hand, yanking her up slightly, up and backward. Sarah's face registered her astonishment. Now Graham crouched next to her, his angry face close to hers as he said, in a voice full of controlled rage, "You don't ever, ever hit Mumma!"

Sarah had wept then, so desperately, for so long, at what must have felt like an unexpected betrayal, a terrible loss—her father! who always, always loved her best!—that they both wound up holding her, trying to reassure her, Annie in particular speaking of her love for Sarah, of Graham's love, explaining it all away: his anger, her blood—all of it nothing, of no importance.

But Sarah was inconsolable. She wept all the way home in the car, she wept as they laid her in her bed, she wept even as she finally fell asleep, shuddering, her eyelashes sticky with tears.

At the time, Annie thought it must have been like a death for Sarah—her first experience of real loss, and loss of the person she held dearest in life.

That grieving little girl was the second thing Annie thought of as she woke on Saturday to the cold coming in from the open window, to the sound of the heavy rain.

The first being Graham.

Sarah arrived in a cab. Annie was still in her kimono and pajama bottoms when she heard her at the front door and came around from the kitchen.

She opened her arms to embrace her daughter, but Sarah shied back. "Ah! No, no! Don't, Mom. I'm soaking. Look." She'd set her suitcase down just inside the door, and now she held her arms out, away from her body, presenting herself. Her jacket was darkened with rain, her hair wet, bedraggled, just from the walk up the driveway. She looked tired too, and drawn, but who wouldn't after taking the red-eye? Annie leaned forward and kissed her cheek carefully, then put her hand on her daughter's chilly, wet face. Sarah closed her eyes for a moment and leaned her head against her mother's warm hand.

After a moment Annie stepped back and said, "Do you want coffee? Or maybe a hot shower first?"

"Coffee. God, yes. And a towel. But I'll get it, I'll get it!" she said, as Annie started toward the stairs.

When she came down, she'd taken her coat off and she had a towel draped on her shoulders, like a cape. Her hair was roughed around her face.

They sat together at the table, each with a fresh cup of coffee. The rain was streaking down the big windows. It was as dark as evening outside. Annie had turned on the lamp that sat on the kitchen counter, and it felt warm and cavelike in this part of the room.

They talked about inconsequential things at first—Sarah's flight, frighteningly bumpy as it landed in the wind and the rain. How good the coffee was. The glamour of the new coffee machine. About Lucas, when he would arrive. About how little Annie had slept.

They set their cups in almost perfect synchrony into their saucers. Sarah looked for a minute at the gray, gray view outside the windows. Gray, and then the deep green of the wet shrubbery.

Her voice was different when she asked, "Where *is* Daddy now?"

The big question. Annie suddenly felt the full weight of everything. She was unable to answer for a moment.

Sarah reached across and covered Annie's hands with hers. Annie's hands were warm, Sarah's cool. Annie turned hers up to hold Sarah's for a moment.

"You mean his body," Annie said.

Sarah nodded.

"Actually, I'm not sure," Annie said at last. "He wanted to be cremated, so that's what will happen. But I don't think it's happened yet—they have to wait a certain number of hours, I forget how long. I suppose it's some kind of legal thing."

Sarah's voice was almost inaudible when she said, "Oh." She sat back in her chair, drawing her hands away from Annie's.

Annie's face changed. "Did you want to *see* him?" she cried. "Oh Sarah, I didn't think of that. I didn't think of it. I'm so sorry." And then she did think about it, everything that had happened around Graham's body, around what had seemed the necessity of its being taken away from her. And of course from Sarah, too.

And Lucas? Would Lucas have wanted to see him? She said, "I'm not . . . I don't think it would have been possible, really."

"Oh," Sarah said. Then, "I don't think I really did anyway. Want to see him." She was frowning, thoughtful. "It probably would have been . . . I don't know really." She shrugged. "Strange, I suppose."

"It was strange," Annie said. The memory of those moments when she was with Graham's body without feeling his presence came back to her, dulled her again. She struggled to think of a way to speak of it. She said, "I felt so much that he wasn't there, that the body . . ." She lifted her hands. "It almost didn't matter to me."

Sarah nodded, frowning—her open, plain face so full of sympathy that Annie felt herself tearing up again. Wrong, she thought. Wrong. You should be comforting her.

But then the tears started, she felt herself giving over to them, and Sarah pushed her chair back and came around the table.

This was the way it held through that day—Annie, often abruptly tearful, Sarah, steady and maternal. Annie was surprised, surprised by herself and a little ashamed; but surprised more by Sarah, who seemed changed. Changed by Graham's death, of course. But perhaps slowly changed too in ways Annie hadn't really taken in before, in spite of seeing her as recently as Christmas. It must have been much longer than that since she'd really looked at her daughter. She watched her now as she moved around, as she got more coffee, as she carried the dishes to the sink. She was the same, but different. Even her body seemed different. She was still big, but now she looked athletic, strong, rather than slow and heavy.

She could stay only through midday Monday, she said, so she wanted to do what she could to help. She began to take charge of things that Annie hadn't even thought of doing—calling Graham's living siblings, and then Annie's. Starting to write an obituary to send to *The Globe*, she said, and the *Cambridge Chronicle*. Answering the door on and off through the morning, as a few of Graham and Annie's friends began to appear on the porch with casseroles or fruit baskets or wine and more bunches of flowers. Annie stayed back in the kitchen, where she couldn't see who was at the door. She could hear her daughter, her rich, velvety voice always the dominant one, sounding gracious and poised. It occurred to her that Sarah had learned this way of being among others, probably from her work at the radio station.

At one point Annie recognized Felicity Rogers's voice on the porch, heard her say to Sarah, "Don't you think it's better that he died before your mother? I mean, honestly."

If she'd been the one at the door, she would just have stared back at Felicity, dumbfounded. But now she heard Sarah say, in a perfectly friendly tone, "I don't quite understand what you mean."

"Oh! Well, I mean, just, he would have been so lost without her, whereas she's so much more . . . self-sufficient, I suppose."

"Of course: Mom. Yeah, I'm sure you're right."

"Thank you for managing *that* one," Annie said when Sarah came back to the kitchen, carrying Felicity's offering, a wrapped box of what might have been chocolates.

"Oh, sure."

"You handled it so much better than I would have," Annie said.

"I'm a smoothie by now, handling people is so much of what I do." Sarah sat down.

Annie said, "What a funny phrase—'handling people.'"

"I suppose." Sarah shrugged. "It *is* what I do, though."

After a moment, Annie said, "I'm just awful at it, myself."

The rain had stopped by now, the sky was lighter, and Sarah suggested they sit outside.

"We'd have to wipe everything down," Annie said.

"Well, let's," Sarah said. She went up the back stairs and came down with two clean, folded towels. Annie took one, and they both went outside. They swiped down the chairs in the backyard. They sat for a while, mostly not talking. The air was even cooler after the rain.

Maybe fifteen minutes after they'd taken their seats, Karen appeared at her own back door. Together, Annie and Sarah watched the old woman come slowly down the stairs and over to their yard. She bared her teeth at them in the rictus that passed for a sociable smile with her. She was wearing a man's raincoat over what seemed like not much else. At any rate, her feet were bare, as were her long, bruised-looking shanks. Her hair was rumpled and wild, as though she'd come to them directly from her bed.

"Well, I know who *you* are!" she said to Sarah as she entered the yard.

"We're even then, 'cause I know who you are too," Sarah said, smiling back.

"Will you sit with us?" Annie gestured at one of the empty chairs.

Karen didn't look at Annie, but she sat down. "You're the girl. What's your name, now?"

"Sarah."

"That's right," Karen said, as though praising a bright child for her cleverness. They all smiled at each other.

Now that she'd settled in her chair, the old woman's knees fell away from each other, and from her vantage, Annie saw that yes indeed, she was naked under the coat, her thin thatch of grayish hair in shadow between her legs, the rest in deeper shadow. She was glad Sarah was next to Karen and didn't have this vista.

"But you don't live here anymore," Karen said. Her tone was almost accusatory.

"No, I'm in San Francisco now."

"*Are* you?"

"Yes."

"I was there once," Karen said. "You know what Mark Twain said about it." Before Sarah had time to respond, she turned her piercing gaze on Annie. "And where's your jolly husband?"

"Graham," Annie said.

"Yes, that nice fat man."

Annie laughed once, helplessly, and let a little silence accrue.

"He died," Sarah said, after the long moment.

Karen swung her head to Sarah. "Oh, come now. That's ridiculous!" she said, her tone haughty. "He's a young man."

Neither Annie nor Sarah spoke for a moment. Then Sarah said, "I thought so too." Her voice was a child's suddenly, and it seemed she might cry. "I thought it was ridiculous too." She inhaled raggedly, a few sharp breaths.

"Oh now, dear, stop that," Karen said. "He'll be back, you'll see. Momentarily."

Annie felt swept by a sudden rage. She stood up. "You know what?" she said to the old woman. Her voice was sharp. "I think I'm going to take you back home so you can get dressed. You're not wearing much of anything under your raincoat, and it would be better if you did."

"Oh!" Karen said. She was surprised, audibly. Perhaps angry too.

"No, let's go," Annie said. She wasn't sure where her own anger came from. Maybe it had to do with Graham. Why should he be dead, when this old woman so uselessly, so carelessly, went on and on?

Or Sarah, she thought. Why should Sarah have to indulge Karen? Karen was their responsibility. Hers and Graham's.

Hers, now. Only hers.

Karen stood up, obediently. Annie stepped forward and would have taken her arm, but the old woman moved ahead of her. One after the other, they walked past the dripping lilac bush and mounted the stairs into Karen's house.

When Annie returned (the messy house, the faint smell of cat, the bare, stained mattress, the old woman's flesh, sagging everywhere—*dugs* the word that leapt to Annie's mind when Karen took her coat off and she saw the long, drooping breasts), she told Sarah she thought she'd lie down for a little while.

She did—she went up to the bedroom and lay down and almost instantly fell into a deep sleep. When she woke, she saw that the clouds outside the window had lightened again. She heard voices downstairs, Sarah's, and then a man's.

Lucas, of course. Lucas with Sarah.

She stood up. She went to the bathroom and brushed her teeth. When she came out into the upstairs hallway, she stood and listened to them talking for a moment or two. She couldn't hear what they were saying, just the easy, familiar alternation of their voices. Siblings, after all. She'd never understood it, how they'd become such friends. Or when. Clearly out in the wider world, away from home. She remembered the first time that Lucas had reported back on Sarah, after he'd visited her in college. How interesting it was, how strange, to hear the way he thought of her, so different from the way she saw her daughter. Completely without the sense of the solitary, unhappy little girl she'd once been, the girl who still haunted Annie.

When Annie appeared in the kitchen, Lucas stood up and stepped toward her. He held her fiercely for a moment. When he let her go and stepped back, she said, "I didn't hear you arrive. I didn't hear the doorbell."

"Oh! I'm supposed to ring now." Even as she smiled back at him—his eyes so like Graham's, disappearing with his smile—

Annie thought, *Yes, yes, you should*: the sense of the house being taken over, of her being somehow no longer in charge of anything.

Then *no*, remembering how it had been, how delighted she'd been when, at age ten or eleven, Lucas began to come over by himself. Not ringing. Just walking in. "Is Daddy here?"

No, she was grateful to both of them, she thought, as they sat together in the living room.

After a while Sarah suggested they take a walk, partly just to get out of the house while the rain held off, and partly to escape the intermittent arrival of people stopping by with food. Annie loaned her a raincoat, just in case, and put on her own almost waterproof jacket, and they went down the driveway and got into Frieda's car—Lucas had driven over in it. Lucas and Sarah sat in front, Annie in back. She noted that the two of them were almost the same height. There was something pleasurable in seeing this—Graham's genes, in Sarah's case triumphing over her own.

They drove to Fresh Pond, parked, and started on the path that ran around the water, three abreast on its wide asphalt, alert for possible dog shit underfoot or the panting footfall of joggers approaching from behind. Even though it was a Saturday, it wasn't crowded—the rain had kept people away. The water in the reservoir moved, gray and sullen, on the other side of the chain-link fence. Ahead of them, the dark woods seemed unwelcoming.

Sarah said, "Lucas and I were talking, Mom."

"Yeah," he said. "We wondered if we shouldn't have a service of some kind."

We, Annie thought. Not *you*. Not *are you going to*.

But it wasn't that, she didn't think, that made her say, "I don't know. Graham might have been appalled." Her *no* was ready, for reasons she wasn't sure of.

"Oh, I'm not talking about a religious service," Lucas said.

Sarah said, "Yes, we didn't mean a *service*, a religious service, so much as a gathering of some sort. At the store, maybe?"

"Can't it wait?" Annie asked.

"You're not ready," Lucas said.

Annie forced a laugh, but she could hear that it wasn't convincing. "I'll say. I don't think I'll ever be ready."

Sarah said, "But a lot of people will want to . . . I don't know. Remember him. *Ceremonially*, I guess you'd say."

"Well, that's just it."

"Too many people." She was asking Annie, her eyes full of concern.

"Yes. Too many people with a claim on him. Too many people for me to deal with right now."

"On your left!" someone called from behind them, and Annie turned just as Sarah caught her hand and pulled her to the side of the path. A whole team of adolescent boys, all wearing identical navy-blue shorts and gray T-shirts, pounded by, large and muscular and overwhelming as a group, a couple of them actually talking through their gasps for air.

Once they were past, Annie and Lucas and Sarah started walking again, Sarah still holding Annie's hand. After a moment she said to her mother, "Your brother asked about it. And so did Daddy's, actually."

Annie could feel it—it had been decided. She knew that. Lucas and Sarah had decided it. They were taking charge of it. Of her. In the name of helping. Of being kind.

She had the sense of things shifting around her. It would be different now, without Graham. She and he together had made an impregnable fortress. They decided what happened next in their own lives. His death would be the end of that. They would speak to her differently now. They would speak to her the way she'd spoken to Karen. More kindly perhaps, but that way. Taking charge.

She remembered her grandmother suddenly, alternately furious and resigned when her children put her into a "continuing care facility." In her tiny room, too full of every possession she cherished—

the spoon set from Grandma Ida, the tea service from Auntie—she had smiled bitterly at Annie and said, "Just wait. It will come to you too."

"Actually," Annie said quietly now, "he didn't want a service, but he said we could have a party if I wanted to. If I had the energy." Annie had read this earlier—yesterday—when she'd found Graham's living will, just before she called the hospital. Maybe a party, he'd written, if she was up to it. And then he'd written, "But absolutely nothing more!"

There was a silence. Annie could feel a shift in the air among them. They'd won. After a long moment, Lucas said, "We could do it later. When you'll have more energy. The party. Sarah and I would do all the work."

"Yes," Sarah said. "We could ask Erica"—the events person at the store—"to put up a poster now, or in the next couple of days, for a, you know, a celebration of his life. Say, a couple of weeks from now."

Annie groaned.

"Okay, a month, then," Lucas said. "A month and a half."

She didn't answer.

"Whenever you want, Mom," Sarah said. "It's just I think people are going to start asking you about it all the time, a service, and this would be a simple, quick answer."

Annie didn't say anything.

"Mother?"

"All right," Annie said. "Let's look at the calendar."

A little after nine on Monday, the day Sarah was to go back to the West Coast, Annie answered the door and the nice young man from the funeral home was standing there, blurry through the old screen with its rusted mesh. Behind him, the sunshine through the leaves of the linden tree in the Caldwells' side yard made a greenish light. "I hope I'm not interrupting anything," he said.

For a moment Annie couldn't imagine why he had come, but then she saw the wooden box, the one she'd chosen for no good reason to hold Graham's ashes. Or really, she thought now, she'd chosen it because it had felt wrong to her at the time to ask them to put the ashes into a cardboard box, which seemed to be the only alternative. It was ridiculous—Annie knew she'd be scattering the ashes, not keeping them. But the thing was, she didn't want to seem cheap—that was it, wasn't it?—so she'd succumbed to it, this large, overweening box.

"No," she said now. "There's nothing to interrupt." She thought that sounded self-pitying, so she opened the screen door. "I see you've brought me Graham's ashes."

"Yes." He held out the wooden box. "Again, our condolences."

"Yes. Thank you." Annie reached out to take the box. She was surprised at how heavy it was.

"We were glad to help."

Now he held up also a cloth satchel, the kind the bookstore would sell you to tote your books home in. This one had no logo.

"What's this?" she asked.

"His clothing," he said. "What he was wearing."

She remembered it instantly, the old T-shirt. She remembered, too, lifting the sheet to see Graham's nakedness below it, her moment of looking at him, his big body, his penis, his long thighs— eons ago, it seemed. Three days. No, four now.

He reached into the bag and lifted a small white box from within it to show her. "And his ring. His wedding ring, I imagine." He dropped it back into the bag.

Annie had thought of none of this, that these things would be coming back to her. It made her feel negligent. She'd let Graham go off to be declared dead, to be burned up, wearing nothing but an old T-shirt, his wedding ring still on his finger. Who would do such a thing?

"Thank you. Thank you for everything," she said, taking the bag from him, holding it and the big wooden box awkwardly as she stepped back. The screen door shut between them, a gentle smack.

"We were honored we could help," he said again, already turning away.

Annie watched him go down the walk. He was dressed as if perhaps he was going to play golf in a little while, green slacks and those brown-and-white shoes—she couldn't think of the name for them at the moment

She could hear Sarah back in the kitchen. She was putting something together for breakfast.

For a moment she stood in the hall, unsure of what to do next, where to put the bag and this absurd wooden box. It seemed to her that there must be some appropriate place for it that she was just not capable of thinking of at that moment.

In the kitchen, Sarah turned the blender on.

Annie didn't want to discuss any of this with her. Certainly not the ashes —it was too soon!—but also not her stupidity in capitulating to this ridiculous, outsize wooden *object*.

She moved to the narrow stairs and started up. She would put the box in the bedroom. If Sarah asked about the ashes, she'd make something up about when they were supposed to arrive, or when she was going to pick them up. They'd agreed, anyhow, she and Lucas and Sarah, to scatter them together up at the cottage before the memorial party, which they'd finally decided to have in the fall, when people would be back from their vacations, their summer homes.

She thought of "the cottage": the little summer house she and Graham had bought as a gift to each other the year after Sarah graduated from college. She pictured it, the world that she and Graham had made there. The world away from the world. She'd like to be there now. Away. She would go, she decided. Soon. She would go alone.

In the bedroom, she slid the wooden box to the back of her side of the closet, amid the jumble of her own shoes. Graham's side was nearly empty—one of the chores Sarah had undertaken yesterday was clearing out his clothing. Annie had been surprised, actually, when she found Sarah laying those things out on the bed, bagging them. Then, after she'd helped Sarah set them out on the front porch for a pickup on Monday, suddenly grief-stricken. She wanted them back, the things he'd worn. The night after he'd died, after she'd gone to bed and woken from a light sleep, she'd gotten up and gone to stand in the dark closet among them, the beautiful linen and wool jackets, the slacks, the soft, worn shirts.

Now she took the ring and the T-shirt out of the bag and started to put them in the top drawer in Graham's side of the dresser. But then she stopped and lifted the shirt to her face, inhaled the scent of Graham it still carried, even as she was aware of this as cliché too, of how often she'd read it, seen it. But how impossible it was not to do these things! These things that so many others had done before you. These were the things you *wanted* to do.

She went to the bathroom to be sure she looked all right—whatever that meant; *normal*, she supposed—before going back downstairs to sit with Sarah, to eat whatever she'd prepared or assembled out of the many gifts of food that friends had brought over.

Annie had checked herself over and over in one mirror or another in these last few days, so keenly did she feel that she must have been transformed. That her emptiness, her shock, must be visible somehow, must have stamped her. And always, always when she looked, here she was, the unchanged face, the graying dark hair framing it, the wide-spaced, slightly startled-looking dark eyes, the thinning lips with the little net of creases above and below. Normal.

She had been pretty when she was younger, pretty in what might have been called a gamine way. Perhaps "elfin," if you were being less kind. She had actually dressed as an elf once, for a costume party early on in her marriage with Graham. He was Santa Claus that night, there was that radical a difference in size between them.

Her old friend from photography school, Natalie Schumer, had said to Annie once that of course they all speculated on the sex between Graham and her, on how it could possibly *work*, mechanically. And though Annie had been startled by the idea of this being discussed openly among her friends, she'd tried to keep her face pleasantly expressionless as she said, "Oh! Very well, thanks."

After a second, Natalie had grinned and said, "You're not going to give me *anything?*"

She smiled now at the memory, at the thought of Natalie, big and solid and almost manly, even in her tentlike dress—"Our own Gertrude Stein," Graham had called her—and watched her face in the mirror grow younger by ten years. Five, anyway.

She tried it again downstairs, smiling at Sarah as she came into the kitchen, and was touched to see relief and pleasure lift her daughter's face.

"Sit," Sarah said, smiling back. "I've made us a lovely brunch out of this and that." And Annie thought again of how changed she was. Of how the Sarah who'd arrived back home this time was not the Sarah she'd expected.

14

ANNIE HAD BEEN relieved when Sarah arrived, but she was relieved too when she left. She was glad not to have to talk. Not to have to do much of anything. There was a sudden sense of freedom in the empty house. She had food, she had wine—mostly Graham's cheap stuff in the pantry, but still, wine, and more than enough.

For a few days, then, she stayed by herself. She didn't cry, in part because she felt that if she started, she might never stop. Later she was unable to account for the time to herself, other than that she supposed that what she mostly did was sit. Either Edith or Frieda called every day—perhaps they'd discussed it, she thought, and were taking turns. She talked to Sarah twice. The landline rang, but she didn't answer it, didn't even check the messages. They would call the office, she thought, and hear from someone else that Graham had died.

She did sit at Graham's desk to sort through the papers on it. She made a pile of things she thought ought to go to the bookstore, but then left them lying there. Danielle called several times on her cell, to tell her that six of the photographs had sold, but Annie didn't return the calls. The condolence cards, identifiable mostly by their size—smaller than a letter—piled up in the front hall.

After three days of this, she called Edith and asked her to dinner the next night, warning her that she would take no responsibility for the meal—she planned just to heat up one of the casseroles still stacked one on top of the other in the refrigerator, and they could nibble on the cookies or brownies or muffins sitting in tins on the counters, most handed to Sarah at the front door or left anonymously on the table on the porch in those first days.

Fine, Edith said. She'd be happy just to see Annie.

Annie had met Edith after her husband, Mike Hodges, had published Annie's photo book *Emergency*, and certainly Annie had liked Edith well enough then, Mike's nice wife; but when he moved out to live with the man he'd fallen in love with, her real friendship with Edith began.

One of the things they talked about was Mike, of course, about the complicating reality that Edith was still in love with him, and he, in another way, with her. He came to celebrate all the holidays with her and the children; they spoke to each other almost daily on the telephone.

Annie had at first been so angry on Edith's behalf that she couldn't understand this. "After all," she said to her new friend, "he was unfaithful to you. Many, many times, in fact, he was unfaithful to you."

"Annie, he was *gay*. He was struggling with that."

"Why should that excuse it? Who cares if it was a man? He was fucking another person—he was *wooing* another person—and he was your husband."

"But think how hard he must have been trying—working really—all those years, to be married to me." Edith's face was anguished with the thought of it. "The wrong person entirely," she said. "The wrong gender, even. It breaks my heart."

Annie had persisted for a while, even as she understood how

judgmental, how small, she sounded. ("So *Protestant!*" Edith said to her once, and laughed.) But over the weeks and months, she came to accept Edith's position, and finally, to admire her for it, for her generosity. As they began to know each other well in the aftermath of Edith's marriage, Annie slowly understood that this generosity, this kindness, was part of what drew her to the other woman.

That, and her physical loveliness—she was at the time possibly the most beautiful person Annie had ever met. She was tall and slender. Her hair then was an unusual bronze color, and she wore it pinned up in a ballerina's bun. Her face had exactly that kind of beauty—a classic, sculpted ballerina's beauty, remote and lovely until she smiled, a smile that even in her sorrow conveyed a kind of pleasure in life.

It seemed she was conscious of this, of her beauty. She always dressed elegantly, if simply—tailored slacks on her long, long legs. Silk shirts. Bright lipstick. But she said all that was to please her patients—she was a pediatrician. It mattered to children, she'd said, how you looked. "Remember how much you loved pretty ladies when you were a child?" she asked Annie. "'Pitty ladies,'" she said in a little-girl voice, and then laughed. "It's only when you grow up that you learn you can love what's ugly, too."

Annie had been unable not to smile—this, from a woman whose husband had been as gorgeous as she was, so that when they came into a crowded room together in the old days, there was an almost collective intake of breath, a kind of group sigh.

Edith called out as she opened the front door, and Annie came around from the kitchen and walked into her embrace. After a long moment, Edith stepped back, holding Annie's shoulders, looking hard at her. "Have you slept at all?" she asked.

"Naps, mostly," Annie said.

"I'm so sorry."

"I know you are. That's why I wanted you here."

They opened the wine that Edith had brought, they talked as Annie heated up the meal, a kind of curried lamb stew. They talked about Sarah and Lucas. About what Annie had been doing. "Almost nothing," she said, and Edith said, "That sounds about right."

While they ate, they critiqued the stew unkindly—Edith was a good cook too. Even so, they consumed a good deal of it, and opened a second bottle of wine when they'd finished the first. As Annie poured a glass for her, Edith said, "I feel he should be here, you know, *pronouncing* on something or other." She had said something like this several times during the meal.

"I do too," Annie said.

"*Opining*, I guess you'd say," Edith said.

"He did love to opine," Annie said. They sat quietly for a few moments.

From outside, they heard a dog somewhere nearby barking loudly. Someone yelled, "Shut up, Bertie!" and the dog barked again.

"*That* worked well," Edith said.

Annie smiled at her. After a moment, she said, "Mostly they were just passing notions, though."

"What were?"

"His opinings. His opinions. Half the time he'd change his mind the next day. He'd take the opposing view." She tried to make her voice deep, Graham-like. "'You know what? I've rethought.'"

Edith smiled. "Yes. A hard man to pin down."

"A fancy dancer," Annie said. She had a sudden memory of him, dancing. Fancy indeed, and so incongruously light on his feet. They had sometimes danced together, just the two of them, in the evenings. Occasionally Annie stood on those graceful feet so he could move her around as though she were a child, he the grown-up.

"I remember when he was on about the Iraq War," Edith said. "Well"—she made a face, she rolled her eyes—"one of the *many* times he was on about that. But the idea was, 'Why did we have to kill a hundred thousand Iraqis just to get Saddam Hussein out of there. Whatever happened to *the wet job?*' Remember?"

"Oh yes," Annie said, and laughed.

"'Ah, the good old wet job,'" Edith intoned, wanting to keep her friend happy a few moments longer. She'd succeeded, Edith—she'd made Annie laugh. Her mobile face showed her pleasure in that.

"Yeah," Annie said, "but then he couldn't stand the drone program."

"Too dry maybe," Edith said. "Not quite wet enough."

After a minute, Annie said, "As much as anything, I think he just liked saying it—'the wet job.'"

Edith smiled. "It does roll nicely off the tongue."

The room was dusky by now. Outside, the backyard was deep in shadow, but the sky above the neighbors' houses was a clear deep blue, and the higher leaves of the trees seemed to shimmer in the last of the sunlight's lingering touch on them.

"Do you remember his argument about fiction?" Annie asked. "About narrative? Another big theory."

"I don't. Probably I wasn't at that party."

"Just, that we read fiction because it suggests that life has a shape, and we feel . . . *consoled*, I think he said, by that notion. Consoled to think that life isn't just one damned thing after another. That it has sequence and consequence." She smiled at Edith. "I think it was more or less the idea that fictional narrative made life seem to *matter*, that it pushed away the meaninglessness of death."

Death. She'd said the word, and Edith's face was suddenly serious. After a long silence, she said gently, "And otherwise it doesn't matter? Life doesn't matter?"

Annie was stopped by the question for a few seconds. Then she said, "Well, look at *his* life. It *was*. And it *was*, and it *was*. And now"— she shrugged—"it isn't. Pfft. There's nothing left." Annie was startled by how angry she sounded. She tried to lighten her tone. "Some narrative," she said. After a moment or two, she got up and fetched some matches. She lit the candles on the table.

Edith was quiet, watching her. Then she said, "That's not true, Annie."

"What?" Annie sat down again.

"That there's nothing. Nothing left. There's *lots* left." She sounded almost fierce.

"Like what?"

"Well, all our memories of him."

Annie didn't want to fight with Edith, who was only being Edith, her good friend. "Okay," she said. Her voice sounded tired.

"That's not enough?" Edith asked.

"I don't know."

"What about Sarah, then? What about Lucas? What about the bookstore?"

Annie started to cry.

"Oh, Annie," Edith said. "Annie." She leaned forward in her chair and reached her hand across the table toward Annie.

"He's just so fucking *gone*."

"I know," Edith said. "I know."

Annie got up to get a tissue from the box on the counter and blew her nose, wiped her eyes. When she was sitting again, she said, "I'm sorry. This is really all about me. It's not about Graham. Or it's only partly about Graham." She blew her nose again. "Mostly it's about how empty and small my life feels now." They were quiet for a moment. Annie said, "I'm so *angry* at him, in a way, that he had so much energy. That he took up all that psychic space. That he took *me* up."

"Well, he did. That's who he was. That's why we loved him."

"But I was just . . . I didn't ask anything of myself. I just went along." Yes, Annie felt, this was it. She should have been more separate, more independent. Then she wouldn't feel so hollowed-out now.

"But who wouldn't, Annie? It was a great ride. We all went along."

"But now that it's over . . ."

"You don't think you were part of it? Part of what made it all work? The ride? The ride was your life together." Her voice was almost angry. "He didn't do it alone. He couldn't have done it without you."

Annie looked at Edith. She didn't know if what Edith had said was true or not—really, she was so lost that there was a sense in which she wasn't sure exactly even what Edith meant—but she was grateful. She knew that. She felt it. "Thank you," she said. 'Thank you for saying that."

"I mean it. Everyone knows it."

It was a few days after Edith came over for dinner that Annie walked past the bookstore for the first time since Graham's death, heading for a routine dentist appointment. She'd thought of canceling it, but she knew there would be a long wait to get another. Also, it seemed to her a small step back into normal life. She was feeling almost childishly proud of herself—Going to the Dentist—as she left the house and started down the long driveway.

She was deliberately walking on the other side of Mount Auburn Street from where the store sat, but even from there, it caught her eye, hanging in the plate-glass window—a huge image of Graham, the blowup of a photograph she recognized as one she'd taken, years earlier. She knew instantly what it was—the poster about the memorial gathering.

She crossed the street then, jaywalked, and stood in front of it, taking it in. It was, in a way, an odd photo for someone to have chosen to announce a party—an uncharacteristically contemplative moment for Graham. But it was arresting, and at this size, compelling. It was a shot of him in the store at night, taken from almost exactly where she was standing now, on the sidewalk. He hadn't seen her through the darkness, the rain, as he stood staring out through the streaked glass, his reading glasses swung up on his head, his arms crossed and resting on the shelf of his belly.

Above this image the poster said simply, GRAHAM. Below it, in smaller print: "Come and Remember Him." Below that, "September 8, 5:00 p.m." The date she and Sarah and Lucas had finally agreed on because it was after Labor Day—everyone would be back from their summer vacations.

Suddenly Annie was aware of a movement inside the store, behind the image. It was Bill, working at the register, his back to her. And then she saw that there was a man beyond him, deeper inside the store, standing fixed in an aisle, reading a book he'd taken off the shelf. And several other customers, too, moving around.

She fled.

Or that's what she felt she was doing. In any case, she walked away as quickly as she could, with the hope that no one had seen her, no one would come outside to call after her, to try to talk to her.

The image, the image she'd made, had startled her and then moved her, coming across it so unexpectedly, coming across Graham as he so rarely looked in life—stilled, thoughtful, unguessable. It stayed with her through the appointment at the dentist's office, the long, strange-but-familiar hour of weird compliance, of accommodating the tools, the fingers, the antiseptic flavors in her uncomfortably open mouth, the sense of drowning in her own saliva. "It's like being waterboarded," she said to the technician, who didn't respond. Was that politically incorrect? she wondered.

It struck her as surreal, this juxtaposition—even in some sense comedic. She wished she could talk to Graham about it, laugh with him, when she got home.

Instead, as soon as she got back, she went to find it, the book in which the photograph of Graham appeared. Graham's book, *Memoir with Bookshop*. It was with the other outsize books—art books, books of travel photographs—on the lowest shelf of the bookcase behind the couch.

Annie sat on the couch and flipped through it slowly. The text accompanying each picture consisted of Graham's comments on what the occasion was, sometimes on who attended, sometimes on odd or amusing things that had happened. Sometimes he just used quotes from the aftermath—the more telling thank-you notes, a couple of written apologies for some outrageous behavior.

Here was that event at the store with Cameron Marx, his third book of poetry, the one that got nominated for something—the National Book Critics Circle Award? The National Book Award? The photo was taken from behind Cameron as he read in his wildly incantatory style, and the upturned faces watching him were rapt, shocked. Graham was in the front row, as usual, and there were tears in his eyes.

How easily he cried! As easily as he laughed. As he kissed.

And yes, sprinkled among the other photographs, perhaps on every sixth or seventh page, was an image of him kissing someone. A few that Natalie had taken of him kissing Annie—once his head bent down to let his lips touch her arm as she leaned over the long table, holding out a platter of something or other. Here kissing Edith, kissing Erica. Also kissing men. Kissing Bill, who'd worked at the store from the earliest days. Kissing Cameron, and Peter. At least as many hugging people, people he swamped and surrounded.

Looking through it, Annie felt pulled back from her sense of smallness, of emptiness. Because as much as the photographs were a history of the bookstore and the parties, they were a history of their marriage. All of it, from the very start. For here was Graham in shirtsleeves at the opening party for the store, wearing the red wine stain down his front, her calling card. And here she was, sitting next to him in the front row at John Arnold's reading, their bodies touching.

What she felt keenly as she turned the pages was how much they had made it together, this world that she and Natalie had recorded— just as Edith had said the other night. And Graham had written a version of that same thing over and over in his comments on the photos. On a photo of him talking animatedly to someone whose back was to the camera, Sarah sound asleep on his shoulder: "At least two of us up well past our bedtime. Annie, the third member of our merry crew, danced until almost dawn."

On a photo of Annie, standing in the bright light of the kitchen, glasses and plates everywhere, Graham behind her wearing his favorite apron, loading the dishwasher. "Cleaning up together when all the fun is over. After this picture was taken, Natalie put the camera down and she and Don stayed on, helping us until everything was done. Then we all had a nightcap and bet on the Nobel Prize in literature, due to be announced soon. Annie, a little less tipsy than everyone else, called it: Nadine Gordimer. I owed her $150. Or so she told me the next day, and I was in no condition to disagree."

When she had turned the last page and shut the book, Annie sat motionless for a long moment. Then she got up and moved to what was almost the center of the open space she and Graham had made of the first floor those years ago. She turned slowly, surveying the room—the living area, the big table, the kitchen that extended into the space under the back stairs. Unpeopled, it seemed bigger than in the world of the photographs. Bigger, and emptier. How could she ever find a way of filling it without Graham?

Come back, she thought. Or maybe she said it aloud.

15

ALMOST FROM THE moment she got onto the highway, headed north toward the cottage in Vermont, Annie was thinking of the things she hadn't done when she left the Cambridge house. No windows were locked, as far as she knew. Probably some had been left open. She hadn't changed the telephone message to say she was gone or where she'd be. She'd left purely on impulse, shoving a few clothes into an overnight bag, grabbing some toiletries from the bathroom.

She hadn't arranged anything about opening the cottage either, so the grass would be unmown, the screens would still be in the shed, the bed would be unmade, the house would be dusty and spiderwebbed and dotted here and there with mouse droppings.

Yet she felt a sense of deep relief to be leaving, to be escaping the neighbors who came to check on her, to offer help, to drop off food. To escape even her friends, with their concern, which she had no adequate response to. She'd felt, over and over, the strain of trying to rise to some kind of sociability. She felt *watched*. She wanted an uninterruptable solitude, and the cottage, she thought, would offer this.

The sense of relief—release, really—grew as she passed the highway markers and familiar milestones, a release that turned into an odd kind of elation. It made her blood pound audibly in her ears, this crazy freedom, but it also made her feel more keenly her grief. She was giddy with both—with the glad escape from anyone's expectations of her, with a joy in being safely alone, but with an awareness the more intense because of that of the long aloneness to come.

She heard herself suddenly, a kind of rhythmic keening she was doing. There were no tears. It wasn't that—crying. It was a kind of protest, something that felt more primal than tears. She gave herself over to it. By the time she was crossing the border into New Hampshire, she was wailing her sorrow. Wave after wave of lamentation, until, finally, she'd worn herself out and she had to stop. Her throat was dry and a little sore. She felt there was nothing left inside her.

As she drew nearer to the border with Vermont, it occurred to her that she would need to stop in Hanover for groceries. She couldn't think what she wanted. She hadn't really cooked since Graham died. What would you make if Graham weren't going to sit down with you and cry out over the food?

Of course he had loved it best when there was company and she made fancy dishes—cassoulet or stuffed bass or Moroccan lamb. But even when there were just the two of them, even if there was just roast chicken or some kind of pasta, he would open a bottle of wine, she would light the candles, and at the first bite he would signal his joy—a hand to his heart, or just her name aloud. Annie remembered his rising once from his end of the table and coming over to her, bending to kiss the top of her head. "You make me so goddamned happy, Annie," he said.

"Ah, it's *food* that makes you happy, Graham," she had answered.

"You *are* food," he said.

In the end she bought just wine and fruit and breakfast things— eggs, bacon, bread and butter, coffee beans and milk.

———

Though the sun was warm on her head and shoulders as she moved across the overgrown yard to bring the groceries and her bags inside, the cottage itself was chilly and smelled of old ashes and damp—the odor of sorrow itself, it seemed to Annie. She plugged in the refrigerator and turned it on, put the perishables inside it, and then went around the three small rooms, opening windows. As she slid one of them stiffly up at the front of the house, she stopped to watch the light move on the lake, spangling it. She could hear a motorboat somewhere, and distant voices, pitched to carry over the engine noise. She could hear the breeze hissing lightly in the pines. The house itself was silent but for the low, steady mumble of the refrigerator.

She called Dan Curtis about the mowing, and he said he could get to it within a few days. She decided to do the cleaning herself—she didn't want anyone in the house with her. She fixed herself some scrambled eggs and toast and coffee, and when she was finished eating, she started in, dusting everything, sweeping down cobwebs from the corners of the ceiling, vacuuming. In the bedroom she opened the storage crate for the bedding, a wooden box lined with wire screening to keep the mice out. She took out the quilt, the sheets and pillows, and made the bed.

When she was done with everything, she went outside and down to the lake. She walked to the end of the dock. She took off her shoes and sat, hugging her knees.

The lake had a pleasant, slightly algal smell. Wavelets lapped lightly at the posts under the dock, a gentle slurping sound. The wood was warm on the soles of her feet.

Graham had loved it here, though he worried at the notion of being a person with two houses. "I've become a fucking grandee!" he said once. They were sitting on the dock with gin and tonics late in the afternoon. Out in the middle of the lake, a water-skier had moved slowly past, behind a white boat.

"To be a fucking grandee, you need something a little more *grand* than a five-hundred-square-foot cottage," Annie had said. "Unwinterized, yet."

Now she dropped her feet into the water. As cold as ever. Only toward the very end of the summer could you jump in without gasping, without worrying about the shock to your heart. She pulled her feet back up, reached down to warm them with her hands, thinking of Graham's hands, warming her.

He had been different up here, as Annie knew she was too. Quieter. The great sociability that marked him in the city eased.

Eased. That was an odd word to think of—as though the sociability were a kind of affliction or burden for him.

Which sometimes it seemed it might be, it occurred to her now. As when his face sagged in exhaustion at the end of an evening with others. As when, occasionally, instead of welcoming an invitation (*Good God, are you kidding?! Of course we have to be there*), he would ask her to get them out of something. "I just can't," he'd say, and it would seem to her he was speaking of a nearly physical impossibility.

Because the cottage was so small that they really couldn't have guests, they just assumed their solitude here. Alone together, they quietened. Whole days passed when they barely spoke to each other. But where Annie had imagined Graham chafing at this, he seemed instead to welcome it. Over time, she thought, to need it.

Their lovemaking had seemed different up here too, not to be generated by conversation or wordplay, as it so often was at home, but by something more visceral—more, again, like need. In the dark silence of the tiny bedroom he'd reach for Annie, move over her, rise up on his knees and enter her, all quickly, quickly. And usually quickly too, he'd come—arched away from her, crying out.

They would lie still in the dark. Later he sometimes turned to her, occasionally bringing her back from the beginnings of sleep, his mouth on her, his fingers sliding in and out of her, her sensations confused sometimes—what was tongue? what lips or fingers? which, moving where? She would teeter for long moments on the edge of coming, the feeling would ebb and then return, and then finally it would begin, a more dizzying, slower version of it than she was used to, the dark and silence around her so complete as to make the experience nearly disembodied, while also being almost purely *of* the body—like a nearly solitary dream of wordless sex they were also somehow sharing. When it ended she felt shaken, sometimes near tears.

They both slept deeply here, and woke with the faint silvery light of first morning, its touch bringing her back to the room, the animal shapes of the clothes on the hooks, the light reflecting on the old mirror like a window where there wasn't one.

Annie stayed for five days. She drank coffee in the morning for energy—three, sometimes four cups. More than once, if she stood up too fast, her heart pounded and she felt lightheaded.

The first afternoon she called everyone who might be worried about her—Natalie and Edith, Frieda and Sarah and Lucas—to tell them where she was.

She tried to order her time. She read in the books that were on the shelves in the living room. The "shelves": just horizontal boards between the exposed studs. They were in the same plane as the studs too, and therefore not really deep enough to hold some of the resting books. Sometimes when Graham walked around too heavily, one or two of the larger volumes would fall out. Volunteers, he called them, and always laid them out to read next, following some obscure rule of his own.

She read Auden. A translation of Catullus that Graham had been reading—funny and, to Annie, surprisingly, amusingly, dirty. She'd taken Latin in high school and read Catullus then. An expurgated

Catullus, she saw now. She read Simic. She read Szymborska, hard and yet somehow comforting about aging and death.

She lay down a lot—it became an activity, a way to pass the time. She lay down on the couch, reading. She lay down on the bed and, while the sky changed out the windows, was overcome by memories. She lay down on the dock and listened to the ever-changing motion of the water. She fell asleep once on the dock, no sunblock on at all, and woke with a painful sunburn, the first one she'd had in decades. (A week or so later, back in her real life, it had turned into a tan. "It's good you went away," Frieda said when she saw Annie. "You look great. You look rested." Annie didn't disabuse her, didn't speak of her long sleepless nights, or nights when she did sleep but had dreams so urgent that she woke already tired.)

She ate only what was for sale at the farm stand in this early season, and scrambled or fried eggs and toast—it seemed like too much work to cook meat or fish, even to make a salad. At night she listened to the radio and drank wine. Half a bottle made it possible to sleep, though she woke then, at two or three, and lay awake, listening to the occasional night sounds. She'd fall back asleep after a while and dream vividly, then wake again with the room full of light, often the nearly iridescent pearly light of sun through the thick white fog that hung heavily on the lake.

She made herself take a daily walk. Once she walked partway around the lake on the path in the woods. Through the treillage of the trees she had glimpses of the expensive summer homes, some of them silent, apparently not yet opened. But at others, she could hear the shrieks of children playing. The next day, toward the end of the afternoon, it was adult voices that floated over to her from an elegant old house, the clink of ice in glasses, the laughter of the cocktail hour. It was hard to come back to the cottage after that, hard to feel her solitude.

On the fourth day she was there, she made a reluctant trip to the little town store—she needed toothpaste and she wanted a newspaper. She thought she might also get some tuna fish and mayonnaise, just to vary her menu.

John Lawrence was there at the back of the store in what she and Graham had spoken of as his "uniform"—jeans and a plaid shirt. She saw that he was lifting boxes from a shopping cart, putting them on the shelves. He called out a greeting. Then, when Annie began to set her things on the counter, he came to the front of the store to ring her up.

"Annie," he said in greeting, nodding once on the word. He stepped behind the counter and began to slide the groceries past himself on its worn wooden surface with his right hand, while his left hand danced on the register, putting numbers in. "I was sorry to hear about Graham," he said. "He was a fine man."

"Thank you," Annie said.

How gracious, she was thinking. That was the way to do it. Simple. Plainspoken. It seemed to her at that moment, remembering the complexity of the sympathy of some of her Cambridge friends, remembering what had felt like the insufficiently grateful or articulate responses she had tried to speak or to write back to them, that there was something vainglorious about their articulate commiseration. Don't tell me what Shakespeare said about death, or Auden, or Tillich, or Annie Lamott, she thought now—she'd had all of these offered to her. Don't make me have to find a way to rise to any of that. Just say what John said, let me just say thank you, and then move on.

She remembered Felicity Rogers's question to Sarah: "Don't you think it's better that he died before your mother?"

And Peter Aiello standing in the front hall later that day, holding her hands between his. "It's like a huge tree has fallen, a tree that was shading us all, and now we're just all blinking away in the sunlight," he had said.

Annie was struck dumb, this was so elaborately unlike what she felt.

"Don't you think?" he'd persisted. What had she answered? She couldn't remember.

Now, coming out into the sunlight with her bag of groceries on her hip—yes, she thought, blinking in the sunlight, but here, now, only because of the contrast with the dimness of the country store—she stopped for a moment to look at the bulletin board.

Unedited for at least several weeks, she noted. Obsolete events: a multifamily yard sale that had happened on May 31. A dinner for seniors in the town hall a week before. But new things too: there was an open meeting of the town selectmen coming up on July 1, a meeting to downgrade the classification of some of the town roads to "unmaintained"—nothing near her, she noted. There was a reading in the middle of August at the town library, a reading by a writer whose work Annie knew and liked. Maybe she'd go, if she were up here.

Would she be up here? She didn't know. She had a sense abruptly of how open, how shapeless, her life was. How empty and without rules. She felt, for a moment, the physical sensation of loss, a wave of it. After a few seconds she shifted the grocery bag to her other hip and made herself focus on the bulletin board again, made herself try to concentrate on the words in the notices.

A lost dog. No date. Somebody with old windows you could take away for free. She remembered then that at some point Graham had spoken of exactly that—acquiring old windows—the idea being that he would build a cold frame off the side of the cottage when he got enough of them, something Annie had been sure would never happen. Graham was full of such projects, begun and then abandoned. The vegetable garden. The studio he was going to make for Annie in the shed. More bookshelves for their bedroom. The bookstore was the only context in which he always finished what he'd started.

There was the announcement of a music program at Lake Scarborough, a program that offered master classes with the members of the quartet in residence. Which quartet would also perform at a public concert—Schumann, Beethoven.

She might go, Annie thought. She would need to start *doing* things at some point. Learning to do things, alone. She looked more closely for the date and saw that it had already passed. Ah. She'd missed it. She looked at the announcement again. The Wadsworth quartet, they were called. The cellist for this quartet, she saw now, was named Sofie Kahn.

She stepped closer to the bulletin board to look at the photo. It was hard to tell, but it looked like the Sofie Kahn she remembered. And how many professional cellists with that name could there be, after all? She felt oddly breathless. She turned away to go to her car. Where she sat for some minutes before she started the engine, trying to order the chaos of her thoughts.

The last time Annie had seen Sofie Kahn's name was perhaps thirty-five years earlier in a *New York Times* review, an almost entirely positive review of Sofie's debut performance at Carnegie Hall. Annie had been young and ambitious for herself at that time, and she had felt a pinch of envy reading the piece: Sofie had made it then, into the world of public achievement, in a way that Annie wasn't sure was ever going to happen for her. But she'd been pleased for her old friend too, pleased that the hard work of music, begun so early in her life, had brought its reward.

Sofie Kahn. She hadn't thought of her in all these years. Their childhood, their girlhood, together.

Which girlhood Annie was calling up in the car all the way back to the cottage, and later, while she unpacked the groceries, and still later than that, while she made her supper in the shadowed kitchen, while she ate it alone on the front porch.

When she lay down to sleep in the cottage that night, it occurred to Annie that this long afternoon of calling up her youth with Sofie

Kahn was the first time since Graham had died that she'd managed to sustain thinking about anyone or anything else for longer than a few minutes. After a moment's almost childish sense of accomplishment, she felt a sudden sweep of grief so strong that she began panting and had to sit up in the dark room to catch her breath.

16

IN THE LATE 1940s and '50s, Annie and Sofie Kahn had been in the same grammar-school class in a public school in Hyde Park, on the south side of Chicago. Sofie was small, like Annie—the other girls and most of the boys in their class towered over both of them—and maybe as much as anything else, this was what drew them together. But they also both had fathers who worked at the University of Chicago, another bond that made them different from many of the other kids.

They lived in different areas of Hyde Park though, neighborhoods separated by the tracks the Illinois Central Electric trains ran on. In order to see each other after school, one or the other of them had what seemed at the time a long walk. But in that other world, where children at nine or ten or eleven could move around unaccompanied, this wasn't a difficulty.

By Sofie's preference, as Annie remembered it, they went to her apartment more often than to Annie's house. That was fine with Annie. She liked the sense of peace at the Kahns'. It felt welcoming to her.

Annie had four siblings, all of whom, unlike her, often had several friends at a time over after school, so that the house was usually full of kids and their activities: records playing, the bigger boys bounding recklessly and thunderously up or down the stairs, Annie's sisters and their friends in one or the other of their rooms, dressing up or trying different hairstyles suggested by *Seventeen*; or gathered in the front hall, using the telephone to pass along school gossip. It must be that, she had thought, that put Sofie off—the noise, the looseness. A looseness that for Annie and her siblings was just part of the sense among them that they were on their own. That their mother had better things to do than fuss with them.

Or other things, anyway. In the daytime, what seemed like her endless chores. Ironing in the kitchen, her cigarette set in an ashtray on the counter nearby, a ritualized pause after each section of a girl's dress or a boy's shirt to drag on the cigarette some predetermined number of times. Typing up a report by Annie's father at the dining room table, or a long letter of her own to her mother, with many carbon copies to go to her sisters.

Sometimes she was literally absent, particularly late in the afternoon, when she went down the street to the Petersons' house, or the Millers' or the Levis' or the Nakagawas' to have cocktails with the other wives—and then the husbands too, as they drifted home from the campus or emerged from their studies at the far reaches of the houses.

Without her, the noise level in the house rose even higher. The records were turned up, the older kids danced with their friends in the living room or tried their mother's cigarettes in the backyard— she smoked Pall Malls, which she drew out of an oval red tin, a hundred to the can. It was easy to pilfer a few without their absence being noticed.

All of this couldn't have been more different from the atmosphere at Sofie's house. Most importantly, Sofie's mother was always present—present in every sense, engaged with her two daughters and whatever friends they brought home. Milk and cookies were served when you arrived. The napkins were cloth, ironed, folded elegantly on one side of the plate. The plate was beautiful, more beautiful than Annie's mother's best china, which had an ivy pattern trailing around the edge and was used only at Sunday dinner and on holidays. The glass that held the milk was thick and cut with patterned shapes. Mrs. Kahn sat with Sofie and Annie and Vera, Sofie's little sister, and asked about their day at school in her faint accent, unidentifiable to Annie at the time.

She seemed genuinely interested in Annie too. *Oh, Annie liked painting? Why? What about it? Had she ever seen Cézanne's still lifes? Oh, she must, she must.* She went off to find a book to show Annie images of these paintings. "Of course, this one is in the Art Institute," she said, pointing.

Oh, yes, Annie said, as though she'd known that, as though she went to the Art Institute regularly—which she knew Sofie and Mrs. Kahn and Vera did.

She had gone once in fact—perhaps twice? she couldn't remember—with her father. Her gentle father, the one in Annie's family who, like Mrs. Kahn, seemed to care about the worlds his children were interested in, though he didn't have the time Mrs. Kahn had to open the doors to these worlds for them. In any case, at that period of clearly defined divisions of labor between men and women, this would have been Annie's mother's role, if she'd cared to play it. Which she didn't care to do. Or perhaps was too busy to do.

When Annie and Sofie went into Sofie's room to loll on either end of her bed and talk or to listen to the radio, Mrs. Kahn would go to the living room and play the piano. Annie could hear the rich, rolling music intermittently under their own noise.

She used to be a pianist, Sofie said when Annie asked about it.

"But she's not anymore?" Annie asked.

"Yah, the war," Sofie said, in a way that seemed so much to assume Annie's understanding that she felt precluded from asking anything more. "The war" was a point of reference in Sofie's house in a way it wasn't at Annie's, in a way that gave it a mysterious power for Annie.

Those afternoons always ended the same way. At a certain point, Mrs. Kahn would knock on Sofie's door, and when Sofie opened it to her, she would turn to Annie and say, apologetically, that she hated to interrupt, but it was time for Sofie to practice.

When the outer door to Sofie's apartment building closed behind Annie and she started the walk home down Hyde Park Boulevard and then across Fifty-Sixth Street to Stony Island Avenue and under the IC tracks, she was aware of the complex and conflicting feelings that flooded her, every time. A real pleasure in moving away from the quiet of Sofie's life toward the freedom of the ruleless, noisy house she inhabited with her siblings; but also a keen jealousy of the rituals, the sense of beauty, she was leaving behind at Sofie's house, a growing consciousness of the high expectations that were clearly set for Sofie and her sister, and of the sense she always had at the Kahns'—the sense that she too might be a serious person, to be taken seriously.

Later Annie came to see that of course money was part of it—the difference between the homes. That her own father, who ran the university's admissions office, was undoubtedly paid far less than Mr. Kahn, who was a physicist. But she thought that the mothers had something to do with it too. The problem being, as she saw it even then, with her own mother, who seemed to have no interests beyond her personal experiences, her own history.

She could remember rushing upstairs to tell her mother of her own rapture with *The Messiah* after she'd gone to hear it in Rockefeller Chapel one year with her father and her oldest sister. Oh, of course, her mother said, dismissal in her voice. She knew it perfectly well. She'd sung it in Chorus in her senior year of high school in Belmont, and Bob Samuelson, who had the tenor solos, had been madly in love with her then and couldn't keep his eyes off her. She remembered what she'd worn for their performances—it was the first time her mother had allowed her to wear black: how sexy she'd looked! She recalled—for herself primarily, Annie sensed even then—the party they'd had after the last performance. Bob had drunk too much from a flask he'd brought with him, and in the car on the way home, he'd tried to kiss her.

She was stretched out on the daybed in Annie's father's study while she was telling Annie this, a paperback mystery in her hand, her cigarette waiting in the ashtray next to the bed, its smoke coiling slowly upward.

But what about the music? Annie wanted to ask.

What about Handel? What about beauty? What about Cézanne?

What about Bach? Whose perfect music Annie had heard Sofie play one Sunday afternoon when the Kahns had a concert for friends in the living room of their apartment. Through the row of windows to the east, you could see the lake—immense, churning, a white-capped greenish gray below the leaden sky on this cold late-fall day. The audience sat in rows of folding chairs the Kahns must have kept just for these occasions. There were perhaps twenty people there. Annie was one of three non-adults present, the other two being Sofie and Vera. She felt both proud of that and terrified of the conversations with the adults that would resume once the performance was over. *You are a friend of Sofie's? How nice. A musician too? Oh. Well, so few people had Sofie's gifts. Or her mother's, for that matter.*

And Annie would find some eleven-year-old's way of agreeing, while feeling confused, ordinary, ungifted. Dull.

17

THE DOOR SWUNG open on the airless, silent front hallway. Annie set her bags on the bench there. She carried the few groceries from Vermont back to the kitchen to put them away. She took her overnight bag upstairs. In spite of her impulse to lie down yet again, she made herself do the responsible, orderly things—dirty clothes in the hamper in the closet, clean ones put away, toiletries returned to the bathroom.

Then she went to Graham's study and checked the messages on the phone there. There were a half dozen or so from various friends. But it was too late, she thought, to start calling tonight.

Instead, she went online and googled Sofie Kahn.

And there she was. There were five or six photos of her on her website. One was of her on a stage somewhere, playing with the other members of the quartet, but the others were publicity photos of her alone. Portraits, really. In two her hair was gray, pulled back in a bun. In the others she was younger, with the luxuriant dark hair Annie remembered tumbling over her shoulders. She was always posed with the cello.

As she moved around the website, Annie was able to guess a little of Sofie's life. Playing with various orchestras around the world.

Appearing with the quartet at music festivals, at concert halls in distant countries, at colleges. Giving master classes here and there. Annie knew enough to understand that this was a hard life in some ways. But she presumed the music made it worthwhile, was the counterweight against everything that was difficult. She hoped so.

She looked under the "Recordings" category. Annie was sure that she and Graham had CDs of at least two of the pieces in the quartet's repertoire. She went downstairs and found a bottle of white wine in the refrigerator. She opened it with Graham's fancy corkscrew and poured herself a glass. Then, carrying the wine, she went into the living room. She opened the CD cupboard.

Graham had separated the small plastic cases into categories— jazz, blues, rock 'n' roll, classical. Within these categories the CDs were arranged alphabetically, the classical ones by composer, the others by performer. A bookstore man to his core, Annie thought. She felt a pulse of urgent, sorrowful affection for him.

They did have one of the pieces—a quartet by Schumann, in this case performed by members of the Emerson String Quartet with Menahem Pressler on the piano. Annie put it on, conscious as she did this that she hadn't listened to music since before Graham died. She turned off the lamp.

She sat in the dark room in Graham's old chair and listened with great attentiveness for ten minutes or so. But then she found herself overtaken by memories. Memories of Sofie again, of her childhood with Sofie—of the large, gracious apartment, the vast green lake stretched to the horizon beyond the windows, the sense of admiration mingled with sadness on her part, something she was aware of feeling even now, listening—the retroactive wish for some parallel sense of beauty, of purpose, on her part. Even now, she thought. Sad indeed.

She and Sofie had drifted apart after elementary school. Sofie went to a private high school on the North Side that focused on the arts;

Annie went to the Laboratory High School, connected to the university. They saw each other a few times, but there was less and less to talk about. Annie was busy anyway, and Sofie even more so, with practice and performances in addition to the heavy standard course load of the school.

But the residue of that friendship lingered for Annie, lingered especially in the newly sharp eye with which she regarded her own family—that gift that often comes in adolescence, when you're suddenly old enough to be conscious of how another family works, of the possibility of other rules, other ways of living, from those you grew up with. The gift that can open a window, a door, into the world. Let air in.

Let you out.

As this gift was at work in Annie, she slowly came to understand that what she had been feeling in her family for a long time was *I don't belong here.* That had helped to free her, to end her puzzlement about her family and her place in it. It had opened up her life, though she hadn't known for years what that would mean for her.

It lingered too in the sense she had that she wanted a life that felt as impelled by beauty as Sofie's was, as Sofie's mother's had apparently been. It lingered in the sense that she might be able to.

The same sense that her first husband, Alan, had specialized in mocking, but which had caused his parents to give her as a wedding present a camera. The camera with which she shot her first serious photographs, the camera that led her to the courses she took, to the growing ambition that did, indeed, push her out into the world.

When the achingly beautiful andante began now in the dark of the living room, Annie came back to the music and listened intently through to the ending, tears in her eyes, tears for Graham's death, yes, and for her aloneness, but also for the beautiful yearning sound singing in the big room. In herself.

Music. Why hadn't she thought of it earlier?

18

WEEK AFTER WEEK, the summer passed. Time itself felt thick to Annie, as if it were a fog she was living in. She would find herself standing someplace in the house—in front of the half-empty closet or in Graham's study or facing the bathroom mirror or at the kitchen windows, looking out—and have no idea what impulse had brought her there, or how long before.

She saw Edith often, sitting with her in her large, airy front parlor on Avon Hill; and Frieda a bit less. She spent a day up in Newburyport with Natalie, walking up and down the dunes on Plum Island, Natalie pointing out the birds they saw. She talked on the phone to Sarah, to Lucas. Friends came by. She went once again to Vermont for a few days, but quickly grew restless there, too. Nothing seemed to matter, really. Even the news that the show had done well, that it had had a quick mention in the *Globe*, singled out in a summary of local shows, didn't awaken her interest.

She waited for evening, when, after a minimal dinner, she allowed herself several glasses of wine while she sat listening to music. Often it was classical—she had bought one version or another of all of the music Sofie had listed on her website as being in her repertoire—but she listened also to the jazz she and Graham had assembled over the years. And to the box of CDs that Sarah had sent her when she told Sarah that listening to music was one of the few things she actually took pleasure in at this point. Then it would be nine thirty or so, and she'd let herself go to bed.

Bed, where, if she wasn't swamped by memories of Graham—of the happy moments, of the shared sorrows, of the occasional argument, of the details (over and over) of the morning she found him dead—she fell into a leaden sleep.

One night, listening to a CD of Sofie's, she was thinking again of the shape of their friendship, the elements she remembered of it—Sofie's mother playing the piano in the afternoons, the lake behind the windows, Sofie herself, her eyes closed as she moved the bow over the cello, almost embarrassingly lost in what she was creating.

She remembered the differences—and the distance—between their two homes. The long walk in either direction.

She was tracing that walk in her mind—*now I go into the tunnel under the train tracks, now I cross Stony Island to Jackson Park*—when she was stopped by a sudden image, another memory. The memory of the bridle path in Jackson Park, the bridle path that was part of the shortcut through the park. And the man there. The man in the park, on the bridle path, when she was walking with Sofie.

Jackson Park was wild and lush at that time, so overgrown that when you stepped into it from the sidewalk, you entered an entirely different world, thick with green.

The bridle path cut through this thick growth perhaps only ten feet in from the sidewalk, but completely hidden from it. She had thought of it then as a *glade*—in her childhood, the word meant exactly that open, sunlit space to her, with the dense green pushing in from both sides. Annie and one or another of her older siblings often cut through the undergrowth and across that bridle path to get to The Museum of Science and Industry or to the lagoon behind the museum, where you could wade in the murky waters and catch pollywogs, or to the bridge over the Outer Drive that led to the Fifty-Seventh Street beach.

By the time Sarah went to college at the University of Chicago, the park had been completely cleared; Annie had noted that when she was driving around on her visits. They'd civilized it, they'd removed all the underbrush to make a kind of grassy plain between Stony Island Avenue and The Museum of Science and Industry. A plain, studded with large, isolated trees here and there, the lake rising beyond it.

But in her youth—and in Sofie's youth—it was different. It was secret. Special.

And one day, when she was walking Sofie partway home, they met a man there. A man, a young man in blue jeans. He had stopped them and asked them to watch the path for a moment for him. He must have seen us on the sidewalk when we turned in, she thought, two delicious little girls. He must have followed us. He'd stepped a few yards away then, Annie remembered, and turned his back to them. They heard the splash of his urine on the undergrowth and looked at each other, trying to contain their laughter. It was naughty. It was *funny*.

When he came back, he squatted in front of them, talking steadily, asking questions— Where did they live? What were they doing on the bridle path? Had they been to the museum? What exhibits did they like there? They had both been answering at first, but Sofie had stopped, Annie realized. She was looking down, not at the man's face. Annie had looked then too, she'd looked where Sofie was looking, and she saw that the man's penis was out of his pants, that he had an erection.

Annie had seen penises before, because she had brothers. They were careless about their bodies, and there was only one bathroom on the bedroom floor of their house—you couldn't help catching a glimpse every now and then. And one of the brothers—Glen, the older—used to like to startle his sisters when they were small by unzipping his pants and waving his penis around. The girls would run away, screaming.

But this was different, this strange, rubbery-looking thing.

He asked them to touch it. To touch his erection.

Sitting in the living room in Graham's chair, the music swelling in the air around her, she recognized this memory. She had known this, she realized. It was familiar to her. It was almost as if it were a film she'd seen. Or perhaps a book—a scene in a memoir of abuse, or a piece of fiction. She had remembered it, at least some parts of it, before. But she had done an odd thing with it, with the memory—she had taken the danger away. She had made it somehow simply a strange event from her childhood, something she had only a vague sense of. It didn't seem real.

He had asked them to touch his penis, and they had, they were such obedient girls. She remembered that. That they had to obey—he was a grown-up.

They touched him, as they were asked to. Quickly. Lightly. But by now, she was uncomfortable. Frightened. When he asked if they wanted to play a game—maybe he'd suggested hide-and-seek, or maybe he said any game, they should choose—Annie had said no. Or something like no. "No, sir," maybe.

And astonishingly, he had let them go. Maybe because there were two of them? Because he couldn't have managed to keep both of them there? Because they wouldn't agree to be separated by the games he'd asked them to play?

In any case, their kindly predator had let them go. It seemed impossible, but it had happened. She had said no, she had taken Sofie's hand, and they had walked together back out of the wooded park and onto the sidewalk that had been right there all along, busy with people, with traffic.

Maybe that was the veil she'd drawn across this event. That it wasn't worth remembering because it had ended well. Happily ever after. The danger they'd escaped from was nothing, in the end. Like Glen, running down the stairs after her and her sisters, clutching his penis while they shrieked and ran away.

The music in the room had stopped by now, but Annie sat as motionless, as if she were still listening. She found herself mentally tracing her footsteps *away* from the bridle path this time. Away from the park, away from Stony Island Avenue, into the dark of the viaduct under the train tracks and out again into daylight on Fifty-Seventh Street, then around the corner to her street and safely home, home to her old house.

Her house, which Sofie hadn't wanted to visit.

Not because of the life within it, as Annie had remembered it. No. Instead, because of the dangerous park and the bogeyman living there, between her house and Sofie's.

Maybe, she thought now, they hadn't drifted apart because they went off to separate schools, separate lives. Maybe they just didn't have a way they could speak together about what had happened to them.

She shook her head, rapidly. How strange, what she had done with it, this event. She'd altered it, transformed it, made it something easy to forget.

How long had it taken, she wondered, before its transformation was complete? Before it was forgettable? Before she forgot it?

Did it matter? She had said no, after all. No, thank you.

She heard herself whisper this aloud, "No!"—and abruptly, strangely, she was remembering, not the man on the bridle path anymore, but the night that she and Graham and Sarah had shouted *no*, over and over again, to the imaginary man who might want to touch Sarah.

How odd. This memory again, the same memory that had come to her in the kitchen the day after Graham died, thinking of him in his apron, shouting, "No way, José!" And of herself shouting "No sir!" to Sarah's imaginary man, the imaginary man who was so like the real man, the man in the park.

Maybe, she thought, she'd been shouting "No" to this, to this buried, lost memory. Maybe she'd been shouting a refusal to be again that girl, that frightened girl. Had she shed the memory in order to escape that self, that version of herself? That fear?

Were you in charge of your memory? Could you will yourself to forget?

It didn't matter. She had said no to him. She had rescued herself, she had rescued Sofie. That was what was important.

Remember that. Frightened as she was, as she must have been, she had said no.

No.

Ixnay, she whispered in the dark, silent room.

Over the next days, the long weeks, she returned to this event over and over. Not even so much the event itself, but the way she'd forgotten it. It seemed threatening, somehow—the notion that you could lose something that at one time must have seemed so central to your understanding of the world around you, to your sense of who you were in it. It seemed connected to the loss of Graham and her almost daily fear of losing him further, in memory—in lost memory. Of losing the sharp, clear sense of who he was, of losing the sureness of her feeling for him.

Could you will it the other way too, memory? Could you make yourself hold it, as much as you could make yourself lose it? She found herself taking *Memoir with Bookshop* out again and again in these evenings, sitting on the couch and poring over the pictures. Using them to remind herself of what she was frightened of losing, what she felt might already be slipping away; and listening over and over to Sofie's music, as if it were memory itself.

19

THE NIGHT BEFORE Sarah arrived to help scatter Graham's ashes, Annie had finally opened the box they came in—the wooden box that had been sitting at the back of her closet for the long summer months. They ashes were held inside it in a medium-size clear plastic bag that someone had closed with a twister seal. This seemed so utilitarian, so honest, such a contrast with the fancy box, that she nearly laughed aloud. It made her remember what Graham had said about his ashes when they were talking one day about their final wishes—that he wanted them scattered in what he and Annie jokingly called "the garden" at the back of the cottage—a stand of irises and roses slowly being overrun by Queen Anne's lace and daylilies. "Think of it as bonemeal," he'd said to her then. "Very expensive soil amendment. That will be me at that point, finally able to be of some use to you."

There had been no surprise, no shock, for Annie in what was in the bag. With one or the other of her siblings, she'd dealt with both her parents' ashes before this, and it was only with the first of them to die—her mother—that she'd been startled by the mealy quality of the ash, and the odd small bits of bone scattered like pebbles throughout it.

———————

It seemed to her now that Lucas and Sarah *were* both surprised—or at least hesitant—as she held the plastic bag out. To make it easier for them, she plunged her own hand in first and then opened her fingers out, letting the ashes filter between them and fall into the mounding clumps of the daylilies, into the weeds. Lucas followed suit, and then Sarah. Jeanne stood at a little distance—she had said ahead of time that while she wanted to be there, she would let them do this. She had loved Graham, she said, but she didn't feel this was something she should have a part in. "It belongs to you," she'd said to them.

Annie had assumed she might feel more with Graham's ashes than she had with her parents', but that didn't happen. She simply didn't have a sense of connection to him through the ashes, or in them. Bonemeal, indeed. It made her recall again the feeling she'd had the morning he died, the feeling that he was not there in the body that was left lying in the bed with her. That the body had no meaning for her anymore.

Lucas and Sarah clearly did have some sense of Graham's presence—or absence, perhaps. Their faces were somber as they passed the bag back and forth. Annie took her turn once again, and then stepped back a few feet to let them take over—Graham's children, after all. She felt a bit like an intruder, watching. She turned away to look at the lake through the trees, busy with boats on this late-summer day.

Then in her peripheral vision she saw Jeanne step quickly forward and put her arm around Lucas. Annie looked over and saw the tears running freely down Lucas's face. She moved to him then too, to put her hand on his shoulder. She turned to look over at Sarah, but she seemed all right, she seemed absorbed in the task. And in spite of his tears, Lucas kept taking his turns, snuffling and breathing irregularly, but reaching in again and again, and watching the ashes fall, slightly windblown, from his long fingers.

When they'd finished, when Sarah had turned the empty bag over and shaken the last of the ashes out, the four of them stood huddled together for a long moment, their arms around one another.

They separated. Swiping at his face, blowing his nose, Lucas went to the side of the cottage. He opened the spigot the hose was attached to, and they took turns watering the ash into the earth around and under the flowers. When Annie's turn was done, she stepped back. Watching the other three, she moved a little to change the angle from which she saw them. She realized abruptly that she was composing a picture she might have taken, and felt a familiar sense of something like shame.

She and Sarah had driven up together, bringing the ashes with them, the wooden box set upright in the middle of the back seat. Glancing over at it from time to time, Annie had had the thought that it looked like some strange, small passenger—an ET, hitching a ride.

Now, driving back to Cambridge by herself, she felt solitary in the car. Sarah had offered to come with her, but Annie insisted she go back to Cambridge with Lucas and Jeanne, who'd driven up from New York to meet them at the cottage in a rental car.

She had thought they might want to talk. As she was packing up the perishables from the cottage kitchen, she'd been listening to the murmur of Jeanne's and Sarah's voices out on the porch. She'd heard Sarah say, "This is so exciting! Do you know what it is yet?"

She had stopped what she was doing to hear Jeanne's answer. "No," she said. "They can't tell you that until a little bit later than this. And quite honestly, I am not sure that's something that Lucas and I even want to know ahead of time."

Annie understood immediately what this was: a pregnancy. Neither Jeanne nor Lucas had said anything about it to her. Perhaps this was something they didn't want people to know yet.

Now, alone in the car, she wondered if Frieda knew.

Then she thought again of how complicated things had become with Frieda. After they got back to Cambridge tonight, for instance, Sarah, Lucas, and Jeanne were going out to dinner with her. They had asked Annie along, but she'd said no, that she'd see them the next day at the parties for Graham, that she thought that Frieda should have her time alone with them, as she had had hers today. She didn't explain that she felt this the more so—this wish to *give* the evening to Frieda—because she'd been relieved that Lucas and Sarah had wanted to scatter the ashes without Frieda. She had some guilt about that. Guilt about the decision itself—which she thought had been mostly Lucas's. And guilt about her own relief at the decision.

In any case, she had let the decision stand.

The plan was that Lucas would be the one to tell Frieda. Annie wasn't able to imagine how he would do it, but she allowed herself to believe that he would know what to say, how to present things in a way that made sense to his mother. That rescued her feelings.

But this was not at all what happened.

One day in mid-August, Annie had answered the phone. It was Jeanne. She wanted to let Annie know that she had told Frieda of the decision about half an hour earlier. That Frieda had called her, "out of the blue" she said, to ask when the scattering of the ashes was to take place, and Jeanne had been forced to tell her both the date, and then that she, Frieda, wouldn't be a part of it.

Frieda had been upset at the news, Jeanne said, and she thought Annie might be getting a call from her. She thought Annie should be prepared for that.

Annie was silent for a moment, thinking of Frieda, imagining her shock. "That must have been difficult for you," she said finally to Jeanne. For Frieda, is what she was thinking.

"Of course it was," Jeanne said. "I did try to put her off, in order for Lucas to be the one to talk to her, as we'd planned, but she couldn't understand why I simply couldn't tell her. So I did, finally. I didn't see how I could reasonably get out of it."

After a long moment, Annie asked, "What did she say?"

"She was upset, quite naturally. Or really, she was angry, though she wouldn't have acknowledged that to me. She asked who had decided this, and I said of course the family had. She asked me if I was in on it—that's precisely what she said: 'in on it,' as though it were a crime—and I said I wasn't. That I hadn't been there for the discussion."

"Did she ask about me? About whether or not I was 'in on it'?"

"She did. And I told her no. But then she asked if you had approved the decision."

"And you said?"

"I said, I think, that you had *yielded* to the others."

"Oh, Christ," Annie said.

"Yes. Well, she got very angry then, although she still wouldn't admit it. I could tell, though. But I must say that I got angry too, Annie."

"At Frieda?" Annie said stupidly.

"Yes. I said you had already shared so very much with her. That I would never have been as generous as you have been. And that perhaps you had a right to the moment just with Graham, just with his children. I told her I understood the decision. That I agreed with it."

Annie said nothing, and after a moment Jeanne spoke again. "She doesn't have the right, Annie, to be angry at any of you. Not you, not Lucas. And I told her so."

Annie was silent. She was shocked. By what? By Jeanne's . . . toughness. By her honesty, really.

Finally she said, "I just don't know if I can do this, Jeanne."

"Do what?"

"Stick with the plan, I guess. Not include Frieda."

Now it was Jeanne's turn to be silent. Her voice, when she spoke, was chilly, Annie thought. "Of course you must do what you need to do, Annie. I know that you're friends with Frieda. I will only say that for Lucas—and perhaps for Sarah too, I wouldn't know—it would be better. Better to stay with this plan."

Annie didn't know what to say. She felt *cornered*, she realized.

"I feel that Lucas has the right to be just with his father," Jeanne said. "That is my stake in this affair. I want for him what he wants. What he needs. It will have a different meaning for him to have his mother there. It will make everything harder."

After a long moment, Annie said, "God, what a choice."

"You mean, for you?"

"Yes, for me."

After a moment, Jeanne said, "But perhaps, in this case, it really isn't your choice. You don't need to feel it is. He was your husband, Annie, of course. I understand that. But Lucas and Sarah are his children, and this is the way they wanted it. Perhaps it was more Lucas, yes. But Sarah too, I think." Jeanne was quiet for a moment, as if to let Annie think about this. Then, the coup de grâce. "And I must say, I feel that today I have borne the brunt of this—isn't that what you say? *Brunt?*"

"Yes."

"Another strange word. Very English. The brunt of it, then. I was the one who had to tell her. Who was honest with her. I faced all of her hurt and her anger, and told her what I thought. So it's done. There don't need to be all these telephone calls back and forth. It's over. *Fini.*" Annie didn't know what to say. After a long moment, Jeanne said, "Let it rest, Annie. It doesn't need to be such a big . . . *drama.* Frieda will get over it."

As soon as she got off the phone with Jeanne, Annie called Frieda. Who wasn't home. She left a message on Frieda's phone, but didn't hear back that day.

She called Frieda again the next day, and again had no return call.

And then she decided not to keep calling. What she felt was that, after all, Frieda had a right not to have to discuss her pain with someone who'd been a part of causing it.

And Annie had a lot to do just then, anyway, to get ready for her part of the memorial events. It made it easier to let it go, to imagine Frieda was perhaps slowly letting it go too.

20

THERE WERE TO be two memorial gatherings the day after the ashes were scattered. The first was the bookstore party, which Peter and Lucas and Sarah had planned with the staff. And Annie had decided finally to host a separate party after that one, back at the house. Hers would be smaller, just family and close friends, but even so she'd had a long list of things to do and order and arrange in the weeks ahead of time. She'd found herself almost grateful for this—for the sense of purpose it provided. And then after the difficulty around the scattering of the ashes, for the distraction it offered from her worries about Frieda.

The bookstore party started off crowded and noisy. It reminded Annie of the party at which she'd met Graham, many of the same people cramming the aisles, leaving their empty or half-full plastic cups everywhere, even among the books on the shelves. Again those shelves had been pushed back to make an open space in the middle of the shop. There were maybe fifty or so chairs set up there, but hardly anyone was sitting in them. They all preferred being able to move around, to talk, to get more easily to the tables set at opposite ends of the space, the tables laden with wine and crackers and cheese and plates of canapés.

Annie, along with Lucas and Sarah and the bookstore staff, was busy greeting people, thanking them for coming. She saw John Norris across the room and waved. She would talk to him at the house—she'd sent an invitation to him with a note saying how much she appreciated his sitting with her the night after Graham died. Natalie and Don Schumer were there, Natalie in a kind of caftan that made her look more enormous than ever. She saw Edith near the doorway. Bill, Rosemary Gregory, Georgie. Dozens of others. She saw Frieda too, but couldn't catch her eye. They would have to talk at some point today, that was clear. It would be too awkward not to. What she hoped was that by now Frieda would have found a way to let go of her anger.

After half an hour or so of everyone's mixing and greeting, Peter went to the microphone set up in the middle of the chairs and asked them all to sit down. He waited, watching them, letting them settle. Annie moved to the back to find her seat. She would have to leave early to get back to the house ahead of the crowd.

When almost everyone was seated, Peter welcomed them on Graham's behalf. It would be a bit like a Quaker meeting, he said—anyone could speak when the spirit moved them.

There was the initial awkwardness of that kind of gathering. After the long silence, Peter rose and went to the mike again. Annie watched him as he choked up, trying to talk of his friendship with Graham. After he sat down, Bill stood up and spoke movingly about the early days of the bookstore, how it was Graham's energy and bonhomie ("I had to look up how to pronounce that," he said, smiling) that made it all work. And John spoke very briefly, about their long friendship and his inability to truly believe that it was over.

Then Frieda got up and walked to the microphone. She was in her usual uniform, a longish skirt, Birkenstocks, and a striped, long-sleeved T-shirt. Annie was suddenly nervous for her, she looked so awkward, so vulnerable.

But to Annie's surprise, as she began, her voice was steady, she seemed completely comfortable. She made people laugh, actually, introducing herself to those who didn't know her as Graham's first wife, the one who "barely escaped alive," she said. "But I'm smart enough to look back on my years with him as the most lively, the most funny, the wildest years of my life, too." She told a few anecdotes about Graham's kindness to her over the years. "Nothing he needed to do," she said. "But he did it." She said what she most admired about him was exactly that kind of thing, because, she said, "he was a person who never wasted a friendship, or a relationship." It seemed to Annie that Frieda was looking at her, but it was hard to tell because of her glasses.

"To Graham," Frieda said then, raising her glass. Then she *was* looking at Annie, directly. "And to Annie, who did so much better a job of it than I."

Unexpected sudden tears rose to Annie's eyes. From across the room, she raised her opened hands ceremonially in a gesture meant to thank Frieda. For the toast, of course. For everything it must have cost her to be able to give it. For making things right again between them. And for weathering for so long the lasting complexity of their entwined lives.

A number of people had turned to Annie, smiling, raising their glasses, and Annie smiled back, nodding.

When the next speaker got up, though, she took the opportunity to make her way to the door, out of the shop, and into the still-hot evening air to begin her slow walk back to the house. As she walked, she was thinking first of Frieda, feeling a near-joyous relief that Frieda had been able somehow to put the pain around the scattering of the ashes behind her.

And she'd been so elegant! Annie had been worried for her as she walked to the mike, worried about how she would *do*. She'd grown so used to Frieda's role in her life and Graham's life that she hadn't thought about Frieda's other life, her life as a teacher, as someone who stood up in front of people every day and talked to them about history, about the movement of peoples around the world in ancient times. She was glad for that too, she realized—for being reminded of this other Frieda.

Then, after a few more blocks, walking past all the houses she'd walked past hundreds of times before, she began to think of how familiar this pattern was —leaving the bookstore before everyone else, in the old days the ones who would stay for the refreshments or the signing, or both. Leaving in order to be home in time to get the party ready.

She had a sense now that this particular departure was the ending of a great many things. It wasn't just that Graham was gone from her life, but that the bookstore too would go away. The life of the bookstore. Peter had talked about this with her a few weeks earlier, his wish to sell. But she had assumed this would happen. The store would belong to someone else. It would change.

Oh, they would welcome her, Annie was pretty sure of that. At readings, at parties. But there would be a slow diminishment of the idea that she was in any way important to these activities. And of course, the after-parties would move elsewhere—the new location depending on who bought the store, who would be running it, and how. In any case, her appearance at those parties, or at the readings, would stop being particularly noted. Perhaps, actually, it would become unwelcome, it would be seen as a kind of sad wish to stay connected to something she was no longer part of, a desire to feel important, somehow.

She could imagine it, at some point someone introducing her as Graham's wife, as his widow, someone else saying "Graham who?"

And that would be that.

No, she'd stay away from the store after this. There were plenty of other literary events she could go to in Cambridge or Boston—at libraries, at festivals, at benefits. She could be as busy in that world, in all likelihood, as she'd ever been, if that's what she desired. But this would be the last of the events at Graham's store for her.

She wasn't even sure she'd miss it. Some of the point for her had always had to do with him, with his outsize pleasure in it all, his animation at the parties, his gratitude at what she'd made for him.

The house looked beautiful from the street, she thought. She walked slowly up the Caldwells' driveway and pushed the gate open. She and Lucas and Sarah had bought a viburnum they were going to have planted in the backyard in honor of Graham, but for now, for the party, they'd left it sitting in a big pot by the front steps. It made a kind of bower out of the stoop.

Inside, the wineglasses set out on the big table gleamed in the early-evening light. All the windows were wide open, and the air moved gently in the house every now and then, carrying the glowing dust motes this way and that in the slant of sun. In the kitchen part of the room, the students in their white shirts and black slacks were talking back and forth, laughing, setting out the food from the caterer Sarah had hired. Annie moved around among them, making room for herself at the counter, room to toss a couscous salad she'd made, room to arrange some stuffed dates on a platter—both dishes she thought certain of the guests might look forward to.

Then she went upstairs to be alone until she heard the first of the old friends arriving.

It was going well, she thought as she greeted people. There were a number of the writers they'd grown close to, and Annie moved around among them. Mike, Edith's ex-husband, had come with her, and Annie was glad to talk with him—it had been months since she'd seen him. John hugged her almost fiercely, and then his wife Betsy took her turn.

Annie was standing near the door, and when she saw Frieda

coming up the long walk, she stepped outside and went quickly to her. They embraced, wordlessly, for a long moment. When they stepped back from each other, both of them had tears in their eyes.

"That was so beautiful, Frieda," Annie said. "Your toast. Thank you."

"I meant it," Frieda said, "I meant it all."

They stood, looking at each other. Then Annie said, "Well, come in. Come on in," making a sweeping gesture of dramatic welcome, and they mounted the stairs together and went into the gathering noise of the house.

Others drifted in. Aaron Lambert was there, and Felicity and Everett Rogers. Don Schumer and Natalie, of course. The Caldwells had come over from next door, bringing their three teenage children with them, all tall and reedy, like their father. The kids stood in a little clot, slim statues, talking only occasionally, and only to each other. Whenever anyone else drew near, they looked awkward and frightened, so Annie didn't approach them.

Everyone from the store had come. The younger of Annie's two brothers had flown up from Philadelphia, and she introduced him around. From time to time she saw him in intense conversations, once, for a long while, with Lucas, who'd always liked him.

Karen was there, fully dressed, mirabile dictu, and with shoes on her feet, even if they were some kind of sneaker, blue with shimmery streaks. Annie had asked Sarah to keep an eye on her, which must have included her going over there ahead of time for a wardrobe check; and Annie saw Sarah or Lucas or Frieda standing next to her every now and then through the evening, one or another of them talking with her, guiding her this way or that with a hand at her elbow.

At some point Annie looked across the room and saw the old woman standing in front of the open refrigerator like someone assessing its contents for leftovers, and she started to go over to try to distract her. But one of the students appeared next to her then, and gently guided her to the table, where she seemed instantly occupied with the food.

"How Graham would have loved this!" someone said, and Annie agreed.

"I can imagine him here, the life of the party, as usual." Yes, she said.

"This is so wonderful. The only thing missing is Graham."

Oh, I know, Annie said. So true, she answered. It wasn't easy, but it wasn't as hard as all the earlier commiseration had been. It made her glad that she'd asked for the delay, the extra months to prepare herself for this night.

And gradually it turned into the party Graham had wanted anyway—really, just a party. She stepped out of the house later in the evening, looking back up at the soft flickering candlelight in the windows, and listening for a moment to the din, satisfied with it, and also saddened by it. Graham *would* have loved it.

They ran out of wine, and she had asked one of the student helpers to get out a case of the cheaper white that Graham had always kept on hand in the pantry refrigerator. ("If we're that drunk, we'd just be wasting the good stuff.") She had already begun to say goodbye to the early departures. Karen had disappeared, and Sarah was moving around more freely, more energetically, perhaps as a result. The student helpers were everywhere too, replenishing the serving dishes, pouring wine, picking up the dishes and glasses left here and there.

Annie went outside again, to cool off this time. There were perhaps ten people on the back patio by now, and Annie lingered out there, talking to Remi Caldwell from next door about e-books, a pleasant, predictable discussion. He was all for them, Annie against—on Graham's behalf as well as her own. Several people came to say goodbye to her during this conversation, which meant the discussion meandered as they jumped in briefly—e-books, yes. But also Amazon, self-publishing—the familiar gamut, the familiar

positions. They also touched on the housing crisis, the impossibility of McCain's choosing Sarah Palin as his running mate. Obama's
chances. Felicity Rogers said that if he won, she would never stop
being terrified that he'd be assassinated, that it was almost enough
to make her hope he *wouldn't* win. The discussion turned to 1968,
the terrible wave of assassinations and the Democratic convention
in Chicago.

When Annie came back inside, needing to use the bathroom,
she saw that there were fewer people in here than outside, maybe
only seven or eight of them left, mostly sitting down now in the
living room, lost in earnest discussion, probably of the kind she'd
just been having. Or maybe just deeply absorbing gossip. Lucas and
Jeanne were among them. Annie had noticed earlier that Jeanne
was one of the few people who looked as though they'd thought
about anything like mourning apparel—in her case, a black silk suit
that made her more formidably beautiful than ever. Now she was
sitting with her bare feet tucked under her on the sofa. She waved
to Annie.

Annie went through the kitchen area, where the student help
was cleaning up—bagging trash, washing dishes—and tried the
handle on the lavatory in the back hallway.

Locked. Someone called out something from within, she couldn't
hear what because of the kitchen clatter, but she decided not to wait
in any case. She went up the back stairs, through the bedroom, to
the bathroom on the second floor.

She'd stood up well, Annie thought, lifting her face to the mirror
as she washed her hands. She'd had a sense of this evening as her
own version of a tribute to Graham, the eulogy in the form of food
and wine, in the form of the kind of party he had always loved.
Now she was glad that it seemed to have worked, and that in many
ways—in many of the old ways—even she had had a good time. She
knew that the silence after everyone left, the solitude—especially

after Sarah went back to San Francisco—that would be hard. But perhaps she'd sleep tonight. She was tired enough. She dried her hands and ran a comb through her hair. She put on fresh lipstick and came out of the bathroom, out into the hallway by the front stairs.

And was stopped.

Stopped by a noise from the front room, Graham's study.

It was *weeping*, she recognized after a few seconds of mystification: that irregular, shuddering intake of breath that accompanies silent weeping.

Sarah, she thought instantly. Annie hadn't seen her in a while downstairs. Of course, Annie had been outside, in back. But she didn't think Sarah had been in the living room either.

It must be Sarah, then, come to sit by herself in Graham's study. Annie had come in here several times herself in the last weeks, come in to mourn for Graham, come in and thought, what was she ever to do with this room? It was his. If he was anywhere, he was here.

And of course, he was nowhere, so it was from here he was most absent.

She went to the doorway, thinking she would hold her daughter, comfort her, feeling a rush of love for Sarah that it seemed their closeness after Graham's death had intensified.

The light was on in the hall behind her; it let her see into the room. There was a figure in Graham's chair, resting her head on her arms, which were set on his desk. The party noise swelled downstairs, laughter, a woman's sharp cry of delight.

"Sarah?" she said, though she knew in the second before she spoke that it wasn't Sarah. This figure was smaller and too feminine—too female.

The woman sat up quickly and turned toward the open doorway, her face lifted to Annie, ravaged by grief, sorrow, and then quickly something else. Guilt. Apology.

It was Rosemary. Rosemary Gregory.

Annie had a moment of confusion, and then of sudden clarity. Followed immediately by a powerful sense of her own stupidity, her own unwillingness to have looked, to have seen.

Rosemary. Of course, it was Rosemary.

21

"DID YOU KNOW? About Graham's . . . lover?"

She'd waited until nine in the morning to call Frieda and ask if she could come over there, to Frieda's place. She didn't want to see Edith, Edith who was too kind, too good. She wanted Frieda. She wanted someone else Graham had betrayed. She wanted someone who would be angry *with* her. For her.

Frieda's face changed. She didn't speak for a moment. She took her glasses off and polished them—carefully, it seemed—with the hem of her shirt, a faded polo. She put them back on. Then she said, very softly, "Yes. I did."

"How?" Annie couldn't disguise her shock. "How did *you* know?"

"He told me."

"He *told* you!" Annie laughed, a sharp, ugly bark. She felt doubly betrayed. Graham, and now Frieda too.

Frieda, who had known and not said anything. Who had held on to this knowledge, this secret with Graham. Somehow, especially after the toast last night, after their embrace, this seemed unbearable, this . . . betrayal.

"God!" Annie said. "I just can't stand this."

Frieda nodded. She seemed ashamed somehow, Annie thought. Embarrassed.

Well, she ought to.

("Perhaps you should wash up," she'd said stiffly to Rosemary. "I think the bathroom is free."

A stupid, stupid thing to say, when what she meant was that Rosemary should get out, get the fuck out of Graham's room.

"Oh," Rosemary had said. Her breathing was audible and ragged. "Sure," she said, in a small, congested voice, getting up, not looking at Annie as she stumbled past her toward the bathroom.

Annie had quickly shut the door to Graham's room; and then stood there stupidly in the hall with her hand still on the doorknob. Stood there, as unsure of what to do next as she was when Graham's ashes had arrived. Thinking about this later, she had smiled bitterly. *Both moments marking the end of something, of course.*)

"But how did *you* find out?" Frieda asked her now.

"What difference does that make?"

"It doesn't. It doesn't, of course. I . . . ." Frieda lifted her shoulders.

"I just know it," Annie said. "She was . . . she was in *Graham's room*, at the end of the party. When I went upstairs. She was crying." Annie closed her eyes for a moment.

When she opened them, she looked at Frieda, who was frowning back at her. Her mouth was slightly open. She looked puzzled. Her glasses seemed just as smudged as before she'd polished them.

"Don't you sometimes just *know* things?" she asked Frieda.

"I suppose," Frieda said, after a few seconds had passed. Then, after a longer silence, she said, "But . . . this is the party last night you're talking about?"

Annie stared at her for a moment. "Yeah?" she said. What was Frieda's point?

"Oh," Frieda said. "I guess . . . uh. I guess I was just confused."

"Huh!" Annie said. They sat there, not looking at each other.

(Lucas and Jeanne had still been there, at Frieda's, when Annie arrived, though they said they were just leaving, that they needed to get back. "I don't mean to drive you away," Annie had said.

"You're not," Jeanne said.

"Are you sure?"

"No, no, no, no," Jeanne said. "Not at all. We really do need to get back. We're supposed to turn the car in this afternoon."

Lucas said, "And you and Frieda need some time together, I'm sure. No, it's fine."

So there'd been the politeness there too. Annie was sick of it. Sick of making nice.)

Frieda said, "If I can just say . . ."

"Say away. It won't make any difference to me."

Frieda took a deep breath. "It's just, I don't think it mattered much to him, in some way."

Annie snorted.

"No," Frieda said. "No, what I mean is that I wish I had understood that when . . . even when he and I were together. Because it was true then too, I think. That it didn't really *matter*."

"Then why do it?" Annie said furiously. "Why take the risk of . . . doing such damage. To you? To me? Of getting caught?"

Frieda was silent for a long time. "I don't know. Of course I don't know. But the way I saw it . . . I've come to see it, I guess, as part of his . . . *Grahamness*. Just his appetite, for everything."

"So *you* forgive him. How generous."

"Annie," she said reproachfully. Her plain face was anguished.

(When she heard Rosemary starting to come out of the bathroom, her instinct was to hide. Almost frantically, she opened the door to the study and went in, closing it quietly, quickly behind her. She heard Rosemary go downstairs, and her body relaxed. She stood there for maybe a minute, her thoughts racing. Then, almost breathless, she stepped across the room and sat in Graham's chair. Her legs were trembling.

It was dark in there with the door closed, but the window was open and she could hear music drifting up from below, music she'd chosen for the party—jazz, one of Graham's favorites: Cootie Williams, his horn rising clearly every now and then. She could hear voices outside now, too.

Sarah, it was. Sarah on the porch saying good night to someone, her voice audible, deep and clear. The other voice was just a low murmuring in response.

Sarah. She could ask her to handle the rest of the party. Sarah could explain her absence: poor Annie, poor grief-stricken Annie.

She went to the window, slid the screen up, and leaned out. "Sarah," she called, and after a moment Sarah appeared in the walk, looking around. Annie called again, and Sarah looked up.

"I need you up here," she said.)

"I hate him," she said now to Frieda.

"That's not true. That's the problem. The problem is you don't hate him. You don't." Frieda's voice was gentle, as though Annie were a child she were comforting.

"No, you're right. I don't. I just want him back."

"Of course that's it."

"*Then* I could hate him. I could *hit* him, anyway."

They were both silent for a long moment. Frieda looked exhausted. "For what it's worth," she said quietly, "he loved you. He loved you very much. You do know that, don't you?" Annie thought suddenly of John, of what he had said to her the night after Graham died. Wasn't it exactly this? That she should remember that Graham had loved her? No matter what else happened? Or maybe, no matter what she heard?

Had he been referring to this, to Rosemary?

Did he know too?

"Did everyone know?" she asked Frieda.

"I . . . I don't think so." Frieda shook her head. "No, no, they didn't."

She leaned forward now and opened her hands out toward Annie, the gesture a bit like the one Annie had made to her in thanks for her toast at Graham's party. "His marriage to you meant everything to him."

Annie laughed again, a sad little noise. "Well, maybe not quite *everything*," she said.

After a moment she blurted, "I just don't know what to *do* with all these feelings." She raised her hands helplessly. "I should be able to just grieve, shouldn't I? I should be able to *have that.*" This is what she had felt last night, sitting up late in Graham's study after everyone had gone home, after she'd heard Sarah go to bed. That this shouldn't be happening now. *Not yet. Not yet.*

Not yet, because in those long days and weeks after his death, she had been feeling her grief as her deepest connection to Graham. While she mourned him, while she felt as fragile as she did, he was still *with* her, in some sense. His death had seemed to her even to draw them closer—maybe because she was so frightened of life without him, maybe because she barely wanted to go on. In any case, she had felt completely engaged with him. He was never not in her thoughts, it seemed.

Now this *insult*—she supposed that's what she felt at some basic, shabby level: *insulted*—this insult separated her from Graham more than his death had. Rage instead of sorrow. Rage, and then jealousy.

What stage of grief would this be, Elisabeth Kübler-Ross? The wish to kill, to punish, the already dead person?

In the dark of Graham's room, in the silence of the house after everyone had left the party, she had remembered a moment at the other party, the party at the bookstore where they'd met all those years ago. The moment when he leaned over her, and she felt *taken in.*

Now she understood that differently, that verb, that preposition. She felt *taken in* differently.

She felt robbed, cheated.

"You might be just as confused if he were still alive," Frieda said.

Her voice sounded almost tearful to Annie. But she wasn't interested in Frieda's sorrow now. "At least I could hit him really hard then," she said.

"Well, that," Frieda said. She *looked* almost tearful too, and suddenly smaller to Annie. Weak.

"But maybe he would have helped you with your anger," Frieda said. "Your sorrow." Her open face, even plainer now in her anguish, was pleading. "Maybe you would even have had angry sex as a way of getting back together. Or maybe you would have cried together."

Annie had a sudden vision then of Frieda and Graham crying together at the end of their marriage. Hadn't Frieda told her once that they did? That they held each other and wept?

She could imagine too his crying with her, she could imagine crying with him—for who he was, for what he'd done. Their holding each other in terrible consolation for both their losses.

It's what she wanted, suddenly—him, holding her, him with her—and it made her weep.

Frieda crossed the room and knelt in front of her, her arms reaching up, encircling Annie's waist. Annie let her. She let her, but some unyielding part of her felt separated from Frieda, angry and unconsoled.

22

JEANNE SAID, "WHAT could they be talking about, do you think, your two mothers?"

They were on the Mass Pike going west, home to New York. Lucas looked over at her. She had tilted the seat of the rental car partway back, and was turned slightly to him, resting almost on her side. Her hands lay still on her belly, which was beginning to show a little, though over the last few days no one except Sarah had seemed to notice, preoccupied as they all were. He loved her hands, which were long and smooth and elegant, the nails unpolished but beautifully shaped. He loved her pregnant belly, the way it pulled her abdomen lower, the way it had already loosened and softened her body. He reached over to set his hand, too, on the slight curve.

"My father, would be my guess," he said.

"Yes?" Her eyebrows arched higher. "They would talk about him together, you think?"

Lucas shrugged and put his hand back on the steering wheel. "They're friends," he said.

"Even so," Jeanne said. She had always thought it was strange, Frieda and Annie's relationship. Not so much that Annie was kind to Frieda—that, she understood. Annie could afford such generosity.

But for big, homely Frieda to be kind to Annie, her pretty successor—
that, she'd told Lucas, she didn't comprehend.

"They both loved him," he said now. "They're both grieving. Who
better to talk to?"

"I should think it would make it harder. It means they are both
thinking of the same things. The things he did with both of them."
She stretched, and was quiet for a minute or two. "I wouldn't care to
share my memories of you with someone who had the same memories."

"No one does."

"No one wishes to share?"

"No, no one has the same memories of me that you have."

She smiled. Then she pulled her chin in and pursed her mouth, a
disbelieving face. She said, "So, you have never made love to anyone
else."

"Certainly not the way I've made love to you."

She laughed, and turned in her seat to face the dashboard again.

After a few minutes, she said, "I would like to know all the different ways you've made love to all the different women you've made
love with."

"Too bad."

"You'll never tell me?" She was smiling, teasing.

"Nope."

She yawned and tilted her seat farther back. "Only Americans
say 'nope.'"

"Of course. It's an Americanism."

They rode in silence for a while. "Do you feel like doing something tomorrow?" she asked. "Maybe it would be good to go out
somewhere."

"Mmm. I've got a couple of things I have to read. But one's a re-
vision, so it won't take all that long."

"I thought we could go to the cinema, maybe. And then dinner?"

He looked over at her. She looked very . . . *particular*, he would have said. She'd pulled her hair back and pinned it into a careless kind of chignon when they got in the car. It made the strong lines of her face—her nose, her large heavy-lidded eyes—seem more prominent. He had never been with a woman he found as beautiful. He said, "Only Frenchies say 'cinema.'"

"That's simply not true." She waved her hand in dismissal. "Elegant people the world over say cinema."

"Nope. Not in the U. S. of A.," he said. "Mooovies."

She swatted him lightly on the arm and settled deeper into her seat, wiggling her butt a little— as if getting comfortable on a nest, he thought. They rode in the sound of the onrushing car for a few minutes. She said, "I'm going to sleep, I think. Whether I wish to, or not."

"Good." A light rain began to dot the windshield. He turned the wipers on. The view smeared momentarily, then opened again.

After a long moment of silence, she said, "I thought Annie was odd about the ashes."

"How so?"

She made a face, thinking. After a moment, she said, "Efficient. Oddly efficient, at least momentarily."

He thought of Annie's face, turning to look at him when Jeanne stepped toward him and held him. The open sympathy stamped on it, the shared pain. "Well, I think they were—they are—the least important part of everything to her."

"Mmm."

"She's very feeling. I've always found her so. She's much more— tenderhearted, really, than Frieda. Or maybe just more available, emotionally. " He was remembering how often he had talked to Annie in the afternoons when he got home from high school. Graham would still be at the store, Annie always at the back of the house at that time of day, fixing dinner.

Where was Sarah in this picture? He couldn't remember. Not there. Or if there, quiet. Irrelevant to him at that age, in any case.

Now he was thinking of one particular afternoon when he'd come to talk to Annie about a beautiful girl, a senior named Lucinda Graver who'd taken him up briefly when he was a sophomore—maybe in amusement at the unlikely situation she was creating: the sophisticated upperclasswoman, the cute but uninitiated underclassman. He had wanted to tell Annie about his feelings for Lucinda, about his anger at Frieda, who had refused to give him permission to go to a party Lucinda was having at her suburban home—refused unless she could speak to Lucinda's parents about how the party would be supervised.

He had said she couldn't do this, embarrass him in this way.

She said that in that case, she couldn't consent to his going.

He was furious with her. No one else's parents cared, he told her.

He had hated the smugness in her voice when she said, "Well, *I* do."

What he had wanted in coming over today was to try to get Annie to take his side, to plead his case to Frieda. Now, as an adult, he could imagine her dilemma, threading her way carefully between his rage and Frieda's rules. He had said to Annie, "I know you don't believe it, but I love her. I really love her."

"Of course I believe it," Annie said. She had set down whatever she was doing when he came in, calling her name from the front door. She had sat across from him at the table.

He'd pushed it. "I want to *be* with her, forever." He'd imagined this, he was recollecting now. He'd driven around then in the poorer parts of Cambridge, picturing himself living with Lucinda—living with her there, in that crummy apartment building—he could get a job, they'd be able to afford it. Or there, in that tiny falling-down house. They could manage somehow, he'd been sure. They'd be together, alone together. And images of sex, which they hadn't quite had, would descend on him and make him moan aloud.

"Of course I understand that completely," Annie had said to

him all those years ago. "It's part of why this . . . party, or whatever it is . . ."

"It's a *party*," he'd said impatiently.

"Right. And that's why—because you love her so much—it's why it's just so unimportant in the great scheme of things. You have"—and here she'd lifted her arm and moved it in a wide arc—"*world enough, and time.*"

A phrase that actually comforted him in the moment. He had remembered it later, all of it, when he came across the Marvell poem in college. He'd laughed aloud then, thinking of the way Annie had reversed the meaning of the thing, with the dreamy, expansive way she'd said the words. A trick, really.

But it turned out that none of this really mattered anyway, because Lucinda suddenly began sitting at lunch with another student, a boarding student this time. Like her.

A senior, like her.

When Lucas confronted Lucinda late one afternoon after a soccer game (November, the dark iron gray of the sky at five thirty before he caught the 6:10 train home, the air raw, the sting of his knee where he'd fallen and skidded on the wet grass during the game, their breath clouding the air between them), she said she was sorry, but she happened to be in love with him, with Eliot. When Lucas started to cry, she said—he could remember it still, the revulsion in her face—"God, Lucas! Get a grip."

"Well, I suppose I can believe that," Jeanne said now.

"Hmm?"

"That she is. More feeling, as you say. Though Frieda too is very sad right now."

"She is. Of course she is."

"Not so much, *of course.* She's often seemed so . . . reserved, to me. You can't tell *what* it is that she's thinking of. Sometimes I think even she doesn't know. For example, when I told her she would not scatter the ashes with us and she was so angry with me, she wouldn't admit that."

"I thought you said she did."

"No, she didn't. She was angry, and I knew she was, but she wouldn't say that to me. I had to be the one to say it—that I knew she was angry—before she would acknowledge it. And even then, she wouldn't speak of it to me."

"She . . . she just has trouble, with her feelings."

He saw his mother in his mind's eye, tall and bony, unfailingly kind, but cut off from him until it was too late by the unreachable sorrow that had seemed to him a permanent part of who she was.

(When he'd come up to Cambridge to tell her he was going to marry Jeanne, she had spoken to him, finally, but glancingly, about her regrets.

It was late. They'd gone out to dinner—his treat—and they were sitting in the living room of the apartment. Out of the blue she had said, "Here's my advice to you," and he thought, *Oh, shit.*

"Just don't leave anything on the table."

He had almost laughed out loud at this slangy language, straight from poker, coming from his tall, dorky mother. She looked like Olive Oyl. She had on multicolored striped socks, he noted then, and shoes with thick, rubbery soles. Who wore such things?

"What's that supposed to mean?" he'd asked.

"You have to work for what you want, that's all." And after a moment, "In marriage."

"And you did?" He was surprised by his own sharp tone, surprised that even in his happiness with Jeanne, he could still react with this old, familiar anger to his mother.

"I didn't. That's my point. I didn't fight for what I wanted."

"What do you mean?"

He wanted to hear her say it, that her pain was her own fault. But she stopped then. Her face changed. She said, "Oh, nothing really. It would be unseemly for me to be offering anyone else advice about marriage, so I won't.")

"You were so sad," Jeanne said.

"When?"

"Well, about the ashes, for one thing."

"Yeah, I was." He looked over at her. "Because it *seemed* sad to me. It seemed awful." He gripped the steering wheel tighter. "That . . . large-spirited person, so big, in every way. Reduced? To white . . . grit? To a few shitty bits of bone?"

Her hand came over and rested on his thigh. His vision was blurred with tears. His throat hurt.

He wiped his eyes with the back of his hand.

"Do you need a tissue?" she asked. He didn't answer.

"I have one." She lifted her body slightly and reached over into the back seat for her purse. She got out a Kleenex, handed it to him.

"Thanks," he said. He cleared his throat. "Thank you."

"You know, I will miss him too." When Lucas didn't answer, she said softly: "I'm so glad you had him for your father." She reached over and touched his leg again. "It will make you a good father, too."

She smiled at him. "A good daddy." She said this in her perfect American accent, the one she could call up easily at any time, the one she used for the voiceovers, for the ads, sometimes for a part, if she was supposed to be playing an American. She also used it occasionally at social gatherings, mostly when she didn't like the people she was talking to.

He had been amazed by this the first time he heard it. She was transformed for him, a different Jeanne, a woman he didn't know, not the woman he was falling in love with. It had excited him, actually, just as the new body she was beginning to have now excited him. He had asked her to keep talking that way after they got back to his apartment—to talk that way to him while they made love.

And she'd started to. But then, when he began to move inside her, she stopped.

"Where'd you go, Jeanne?" he'd whispered, making his own accent broad, midwestern, the way he'd said "movies."

"Je suis ici," she breathed.

"Yes," he said, rocking in her slowly, his elbows on either side of her head, her knees touching his shoulders.

"Oui," she answered softly. Or he thought she answered. But she was starting to come then, and afterward it occurred to him that it might have been just a noise of pleasure she was making on account of that.

23

WHEN HER MOTHER came back from Frieda's, she seemed distraught to Sarah, her sorrow renewed, or deepened somehow. She had clearly been crying—her eyes were reddened, the lids swollen. For a moment Sarah felt a twist of jealousy: her mother had shared her sorrow with Frieda in a way she hadn't, or wouldn't, with her own daughter. It felt too familiar, this exclusion from the world of the grown-ups, and for a moment the old resentment of that touched her again.

But after all, she told herself, Annie must feel easier mourning with Frieda—someone her own age. Frieda, who had perhaps loved Graham in some of the same ways Annie did. (She had asked Frieda about this once, when she was still young enough to be insensitive to the pain it might cause Frieda. This was in the period when she was closest to Frieda, when she occasionally spent a weekend night at Frieda's house, baking or doing a picture puzzle before watching *Saturday Night Live*, which Frieda called "our favorite." She couldn't remember how she'd phrased her question, but what she wanted to know was whether Frieda's relationship with Graham was as private, as much a secret, as her parents' relationship seemed to her.

Frieda had laughed, and said she didn't think so. "We were younger, you know. We were awfully young." Frieda's face had looked sad in a way that made Sarah aware of how long ago it had been. Anyway, Frieda had said then, love was always different. What she had said exactly—and Sarah never forgot this—was "Love isn't just what two people *have* together, it's what two people *make* together, so of course, it's never the same.")

After Sarah had fixed her mother another cup of coffee, after her mother had drunk it—slowly, not talking much—she set it in its saucer and said, "You know, I think I'm just going to go back up to Vermont." She looked across the table at Sarah. She was frowning, anxious-looking, as though Sarah might not give her permission. As though she were someone who had permission to give, which startled Sarah. "Do you mind, sweetie? I really need to be alone, I think."

"You don't need to go all the way to Vermont to be alone, Mom. God, *I'll* go. I can change my flight. It's not a big deal. I mean, this is your house. You ought to be able to be as alone as you want right here."

They argued it back and forth, but finally Annie convinced Sarah that she actually wanted to be in Vermont, in exactly that place. That she wanted the more complete aloneness of the country, the cottage. "Plus, you're not obliged to *do* anything up there," she said. "You can just sit outside and look at the water, or the trees, and not feel you're wallowing. No, no, no, no: you're *in nature*." She rolled her eyes dramatically for Sarah. "You're *noticing* things." Her voice exaggerated the words, and she smiled at her daughter, at her own little joke.

While her mother went upstairs to pack, Sarah made her a sandwich and wrapped a few of the cookies left over from the party. Annie came back down and set a small, overnight-size bag on the table.

"That's all you need?" Sarah asked. Something about it seemed pathetic to her. Her mother, so reduced.

"Yeah," Annie said. "I have a couple of changes of clothes up there." She put the sandwich and cookies in at the top of the bag. "Daddy does too, actually."

"Oh," Sarah said. "Still?" She should have offered to help with that while they were all up there, she was thinking.

"Yes," Annie said. "I haven't done a single chore there this year." She laughed, humorlessly. "Not even put the screens in this summer."

"But it's not worth it now, is it? The screens, I mean."

"No. No, I won't do anything until next year."

"And maybe next year Lucas or I could help you," Sarah said. "You need to ask, Mom. We want to be *useful* to you."

Annie looked over at her, and Sarah watched her face soften, some tension or sorrow easing. "You are," she said. "You always are. Even just your being here now is a help."

They walked together down to the curb, talking about the party: how well it had gone, the various people who had come and what they'd said to one or the other of them. Sarah was aware of her mother's slow responses, of her own busy chatter. She said, "God, that Rosemary what's-her-name took it hard, didn't she?"

"Oh?" Annie said. She turned away from Sarah to open the passenger door on the old Citroën and toss her bag in.

"Oh, yeah." Sarah nodded. "She was starting to get weepy at the bookstore, I noticed. And then at the house, she had to go upstairs at some point—I saw her actually *fleeing* the room."

"I'm sorry to hear it," Annie said, her voice somehow cooler than Sarah would have expected.

"Yeah. Did you know her well? You and Daddy?"

"Well, pretty well," Annie said. "He might have known her a little better than I did."

Sarah nodded. After a moment, she said, "It's just, you know, he was so *important* to people. It feels good to know that, don't you think?"

"Yes," Annie said.

They stood there awkwardly for a moment. It had started to sprinkle lightly. Finally Sarah said, "So, the party didn't help, it seems like." She had put her hand gently on her mother's arm.

"No, it didn't. It sort of . . . brought it all back, I suppose."

It occurred to Sarah that she'd never seen her mother look so tired, not even right after Graham had died. Then there had seemed to be a kind of a fuel of disbelief that fed her, that gave her a strange fragile energy. "Well, for me too," she said to her mother. "But I thought it was a lovely . . . send-off, I guess you'd say."

"Oh, it was! You and Lucas did a wonderful job."

"And Jeanne, don't forget. And Bill and Peter and Erica."

"Yes. All of you. I'm very grateful."

"And you, Mom." Sarah put her hand to her mother's cheek for a moment. "Here at the house. You did too. It was just lovely. I felt he was . . . Well, he would have been pleased. He would have loved it."

"Yes, I think he would have. All of it." She smiled at Sarah. ("The most joyless smile I've ever seen," Sarah said to Thomas later.) She reached her arms up to Sarah and they hugged, the tall daughter and the small, slender mother. Then Annie went to the other side of her absurd old car and got in. Sarah stood watching, waving, until the van went around the corner at the end of the street and disappeared behind the huge oak tree there. She turned then and walked slowly back up the driveway, lifting her face to feel the light rain on it. She opened the gate and stepped up to the house.

Her old house. She came into the living room and sat down, looking around consciously for the first time in a long while at this space she'd grown up in, surrounded by books and records and CDs and paintings and photographs and odd things that had pleased one or the other of her parents over the years. There on the shelving running along one wall was the beautiful but unusably delicate bowl her father had given her mother because of its color—a blue so pale it was like the sky just before dawn. A collection of tiny shells was spread out next to it, pink or flecked or pearly. They'd gathered them together and separately over the years from various beaches they'd walked on. In front of Sarah, on the trunk they used as a coffee table, was an ornate silver platter, given to her great-grandparents on the occasion of his retirement as the pastor of a church in Minneapolis. The bookshelves from floor to ceiling on two walls of the room sagged in the middle with the weight of the books, some tucked in horizontally along the tops of the ones that stood in rows.

Years ago her parents had painted the room a pale ochre that had faded over time. Sarah couldn't think of the word that would give a sense of its color now, a color she had thought of in her childhood as rich and elegant. Now it was worn, a brownish white. The floors were scuffed, she noted, and stained here and there. Annie's photographs hung everywhere, or were propped on the shelves in front of the books, including many shots she'd taken of Graham and Sarah and Lucas, of various friends, many of groups of people at parties. There were paintings on the walls and shelves too, most of them by artist friends of her parents.

It was shabby, you could see that clearly now in the daylight— transformed from the loveliness Annie had created last night with the flowers, the softer lighting, the candles everywhere. Sarah hadn't known that, growing up—that the house was shabby. She hadn't noticed how different it was from the grand houses around it. Small, square, the one big room downstairs, four small ones up—it had felt capacious to her. It had felt perfect.

But once a friend from college had stopped as she came into the big room and said, "Wow! This is so . . . funky. Or bohemian. Or something. So . . . sixties. There's just so much *stuff.*" Sarah had seen it clearly then, that it wasn't beautiful, as she had thought it was. But maybe that was after things in the neighborhood began to get elegant—the houses that had been divided into apartments reclaimed as single-family homes, shutters hung, clapboards repaired and painted in rich colors, gardens established. Maybe it was then that she began to see that her house didn't belong on their grand street, among the big Victorian houses with their wide porches, their cupolas.

Would Annie stay on here? she wondered. Could she even afford to?

It occurred to her that she had no idea of her mother's finances. She couldn't earn much of anything from her work—maybe, actually, not even enough to pay for the studio, maybe not enough for the developing—which, since her mother had moved to the large color prints, was almost prohibitively expensive, she knew.

Did they even own the house? She knew they'd gotten a second mortgage to pay for her college, but she had no idea how much of that they might still owe. Or even whether the first mortgage had been paid off. She hadn't asked her mother any of this, hadn't thought about it until just now.

She couldn't imagine Annie anywhere else, she realized. Even as she also realized that this feeling had to do not so much with her mother as with herself. Really, what she couldn't imagine was not having this home. Of course this home to come back to, yes. But also, she understood, to be gone from. The place she could call up from far away in her own life when she thought of *home*—this room, and everything in it.

She got up and went back to the kitchen. The breakfast things and their later coffee cups were still in the sink. She cleaned it all up—loading the dishwasher, wiping the counters and the end of the long table where she and Annie had been sitting. When she was done, she went into the living room again. She moved around, looking more closely at everything there, touching things. She stood in front of one of the framed photographs of her father. He was looking at the camera—at her mother—with a gentle smile, his eyes announcing all that he felt for her. There was a smaller picture of herself that she'd always liked—she was in the sandbox that had predated the brick terrace in the backyard, dirty, wearing just shorts, a clear stripe through the dirt on her belly where she'd drooled on herself, waving a plastic shovel at her mother. Or at the camera, anyway.

Before she left the room, she stood for a moment, turning in a slow circle. Then she went quickly over to the low shelf. She reached down and slid about a quarter of the tiny, beautiful shells off it and into her hand. She put them in her jeans pocket. Then she went to the kitchen area again and up the back stairs, up to her parents' bedroom.

She stood for a moment in the doorway, surveying everything. She crossed the room and sat in the big chair at the foot of the bed, her father's chair. Part of her had been glad when Annie left, she felt it now. Yes, glad to have the house to herself. Glad to move around in it, to remember her father here, without her mother's sorrowing presence.

She smiled. Glad to have a chance to take something that connected to him without having to ask her mother's permission, without even having to let her know she'd done it. A secret.

She put her feet up on the bed as her father used to do in the mornings when she was a little girl. On the weekends especially, Sarah had sometimes joined her parents in here, climbing into bed with her mother or sitting on her father's lap while the two grownups went on talking and drinking their coffee.

Through the open window now she heard the rain intensify, she smelled the dampness of earth. She remembered the sense she often had when she came into this room—the sense that her parents had been telling secrets to each other, that there was something between them, maybe everything, that she didn't know about. Her strategy for making room for herself between them then had been to throw herself at one or the other, to be wild, noisy. Her father always responded, tossing her around, roughhousing, making her shriek with joy.

Her mother was not as much fun—on those mornings when

Sarah started being too rowdy, she simply withdrew. She'd get up out of the bed, tying her kimono tighter around her, and head for the bathroom. Which ended everything.

How obvious it was to her later, thinking back on it—embarrassingly obvious—that often enough it must have been sex that she'd interrupted.

She had a memory now of waking in the night in her own room. She must have been seven, maybe eight. She'd heard something, a cry. A moan. She had lain there, listening intently for a long, silent interval that frightened her.

But then her parents' voices began, that familiar rhythmic flow between them. His deep rumble, whispering. Her mother's higher, gentler voice answering him—rising, falling. They laughed softly. Sometimes her mother's voice was so low she couldn't really hear it. But she could still somehow *feel* it, the special way of talking she saved only for him.

Sarah had started crying in her bed then, at first just for herself, a nameless, private grief that at that age she didn't ask herself to understand. But then more loudly, wanting someone to come to her. After a minute or two, her mother did, sitting on the edge of the bed. Pushing Sarah's hair gently off her face, she asked whether Sarah had had a bad dream.

Sarah remembered willfully intensifying her sorrow then, moving into a kind of hysteria that became real as she enacted it.

Finally her mother left and her father came in, the one she had wanted all along, apparently. He sat with her, stroking her hair as her mother had, whispering to her in a kind of song, "Hey, little girl, hey, little girl." When he lay down next to her, she began slowly to calm herself, until finally she fell asleep.

She had talked about this with Lucas once much later, her wish, her "classic wish," as she described it to him, to interpose herself between Graham and Annie. To triumph over her mother. So embarrassingly oedipal.

Or Elektral, he said.

"Whatever," she said. She'd asked him if he'd ever felt anything like that.

"Toward Graham?" he'd asked.

"I suppose."

"Well, as you know, Annie was not my mother, so everything was different for me, I think."

"I guess so. Yeah."

"I *liked* her being with Graham. I liked Graham's being with her. I wanted her for my mother. I wanted him for my father." He grinned at her, his famous Lucas wolf-grin.

"But he is your father."

Lucas had looked at her and nodded, the smile still on his face. "I wanted both of them," he said. "For me, I wanted them together. Don't you get it? What they had together. I wanted this very *house* to be mine." He looked around, as if newly taking it in. They were sitting at the kitchen table, where everyone sat when they talked. He laughed then and said, "I wanted exactly what you had, sister Sarah." He made his hand like a gun, pointing his finger at her. "I wanted your life."

"And I wanted yours," she almost said. But of course, that wasn't true. Because though she would have had Frieda then—so steady, so safe, so much *the same*, always—she wouldn't have had Graham. And that was at the heart of what she and Lucas had been talking about, really, she thought now. They both wanted the same thing. And for different reasons, neither of them could have exactly what they wanted.

She could feel the tears rising to her eyes, the cottoning in her throat. She got up from the oversize worn chair and went into Graham's office. She lay down on the daybed there and looked up and around at everything there—the books crowded onto the shelves, in places two deep. The books stacked on the floor, on his desk, on the table. The papers with his backward-sloped handwriting on them. The photographs—of Annie, of Lucas, of her. The room actually held his scent somehow, though you could as easily have said that Graham had held the room's scent—the scent, that is to say, of books, of paper. Everything, down to the fraying cushion on the daybed where he lay to read. Where she lay now, beginning to cry.

Throughout the summer, Sarah had been intermittently overwhelmed by her grief for her father—always taken by surprise, in ways that felt like a siege sometimes.

Not right away, no. When Annie called to tell her he had died in the night, in his sleep, she hadn't seen her father for six months, not since Christmas. His death had hardly seemed real, it had happened so far away from where she was then, in distance, in time. Not seeing him was the norm in her life, and in some ways it was hard for her to believe he was any more gone now than he was from her every day. She wept a little, even then feeling constrained by Thomas's presence. But also because there was just so much to do. Getting the ticket right away, arranging for her absence from work, packing.

And then, when she was in Cambridge for those few days, there was her mother, so lost in sorrow that Sarah felt obliged to be strong. It didn't seem that this was the time for her own grief.

Once she was back in San Francisco, though—oddly, once again so far away from her father, from the place where he'd been so alive—it came to her unpredictably and illogically at odd moments. She was making a solitary dinner for herself one night in the middle of the summer, and the thought occurred to her, as though she hadn't really taken it in before, that she'd never see him again, never hear his voice, that joyful, deep voice.

She carefully turned the burners off, taking an absurd kind of pride in how responsible she was being, and sank to her knees on the floor, rocking herself back and forth as she wept.

And one afternoon at work as she walked past the staff room, she first heard, and then saw, that there were three people in there, three people cracking up over something, laughing uproariously, one of them bent over and pounding on the table, so carried away was he in the hysterical hilarity of whatever the joke was. She had felt such a wave of rage at them—for laughing, for not *knowing*—that she had to go directly to her office and shut the door to calm herself, to wait for her hands to stop shaking.

And the first time she and Thomas made love after she was back from the June trip home, he was treating her so tenderly that she couldn't stand it. She wanted to disappear in sex, to be no one, to be just her sensations. She pulled him down next to her, turning under him, directing him with her body, her hands, to enter her this way, that way, pushing her body hard against him over and over until they were both slick with sweat, until she'd exhausted herself.

Afterward Thomas had held her and stroked her damp hair back off her face. Had whispered, "What are we doing here, Sarah? Why are we doing this now?" and she had burst into tears and cried out, "Because we're *alive!*"

What did she mean? Thomas didn't ask her to explain again, he just held her. But later she had asked herself, what *was* she doing? Was she mourning her father in this crazy way?

She didn't know, and it shook her—her inability to understand herself in that moment, and the way she'd let Thomas see that intimate confusion.

She'd stopped crying now. She sat up on the daybed. She'd been wrong—she didn't want to stay here alone. She got up, turned on Graham's computer, and began to look for flights later in the day for San Francisco.

When she got home, a little before eleven, she dropped her bag in the hall just inside the door. She went down the long hallway to the bathroom to wash her face, to brush her teeth. In the bedroom, in the dark, she took off her shirt and dropped it on the floor. She undid her jeans and lowered them quickly. The tiny pale shells she'd stolen from home fell out of her pocket and scattered themselves with a gentle, scuttling, animal sound over the floor, under her bed.

24

AS ANNIE TURNED off the engine, slowly looking around her at the overgrown field the cottage sat in, she felt it deeply: it was a mistake to have come up here. It wasn't going to help this time—being alone.

But she couldn't have stayed with Sarah a minute longer, she felt. She couldn't go on pretending her fury at Graham didn't exist.

She opened the door and crossed the yard from the car. Under the gray sky everything looked unwelcoming. The cottage itself needed paint. The stepping-stones laid by Graham the first summer they owned the house were almost hidden in the wet grass. The leggy plants where they'd scattered his ashes were losing their petals, turning to dry stalks.

When she stepped inside, the house was chilled and musty. The very opposite of a refuge. She set her purse, her overnight bag, her keys, on the table and then stood there in the main room, overcome by a nearly bodily sense of irresolution. Because there was nowhere else to go—that was it. No place to escape herself, to escape her brain, which kept going over and over the thing she didn't want to remember—Rosemary, lifting her face from Graham's desk, offering her grief to Annie. And the other visions, the imagined ones she couldn't stop from pressing in. Graham moving over Rosemary, Graham pushing her legs apart, Graham laughing with her, Graham sitting across a table from her, talking.

When she'd come up here those few weeks after he'd died, she hadn't been able to stop calling him up either, all her memories of him. Her face twisted into a bitter smile at the thought, at how much she'd *wanted* to remember him then. She'd wanted to remember everything so she could feel him with her and be comforted by that. She'd sought those memories, they were the balm she needed. And of course they were exactly also the wounds she needed balm for. She'd thought again and again during those days of everything—of the darkness when they'd made love here, of the daily quiet and ease between them. His warming her lake-cold feet with his hands. His hand on his heart, thanking her for dinner. Even the old dishes she ate out of by herself seemed dear to her, seemed to bring him close. Imagine it, she thought now—my fear of losing all that, of forgetting him.

Now what she wanted was to forget him, was for her brain to stop its circuit of all these images.

There's nothing there to comfort me, she thought.

"Everything I remember is . . ." She shook her head fiercely, "Shit."

Shit, because each of those memories came trailing pure bitterness. Trailing too its own corrective—the imagining of the other person he might have been thinking about when they did *this*, or *this*. How he had done these very things with someone else. Again and again the thought of Rosemary, turning her face to the light falling in from the hall.

Suddenly, quickly, she crossed the living room to the line of books sitting on the horizontal boards in the wall. With one long swoop, she knocked all of the books between two of the studs to the floor, welcoming the loud thudding. She was panting. She spun around and walked over to the kitchen. She made herself stand still there, facing out the window over the old kitchen sink, gripping the edge of the counter, looking at the glitter of the lake and not seeing it. Not seeing the trees on the opposite shore, not seeing the touch of yellow and cerise on their leaves.

Who is this version of me? she thought. So jealous. So full of rage.

She was lost. She'd lost herself. When? It had happened, what she'd been so afraid of when he was wooing her. She'd given over to him, to being married to him. She was like Frieda now—the jealous wife.

She remembered Frieda, what Frieda had said about Graham's infidelities—that they weren't important to him, that Annie should understand that, that she had understood it too late for herself. But Frieda had had the great privilege of agreeing to it at the time, even if she'd come to regret that later. She had agency, of some sort. At any rate, he'd *told* her what he was doing. She had known. She didn't need to find out after the fact. She didn't need to be shocked by it. Damaged by it.

"And what if he'd asked me?" she said aloud. What if he'd said to her, "Annie, I want to do this. Do you?" Or just, "I want to do this."

But he *hadn't*, she thought. He hadn't asked. He'd kept it from her. A secret.

And told Frieda all about it. Frieda. Her friend. She made a funny noise, a moan.

She opened the door to the screened porch and went outside.

The air felt cool, almost cold. What time was it? Midafternoon, anyway. The sun had come out from behind the clouds for a moment, and there were deep shadows in the woods around the house. The air stirred, and she heard raindrops falling from the trees onto the bed of dry leaves below them.

She had to leave. She had to get the fuck out of here. She felt it as a physical necessity. Her breath was coming short, her hands shaking. She went back inside the cottage, shutting the porch door behind her, locking it. She picked up the things she'd set down on the kitchen table and crossed the room to the front door. She went back out into the cool, wet air and locked that door behind her too. Something felt final about this.

She stood for a long moment in the yard, looking around again. Everything seemed sad to her. Everything cried out for work. It exhausted her just to look at it. How could she have imagined this would be any kind of haven? She looked down the long dirt driveway she'd come in on, the tunnel between the trees that arched in on either side—the trees that brushed the sides of the car when you drove through them. The driveway curved slightly; you couldn't see the end of it. There was nothing to do but get in the car and go back down into that endlessness, to go back the way she'd come. There was nowhere to be that would be any better, that could help her with what she was feeling.

She got in the van and turned on the engine.

Twice she stopped. The first time because she realized that she didn't know where she was, she was so distraught. Nothing looked familiar, and she had no sense of how long she'd been driving. Finally she saw the sign for the rest stop near Exit 10, but it didn't help—she still felt so wildly disoriented that it frightened her. She pulled off when she came to it, and drove past the few cars to the very end of the parking area. There was a truck there, off to the side, but she didn't see anyone in it. She cut the engine, rolled down the windows, and sat, trying to breathe slowly and deeply, until her body seemed calmed.

The second time she stopped was to get gas—she had noticed just in time that she was almost out. This frightened her too, the idea that she might have driven until the gas ran out and then have had to wait for help. That image of herself, alone and lost and useless at the side of the road, waiting for some form of rescue, seemed so terrible that she wept for a few minutes in the gas station after she got back into the car.

———————

At home, the door was locked. She let herself in and called for Sarah, even though she could tell by the sense of stillness in the air of the house that she wasn't there. Then she saw the note on the floor, a book set on the edge of the paper to hold it in place.

"I changed my mind about staying," Sarah had written. She'd headed to Logan to get on a waitlist to return early to San Francisco. She hoped Annie would find her stay in Vermont "a comfort." Annie made a noise.

She took her jacket off and draped it over the newel post. She went into the living room and sat down on the couch. The light was almost gone in here, and in the shadowy room everything, all these things she'd chosen as . . . what?—emblems of her life with Graham, with Sarah?—they all seemed alien, unappealing. She closed her eyes. She was glad Sarah had left.

After a minute or two she got up on her knees and bent forward over the back of the couch, reaching down to the oversize books on the shelf behind it. There it was, where she'd left it—*Memoir with Bookshop*. She brought it up and sat down again, sinking into the old pillows with the book on her lap. She turned on the lamp next to her and opened it, feeling her anger swell. Her hands were trembling.

25

FRIEDA HAD BEEN taken aback by her conversation with Jeanne—the conversation in which Jeanne had told her that the scattering of Graham's ashes was just for the immediate family. In its aftermath, she had felt roughly treated. She went over and over what Jeanne had said, and it seemed to her that nearly every word was a blow. It took her several days to recover.

But as she gained more distance on it, she began to think that Jeanne was right—that of course Annie had a right to keep the ceremony small and intimate, if that's what she wanted. To make it, after all, about the death of her husband—the marker of the end of her marriage to Graham.

And in what seemed like the logical next step after that, she actually began to admire Jeanne for her role in all of this. How unapologetic she'd been! How clear and unflappable. How fierce, in her defense of Lucas's interests. That part helped Frieda to see their marriage anew, and she felt glad for him that he had someone so powerfully loyal to him.

She came to feel, too, that perhaps she *had* taken advantage of Annie in some ways. She'd never considered it, because of Graham, she supposed. Because he had seemed to take it for granted—as she had also, in the end—that she would always be part of his life with Annie. She began to wonder, in those days after she'd talked to Jeanne, what it might have cost Annie to be so *generous*, as Jeanne had said.

She thought for the first time too of the way in which her presence at so many important moments in Annie's life with Graham might have been intrusive. Unwelcome. She actually began to feel an element of embarrassment for herself—she must have seemed so needy sometimes, so desperate.

What she seized on to help her with all this was that she needed to make some kind of apology to Annie, an apology that she hoped might rebalance their relationship.

Or perhaps not an apology, she thought. It might be difficult to discuss it directly with Annie. Surely she wouldn't want to acknowledge feelings of irritation or anger toward Frieda. Feelings that might, after all, be unconscious on her part. Or if conscious, certainly awkward to confess to her, to Frieda.

She began to focus on the toast to Graham that she wanted to give at the bookstore party. She thought she could write it so that Annie would understand it as her way of saying how sorry she was, but in a way that would put no burden on her.

She had written it out, and then gone over and over it, discarding whole paragraphs, changing a sentence here, a word or a phrase there. She had read it aloud and then spoken it five or six times to be sure she was saying exactly what she felt, to be sure that it was clear, that it was, itself, generous enough.

As she made the toast, she had felt with deep pleasure that it was working. She watched Annie's face open to her, her hands too opening in gratitude, in blessing. She felt it again as she and Annie embraced later in the evening—and she was grateful to Jeanne again for having spoken as she did.

———

So much of that was just swept away starting the very next day after the toast—swept away by Annie's shock and anger at what she assumed was Rosemary's affair with Graham; and by the way Frieda was complicit in that affair, as Annie saw it. Complicit in having kept it a secret from her.

Frieda was crushed. She had been so hopeful that she and Annie could somehow begin again. Annie's deep anger—at Graham, at her—had made that seem impossible. It haunted Frieda—partly because of her guilt at confirming Graham's affair with Rosemary when what she'd meant to confirm was that long-ago affair he'd had with Linda Parkman.

She had tried once in the fall to talk to Annie about all of this, to suggest to her that perhaps Rosemary was simply a sad friend of Graham's. She said she wasn't sure that Graham had, in fact, been unfaithful to Annie with Rosemary—Annie's evidence for it seemed so tenuous, really. So much a matter of her interpretation of Rosemary's grieving. It was just as likely, wasn't it, that Rosemary's grief was for the loss in her own life that Graham's death had reminded her of? Hadn't she just been divorced? Hadn't Annie said that? Frieda knew that emptiness, that sorrowful void—in some ways worse than a death. A failure. A defeat. A deep, deep defeat. It had been so harrowing a loss for her that she could imagine Rosemary's being reminded of it by Graham's death.

She said this to Annie on one of the occasions Annie had come over—she had taken to appearing at Frieda's apartment once or twice a week through these months. Frieda was the only person she could talk to about this, she said. It was too painful, too humiliating, to discuss it with anyone else. She didn't want to ruin anyone else's memories of Graham, either.

When Frieda began to make her suggestion that perhaps Rosemary was just another mourner, not necessarily a lover, Annie had sat upright and stared across Frieda's kitchen table at her. Frieda faltered and stopped talking. Annie waited a moment and then said,

"Did you, or did you not, sit there and tell me that you knew they were lovers?" Her dark eyes seemed to snap.

How could Frieda have said then that she was talking about *another* lover? A lover from earlier in Annie and Graham's marriage? How could she have added *that* to the complication of rage and sorrow Annie was feeling?

"I did tell you that," she had said then to Annie. "You're right, I did. I'm sorry, I just . . . suppose in some way I just can't believe it myself."

"*You* can't believe it!" Annie said, bitterly. "Imagine how I feel."

"I know. I know, Annie."

"And I have to behave as if I *don't* feel that way. I have to act my part—my part being the grieving widow. And I *hate* that, Frieda." She smacked the table, hard, and Frieda started back. "I hate it. That I have to pretend." Her voice was almost breaking.

"I know," Frieda had said. "I understand."

It was then that Annie had said that Frieda was the only person she could talk to.

What about Edith? Frieda had asked. Couldn't Annie talk to her? But even as she began to say the words, she understood how selfish she was being.

In any case, Annie had said no. She didn't want to tell anyone else. She shook her head fiercely, her teeth bared. There was nothing pretty about her. "That's how it becomes gossip, that's how it happens," she had said. "You tell one person you trust, and after a while they're not able to keep it to themselves. They tell one person *they* trust, and maybe that person doesn't care as much about you, about the *principals* in the event, as it were. And it's such a delicious story, they can't help but pass it on. And pretty soon you've got a universe of people in on the secret." She laughed, humorlessly. "Yes, in on it, but anxious that you shouldn't know that, you shouldn't know that they're in on it. And so they start acting too, and before you know it, you can't tell a fucking thing about anyone anymore.

About whether they might know, or whether they don't have the foggiest."

Frieda sat, silent, at a loss. She felt the accusation in everything Annie was saying.

Annie leaned forward, almost smiling. "And then someone, somehow, eventually tells someone who knows Sarah, or who knows Lucas, and wants to talk to them about it, or maybe just accidentally mentions it—" She sat back. "And then they're mired in it too. And their sense of knowing their father—it's done."

Frieda needed to say something.

"I don't think that's right," she offered. "I don't think anyone would ever mention anything about it to Sarah or Lucas."

"No? Didn't you, in fact, mention it to me?"

"You *asked*, Annie. I assumed you knew already."

There was a silence. Then Annie said, "But what if I hadn't known, Frieda? If I hadn't known for sure. What if I expected you to say, 'No, that never happened. No. You mustn't believe that about Graham for even one second.'"

Frieda had felt trapped, really. Closed in with Annie's grief and rage.

And she was angry too, she realized. When what she most wanted was to mourn Graham for herself, to remember what had been sweetest in their falling in love, in their early marriage. To remember his generosity to her over the long years, his unfailing loyalty. Every year on her birthday, he came over with champagne and gifts. When her father died, he stayed with her three or four evenings in a row, until she felt she might be able to sleep.

Sometimes he just stopped by, for a game of Scrabble or a beer, and they talked—about Lucas, about Sarah. About books or movies. Stupid things—the price of real estate. A good joke he'd heard.

Why couldn't she have had her own tender sorrow about all that? Why did she have to be plunged into what Annie was feeling? Why did she have to listen to Annie going over and over her betrayal?

Sometimes she wanted to ask her that, or to tell her to stop, to tell her not to come over again. Once she sat upstairs, unmoving and silent, while Annie rang the bell again and again down in the foyer. The shrill of the bell itself seemed full of rage to her, but finally Annie left. And then Frieda felt guilty about that.

It had ended, though. Perhaps Frieda wasn't able to offer Annie enough of what she needed. Perhaps Annie had a sense of Frieda's resistance to her view of things. Perhaps Annie *had* begun to talk to Edith, or to someone else, and was taking comfort there. For whatever reason, as the fall wore on, as the days grew darker, Annie stopped coming over to Frieda's so much, and then wasn't coming at all.

What Frieda felt at first was mostly relief. But then she began to worry about Annie. Her dear friend, after all.

So Frieda called her, finally, in early December, to ask how she was, how she was managing. "Very nicely, thank you," Annie said. Then she'd laughed, unconvincingly. Not even intending to be convincing, it seemed to Frieda.

But Frieda kept trying, kept calling. She reminded herself of the way Annie had responded to the toast at the bookstore party. Of the way she had been feeling about Annie and herself as she planned the toast. She kept calling, and slowly, gingerly, over the holidays and the long dark months of deepest winter, there seemed to be a kind of rapprochement between them. Or so Frieda thought. So she hoped.

Not exactly what she had wished for. That would take time. But she had plenty of that.

In late February, Jeanne gave birth to a girl, Claire, named after an unmarried aunt of hers, the aunt who had favored Jeanne among all her nephews and nieces. Who had paid for the classes at the drama school Jeanne had attended in Paris before she moved to America.

At Lucas and Jeanne's invitation, Frieda went down to New York to help out the day after Jeanne came home with the baby. She felt this invitation as a gift, a reassuring affirmation of her place in the family, of her unique role as Claire's grandmother. Her happiness about this touched everything she did with meaning in those days at the apartment.

She stayed for a week, sleeping on the couch in the living room and getting up in the night when Claire began to cry. Or not to cry exactly, but to make a noise that sounded to Frieda like the creaky hinge on a door that was swinging open and shut slowly, over and over.

She would go to Claire's crib, just off the dining room. She'd pick her up and hold her until she calmed, singing softly to her, songs she'd sung to Lucas long ago. She'd set her down and speak to her while she changed her wet, sometimes shitty Pampers. She'd clean her bottom, change her sleeper if it too was soaked through. Then she'd pick her up again and take her down the long narrow hallway to Jeanne and Lucas's bedroom.

When Frieda opened their door, she was aware of the closed-in, humid air. It smelled of birth and milk and old blood and the heat of their bodies, Jeanne's and Lucas's. It felt almost shockingly intimate to Frieda the first time she came in. She bent forward to touch Jeanne's shoulder, holding the weightless curl of Claire's body against her own. The tiny girl was already turning her head back and forth across Frieda's front, in quest of the nipple.

When she went back alone to the living room to lie down again on the couch night after night, Frieda was flooded with memories of how it had been when Lucas was a baby—that same sense of being closed up inside a life that had been magically and completely altered.

She had never been as happy as she was then—Graham had seemed so enchanted with Lucas, with her. She had thought this was the miracle that would bring him back to her, the miracle that would make their world—the three of them, the three of them in bed—enough for him. She couldn't imagine that he didn't feel, as she did, the joyful sense of having made something whole again that had been broken, having completed something. For a while, it had seemed to her that it might be possible, that miracle.

She didn't know when it started again, the other women. She didn't know, actually, if it had ever stopped. She wouldn't have known, she'd been so inward-turned, she'd felt so safe, so happy.

Until she wasn't.

She tried not to allow those thoughts to rise. She reminded herself how lucky she was to be here, to have been asked. She focused on the pleasure of being with the baby, of helping Lucas and Jeanne. She did everything for Claire when the little girl was awake. When she needed changing, or a bath. And when Claire slept, there were plenty of chores Frieda could occupy herself with—the shopping, the cooking, the cleaning up.

And at night, the endless piles of laundry. (The trip down in the ancient elevator with the smelly crib sheets and changes of clothing, with Jeanne's milk-stained blouses, her blood-stained underpants. Then the cramped laundry room. The insult of finding your damp things set out on the folding table and someone else's clothing flopping around in one of the dryers.) It felt good to be so utterly taken up, moment by moment.

Frieda had thought she and Lucas might talk in the evenings after Jeanne went to bed, but he usually went to the dining room table then and spread out his papers. Frieda was tired all the time anyway, so on those evenings, she would take her turn in the bathroom and then lay her bedding out on the couch again and lie down, the light from the dining room falling in through the French doors Lucas had closed. She could watch him as he sat there, his back to her, flipping the pages over from one pile to the other, stopping sometimes to write something on the sheet in front of him. Sometimes she woke to hear the French doors to the dining room open—the click of the latch, the complaint of the hinge—and opened her eyes to see Lucas's dark shape move across the living room into the mouth of the long, dark hallway.

But two nights before she was to leave, Frieda went to the closed dining room doors and knocked gently on one of the glass panes. She could see Lucas startle before he turned around. He got up and opened the doors.

Frieda came in and sat at the end of the table. Lucas closed the doors carefully and came to sit in his chair, pushing the two stacks of paper, one of them half the height of the other, to the side. He did this unhesitatingly, it seemed, and Frieda thought of how gracious he was being—how gracious he had been through her whole visit. How much he had to do, and yet the implication that he could simply push his work away to take time for her. His face, when he turned to her, seemed older, worn. Her beautiful son.

"You can't sleep?" he asked, his voice nearly a whisper in order not to wake Claire. Her room, the butler's pantry between the kitchen and the dining room in some earlier era—a room that had been Lucas's study until a few weeks before—was open to the dining room, and Frieda could see the little girl in her miniature crib, a tiny rounded shape in her yellow sleeper.

"Well, I will, I'm sure," she said. "How about you? Do you plan on sleeping tonight?"

"I just want to get through a few more chapters. If I can. If you hear my head hit the table, you'll know I didn't make it."

Frieda was silent for a moment. Then she said, "Well, that's sort of what I wanted to talk to you about."

Lucas looked puzzled. "What?"

Frieda looked at her hands folded on the table in front of her. She had been intensely aware of them this last week, the raised, lilac-colored veins, the spotted papery skin stretched over them, the lines circling each knobbed joint—they had seemed so crone-like as she moved them over the baby, whose skin was so perfect, so unmarked.

"There's so much you have to *do*. It seems like too much. I just wondered if perhaps I shouldn't . . . stay on for a bit longer. To help."

Something changed in Lucas's face. Then changed back—she could watch him recover from his first response, which, she had seen, was dismay. Or worse.

His hands moved to the closer stack of paper, as if it offered a kind of support. "Ah," he said. "Well, you know, you've been helpful beyond words, Mom, but honestly, I think we're looking forward to figuring out how to manage on our own." He nodded several times.

When she didn't answer right away, he said, "This part of it, God, I mean, we're so grateful to you." He'd regained his composure, his smooth, fast voice. "You taught us, really, how to do it. Taught me, mostly. You've showed me how to do it. How to be of use to Jeanne, which I'm not sure I would have been, otherwise. But I honestly . . . really, I think I will be—*we* will be—if not fine, exactly"—he grinned, the charming smile that he'd inherited from Graham, the smile that looked so different, so much more rakish on him—"at least okay."

In the train on the way home, Frieda found a seat by the window on the right-hand side of the car. While they were still in the city, while the window was still showing the city's rump side to the train as it sped by, Frieda read, looking out only intermittently. But when they began to pass the small towns in Connecticut that opened out to the ocean, she closed the book on her lap. She watched the water, the beautiful swaying grass. She was aware that she had had exactly this consolation in mind when she chose her seat, and she was grateful now that she could feel it working.

This was how you did it, she thought. How you managed in life.

And she had, hadn't she? Right now, the conscious noticing of the sun over the beautiful sweeps of pale-gold spartina, over the dark sea, the faraway boats. These last days, holding the baby, singing to her. At home, the careful preparation of the meal for one. The ritual glass of wine. The slow making of music from the patterns of notes on the lined page.

All in the service of some sense of . . . what? Purpose, she supposed. Order.

Or loveliness. A sense of loveliness that made everything possible. Why shouldn't you have to work to hold on to it?

26

IN THE DAYS after Claire's birth, Lucas had been afraid that he would never be able to love her. Some of it was simply physical—he couldn't help it, he found her unappealing. She had dark, oily-looking hair that stuck to her head in thinning clots. She herself was thin, and her legs bent in curves that made them resemble an old cowpoke's. The un-Gerber baby. Her flesh was red and blotchy and angry-looking; her hands with their tiny, sharp nails seemed large for her size. Her size: six pounds two ounces. They'd roasted chickens larger than that, he'd joked to Jeanne.

"Not funny," she said coolly, announcing her distance from him, her loyalty to Claire.

He understood it, of course he understood it. He wished he could feel it too, the unswerving interest she had in the baby, the love that he couldn't understand the source of.

He didn't *get* it, that was the problem. Claire was unseeing, un-responsive except to her own internal signals, all of which were invisible to him. "She's just shitting," Jeanne would say when he wondered why she was crying. Or not really crying, but making her dry squawk. "See? She's turning red, a little bit."

But she was always red, as far as he could tell.

Or she was hungry, and Jeanne would open her blouse and fetch out a newly enormous, leaky breast, which tiny, ugly Claire would attach herself to, making slurpy, grunting animal sounds, amazingly loud for someone her size. And then almost immediately fall asleep, flopping back, her mouth open, whitish inside with the thin milk.

She was cold. Or she was wet. Jeanne seemed to understand all these things. His mother had too, when she arrived to help out, which was a kind of news to him: his mother, so at ease with Claire, so gentle. He was in the kitchen making coffee one morning when he heard her talking to Claire, just describing what she was doing ("We're going to get this wet nightie off you, yes, we are"), but in a voice so suffused with love that it startled him.

He was, he supposed, disappointed in the experience of fatherhood. Mostly in himself as a father. Why did he feel nothing? Or not quite nothing—a kind of revulsion, really. Was he as cold as he seemed to himself to be? Was he as jealous as he knew himself to be when Jeanne turned all her attention to Claire, when she was forbidden to have sex yet, when she didn't seem to be interested in any intermediate activities? Or in him, as far as he could tell.

He stayed later at the office. He found people to have a drink with after work. He was aware that he was waiting for the middle of April, when Jeanne was taking the baby to France for a month to introduce her to her family. When, as he felt it, he would reclaim himself, his life. Or at least shed the daily guilt he felt for being so uninterested, really, in his own daughter.

On the way home from seeing Jeanne and Claire off at the airport, he stopped at the bistro on the corner of their quiet street. He felt young, unencumbered. He didn't even have his briefcase with him—he'd come home early from work and left it at the apartment when he went with them to the airport.

He sat outside by himself at one of the three metal tables on the sidewalk. The new, small leaves of the trees that bent over the street were the tenderest of greens. It was a mild evening, and the big folding windows of the restaurant were pushed back, releasing the noise from inside. This lifted his spirits. When the waitress came out to take his order, he asked for a dirty martini and oysters, a half dozen.

While he ate and drank, he watched the couples inside. Slowly his sense of exile from the world evaporated. The waitress came out to ask him if he needed anything else, and he ordered an expensive glass of white wine and another half-dozen oysters.

The sky was lavender above him. Yellow lights were coming on in the apartments in the houses across the street. The rooms they revealed seemed full of promise and mystery. Had there been, ever, such a beautiful evening? Everything felt strange and new to him.

The color in the sky deepened, and he asked for his check. When he looked in his wallet for his credit cards, he felt a little shock at seeing the American bills there—it seemed to him that he should be carrying some other currency, he was at such a distance from what he felt was his life.

He walked slowly the half block home. As he entered the dark apartment, he thought of Jeanne. He remembered how she had looked, standing in the line to go through security—Claire just a bulge in the baby carrier on her front, her purse on one shoulder, the big overnight bag, full mostly of Claire's necessities, slung from her other shoulder. She had turned to look for him to wave good-bye, her eyes searching the crowded space, and in that moment she had looked so alone, so burdened, that he was sorry he wasn't going with her. He raised his hand and waved it wildly over his head until she spotted him, feeling a desperate wish to make up for how separated from her he'd been. Her face softened, opened. Awkwardly, she shifted the overnight bag so that she could blow him a kiss.

He thought of that moment often during the weeks she was away, weeks when he swung from the kind of easy pleasure of that first night alone (he ate out almost every night, he drank much more than he usually did) to his dread when he thought of his sense of distance from Claire. His repulsion, really.

He made promises to himself. He would help Jeanne more. He would act as though he loved Claire, in the hope that it would open a way for him to feel that love. He thought of his mother, not his mother with Claire, but what he remembered from his own childhood—her inexpressiveness, what seemed her lack of feeling. He didn't want to repeat that. He could not allow it, allow himself to feel so cut off from his daughter. He would be like his father, like Graham, joyous and loving.

Did you get to choose? It seemed to Lucas this must be possible, that this must be some of the point of living in a family. You could look at different ways of being in the world, you could exercise some will.

He watched children when he was outside, and he was outside often—the weather held steady in its beauty from that first night on.

Four days before Jeanne and Claire were to return, Lucas left work late and was walking home from the subway in the pale twilight. There was a woman walking slowly toward him on West Tenth Street, pushing a stroller. Even from a distance, he could hear a kind of mindless chanting arising from within it, and when he got closer, he saw the child making the noise. It seemed to be a little boy, though Lucas couldn't be certain of that—his hair was longish and curly. He might have been somewhere a bit over two. He was singing—*mnh, mnh, mnh, mnh*—moving up and down again and again through just a few notes. He was holding a badminton racket across his lap, and he was *playing* it, his left hand holding the handle, his right hand strumming wildly across the stringing of the racket's head.

He looked directly at Lucas without self-consciousness, without even *seeing* him, really, so lost was he in the music he imagined he was making.

As they were about to pass each other, Lucas's eyes swung up to meet the mother's. She met his gaze and lifted her shoulders, making a quick sly face, a face that indicated both a relinquishment of any responsibility for the little boy's behavior and an amused pleasure in his game.

It was a vision for Lucas, a vision of the fact of the inner life, even in someone so young. A vision of the way Claire too might come to have a *self*, independent of him or Jeanne.

That night he dreamed of Graham. He was dancing in the living room of the Cambridge house with each of them in turn, but each of them as a child. He bent tenderly first over Sarah, Sarah at the same age as the boy in the carriage—her hair still shortish around her head, her sturdy legs stomping on the old wooden floor of the big room. Then Sarah slowly turned into Annie, a small, dark child; but he knew it was Annie because there was something mysterious, something sexual, that was part of her dance with Graham. Nothing explicit—Lucas felt, rather than saw, the strong erotic element working between them.

Then Lucas, although perhaps because he couldn't actually *get into* this dream, since he was seeing it from outside, Graham was dancing with a creature, an animal of some kind—feral, it seemed in the dream. But he knew this creature to be himself.

And last, Frieda, whom he treated more tenderly than anyone else. They waltzed, prettily, gracefully, his father leading Frieda gently. His kindness, so entirely in character, was unbearable to Lucas. It made him uncomfortable, ashamed; and it was then that he woke up.

The aftermath of the dream, though, was relief, a sense Lucas had that Graham had come in his dream to help him, to show him the way, so that he would know how to do it too, to love easily, generously, those who were close to him. To dance with Claire, with whoever she was. Perhaps also the sense that she would simply *be* who she would be, as each of the dancers with his father in the dream was. As the child in the carriage had been. That he didn't need to worry about that. It would be all right.

He hoped it would be all right.

Jeanne's plane got in at one, but she had insisted he not take the time off from work to meet them. She said she could manage it all—the baby, the luggage, the cab. She would call their neighbor David when they got close, and he could come down and help her bring things up.

So Lucas arrived home from work at the time he usually did. He was just putting his key into the lock when he heard the latch click free from within. The door swung open, and there was Jeanne.

She stepped forward, into his arms, and it was as though the tension of the months after Claire's birth had never been. He felt the full length of her strong body pressed against him. He felt *rescued.* After a moment, he held her head in his hands and tilted his own head back to see her face. She seemed to be laughing, and then he saw that she was also crying. He kissed her eyelids—the salty taste—and then her mouth, open and warm. "You're here," he said.

"*You're* here," she answered.

They rocked together side to side, a little like the dance Graham had done with Annie in Lucas's dream.

"Is Claire napping?" he asked after a moment.

She stepped back, wiping at her eyes with the heels of her hands. She shook her head. "No," she said. "Go and see." She smiled. "She's in the living room."

Lucas made his way down the hallway toward the light that was the living room. And here she was, lying on her back on the floor in a yellow shirt and diapers, looking up intently at a kind of mobile that arched over her, its legs on the floor around her. Her hands, fisted, worked in the air above her, as if she thought she could reach the suspended cloth animals if she tried hard enough. Her bare feet worked too, dancing and kicking, and she made gentle noises of effort.

He saw instantly how changed she was. He knelt next to her. He could sense Jeanne behind him, watching them.

He bent over her. "Hello baby," he said. "Hello, Claire." Her head wobbled a little from side to side, looking for him, and then her eyes found him.

He said it again, smiling down at her. "Hello, Claire."

She looked up at him gravely, focusing hard on him—he thought for the first time that she could actually see him. And then her whole body answered him, her arms and legs doing their dance, for him this time. A wide, toothless grin transformed her face, and he felt something inside him lift, change, in response.

Father, he thought.

27

IT WAS SATURDAY, about 5:30, and Annie was making a warm
frisée salad with new potatoes and bacon. Nothing heavy, she'd said
to everyone. "We'll all be in recovery from Thursday." (Thursday,
Thanksgiving, when she, Sarah, Lucas, Jeanne, and Claire had all
spent the day at Frieda's, the adults eating a meal of the traditional
dishes Frieda liked to make—a huge turkey with stuffing, sweet
potatoes with marshmallows, both apple and pumpkin pies.)

Today Annie had set the table for nine adults, and asked Lucas
to bring down the high chair that had been Sarah's from the closet
on the second floor. She had put candles in a row along the center
of the table, the way she'd always done for the big dinners she and
Graham had given. She felt light, actually cheerful, she realized.

For the last two years, the holidays had been difficult for Annie;
she was still so entwined with Graham's death and then her anger
at him for all that had happened afterward. The first year, Sarah
had come home for both holidays. And last year, Annie and Frieda
had gone together to New York on the train, just for Thanksgiving
Day, and Lucas and Jeanne had hosted them. No turkey, Jeanne had
insisted. ("Turkey is an American invention. Unknown elsewhere.")
They had small game birds instead, and the meal was spare and

delicious, as if in defiance of the American notion of excess. Afterward they had sat in the living room with cognac and passed the baby around until it was time to go to the station. Annie had been grateful for this, for the way the baby made it unnecessary to sustain a conversation. She felt—she had felt for months—that she had nothing of interest to say to anyone.

In the taxi on the way back to Cambridge from the train station in Back Bay, she and Frieda had both fallen silent. Looking over at Frieda, Annie had seen stamped on her face the exhaustion that she felt herself. *Here we are,* she thought. *Two old ladies. Stuck together.*

This year, having ceded the Thanksgiving meal to Frieda, she'd decided to have a small party two days later. At the moment, just the family had arrived. They were all waiting for the others—Natalie and Don, who'd been in New Jersey for Thanksgiving with their only child, an associate professor at Princeton. Edith, of course, after the huge Thanksgiving she'd been in charge of at her house for her children and grandchildren and Mike and his partner. And Peter, who had just returned to Boston from a long, wine-focused trip to California.

Lucas had started to assemble various bottles on the kitchen island, and to open a few of the reds Annie had set out. Frieda and Sarah were in the living room with Claire. She was toddling across the room from one of them to another, playing a game she'd invented. She would hand a wooden spoon over to one of them, and it was Sarah or Frieda's job to hold on to it and let the little girl tug at it for just long enough so that when it was released, it felt like a triumph to her. She would laugh, a hiccupping squeal of joy and triumph that sometimes convulsed her so thoroughly that she would sit down, hard, on the floor—which itself seemed funny to her, made her cry out again with a gurgling pleasure. Jeanne was there too, taking the opportunity of the other adults' engagement with Claire to flip through the newspaper.

Peter arrived, bundled up, his cheeks pinked by the chill, so that for a few moments he looked like someone else, not the dark, brooding version of himself he usually presented to the world. He'd brought a cake with him, from the new branch of the local bakery that was everyone's current favorite. He handed the white box to Sarah so he could take off his coat. ("What a shame you wasted your time making that perfectly *ordinary* chocolate mousse," Sarah said to Annie as she set the box on the counter back in the kitchen.)

Jeanne roused herself and carried Claire off, back up to the guest bedroom, to change her diaper. The little girl shrieked her protest all the way up. While she was gone, Edith arrived, walking in without ringing the bell, stopping to greet Frieda in the living room before she went back to the kitchen to kiss Annie. She'd brought a fancy sauterne for after dinner.

The kitchen suddenly seemed crowded, people greeting one another, embracing, getting drinks. Annie chased them all into the front of the house—"I'm trying to get a meal on the table here!"

When Jeanne came back downstairs, she brought Claire to the living room again. The little girl looked silently but cheerfully around at all the new adults: so many fresh playthings. Then she picked her spoon up from the floor and the game began again, all of them sitting in a kind of circle around her.

The last to arrive were Natalie and Don, apologizing as they came in. They'd been having a long walk on Plum Island and hadn't noticed the time. They too brought wine, and a wooden box of clementines.

"Oh, what a beauty!" Natalie said when she'd hung her coat up and come back into the living room. "What a *cutie!*"

"But of course," Don said. "Look at her antecedents."

Jeanne curtsied her head, making light of the compliment, but Annie could see, even from the kitchen, that she had flushed in pleasure.

Lucas offered them their choice of drinks—champagne, mimosas, martinis, scotch. There was a pleasant buzz of conversation that Annie heard snatches of while she warmed up some small fennel rolls she'd made earlier, tilting them back and forth in a pan of olive oil and then salting them. She put them in a straw basket under a cloth and took it to the living room, setting it down on the table along with some napkins.

Peter and Lucas immediately reached for the rolls, Lucas even as he was pouring a glass of wine for Annie.

"My god, these are wonderful!" Peter said, his mouth full.

Annie blew him a kiss.

Claire picked up a roll and chewed on it for a moment, then put it down on the table, spitting the bit of dough out. "Too sour!" she said, making a face.

"Not sour," Lucas said, reaching for another one. "*Salty.*"

"Salty," she echoed. She watched him steadily as he ate, exaggerating his chewing motion for her.

They reviewed their holidays. They bemoaned the difficulty of travel. They discussed the weather and compared it with the Thanksgivings of years past—the unseasonably warm, sunny one, everyone out walking around outside without coats. The heavy snowfall another year that kept people from having to travel.

When Annie called them to the table, Lucas brought Claire and set her in the old-fashioned high chair, offering her several spoons to bang on its wooden tray. Natalie unpacked a clementine and rinsed it off at the sink. She set it down on the high-chair tray also. She began to show Claire how to peel it.

The salad was passed around the table, and the rolls. They started to eat. Lucas moved behind each of them, pouring wine.

"So, what have you done with the cat today?" Frieda asked Annie.

"Well, the good thing about cats is, you don't have to do much of anything with them."

"What cat?" Lucas asked.

"Did I not tell you?" Annie asked, looking up at him. "About the cat?"

"No," Lucas said. "You certainly did not."

She seemed puzzled. "I didn't tell you Karen died?"

"No. God!" Lucas said. "No! You didn't."

"Oh, I'm so sorry." Annie sighed. "Well, she did. She died. It was about three or four months ago now. Four months."

"Ah, that's too bad," Lucas said. "She was such a fixture in our lives." He set the wine bottles on the table and sat down.

"What did she die of?" Don asked.

"Old age, I suppose you'd say," Annie answered. "I don't know, actually. I assume, heart failure or something like that. She was over ninety, so I don't think they did an autopsy or anything like that. And she died at home."

"But what has this to do with the cat?" Jeanne asked.

"He was Karen's." Annie looked over at Sarah. "Sarah remembered him." Sarah nodded. "You don't, Lucas?"

"Not so much. I've been gone kind of a long time, as you will recall."

"So you took him in," Jeanne said. "The cat?"

"Well, it's a little more complicated than that."

"Tell," Peter commanded.

It was a long story, as Annie told it. She was interrupted often by someone asking someone else to pass the wine, or the salt and pepper, or the salad bowl.

She had been bothered one night by Karen's cat, she said, yowling almost as if he was in heat. "But of course, he's a male cat. Altered, but male. So I assumed, well, maybe she was keeping him in because there *was* some cat in heat nearby. But it went on and on through the night—well, *off* and on—and then the next morning, it started up again.

"When I looked over, I could see him inside there, at the kitchen window this time, hanging by his claws on the screen, and really,

I knew right then. I tried telephoning, but of course there was no answer. I could hear it ringing and ringing. It was about seven in the morning by then, so I called nine-one-one and the ambulance came."

"I thought you had a key," Edith said.

"I do. But I didn't think I could bear it, if something had happened. I just didn't want to . . . to be the one in charge, I suppose."

And that was true. But it was also true that she *had* been in charge of Karen, increasingly so as the months went on. To the degree she could, she monitored the old woman's appearance. She always checked in with her before she went to the grocery store. She picked up things that Karen would be able to fix easily for herself—canned soups, bread, eggs. Sometimes prepared food from Formaggio—a roast chicken or pasta salad. And at least once a week, she had the old woman over for dinner, though Karen ate very little on these occasions. Mostly she just wanted to talk—to discuss with Annie her confused version of the world. The people who came and looked through her windows at night. Who stole her money and her books. The houses on the street that had burned up. And once, tearfully, she broke the news to Annie that Graham—she called him "that fat man you live with"—had died. "I didn't want to tell you," she said to Annie. "But then I talked to your mother, and she said I *should*." She pulled a crumpled Kleenex from a pocket in her skirt and blew her nose. "I couldn't be sorrier," she said.

"It's all right," Annie had said. "I'm almost used to it."

Now she went on with her story of the morning of Karen's death. "There was a niece, though, I remembered that—somewhere on the North Shore. So after the ambulance took her away—"

"She was already dead, then?" Lucas asked.

"She was. They wouldn't say much to me, of course—I'm sure they saw me as just the nosy neighbor who let them in. But they did tell me that. And that they were taking her to the hospital. To Mount Auburn. I said I'd try to find someone—some relative or something. So anyway, I looked up the niece—I knew it was Ips-wich or Gloucester, one of those towns—and she had the same last name, thank goodness. So I told her Karen had died, and where to call."

She and Graham had wondered about this niece every now and then. Was she real? Or maybe just a figment of Karen's imagina-tion? They suspected the latter, having been witnesses to the long solitary life next door, the cat and his two predecessors seemingly the only companions the old lady ever had. So Annie had been a bit startled when she found this niece so easily.

"She seemed . . . put out, I'd have to say." ("Christ!" the woman had said. "Well, it was bound to happen sooner or later.") "But she turned up later that day. She came to get the key from me so she could get in. I think she'd already been to the hospital. I was glad, I suppose, to shed my responsibility for her. For Karen, I mean. Hor-rible as that is to say."

They were all silent for a moment.

"It seemed the niece just wanted out too, really. The whole thing seemed beyond sad to me. Though she did come back over to ask if I'd take the cat in for a few days. She needed some time to straighten things out, was what she said."

"So now you're stuck with him?"

"Not stuck, really. Because it turns out she'd *left* him to us. Karen had. In her will. To Graham and me. At some point he apparently agreed to it. I knew nothing about it."

When Annie had told her the story, Sarah had imagined it, Karen asking, her father reassuring her. *Of course! Of course! Sam's like a brother to me.* Or maybe, *It's easy enough to say yes to you, Karen, be-cause you're never going to die anyway.*

"But you *are* stuck, still," she said to her mother now.

Another silence. After a moment, Annie said, "Well, she left quite a bit of money, too."

Sarah hadn't heard this before.

"She left you money?" Edith said.

"Well, not to me, exactly." She seemed embarrassed. "But to me, yeah. To take care of him. Sam." She made a funny, guilty face, and nodded several times. "The cat."

"To take care of the cat?" Lucas echoed.

Annie nodded. "Yeah," she said.

"How *much* money?" Sarah said. "If I may ask."

She turned to Sarah. "A ridiculous amount."

"How much?"

She smiled, ruefully. "Fifty thousand dollars."

Those at the table seemed to move as one, though in different directions, some leaning forward to look at Annie, others pulling back, surprised.

"My god, Mother! You didn't tell me that part of the story."

"Well, it's the embarrassing part, really. Isn't it?"

"It *is* a whole lot of Meow Mix," Don said.

"I know." She laughed and lifted her hands, helpless. "And he's fifteen years old. He won't live long enough to eat a tenth of it. Less than that. But she really loved him." Her face sobered for a moment, and then she shrugged. "So suddenly I'm a rich widow with a cat. A cliché."

This was, relatively speaking, true. Sarah knew the details. Graham had left a life insurance policy for $200,000, and Peter had a buyer for the store—he didn't want to hold on to it without Graham. He'd told Annie, and Annie had told Sarah, that he thought she'd get about $80,000, after taxes and everything else.

"But the funny thing is, I like him," Annie said.

"Who?" Jeanne asked.

"The cat."

"I thought you didn't like cats," Lucas said.

"Did I say that?"

"More than once."

"Well, I suppose I did." She looked pensive. "They're all a little bit *snotty*, really. And Sam does have a certain . . . hauteur, I guess you'd say. But now that Karen isn't there anymore, he's more or less dropped *that* pose. With me, anyway. I think he realizes he can't get away with taking that tone now. He's actually quite affectionate."

"I don't like them," Natalie said. "Cats. I just can't like them." She made a face, shaking her head. "Because of birds. Because I'm a birder." She was holding her hand out toward Claire, so the baby could slowly pass her the little pieces of clementine peel she'd managed to get off. "And cats, who aren't even native to this country, kill billions and billions of birds a year."

"Billions? You're sure?" Sarah asked. "That sounds like way too much. Not millions?"

Natalie shook her head. "Billions," she said emphatically, angrily.

Claire looked at her, interested. "Biyuns," she said quietly, as if to herself. Then, louder: "*Bee*yuns!"

"I would have felt the same way," Annie said. "I did feel the same way, Lucas is right. But I think just taking care of something—someone—endears them to you."

"Oh!" Natalie said. "Don! This explains you." Several of them laughed, Don included. Claire looked around benignly, eagerly, her smiling mouth opened expectantly, as if someone might let her in on the joke. You could see the stubs of two lower teeth clearly.

"So where is he now?" Frieda asked again. "The cat."

"Oh, I put him back over at Karen's for the day. I wasn't sure how he'd be around Claire. It seemed better not to risk it."

Peter started on a story about an uncle of his, the big family fight that resulted from his leaving all of his money to a particular niece. The one who'd taken care of him as he aged, sure, but still . . .

They talked about wills, who had one, who didn't. Lucas said all of this reminded him to get on it. "But it seems like such a concession to death."

"Yeah, it does," Peter said. "It *is*. But you just can't keep saying 'Who, me?' forever."

"I know. But I'm just not ready yet."

"Ready to make a will, or to *die*?" Sarah asked.

"God, Sarah!" Peter said. "What about . . . *tact*?"

"The latter," Lucas said to Sarah. "I have a few things I'd like to do first."

"Ah, I've always wanted to see Paris before I die," Don said, in his best W. C. Fields voice.

"What kinds of things?" Sarah asked.

"I don't know, really. Just . . . you want to leave something behind, don't you? Something to be remembered by?"

"Annie and Nat have it all over the rest of us there," Don said. "Pictures. Actual *things*. And then also the particular way of seeing the world they offer us."

"Mine scattered widely over about two, or maybe three, living rooms in Cambridge, Massachusetts," Annie said.

"Oh, come on, Annie," Natalie said.

"Well, but you do always compare yourself, don't you?" Annie said. "Don't you?" she asked Natalie.

"To whom?" This was Frieda.

"Well, in my case, to people who have a more . . . *singular* vision, I guess you'd say." And suddenly the image of Sofie Kahn came to her—Sofie, the lake behind her, her head tilted back as she swayed slightly to the deep, thrilling sounds she was making. "I wish I did." And then, because she'd sounded so wistful, even to herself, she changed her voice. "See, I don't, if you really look at the whole *oeuvre*." She exaggerated this word, to make it seem pretentious. "I've just . . . gone around, trying this and then trying that. Jumping around. But then you notice that someone else, Nan Goldin, say, or Bill Eggleston, or Diane Arbus—they have some one thing they're *doing*, always. Something they must *need* you to see."

"That doesn't sound so bad to me—a wide-ranging talent," Frieda said.

"That's kind of you," Annie said, looking down the table at Frieda. "A very kind spin to put on it."

"Well, there are other things anyway, besides work," Lucas said. "Maybe you'll be remembered for the parties."

"Certainly I'll remember those," Peter said.

Don said, "This meal ain't half bad either."

"Thank you. Thank you all." Annie bowed her head to each of them around the table.

"And Diane Arbus is creepy anyway," Sarah said.

"Do you think so?" Natalie asked. "I really love her work. It's like *information* from another planet, almost."

"That's what I mean," Sarah said.

They'd finished eating by now. Natalie asked Sarah about *her* work, and Sarah started to explain it to her and to Don. Frieda was taking her turn passing things back and forth to Claire now, her face open and eager as she leaned toward her granddaughter. Peter and Jeanne were talking earnestly, about wine, Annie thought. She went upstairs to get her camera. When she came down, she began moving around the table taking pictures, entering the conversations only occasionally.

It was photographing Claire that had started Annie's turn back to taking pictures of people, as well as to her old camera; and because of that, to developing film again, in a tiny darkroom she'd made in the old pantry in the back hall off the kitchen—she'd had to move out of her studio when the building sold.

It had felt like a kind of homecoming to her, working in the darkroom again. Everything about it was dear and familiar, even though the room was really too small to work in easily. But she loved it. She'd forgotten how she loved it. The sharp smell, the unreality of the red light, the slow emergence of *this* version of the image, now *this other* version—the control you had over that, over the way you saw things and wanted to remember them.

What she had wanted initially was just to record the little girl as she changed, to remember all the versions of her, some of which seemed to last for only a few weeks. She'd gone to New York every few months, and tried to see Claire every time Jeanne and Lucas came up to stay with Frieda. Most of the pictures she took were black and white—she wanted the more intimate sense of Claire that offered, she felt, as she worked with the film. She thought with sorrow of how she had let Sarah grow up without taking many photographs of her. Maybe if she'd *looked* at her more, looked at her more with the camera—that intense kind of noticing—everything would have been better for Sarah. And might have been better for her as well. Sometimes, watching Claire, she remembered laying Sarah across her own mother's lap, and was astonished at the version of herself that could have done such a thing. She remembered Sarah, more or less balanced there, lying so still, as if she knew even then that no one would catch her if she started to fall.

She'd thought of herself as making up for all that with the photographs of Claire. She'd taken pictures of the little girl asleep, of her crying, of the curve of her naked back from behind as she squatted on the patio, watching the path of ants across the brick. Of the back of her head, like a beautiful rounded jug, her too-big ears with their intricate curves on either side of it. Of her hands, fat and yet somehow delicate. Of her blank face as she began to succumb to sleep.

It had turned her to the others in her life too. She had what she thought was a wonderful series of shots of Don and an opinionated friend of theirs named Anders having an argument one evening, the back-and-forth, the impassioned expressions. She shot Jeanne as often as she could, her heavy-lidded, almost exotic beauty. She shot Frieda, holding Claire, her plain face transformed by love. And Edith, whose beauty had begun to fade, becoming more fragile, less remarkable, but to Annie, more moving. She photographed Sarah standing in the bathroom, looking intently at her own reflection in the mirror over the sink.

She felt she was seeing them all more clearly. That the pictures were a form of intimacy with them. There was no narrative she was trying to shape, no story she was trying to tell. Just these people, so familiar to her, and the different ways she could see them. Her family, her friends, and the camera. She felt invisible. A medium. And that's what she wanted, apparently.

Peter was watching her now. "*This* is different," he said.

"What is?"

"Or maybe it's not so different. It's like the old days, actually, when you used to hide behind the camera at parties."

"Did I? I didn't think of it as hiding, exactly."

"Yes!" Edith said to Peter. "When she used to shoot all of us, remember? I hadn't thought of that." She'd turned to Annie. "So here's a question. I thought you were through with photographs of people. Didn't you say you were done with that?"

"And I was, for quite a while." She gestured at the big color print on the wall above the table, a stubbled brown field with a distant, collapsing red barn. "But that's changed."

"Yeah?" Natalie asked. "How?"

"I don't know. I guess it's like a way of . . . *remembering* all of you." She smiled, almost shyly.

"Aww," Lucas said. She made a face at him across the table, and he grinned back at her.

The conversation broke up again now, people returned to talking by twos—Peter and Don, Natalie and Sarah. In the midst of this, she heard Edith say to Lucas: "Give me the names of a couple of good books, Lukie. I need some Christmas presents."

He turned to her. "Sure. I've got more than a couple. But a few of them won't be available until after Christmas. Anyway . . . let's see." Lucas's voice was quick, smooth, a lighter timbre than Graham's.

"Okay, I love this one. It's terrific. A fictionalized version of the life of Olga Knipper."

"Who is Olga Knipper?" Peter asked. He had looked over when Lucas starting talking, and now he was extracting a small leather notebook and an expensive-looking pen from the inside pocket of his suit jacket.

"Chekhov's wife," Lucas said. "But they weren't married for very long before he died—a few years maybe. Then she lived on and on and on, without him. Well into the Soviet era."

"That's so sad," Frieda said.

Sarah looked at her mother, standing behind Claire's high chair, but Annie's head was bowed to look down into the camera.

"She was an actress, actually. He wrote a couple of plays for her. And this story—this book—is wonderful. Wonderfully done. Some of their letters to each other . . ." He shook his head. "Extraordinary. So . . ." He made a fist. ". . . *present*." Peter seemed to be writing all of this down.

After a moment Lucas went on. "Then . . . Then we've got a sort of mystery. Better than that, though. Very complicated. Very funny, actually. Very British. The plot isn't really the point." He described it, and then leaned forward to give Peter the title, the author's name.

He sat back again, frowning, thinking. "Ah, yeah. I've also got a wonderful father-son novel coming too. Not until January, I'm afraid. But, boy, a book after my own heart, you might say."

"If you were someone who really, really liked clichés," Sarah said.

Lucas made a moue in her direction and went on. "It's written from the perspective of the son, the son as a teenager, at the height of some rebellious behavior. Though the narration jumps way forward in time at the end. The kid as a man, remembering. But it's so assured, the voice—the teenage voice. And so smart, psychologically. So skillful about what the kid *just won't recognize*, in himself, as well as in his father. Then the great leap ahead, long after the father's death, long after the boy has come to understand it all."

Peter asked for the name of the book.

"That's the bad part," Lucas said. *"Young and Easy."*

"Yuck," said Annie. She was standing behind Peter now.

"Young and Easy?" Peter said. He sounded incredulous.

"I know. A really shitty title. I tried to talk him out of it. It makes it sound like some kind of . . . teen *porn*, really. But he was adamant. And if you know the reference, it does make perfect sense."

"What is the reference?" Edith asked.

"Dylan Thomas, 'Fern Hill,'" Lucas said. He made his voice incantatory: "'Oh as I was young and easy, in the mercy of his means, Time held me green and dying, da-dat, da-dat, da-dat . . .'"

"Oh, I knew that once!" Edith said. "Once." Her voice was rueful. She nodded her head several times. "But you're right—it *is* a bad title. It's awful, really."

"You could call it *Green and Dying*," Frieda said. She frowned. "Or not, I guess—that's pretty bad too, isn't it?"

"Yeah," Lucas said. "I'd have preferred something that emerged from the text. Still, he's the boss. . . . But here's the interesting thing. He came to the office to meet me—this was after we'd taken the book—and I was expecting this young guy. Or youngish, anyway, the voice of the novel was so convincing. And I was astonished. He's old. Older than Dad was, for sure."

"Oh, *ancient*," said Annie. She was sitting at the table again. She'd set the camera on the kitchen counter.

"Well, you know what I mean," Lucas said. He grinned. "But he *is*, he's really old. He had a couple of books when he was a whole lot younger that did very well then. Critically, anyway. I'd never heard of them, but I guess I was too young to have read them. Then this long, long hiatus, until now."

"What's his name?" Edith asked. "Mister Young and Easy. Not that I'll remember. You're writing it all down, Peter?"

Peter nodded, and Lucas said, "Pedersen. Ian Pedersen."

Sarah was looking down the table at her mother then, about to signal that she wanted her to pass the wine. She saw Annie's face shift, her mouth open, just slightly.

"Peterson," Annie said to Lucas, frowning.

"Yeah."

"How do you spell it?" she asked Lucas.

"With a *d*. Pe-der-sen." He pronounced it more carefully this time, so you could hear the *d*, and the final *e*.

"Ah," Annie said. Her face had changed again, Sarah thought. She looked frightened. Was that it? Frightened? *White around the gills*, her father used to say.

"Have you read him?" Lucas asked, leaning forward to meet Annie's eyes.

"I did," she said. "A long time ago. Those early books." She nodded. "Actually," she said, "I *knew* him."

"Oh, you *knew* him?" Lucas said.

"I did," she said.

"From the store?" Peter asked. "Did he read there?"

"No, I don't think so." She shook her head. "No, he didn't. I'm certain of that. No, I knew him from MacDowell."

"What is this—MacDowell?" Jeanne asked.

Annie turned to her. "An artist colony." She gestured dismissively. "It's like a summer camp, but for adults." She laughed, self-consciously, it seemed to Sarah. "Adults in the arts. Writers, photographers, painters. One composer during my time, as I remember it."

"I don't recall your going to a colony," Sarah said.

"No, it was long ago. Before you were born, actually."

"Damn it, everything interesting happened before I was born," Sarah said. "I'm sick of it."

"For instance, all the rest of *us* were born," Lucas said, smiling his teasing smile across the table at her.

"Well, now I have Claire," she said. "At last, somebody younger."

"No, *I* have Claire," Lucas said. He'd made his voice like a school-yard taunt. "Get your own somebody younger."

There was a little silence. Lucas heard in it what a possibly cruel thing he'd said.

But Sarah rescued him. "Maybe I just will," she said, squinting her eyes at him. The room seemed to let out its breath, she thought.

Annie pushed her chair back to start to clear, but Lucas insisted she sit, and when he got up, Peter and Don joined him, as if by agreement, ferrying the dishes to the kitchen sink.

When they were done, Annie got up again and brought Peter's cake and then the mousse she'd made to the table. Sarah got bowls and plates. Annie took orders, and the dishes went up and down the table in the scattered conversation.

When at last the sauterne was served, Lucas ticked his fork gently against the delicate glass. "Ahem, ahem," he said. Then, when everyone was quiet: "Let's drink. Let's drink to the missing member of our gathering."

"Oh yes! To Daddy," said Sarah, and Lucas smiled and reached across the table to touch his glass to hers. They made the lightest of *pings*.

"The one who's always here, in spirit," Peter said.

"To Graham," Edith said, raising her glass.

"To Graham," said Natalie.

"To Graham," said Frieda.

"To Graham," Jeanne echoed, raising her glass and turning to Annie, sitting on her left.

Annie's fingers were resting on the stem of her glass, but she quickly raised it too and clicked it gently against Jeanne's. "To Graham," she said.

Frieda was watching her. And Sarah.

Shortly after this, Jeanne and Lucas got up and began to assemble Claire's things. Jeanne laid the little girl on the living room couch to put her into her snowsuit, which made her protest. She didn't *want* to go, she said over and over. Frieda got up too, and Natalie and Don, who had a long drive home, back up to Rowley.

The front hall was full of people then, people putting on their coats, people moving around to embrace one another. Claire stood in her snowsuit, almost in the center of a rough circle that had formed. She was looking up at all these grown-ups in her life, smiling her openmouthed smile. When a little silence fell, she clapped her hands and shouted, "Ebbrybody JUMP!" her hands rising, opened, at the command.

For a second no one knew what to do, though they were laughing, delighted with Claire, with her having thought of this. Then Jeanne took Peter's hand in hers on her left side, and Annie's on her right. Quickly they all started to hold hands, Frieda's hand in Lucas's, Edith's in Don's. When they had formed a circle, Peter counted to three, and they all jumped.

As they went out the door and down the walk, they were all talking, laughing with one another. Annie and Sarah stood at the door, calling goodbye over and over, and then came back to the table, where Edith and Peter were sitting down again.

They sat too. They talked about Claire for a moment, how bright she was, how much fun. Then Sarah rested her arms on the table and dropped her head onto them dramatically. "Pffff," she said. She raised her head again. "I am so wiped out."

"The holidays will do that," Edith said.

"Yeah," said Sarah. She looked over at her mother. "If only we had Daddy here to help us clean up. Remember, Mother? In that crazy old apron of his?"

"Yes," Annie said.

Sarah stood up to start to clear the table.

"Oh, wait a minute for that, sweetie," Edith said. "We'll help. Let's just sit for a little longer. Do you want some more sauterne?"

Sarah shook her head. "No. No thanks."

They were all quiet for a moment. Sarah turned to Annie. "I was thinking—do you remember this funny time, Mom, when Daddy was in that apron and we were all shouting, 'No!'?"

"I do," Annie said.

Sarah frowned. "So what was that *about*? What were we doing?"

Annie lifted her hands. "We were saying no to an imaginary molester, of course."

There was a second or two of silence. "You could enlarge on that," Peter said.

"Oh, it was just this thing at Sarah's day care," Annie said. "We—we parents—were supposed to be teaching our kids about how to protect themselves in case some evil person tried to do horrible, sexual things with them."

"Well, *that's* really crazy," Sarah said.

"It *was* crazy," Edith said. "It was utterly nuts. It had to do with this whole recovered memory thing then," she said. "With little children."

"Oh, yeah, we all know about that," Sarah said. "Recovered memory. As in, Catholic priests." She frowned. "But here's what's interesting, I think. Why is it always the bad stuff? Everything you recover."

"Interesting," Peter said. "I hadn't thought of that. Yeah. Why don't we ever work on recovering memories of the good stuff?"

"Because you don't forget the good stuff," Edith said.

"Sure you do," Sarah said. "There are people who specialize in that. Only the memory of everything awful. Gloom and doom."

"Well, in *this* case," Edith said, "these very dubious child psychologists were working exclusively on the bad stuff. They got the kids to testify that they'd had terrible things done to them by their day-care teachers."

"Virginia McMartin," Annie said. "Remember her?" she asked Edith. She turned to Peter and Sarah. "This dumpy, elderly day-care person. A Satanist, if ever there was one." She looked at Edith again. "And around here, there was the clown."

"Yeah, the wicked clown."

Annie explained to Sarah. "This was a day-care teacher, a man, who was supposed to have dressed up as a clown and taken the children into a mysterious room—a room which, by the way, no one could ever find—and done nasty things to them."

"*I* remember the clown," Peter said. "Somewhere in Medford, I think."

"Yes, I think that's right," Edith said.

Sarah said, "I *knew* there was a reason I didn't like Medford."

"*Anyway*," Annie said emphatically. "We had these instructions, the gist of which was to teach you kids to say no to people like these clowns. So we made a game of saying no one night after dinner, and Graham was there, cleaning up in his famous apron."

"What kind of game?" Edith asked.

"Oh, nothing really. It was dumb. Just, we shouted out every word for *no* we could think of. Sarah loved it."

"I did," Sarah said. "That's what I remember. Just that part of it."

Annie was thinking of how odd it was that this had come up again, this memory that had also come to her the day after Graham died. The connection it had to her remembering the man in Jackson Park. She thought of telling Edith and Peter and Sarah that story now, the story from her own past that she'd forgotten and then *re-covered*. The story of Sofie Kahn, of Sofie and the molester.

But Edith was expanding on the recovered memory phenomenon and how insane it was—her word—to rely on little children for accuracy. She began to explain the way memory worked in young children, its pliability, its responsiveness to adult expectation.

Annie wasn't really listening. She was recalling the night of the *no* game. Remembering that later, after she and Graham and Sarah had finished playing it, after Sarah was in bed and the kitchen cleaned up, she and Graham had gone to the living room to sit, each with a glass of wine, and out of curiosity, he'd gotten up to look up the derivation of the word *molester*. She remembered watching him cross the room. He had turned on the lamp and bent over the dictionary they kept open on one of the shelves. The thin pages had made a faint fluttery noise as he flipped through them. The lamp was behind him, and he was in profile to Annie, almost silhouetted. After a minute or two, he had stood straight and turned to her, grinning, his whole face alive with delight.

"It comes from the Latin," he had said.

"The Latin for what?"

"For the verb *to irk.*"

They had both laughed. "I'll say," Annie said.

He shook his head slowly, and said, "You've got to admire the understatement there."

He had turned the light off then and come back to sit across from her in the slightly sprung wingback chair she'd sometimes called his throne. They still had that chair. Peter had been sitting in it before dinner.

She felt an unfamiliar pang, a feeling she hadn't had—hadn't allowed herself to have—in a long time. Not since Rosemary.

She missed him, suddenly. She missed Graham.

28

WHEN EVERYONE HAD finally gone home and only Annie and Sarah were left, Annie went out the kitchen door and across the yard to bring Sam back.

"And here he is," she said to Sarah as she came in. She set the cat down. While she was opening the can of his food, Sam circled her legs, his tail twining around them—as it used to twine around Karen's, Sarah thought, looking carefully at her mother, thinking of her as *old* in a way she didn't often. Annie set Sam's bowl on the floor under the tall windows, and he hunkered over it to eat, his head moving down and then quickly up as he tossed the chunks of food to the back of his mouth.

They both watched him, Annie leaning her butt against the kitchen counter, Sarah still sitting at the table.

After a moment, Sarah said, "Does this bring it all up again?"

"What do you mean?"

"The cat. Karen's death. Does it remind you of Daddy dying?"

"Oh!" Annie shook her head. "Not in the least, sweetie. I'm sad about her death, of course. And sorry. Sorry that she was so . . . alone, it seems. Mostly that." Annie came and sat opposite Sarah. "But she was old. And she was failing. I'm sure you'd noticed. I was glad things hadn't gotten worse. And I was glad for her that she'd more or less managed things on her own up until she died. That's an achievement. One I hope I'm capable of."

Sarah made a noise, a raspberry. "Come *on*, Mother," she said.

"Well, you know what I mean." Annie looked over at the cat. She shook her head. "No, your father's death was completely different. It was way too soon. It was untimely." She turned back to Sarah. "There were things . . . some things I would have liked to talk to him about, I suppose."

"What kinds of things?"

"Oh. Just. Married things. How we would . . . have gone on being married, I suppose."

"What do you *mean*?" Sarah's voice was alarmed.

Annie heard it. "This is . . . kind of personal, isn't it?" She laughed. "Very personal. Why don't we talk about the cat?"

"But *you* brought it up, Mom."

"Not really. It *came* up, I would say. And then you asked."

Sarah stood and began to pick up the glasses, the delicate little glasses that had held the sauterne. "Well. I'm sorry. I didn't mean to be . . . personal. Or I did, actually. But . . ."

"Oh, hon," Annie said, "I'm the one who should be sorry. And I am. I'm sorry."

"But . . . what *do* you mean?" Sarah had set the glasses in the sink, and now she turned to face her mother.

Annie inhaled sharply, and then let her breath go. After a moment she said, "Just, there were things I would have liked the time to talk to your father about."

"But you talked all the time," Sarah said, remembering their voices in the night. The laughter, the music downstairs after they'd put her to bed. The way he turned to her, expectant, smiling, when she spoke.

"Yes. Of course, we did. But some things . . . There were things, things we didn't have time to talk about."

"How could you not have time? You had years."

"Well, I suppose you put things off, don't you? The hard things."

Sarah was about to ask, "What hard things?," but she didn't. Later she thought that she must have been afraid. That she didn't want to know, whatever it was. Whatever they were. She turned back to the sink and began to wash the little glasses by hand.

After a long moment, she said, "How well did you know Lucas's writer? The guy you met at the artists' colony."

"Ian?"

"Yeah, Ian. What was his last name?"

"Pedersen."

"Right. He was a friend?"

"Well, it was kind of a strange setting." Annie had poured herself another tiny glass of the sauterne. She was twirling it slowly by its stem. "You got . . . very intimate, very fast, in a kind of unreal way. So yes, I knew him well, in exactly that way. That odd way." She laughed, quickly. "He *was* a friend. I suppose I had a little crush on him or something like that."

"When? This was before you met Daddy."

"No, it was after. After we were married, actually. But it was one of those . . . just lovely, fizzy things. Nothing happened."

This phrase struck Sarah, all the parts of it. First, of course, *fizzy*. A fizzy thing. Something she'd never had, as far as she knew. Certainly not with Thomas, things had gotten so serious so fast. Because of her father's death, she supposed.

Or maybe because she wasn't *fizzy*. Maybe because she just wasn't a fizzy kind of person.

Then, "one of those." *One of those* lovely fizzy things. Implying—did it not?—that there were other lovely fizzy things her mother had lived through. Implying another life for her. A life beyond the whole, complete, private world she'd created with Graham. The world Sarah had grown up sensing all around her. The world that she'd felt shut out of.

"I'm going to head up, I think," Annie said. She tilted her head back to drain her glass, and then brought it over to the sink. She crossed to the door to the back stairs.

"Okay. I'll follow in a bit." Sarah said. "I'm still sort of on West Coast time."

Annie stood at the door for a moment, looking back pensively at Sarah. Then she said, "You shouldn't hold your father too dear, sweetie."

"What do you mean?"

"Just . . . oh, I don't know. He was . . . human, after all. And maybe it keeps you from looking around. At, other men, I suppose."

Sarah waited a moment before she said, "*Now* who's being too personal?"

Annie bowed her head, as if conceding the point.

Sarah felt her anger fully seize her. "And I'm allowed to, anyway. Children are allowed to hold their parents too dear. As *dear* as they want to."

Annie must have heard the anger in Sarah's voice. She said, "They are. They are allowed, of course. I'm sorry." She came across to Sarah and hugged her. Sarah barely responded, holding her mother loosely for just a few seconds. Then Annie turned and went up the back stairs, Sam trailing behind. Sarah heard the door to her bedroom close.

Sarah was still thinking of this, and of the evening generally, as she finished clearing up. As she loaded the dishwasher and set it going, as she covered the leftover cake and chocolate mousse and put them in the refrigerator. As she wiped down the table and the counters.

She turned off the kitchen lights and went into the living room. She sat down.

Claire's wooden spoon was on the floor in front of her, and she bent over and picked it up. She stretched out on the couch, the spoon in her hand, tapping it on the top of the couch back. *Tump, tump, tump, tump, tump.*

A strange night, all right. Her mother and Lucas's writer. The way her face had changed across the table when Lucas said the man's name. His *fizzy* writer's name. What would the right words be? That it . . . what? Became *guarded*, maybe.

She thought of Claire then—of her sweet unguarded face, of the game she'd thought of, born of what must have been her idea that the adults had made a circle so they could jump. She had been looking at Lucas when Claire yelled, and saw his face change in pleasure, watching his daughter.

Abruptly she thought of his embarrassment after he'd said she'd better get her own small person. As though he was pointing to something that was clearly an impossibility for her.

And what was her mother talking about at the end there? As though Sarah would be, maybe *had been*, damaged by loving Graham too much. As though it had unsuited her for someone else. For love.

Always, always, that fucking implication—that her life was empty, that she had no one. It made her angry at her mother whenever she caught this glimpse of how Annie saw her. Tonight, angry at Lucas too. It had been clear to Sarah that he felt he'd pointed out what he must have seen as a *problem* of hers. Her unpartnered life.

She remembered Thomas's body suddenly, his turning her over as they made love, pulling her hips up to him, coming into her from behind.

Her hand had loosened on the spoon, and it clunked to the floor behind the couch. "Shit," she said. She rose on her knees and looked down. There it was. She tried to reach it, to retrieve it. Too far.

But her glance had fallen on a book, the book her father had written—or the book her mother had taken the pictures for. The memoir. It was lying on top of a bunch of other coffee-table-size books on the lowest shelf behind the couch. She could easily reach it, and she did, pulling it up, already anticipating these old familiar pictures—like a history of her life here, in this house, the way it had been.

Her father and mother, their friends—all the writers, the artists, the photographers, the parties she'd fallen asleep listening to. She hadn't looked at it in years.

The book felt odd, thickened and misshapen. Had it gotten wet, somehow? She opened it, and took an audible breath. Page after page, perhaps a third of them, had been ripped out. Some fell on her lap.

It took her a moment to get over her shock. Then, slowly, she began to look at it, at the damage.

There were many pages—from about halfway through the book on to the end—that were intact, so it wasn't as though someone were removing the images systematically to do something with them. Anyhow, the rips were uneven, incomplete, chaotic. Sometimes a page was gone completely. Sometimes four or five pages had been ripped at once. Some were ripped only halfway through.

How could this have happened? Could Claire somehow have gotten hold of the book and started tearing it apart?

But Claire couldn't have managed this. She didn't have the strength for any of it. She would never have been able even to hold the book, let alone tear a page out, or tear multiple pages at the same time.

Her mother, then.

Yes, her mother, the only possibility.

It must have been after her father died, Sarah thought. The despair, and clearly some kind of rage—at what?

Her abandonment?

Or maybe some of those *hard things* she never got to talk about with Graham. Things hard enough, difficult enough, unresolved enough, to make her tear at this record of her life with him? To make her try to ruin it?

She couldn't imagine this. She didn't want to imagine it. She wanted the old version, the old, familiar sorrow. Not this new story. This new sorrow.

She lifted her hands to her face and made a noise at the thought of it.

The book slid off her lap to the floor, the loose pages scattering. She sat up and looked down at the mess.

Then she got up. She went to the stairs and up to the bedroom that used to be hers, the one that had become her mother's office after Sarah moved to the West Coast. Though the bed was still there, and the bureau, and the desk—covered now with Annie's papers.

It was completely dark outside the windows. Sarah turned on the bureau light and fished her phone out of her purse.

Thomas's voice warmed when he heard hers, and Sarah felt some of the anger and confusion leave her. They compared their holidays—he had spent his with his parents, at their retirement community in Seattle. They'd eaten in the common dining room, he said, among the other residents and all their visiting children and grandchildren. "The point *there* being," he said, "to make me feel guilty for shirking my job—for me to see what the others had that my poor parents didn't."

"And did it work?" she asked.

"Oh, it always works," he said dismissively. "And then I get pissed about that, because it *has* worked, and it's made me feel guilty when I don't want to. And then they get sad. Or my mother gets sad, sad that I'm pissed. And then my father gets pissed that I've made my mother sad. And then we all have another cup of coffee and say goodbye."

"No fun," Sarah said. "I'm sorry."

"Oh, it wasn't as bad as all that. It's almost like a predictable routine we go through at this point. We all know how to play our parts." They were silent for a moment. Sarah thought she could hear him breathing.

He said, "Yours does sound like fun, though."

"It had its complications too."

"What kind?"

"Well, every kind, I guess. But I'll list them for you when I get home tomorrow." For now she just wanted this ease, this comfort—his voice. His breath.

"But it was also fun. Yes?"

"Parts of it, yes, I have to confess." She was thinking of the big table, the familiar faces around it. Of Claire. She said, "But of course we *did* have the grandchild, so that wasn't an issue."

"Touché."

"I'm only teasing."

"I know."

When he spoke again, his voice had changed. It was quieter. More intimate. "May I tell you this? It's your voice. Just hearing you say hello. It thrills me."

She laughed.

"I mean it."

"Well, we could always keep the light off when we're together, and you could just listen to my thrilling voice in the dark."

"Oh, Sarah." He sounded tired suddenly, and she felt it then, what she'd done. Again. Again she'd made a joke out of a gift he was offering her, a compliment.

She thought of the way he looked—his watchful dark eyes under the smooth flat flesh of his eyelids, the lines of age just beginning at the outer corners. The thick black hair, going slightly gray at the temples. The squarish chin, the strong, graceful body, the lovely light-brown skin. The surprise of his smile, his ready laughter.

Why couldn't she just let it happen to her, let him say it, let herself feel it—what he meant?

After a moment, she said, "But then, of course, I couldn't see you. And that's what *I* love."

"Do you?"

"I do," she said. She laughed, lightly, and said it again. *I do.*

In the mirror over the bureau, she watched her own face, the way it had softened, become, it seemed to her, almost pretty.

After she'd said good night to Thomas, she stood there, looking at herself. She had thought, when she came east, that she'd finally tell her mother about Thomas—or maybe she'd tell all of them.

What would she have said? That she was *involved* with someone? No.

That she loved someone, she loved Thomas. That he loved her.

She'd had an image of announcing something like that at the table at Thanksgiving, she realized. She'd actually spent some time imagining the various responses.

But she hadn't done it, and now, standing at the bureau, thinking about the evening that had just passed, she thought she understood why not. Because her mother—and Lucas too, she thought—had revealed to her their unchanging, unchanged version of her and her life. Her announcement of her happiness would have seemed to them defensive, something she was offering as a kind of pathetic corrective to their understanding of her. It wouldn't have the meaning for them that she'd wanted for it. The cleanness, the pure joy.

And it would have become *theirs*, she thought. They would see her happiness as a kind of capitulation to their expectations, their way of living. They would see it as the beginning of a life like theirs. Married, like all of them—her mother, Frieda, Jeanne, Edith, with all the sad stories they had to tell about that.

Well, maybe not Jeanne. But even her mother, it turned out. The *hard things*, the doubt about whether she and Graham could have gone on being married. The surprise of it!

She didn't want to think about it. She didn't want to change her version of things. Their voices in the night. Their safe, private world.

She thought of her childhood, and Lucas's, each of them yearning for what they thought the other had. She thought of the sense of isolation she had as a kid, the isolation she had so deliberately and slowly fought her way out of. She thought of Thomas, the miracle of having him in her life, the *reward*, she couldn't help feeling some-times, for her long struggle.

And perhaps they *would* end up married, she and Thomas. Maybe they'd even have a child. But for now, what they had—the deep con-nection between them—that was exactly what she wanted, was all she'd ever wanted, she felt. That solace. That safety.

Not marriage—not all the other promises to be made, and then broken. Not the children, the difficult growing up. The wounds in-flicted, back and forth, the inevitable disappointments, the unbridge-able distances.

Not that.

Not monogamy.

She went back downstairs. She gathered the scattered, mutilated pages of *Memoir with Bookshop* and put them back into the book, closed the cover over everything. She put the book back in the pile of other outsize books behind the couch, on top of the one with photographs of the Galapagos.

Then she lay down on the floor in front of the couch, and with the tips of her fingers, found Claire's wooden spoon and drew it to herself.

29

CLAIRE FELL ASLEEP in her car seat on the short trip home. Frieda, sitting next to her in the back seat, watched her fight against this, watched her repeatedly jerk her drooping head up, struggling to open her heavy eyelids over unseeing eyes . . . until finally she yielded and slumped forward, limp against the harness that held her in her chair. There was something so touching about this, about the little girl's hopeless wish to stay awake, to stay a part of things, that Frieda felt flooded with tenderness toward her.

Lucas and Jeanne were discussing it as Lucas parked the car—the problem Claire's conking out presented. Should they wake her to change her, to put her sleeper on? Would she resist going to sleep again if they did?

She might, they agreed. The plan then, decided upon as they climbed the stairs to Frieda's apartment—Lucas carrying Claire—was to let her sleep, even though she'd probably be very wet in the morning.

"Should I take the snowsuit off?" Lucas asked Jeanne.

"No, just unzip it so she doesn't get too hot." As Lucas headed down the hall to the room that had been his as a child, she called, "But take her shoes off."

Jeanne and Frieda put their coats away and went to the living room to sit down. When Lucas came back, Frieda offered them a drink, or coffee. She had decaf, she said.

"Oh, I couldn't!" Jeanne said. "I am *stuffed*." Adding perhaps two extra *f*'s to the word, Frieda thought.

Lucas said he'd have tea, if Frieda had any, so she went into the kitchen to prepare a pot. As she was setting the kettle on the burner, she heard Jeanne say, "How astonishing it is, isn't it? That Annie should have known your Mr. Pedersen."

"Mister Young and Easy, as Edith calls him."

Jeanne laughed, her full, throaty laugh. "Yes."

She sighed then, and Frieda could imagine her stretching. She was like an animal, it sometimes seemed to Frieda. A large cat. A tiger, even. She thought suddenly of their telephone conversation about Graham's ashes, of Jeanne's strength through that. A tiger indeed.

Now she heard Jeanne say, "I wonder if he and Annie might have had a little . . . fling. Whatever."

"I doubt it," Lucas said.

"Why would you doubt it?"

Frieda couldn't hear his reply. The kettle was boiling. She rinsed out the teapot with hot water.

When she came back in to the living room, carrying her tray, Jeanne looked up at her, her wide mouth open in an eager smile. "We would like you to vote, Frieda. Do you think it is possible that Annie had some kind of affair with Lucas's writer, Mr. Pedersen?"

Frieda set the tray down. "She didn't, I don't think."

Frieda poured out Lucas's cup and then her own. They watched her.

"Why don't you think so?"

"I think she would have told me. We've been friends for a long time."

She went over to the chair she usually sat in, next to the purely ornamental wooden mantel, the fireplace closed in with plaster at some point in its past. She set her teacup down on top of a stack of books on the little table there.

"And she would tell you a thing like this?" Jeanne had taken her shoes off. She'd stretched out, and her feet, in their black stockings, rested in Lucas's lap.

"She has told me lots of things a lot like this. None of them involving her sleeping with someone else."

"Ah!" Jeanne said.

"Told ya," Lucas said to her.

After a moment, Jeanne said, "Still, she seemed interested."

"Well, yes. Even I could see that," Lucas said.

"Well, *maybe* interested. But maybe just surprised," Frieda said.

As if Frieda had said nothing, Jeanne said to Lucas, "Perhaps you should somehow let him know about her. He is divorced, isn't he?"

"Oh, is he?" Frieda asked.

"Yeah, for the third time, actually," Lucas said, looking over at her. "A bit of a rake, I think."

Frieda smiled. "'And a rambling boy,'" she said.

"What do you mean?" Jeanne asked, frowning.

"Oh, that's just a song. An old folk song. I think Joan Baez sang it."

"Oh, of course, I've heard of *her*," Jeanne said. Then, to Lucas, "But she is too much alone, don't you think? Annie? Do you think she would be ready to . . . I don't know. *Date* someone?"

"I don't know," Lucas said. "But I'm not eager to be the one setting up anything like that."

"Yes, that would be . . . uncomfortable," Frieda said.

"*Yucky*, I would say." Lucas. This time Frieda laughed—the word that had entered the whole family's vocabulary now that Claire was talking.

They moved on to other things. A job Jeanne thought she might get, the first one she'd tried for since Claire was born, a bit part in a television soap opera. "I'm wicked in this role—evil, evil, evil. And the proof of this is that I speak with a French accent. It wasn't supposed to be that way—I was supposed to be American, and I read for the part with an American accent—but when I spoke in my normal way, with my own accent, they were wild with excitement. *Much* better, to have the bad person be from France."

"Well, of course," Lucas said.

Then *he* talked, about the possibility of a change in his own life. He told Frieda that he didn't see how they could manage in New York on his salary with all that would be coming at them—Claire and school and within a year or two, surely a new, larger apartment. He said that he was thinking of becoming a literary agent, that he'd spoken to one of the agents he admired, who'd encouraged him.

Frieda listened and commented. Yes, how funny about the soaper part! Yes, yes, she understood the financial strain of life in New York.

But while she was talking, making herself so agreeable, she thought about those subjects, and then all the other subjects everyone had raised at dinner, all the things that everyone had talked about these last few days, and the way they never centered on her.

She would have liked to talk, of course. About her life. About how torn she was at the thought of retiring. How would she spend the days? When would she see the colleagues who had become friends, most of whom lived in the little towns west of Boston, closer to the school? And then, should she sell the apartment, maybe move to someplace cheaper? Arlington? Somerville?

Sitting in the dark in her bedroom after they'd all said good night, waiting for Jeanne and Lucas to be finished in the bathroom, she thought of what they'd just been talking about—Annie, their concern for her. Of course it was because Annie was newly alone, Frieda knew that. But still . . .

She thought of that, she thought of all the other subjects everyone had talked about these last few days, and the way they never focused on her.

She had felt a kind of invisibility today, that was it. First at the party, and now here at home with Jeanne and Lucas. She thought about how differently the day would have gone if Graham had been here.

She missed him. She missed his cry of pleasure when he saw her. "Ah, Frieda! The first Mrs. McFarlane," he'd say when she arrived at a holiday dinner. And then, holding her hands, smiling at her, "How did I ever let you go?"

And she would answer, "You had no say in the matter," and he would throw his head back and laugh.

She thought again of the way he'd kept her in his life. The questions he always had for her. About her father, who'd lived well into his nineties. About her piano lessons. About the books she was reading, about her teaching. About what she'd heard from Lucas.

He knew her as no one else did, she thought. She had relied on that. On him.

Too much, too much, she saw now. She'd gone on loving him for too long. He had been too important for her—she hadn't tried, really, to have another life, focused somewhere else.

Now she was remembering something he'd said at a party one night—she couldn't recall where, or how long ago. He was talking to someone—Aaron Lambert, she thought it was—about how impossible it would be for him ever to move away from Cambridge. He'd listed his reasons. The store, she remembered. "I hope I'll be standing at the register, book in hand, and just keel over one day." The house, which he loved and would never leave voluntarily. He'd mentioned a few other things. Then, "My two children, of course." Followed quickly by, "My two wives."

Everyone had burst into laughter. Annie and Frieda had laughed too. At the way he'd exposed himself, she supposed.

Graham had blushed, she remembered that now. In embarrassment? In shame? But then he had laughed too, at himself.

Thinking of this, she was uncomfortable, she shifted on the bed.

It came to her then, almost as a shock: *he had relied on her for too long, too.* Her life at the margins of his marriage to Annie had been something that he wanted, that he had made happen.

He had held her too tight, he had kept her from other possibilities. *The first Mrs. McFarlane.*

Suddenly she was thinking of Annie's misplaced anger at her for what she understood as Frieda's having kept Graham's secret about Rosemary.

But that wasn't the problem, she thought. The problem wasn't that she'd *kept* Graham's secret. It was that she had been *told* Graham's secret.

She shouldn't have been told. He shouldn't have told her things he didn't tell Annie. She shouldn't have been his confidante, his second wife. It wasn't fair to Annie.

It wasn't fair to her.

Her throat tightened.

30

HE'D LOOKED NOTHING like a writer, Annie had thought when she met him. Ian.

She'd spent the afternoon, her first at the colony, out at her studio, unpacking her stuff. It was getting dark when she walked slowly back up the road that led to the main building where they would all gather to have dinner—and where, on the second floor, she had a tiny, monastic bedroom. She stopped several times in the dimming gray light to listen to the rustling noises in the woods on either side of the dirt track, spotting only a chipmunk once, and then, as she rounded a curve in the road, a group of wild turkeys, frightening in their size, in their primitive ugliness. They didn't even bother to hurry away from her, just moved off at the same glacial pace toward the woods, lifting each leg with what seemed like dramatic deliberation, slow-motion monsters.

As she came up the porch stairs, she heard the hubbub of many voices. Earlier in the day, when she'd come to the main building to announce her arrival, there had been one person in the large living room there, reading. He had looked up briefly to answer her question about where the office was.

Now the room was crowded, the noise of the voices almost overwhelming as she opened the door. She hung her coat up and started to try to mix with the others.

There were too many people there for Annie to remember names, but after they were called into the dining room, Ian sat at her table and introduced himself again. He was slender, clean-shaven, pale, with disorderly brown hair. His voice was soft—faintly southern, she thought. (This was wrong, it turned out.) He was handsome in an almost androgynous way. A writer, he said. Fiction.

She said she was a photographer, and he asked about that, about how she would characterize her photographs, about what she planned to work on while she was here.

He spent some time then talking to the woman on his right, Amelie, also a writer. She was beautiful, Annie thought, in a wiry, tense way, her skin tanned a dry, nutmeg brown. She'd "broken the back" of a chapter in her book that day, she said, and for a moment Annie didn't understand what she could possibly mean. But Ian apparently did, and he spoke with enthusiasm about it to her.

Were they a couple? she wondered. It seemed possible. There might be something sparky going on there.

She watched them for a moment, and then turned to talk to the young woman next to her on the other side. Melinda. A painter. She was flippant about her work, nearly every sentence punctuated by a breathless short laugh, a dismissal of whatever it was she'd just said. She was into glazes, she told Annie. She did a lot of still lifes, then glazed them over and over. "Which will get me nowhere, of course." The laugh. "I mean, who even does glazes anymore? Me. Little me. The only one."

But Annie was intrigued. It seemed to her it might be a bit like developing a photograph, the slow changing of the tone and sense of depth that a glaze would create. "I'd love to see them," she said. She and Melinda arranged a time the next afternoon when she could stop by.

She had scattered conversations with others at the table. There was the composer, elderly, originally from Poland. He had an accent so thick that it was hard for Annie to understand most of what he said, but she smiled and tried to respond when it seemed he'd asked her a question. There was a printmaker from San Francisco, and an African guy doing a book on the damaging side effects of international humanitarianism.

After dinner, nearly everyone went back into the big living room, which was divided into two areas. In one, a large fireplace with a big couch and chairs arranged around it. In the other, beyond the couch, a pool table took up most of the space. Melinda was over there, beginning to teach the game to Samuel, the African guy. A group of about six people was milling around, gathering their coats. They were going to a movie in a nearby town, clearly something planned ahead of time. There was another cluster of people settling in around the fireplace, but Annie would have had to ask someone to move over to make room for herself, and she felt a sudden, nearly adolescent sense of social incapacity. She'd go back out to the studio, she thought. Finish organizing things there.

She got her coat and waved goodbye to the room—jauntily, she hoped. When Josh, the printmaker, noticed her, he waved back. Then, just as Annie turned to go, several of the others looked up and called goodbye or waved too. "See you, Annie," Melinda called from the other side of the room. "See you tomorrow."

She was on the dirt road, flashlight in hand, watching the circle of white light dance ahead of her. She was scaring herself a little—the city girl, imagining bears, imagining a vaguer, more ominous animal life—when she heard footsteps behind her. Running. She turned. A man.

"Hey," the figure said. She flicked her light up, to his face, and he lifted his arm to shield his eyes. It was Ian.

What she remembered their talking about that night—he'd invited her to his studio, where he had a bottle of wine and some glasses—was mostly work. Though he also offered her information on some of the other residents. "Campers," he called them. He'd been there for almost a month, and he knew everyone pretty well. He had another month to go.

"Two months!" she said. "I'm only here for three weeks myself. Any longer, and my husband would shoot me." (Why had she been so quick to bring it up, the fact that she was married?)

Ian was squatting by the fireplace now, trying to start a fire—balling up newspaper, jamming more in under the kindling each time the paper fire dwindled. Annie watched him for a minute. She felt conspicuously useless. She began to move around the room, looking at everything. There was an old wooden desk in front of the windows, a typewriter on it. Next to it were several stacks of paper, covered with print that had been scribbled over in ink here and there. The room had unfinished wood walls, walls that were studded with Post-its, a line or two on each in the same nearly indecipherable longhand. "Isaac needs to be more comfortable with himself." "Changes in the scene with Ruby—she's the angry one."

"*There* we go," Ian said, and she turned. The fire had caught. He gestured for her to take the armchair set by the fireplace, and he pulled his desk chair over on the other side of the hearth. They sat in silence for a moment, a moment that stretched out too long. Annie was aware of the noises of the fire. They both started to speak at once, they both said, "You . . . ," and then both stopped.

He smiled and said, "Okay. Really: *you.*"

She made *comments* then, as she thought of it later. How little stuff he required for his work—gesturing at the desk. How it was just a matter of him and the paper and the typewriter. "That must be so lovely," she said.

"Yes. *Lovely*," he said, exaggerating the word. "I don't usually think of it that way, but there it is."

She began dramatically listing everything she'd brought with her, all the equipment.

He seemed to be amused, sitting, listening.

The fire popped, noisily, and little embers jumped onto the outer hearth.

Why was she going on and on? Annie thought. It occurred to her that she didn't know how to be alone with a man anymore.

Or maybe not exactly that. She was fine with male friends, with the writers and photographers she knew. With other women's husbands. She was thinking she'd be fine, she'd be comfortable with Ian, if they were both single, if sex were going to be a possibility. There was just something anomalous about this situation in her life—not knowing what the possibilities here were. Or weren't.

Were there possibilities?

In the next silence she said, "Why did you ask me here?"

He raised his eyebrows. "Oh! Well, I guess I supposed you might like some company on your first night." He smiled. A slight smile, though. "You don't have to stay, you know. I like sitting by the fire perfectly well on my own."

"No, I *do* like the company."

"Well, I'm glad then. Glad I asked." He was still holding the poker he'd used earlier to push the paper under the kindling. Now he leaned forward and nudged one of the logs back with it. "You seemed . . . lonely. You seemed *new*, in any case. I suppose I feel like the old hand."

"A welcoming committee of one," she said.

"Yes," he said.

A silence accrued again. She was more comfortable in it. Still, she was the one who broke it. "What are you writing about?" she asked.

"Oh, it's not interesting to describe it."

"I'm interested, though."

He waited a moment, and then he said, "A marriage."

"That could be anything. It could be . . . Henry James. It could be Updike."

So he explained it to her. An older man. A younger woman—a

divorcée, with a little boy. He knows almost right away that the marriage is a mistake for him, but he has come to love the boy, so he does nothing about it. The woman understands this finally, and is wildly angry. "She starts to lead her life more and more away from him, away from the child. And finally she leaves, but she leaves the child with him."

Annie was thinking of Lucas, the little boy she loved. The boy who already had a mother.

"Is it a happy ending, then?"

"I suppose you could call it that, if you felt it was."

"But do you?"

He shrugged.

"Ah, you're impossible." She laughed.

"Well, you asked what it was about, and I told you. I told you, basically, the plot. But I don't want to tell you what I think it's most deeply about, or what *you're* supposed to think about what it's about. That's something I can't control anyway."

She said, "It's about Isaac and Ruby."

"That's it. The boy and the girl. Same old, same old." They were quiet for a moment, and then he said, "Now you have to tell me what your work is about."

"Ah! It's even harder for a photographer, saying what it's *about*. What you see is what you get."

"And what would I see?"

Annie had just started to work from the negatives of the images she'd taken of her mother then, most of them of her face. She was, as she put it now to Ian, going to fool around with what she wanted from these shots. "*Then* I'll know what they're about."

Annie had been angry with Graham when she left for MacDowell. It was at a time in her life when she wanted to move to New York. What she said to Graham was that she thought it would help her professionally, she thought it would be a more sympathetic place for a person like her. And she was tired, she said, of Cambridge.

This was before they bought the house, before she had Sarah. And it was after her first show did so well, when she had thought that this meant that all the shows would do well—all the future shows—and that her life would change as a result, she would *belong* in New York. She said this to Graham. "I think New York would be a much better place for me. For my work."

But her tone when she spoke was deliberately careless—so careless that Graham must have thought it was just a kind of daydream she was talking about, a sort of joke.

"Yes, isn't it pretty to think so?" he said. Then he laughed.

Annie's plan had been to ask him to consider her idea while she was away at MacDowell, and his response felt like being slapped—so that by the time he understood how serious she'd been, the damage was done. She had turned away from him, wounded and furious. When he offered his real objections, having to do with Lucas, with Frieda, having to do with the bookstore, having to do with the impossibility of starting up all over again in Manhattan, she was unable to summon any sympathy for his point of view. He seemed to her, suddenly, small-minded. Everything he did, his *pleasure* in everything he did, was offensive to her. Unbearable. Only later did it occur to her that her proposal to him, taken seriously, would have felt like a dismissal of his whole life and what he'd made of it.

At the moment, though, she wasn't capable of thinking about how she had sounded. She felt, listening to him, that she was hearing doors shutting, that she was understanding, for the first time, how confined his life was. Confined by the small size of his ambition, and by his actual enjoyment of all of his familiar, repetitive routines.

And that meant that her life was confined too. The fears she'd overcome to be with him, the fears of being eaten by him, absorbed by him, by his appetites, seemed suddenly confirmed.

"Annie," he said, his voice serious now. "We settled on this, long ago."

"We settled *for* this," she said.

There was a moment of silence between them. They were looking at each other, hard.

"You know there's such a thing as money, right?" he said, finally. "There's no way we could even begin to swing it."

They had a chilly month and a half, and then Annie went off alone to MacDowell.

After that first glass of wine in his studio, Annie and Ian began to seek each other out. It started a few days later when Ian asked her at breakfast if he could hitch a ride with her to town, to Peterborough. He didn't have a car here, and he needed a few groceries for his studio. To make it worth her while, he'd buy her coffee. Or a drink. Whatever she liked. So they went into town together and walked around, looking at shop windows, looking at houses and gardens, and then they sat and had coffee at a lunch place.

Ian had a slow way of talking. He seemed to her at first quiet, almost inexpressive, accustomed as she was to Graham's exuberant assertiveness.

What was the affinity, then? There was one, and they both felt it, it seemed. After that first afternoon together, they often sat next to each other at dinner. They fell into the habit of walking back to their studios together after breakfast. Occasionally they met in the afternoons and walked around the grounds, or took long drives in Annie's van, weaving through small towns in northern Massachusetts or western New Hampshire. Sometimes they listened to music together in the building called the library.

They touched each other carefully, Annie's hand on his arm, on his shoulder, calling attention to something she wanted him to see. His arm across her shoulder, guiding her across a street, or into a bar. It felt a bit like high school, she thought. But thrilling, in that same way.

There were several parties while she was there, parties in other people's studios. They danced together a few times at these parties, and she was intensely aware of his body, so slender and muscled against her, his hands on her back so strong, so in control of how they moved.

She recognized that something was happening between them. That she wanted something to happen. And didn't, too. But she allowed herself to have fantasies about it—about an escape from her life with Graham. About an affair. She told herself this was all right, because she wasn't going to do anything about it. It was just a way of adjusting the balance between them, between her and Graham.

Though she didn't think of it then, she realized later that it was a kind of *revenge* she was exacting. A private revenge. One Graham didn't need to know about.

Late in the afternoon four or five days before she was to leave, she was startled by a knocking on her studio door. When she opened it, Ian was standing there in the cool, damp air under the little roof that protected the doorway. Behind him, droplets from the eaves fell, a kind of silvery scrim. All around was the rustle of light rain landing on the carpet of bright leaves that covered the ground everywhere.

"Oh, no," she said, already shaking her head. "No, no, no, no, no. You're not here. You're can't be here." This was the rule of the colony. No one arrived at anyone else's workplace without a specific invitation.

"On the other hand, I *am* here."

He waited for a moment, as if for her answer. When it didn't come, he said, "I think you know why."

Annie looked away, as if she were ashamed. "I do," she said. Then back at him. "But . . . I just can't." She shook her head. "This is not something I can do."

"Just let me in," he said. "We can talk about it."

"I don't want to talk about it."

"We can talk about something else, then. Anything you like."

So she let him in. For a while, they did talk. He sat slouched in the only chair in the room, his long legs stretched out in front of him. She was propped up against the pillows on the daybed she'd napped on sometimes in the afternoons. Photos she'd developed of her mother's face were everywhere on the walls, looking blankly down at them.

She'd turned the lights off when he came in, in case someone should pass by on the dirt road, out for a walk in the rain. The day was dark anyway, and with the lights off, the big room was shadowed—though outside, the yellow leaves of the birch trees that surrounded the studio seemed nearly to glow against the deep green of the pines.

Ian talked about himself. He hadn't before, not really. What she'd learned about his life were just odd, unconnected facts she'd had trouble fitting together. Now he spoke of living in New England for a while as a young man, having come to college from Phoenix. "It might as well have been another country," he said. He spoke slowly, as always. Sometimes there was a long pause between sentences, but Annie was used to this by now. She'd learned to wait for him.

He'd gone back to Arizona to try to make a life there when he was through with college. He'd lasted about five years, he said, the whole time missing the East. "Especially this time of year. The town greens, the leaves, the white houses." He'd yearned for it, he said. Even for the women, who seemed to him as different here as every-thing else was.

"So I came back. Tried the Vermont life, along with the other thousands. Everyone who wasn't in . . . Copenhagen. Or Marra-kech." He seemed to be smiling. "San Francisco." He nodded, several times. "I actually got married. Which turned out to be a great mistake. And when it all ended, I felt exiled. From Arizona. From New England. So I went where everybody goes to escape where they're from."

"That being New York?"

"Yes."

She could hardly see his face, the shadows in the studio had deepened so.

"It's just about killing me to be here again." His voice hitched, and she realized that he was weeping.

"Oh, Ian," she said. "Why don't you come over here?" She patted the bed.

He came and lay down next to her, directing her with his hands to make room for him. Then to slide down and lie beside him.

"You know I can't do this," she said again.

He was turned to her. "We're talking. I'm crying. You can do this."

They did talk some more. But then, of course, as she had known would happen, they began to touch each other. His hands slid along her back, and in response, she held him too. She was almost trembling, his bones under the flesh felt so different from Graham.

Then he was moving over her, moving onto her. His hands started to slide under her sweater, and she stopped them. They moved to the waistband of her jeans, and she stopped them. But her body kept responding to him, rising up to him, moving in what felt to her like slow waves that didn't seem stoppable. She became aware that he was moving too, slowly at first, and then more definitively, moving toward a climax.

Which happened, quietly, a final tightening of all his muscles as he pressed against her, several catches in his breathing, then a long exhalation, and the gradual easing of all the tension, his weight sinking fully onto her. They lay in each other's arms, loosely. Then he slid off her. She turned toward him. In the dim light, she could see the tightening of his mouth, the slight twisting that meant he was smiling.

After a few moments, he cleared his throat. He said, "This is not a grown-up thing to be doing." She heard in his voice that he was still smiling.

"Yet you did it," she answered.

"Oh, but you did it too," he said. They were speaking softly, as if there were someone nearby who might hear them. After a minute, he said, "I feel like a teenager. And I don't mean that in a good way."

She laughed, a quick, small sound.

"Actually," he said, "it *was* sort of fun. In its way." After a moment, "Anyhow, it's always nice, isn't it?"

"Always?" she whispered. "You do this a lot?"

He laughed. "No, I don't. I never do this." He pulled his head back, to look at her. "Who would do *this*?" Then he relaxed again. He spoke close to her ear. "No, what I mean is just *coming*. Coming is nice. That release. And actually, there was a sweet quality to this particular one, I thought." She couldn't tell if he was serious. After a moment he said: "Sticky, though," and she could hear that he wasn't.

"I suppose." She turned onto her back. "Of course, I didn't have that 'sweet release.'" She emphasized the words, making fun of him.

He reached for her. "I'd be only too happy to—"

"No. No, really, I can't." And felt how odd it was to say that, how different from everything she'd understood as her own sexuality.

After Ian left ("I suppose we should show up separately for dinner, yes?") she lay on the bed for a while, watching the dark gather around her studio, thinking about what had just happened. And then about Graham, about the first time she'd had sex with him.

There were only four days left in Annie's stay after they lay down together. They talked as much during these days, sitting in a corner of the big main room, or having some wine in the library after someone's reading, but they seemed to be trying not to be alone together. At least Annie felt it was mutual. They seemed, she thought, to be acting out a kind of sweet, stupid *companionship*, as though their attraction to each other had become a kind of joke they shared.

It occurred to her only much later that he might have lost interest when it was clear that they weren't going to fuck. That he was perhaps being only polite after that, while basically waiting for her to leave so he could try his luck with someone else. She'd heard about people like that at artists' colonies. Serial romancers for whom the assembled writers and artists were just so many opportunities.

In any case, it was easy enough not to be alone. There were always people around, and she had come to know some of them, to like some of them. Melinda, the painter, had left after Annie's second week, but she'd grown close to a sociologist named Gertie Grant, who was writing a history of federal housing policy and its impact on the black community, "For a general audience," she said. "And all that really means is that I'm hoping for some dough with this one."

Gertie walked into the main building one afternoon about an hour before dinner to find Annie and Ian sitting together in front of the fireplace. They'd been talking, but they stopped when she came into the room. She stood frowning at them both for a long moment. She said, "What *is* it with you guys?" Gertie was tall and of ambiguous sexuality, with a pug face, everything a little bit flattened-looking. Still, there was something appealing about her.

"There is nothing with us," Ian said. "We were happily alone here, until you arrived."

As seemed to be the tradition, at least in the group at the colony while Annie was there, on her last night she had a party in her studio. She had resolved that she wouldn't let Ian stay on with her afterward, but it seemed he must have resolved it too—he left with the last group to go, stopping to hold her face in his hands on the front stoop, to turn it and gently kiss each cheek.

She was disappointed, in spite of her resolve. She was also a bit drunk. She sat down on the edge of her daybed and messily cried for a few minutes before she started to pick up the room.

He wasn't at breakfast the next day, but he'd left a note in her mailbox. Since she didn't check the mailbox before she left, though, the note came forwarded to her at home after about ten days. She was back in the routines of her life by then, but not so much so that the thought of Ian had begun to seem as unlikely to her as it did later on.

You almost broke my heart, Annie. And you could have, if you'd wanted to.
I'll hold all this time close to me.
Ian

One day, months later, when it felt safe to her, when the time with Ian had already begun to fade, she asked Graham if he'd ever read anything by Ian Pedersen.

Oh yes, he said. He had. He'd read both of the novels, and he thought they were first-rate. Why did she ask?

She was using a neutral, tempered voice, in spite of the perverse excitement she felt. She tried to make it no different from the voice in which she would have discussed any other writer. "Oh, he was at MacDowell when I was there, and I just wondered what you might think of him. Of his work, I mean. I thought I might try him."

Graham was looking at her, curiously, she thought. "Well, that's what I think," he said. "Of his work."

As he turned away, she had the sense that she'd betrayed him more with what she'd just done than with anything that had happened at MacDowell.

31

SINCE THE DAY on Thanksgiving weekend when Lucas had first brought up Ian's name, Annie had thought of him and of her time with him at MacDowell often. She mentioned him in an email to Gertie, the one friend from MacDowell she'd kept up with. Gertie lived in California, but whenever she was in New York, Annie tried to go down to see her.

In her email, she told Gertie that Ian—"Remember Ian Pedersen?"—had another book coming out after all these years, and by an amazing coincidence, her stepson Lucas was his editor.

Well, Gertie wrote. *Here it is, your unencumbered chance to pick up where you left off.*

We were just friends. That's where we left off.

Har, har. So you say. So you said then. But none of us believed you.

So I say now. And who's this "us," as in "none of us"?

Did you not know you were the object—or is it the subject?—of gossip? We were all sure you were fucking.

Well, we weren't! she typed.

But then, startled by her own quickness to respond, to respond so emphatically, she began to think about it, her afternoon with Ian, remembering it more and more clearly through that day, through the next few days. The visual images arrived first—the silver drops falling behind his dark shape on the porch. The golden light on the leaves of the birch trees. The deepening twilight inside the studio as they talked.

And then the other details. ("Sticky," he'd said.)

It came to her that the difference between fucking and what they'd done was what Graham might have called "pretty technical."

How ridiculous, then, her prideful response to Gertie! In fact, the whole thing slowly began to seem laughable to her. And as her memory of the events sharpened, she recognized that over the years she'd created a particularly self-forgiving version of it for herself. That she'd been attracted to Ian, but had said no. It's what she had confessed to Graham much later, *her noble, noble confession.* It's what she had told Edith. And wasn't it essentially what she'd said Thanksgiving weekend to Sarah, too? *A sweet flirtation that hadn't meant anything.* Something like that.

But now she was remembering more and more her own part in it. How exciting the slender, muscled quality of his body had felt to her when they danced, when they lay down together, the *otherness* of it. She remembered, with a sense of surprise, that she had argued with herself about whether or not to sleep with him over the days that preceded the rainy afternoon.

She remembered the last night she saw him, wanting him to stay with her. Not wanting it. But really, wanting it. Crying when he left.

She remembered too asking her question of Graham those months later—the question about Ian's books, and the sense she had immediately afterward of having done something wrong to Graham.

In late January, Lucas emailed Annie to say that Ian Pedersen was going to be reading at the bookstore. *Just FYI,* he wrote. *No need for you to go. I didn't mention anything about you to him. But just in case you want to see what "really old" looks like . . .*

Then the postscript: *The book, by the way, is doing okay. Not quite as okay as we had hoped. But then that never happens.*

At first she didn't plan on going. She had no wish to confront the version of herself that had been interested in Ian. *Interested in Ian because she'd been furious at Graham.* She had remembered that detail also—her anger.

Which brought with it its own humiliation when she recalled the reasons for it: she'd been so sure that her life was moving in a different direction from Graham's, that he was *holding her back.* (It was at this point that it occurred to her that she might have thought of Ian at the time as a handy instrument of revenge. Admittedly a strange, private revenge. One she wouldn't reveal to Graham. But was that part of the *affinity* between them, then? The use she might make of Ian in her anger at Graham?)

She suspected that Lucas was at least in part just trying to get her out of the house when he wrote to her about the reading. It seemed her friends took turns at this. But she reminded herself now that there had been also increasingly the sounding out of her possible readiness to meet someone. The odd tentative suggestion. Perhaps someone's widowed brother? (This from Edith.) Or divorced friend? (Don.)

Her *no* to these invitations had been automatic, but now, with Lucas's quasi-invitation, she began to consider it. And in the end, she decided she would go. Go, to see how Ian had weathered the years—she recognized her curiosity about that. Go, to see how she might respond to whatever the new version of Ian would be, without the complication of being married to Graham. It had been long enough, after all. It would have been long enough even without Graham's affair with Rosemary, but perhaps that gave her a more powerful permission.

Why not? she thought.

Why not?

And maybe he'd have no memory of her. Fine. She was curious, anyway—or at least interested—to hear him read what Lucas had admired so, to buy the book.

And if he did remember her, if he was interested in her, they might have a brief conversation. That was probably the most likely outcome. A brief conversation.

But even that she looked forward to, she realized. An evening out, a conversation with a probably perfectly safe man. Any other possibilities seemed unlikely, and she tried not to let herself entertain them.

Annie was sure she'd be late. Just as she was leaving the house, she remembered that the cat was outside. She went onto the back stoop and called and called, her breath pluming thick and white in the light over the back door, but Sam didn't turn up.

She didn't really worry about his wandering. He had disappeared occasionally before, but he never went far from the yard—he hadn't in Karen's day either. Still, it would be a long time for him to be out on a cold night. She felt bad about leaving.

And then she felt anxious because she was going to be late, which made her realize how much she'd been looking forward to this evening, to seeing Ian again. She hadn't fully acknowledged that to herself, she understood now, walking too fast to the bookstore over the icy sidewalks. She was breathless and frazzled by the time she arrived—a bit early, after all. She bought the book, she went to the open area for readings at the back of the store to find a seat.

There was a decent audience, Graham would have said.

Disappointing, Lucas would have said.

But the new owners (she'd met them, Sid and Olympia, a youngish couple) were as smart as Graham had always been about the number of chairs set up—never as many as you suspected you might need, in case it turned out you *didn't* need them and the place wound up feeling disappointingly underpopulated.

In this case they'd set up about ten rather narrow rows, rows that were already about two-thirds full when she arrived. She waved to a couple of people she thought of as "Graham's writers," and sat near the middle, in a row with two or three empty seats.

Something about the store felt different to her. She had the sense that things had been rearranged somehow since she'd last been here. She looked around, but she couldn't quite figure it out—what the difference was. It was a bit disorienting, so she stopped trying. She took off her coat. She opened the book to the back flap to look at the author photograph.

She wouldn't have recognized him. His hair was white and cut close to his head, which made him look quite *other*. Tougher, she thought. None of that androgyny stuff anymore. She read the short bio, then the acknowledgments, then the dedication. There was nothing that signified *wife* to her, or even *lover*.

She felt self-conscious, suddenly. Foolish. She shut the book.

The rows had almost filled, and now a couple of store workers were setting up more chairs, the metal clanging and clattering. She watched the people arrive, and she waited.

At about five past the hour, Sid, the new owner, moved up to the podium, trailed by a tall, lanky man—the new, white-haired version of Ian. Sid welcomed people and read through the announcements of upcoming events. He had none of the palpable energy and enthusiasm Graham had brought to this task—the asides, the jokes. She thought of the way he used to worry before each of these evenings. Then his happy, busy hosting of things once they got started.

Sid introduced Ian. She'd been watching him the whole time. He looked the same in some ways—in many ways. His face was lined, she could see that even from where she was sitting, but it was lined kindly, gently, as if a faint netting had been set evenly over his features. He was dressed a bit like a cowboy (jeans, boots) but then wearing what looked almost like a woman's shirt—white, slightly belled, no collar—and over that, a brown tweed jacket so old it was almost shapeless. He'd grown a mustache, which enhanced the cowboy look. (She remembered then how contemptuous Graham had been of mustaches when they came into vogue in the 1980s. He thought they signaled an absurd kind of vanity. Well, what about the mustache and beard upon his own face? she'd asked him. Completely different, he said. This was the way facial hair was *meant* to grow. A mustache by itself—he'd shaken his head pityingly—was an *artifice*.)

She'd forgotten Ian's voice, how soft it was, how gentle. "Can you hear me?" he asked, and almost everyone more than three rows back called out "No!" in a ragged chorus.

He adjusted the mike so it was closer to his mouth. "Better?" he asked.

A more organized chorus this time. "Yes!"

He began. No introduction, no explanation of inspiration, of *process*, as it was called in this universe. He read for about twenty-five minutes. As Lucas had promised, the story was a boy's, told in a voice that combined the boy's and the grown man's perspectives, moving easily between the two.

In the section Ian was reading from—the very beginning of the book—the boy explained his father, a patient, disciplined man, the editor of the only newspaper in a town of about five thousand people in Arizona. A man who would listen to you, question you patiently, even when you'd done something foolish or just plain wrong. Who'd want to hear your explanation for your behavior. Who always assumed you would have one. "Nothing made me angrier at him than that quality of my father's," Ian read. "His unforgivable readiness to understand me, to see me as a rational human being."

This first chapter set up the tension and foreshadowed the way the conflict between the two, father and son, would play out. The boy, driven to wilder and wilder misdeeds; the kind, slightly abstracted father willing to find a reason to forgive the son every time; the mental instability of the mother obviously the battlefield on which the conflict would play out. It was quiet, a bit slow, and entirely compelling to Annie.

There was generous applause after Ian closed the book. He took off his glasses and lifted his face to the audience. She remembered again the way it had looked the afternoon they lay down together.

"I'll take questions," he said.

There was the usual awkward pause before they began, but finally someone about three rows back raised her hand: How much of what he had read was autobiographical?

"Pure invention, all of it!" he said, smiling. Cue the laughs.

The smile made him more recognizable, the pursing of the lips first, their slight twist sideways. He was an old pro, she thought. And clearly enjoying himself.

Why the silence of so many years?

"You'd have to ask that question of any number of unreasonably picky publishers."

It was hard for Annie to figure out what to make of this. Some people laughed, but she thought there might be a bitter quality to Ian's voice.

What were his writing habits? someone else asked, perhaps intending to change the subject.

"Diurnal," he said, and turned to point to another raised hand.

There was a series of familiar questions then, ones Annie had heard many times at other readings she'd come to—they didn't seem to change much over the years. *How did you get started? When did you know you were a writer? How much does* place *figure in your work? What kind of research do you do for each novel?* Ian's responses were more interesting than the questions, but they also seemed familiar.

Someone asked once more about his long silence. He paused for a moment, as if making a decision about how to respond. Then he began again, differently this time. While he was speaking, the humor fell away, and she heard clearly the anger he'd masked with his first, joking response—which had been the one he was used to offering, she supposed.

He spoke of his years "out in the cold," as he put it, starting with his third novel. There'd been a crappy review in the *Sunday Times* of this book, "possibly my strongest novel to date at that point," he said. Then they piled on, the reviewers. Some of the later reviews actually echoed the language of the first one. He paused and smiled, a mocking smile. "Apparently a case of monkey see, monkey do," he said.

He went on. His publishers backed away from him—they dropped him, dropped the book. No ads, no pushing it. Several radio interviews that would have made a big difference were canceled. "Let's just call it a clusterfuck, pardon my language." But as a result of all this "bad faith," he said, the book didn't sell. "And that follows you around," he said. "It makes everything harder.

"Plus, it didn't help to be a white man either at that particular point in time. I actually had someone say to me that if my fourth book—my very unpublished fourth book—had been written by a woman, almost any house would have taken it."

There was an uncomfortably long wait, and then another hand went up. What effect did all this have on his writing?

"On the writing itself, I don't know." Then he shrugged, and his face changed. The charming half smile returned. "But who knows? It might have been useful to me personally, in the end."

How, useful?

"Well, it brought me to my knees. And that is always useful, for a person like me."

"What kind of person is that?" someone in back called out.

The audience laughed, a bit uneasily. Was this too intimate a question?

"An arrogant son of a bitch." He offered the smile again. "Or so I've been told."

There were a few more questions, and then a silence. No hand went up to break it. Stepping back, he nodded his head several times. "Okay," he said. "I'm here to sign." As the applause rang around the room, he opened a questioning hand out toward Sid, who had been standing behind him while he read, leaning against a bookcase.

Sid directed him to the table off to the side of the space the podium was set in. Ian sat down, and people began to rise from their seats and move slowly toward the ends of their rows. A line started to form in the aisle, a line that shuffled and shambled and then pulled itself into a kind of disorderly order, winding around the side of the rows of chairs and beginning to move very slowly forward, toward where Ian was seated now.

Annie was standing with the others in her row, waiting to move toward the aisle. She was watching Ian, who was looking out over the room as the line formed, perhaps counting the house. For a moment, their eyes met.

He recognized her. Or at any rate he was trying to place her— she could see that: the frown, the mouth that opened, just slightly. But then he turned away to look at the first person standing by the table, holding out her book to him.

Annie inched forward toward the aisle end of her row, looking over several more times at Ian. He was mostly engaged in conversation or looking down to inscribe a book, but their eyes met again once and he smiled his ironic smile and nodded several times, as if to say yes, he recognized her. Yes, he was waiting for her. She was aware of standing up straighter, of a kind of pleasant breathlessness.

As she reached the aisle and turned toward the table where Ian waited, she saw that Olympia, Sid's freckled, redheaded wife, was standing at that side of the room, asking for the correct spelling of people's names and writing this down on Post-its that she handed to them to affix to the front of their books, a time-saving courtesy to the author that Graham had always insisted on too. Olympia looked up and smiled as Annie reached her. "You don't need to tell me *your* name," she said to Annie, and wrote it down. As Olympia handed over the slip of paper, Annie felt someone grip her arm. She turned. It was Bill, skinny, gray-haired, ever the same. He leaned forward and hugged her quickly, shyly. "It's so good to see you here," he said. "You should come more often."

"I know. And maybe I will once the weather makes it a bit easier."

"Yeah, this is always a tough month," he said. They talked for a few minutes more, Bill moving forward along with her, and then he said he had to get back to the front desk. Annie reached up to hug him, to kiss his cheek before she stepped away.

She finally reached the table and stood waiting while the couple in front of her finished talking with Ian. As they moved on, Ian looked up and saw Annie. He stood quickly, reaching his hands across the table to take both of hers. Awkwardly, she set the book down to let this happen.

"God, it's *so* good—it's just amazing!—to see you again," he said. He leaned toward her to touch his cheek momentarily to hers on one side and then the other.

"It is," she was saying. "It's wonderful to see you, too."

He kept standing for a moment, looking at her, grinning. "I recognized you right away," he said. His mouth twisted slightly. "'Across a crowded room.'"

He sat down, sliding her book toward him while he looked up at her. "You live near here?"

Yes, she said. A couple of blocks.

He smiled at her for a moment, nodding his head slowly. He said, "It was Yaddo, wasn't it?"

"Almost Yaddo," she said, smiling back. "MacDowell."

"Right. Right. Right." He nodded several times again. "But I mean, Christ! How many *years* ago was it?"

"Maybe thirty?" she said. "Shockingly enough. Since we're both so young."

He laughed. He shook his head then and said, "It's just so fucking good to see you, Annie."

She smiled back at him. "And you," she said.

He took the Post-it off the book and opened it to sign. "Just your name is fine," she said, and he signed it quickly—illegibly, she noted. A big scribble. They talked for a minute or two more, Annie increasingly aware of all the people behind her. Remembering it later, she wasn't even sure what they had said, but she was waiting through it anyway, waiting for him to say what he did then.

"Look, Annie," leaning toward her, lowering his voice. "Why don't we get a drink somewhere when I'm done here?" He was holding the book out to her. "It'd be nice to take a break from the never-ending enforced politeness of the book tour. That's hard to sustain for someone like me." He grinned again. "Plus I'd love to catch up."

Annie looked over at the long line. "You won't be done here for a while," she said. "Maybe we could meet somewhere close by?"

That sounded excellent, he said, and she suggested the bar in the restaurant of the Charles Hotel, a couple of blocks away. "It's a nice bar. Quiet. Come up the staircase from the lobby. It's easy to find."

Before she'd even turned to go, the man behind her was pushing his book across at Ian, asking if he could inscribe it to a friend.

Outside, the bricks were wet and whited with the salty residue of the snow. The shoveled hillocks stood at the edge of the sidewalk, stained here and there with dog piss. Annie walked slowly, thinking about Ian, about how this might go. She was, she would have said to anyone who asked, excited. But also anxious. Maybe a bit scared.

Well, she would see, she thought. And if things weren't going well, if things were awkward or difficult somehow, she had an excuse ready—that she couldn't stay too long, on account of the cat.

But what if things were going well?

She could offer him a drink at her house, of course. The cat could be useful in that case too—*she needed to get home to let him in.* It wouldn't be hard to invite Ian to come with her.

Inside the hotel, the ground-floor lobby was almost empty. She mounted the wide, carpeted stairs and went into the bar. She could hear the hubbub of conversation from around the corner, where the restaurant opened out. The bar was quieter—there were only two tables occupied out here, one by a couple, the other by a solitary man. Japanese, she thought, in an expensive-looking suit, having his dinner. The wall of windows behind him looked out on the vast, empty courtyard, the only light out there the tiny white bulbs wrapped around the trees, leftover Christmas decorations.

She ordered a whiskey, rocks on the side. When the drink came, she sat sipping it and looking out at the dark night, at the twinkly lights.

Then Ian was there, at the top of the stairs, glancing quickly around to see which way to go. He saw her and grinned. Even as he threaded his way around the unoccupied tables, he was smiling at her.

He leaned forward and touched her cheeks with his again before he sat down opposite her. He was glad she'd already ordered for herself, he said, and turned to signal the waiter. He asked for a beer.

While they waited, they expressed amazement once more. He asked about the guy she'd been talking to in the line. Oh, an old, old friend of hers and her husband's, she said. He worked in the store.

Oh, yes. He remembered: she was married. And he smiled again, his minimal, sly smile.

"I was," she said. "I'm a widow now," she said, surprising herself.

Clearly surprising him too. His face changed. "Oh, I'm really sorry."

Had she wanted to do that? To startle him? To catch him off guard? Was she using Graham, Graham's dying, for that?

"Well, it's been a while," she said.

"Still . . . ," he said. He talked about his divorce then. "Not that it's comparable in any way." He'd gone into a funk, he said. "Technically, I suppose, a depression." He'd stopped writing for a while. He described his slow recovery, the sense he had of returning to his work changed, strengthened in some way.

His beer came, and he raised his glass. "To . . . reunions, let's say."

She raised her glass too, and they clicked them together over the table.

They talked about the reading then. She said how much she'd enjoyed it. He talked about the difficulty of choosing a passage to read, he described a couple of the possibilities he'd rejected, and explained why. She asked about the book tour—how long? Where? How was it going?

He spoke easily of the various cities he'd already been to. The bookstores. The size of the audience. Where he was going next. How long he'd be "on the road," as he called it.

He was enjoying it, he said. He'd done almost nothing for his earlier books, so this felt like an opportunity. "To, you know, give it a boost if I can. And of course, given the isolation of the work I do, 'the solitary life of the writer'"—he'd made his voice pompous— "it's kind of a treat, really. To be out and about." He looked at her and then smiled, leaning forward toward her over the table. "But you must understand that—you live the solitary life too. You're a painter, am I remembering that right?"

She had a quick small shock at his mistake. But then it seemed reasonable, it was so long ago. "You're in the realm anyway," she said. "The visual arts. I'm a photographer."

"Ach!" he said, and hit his temple lightly with the heel of his hand. "The old errant brain." He smiled. "Do you find it happens more and more to you, too?"

They talked about it for a while, a conversation she'd jokingly had with various acquaintances. The familiar litany of forgetfulness— where had you parked the car? why had you come into this room? what was the name, goddammit, of this very person you were exchanging pleasantries with? where had you left your glasses?

They laughed. They moved on. He spoke of his sense that he had one more book in him, and as part of that discussion, she learned his age—seventy-four. He said he had a wonderful young editor— "Young to me, anyway"—and that this guy had given him hope, at long last, for his future in the publishing world.

They were quiet for a few seconds. It seemed too long to Annie. She said, "I have a coincidence for you."

"Good. I love coincidences. I'm a writer, after all."

"Meaning?"

"Meaning, what would we do without them—coincidences— those of us trying to make fiction?"

"But they're useful in life too, aren't they?" she said. "Or interest- ing anyway."

"Yes, they are. Sometimes very interesting. This evening being a prime example."

She felt shy suddenly. She sensed she was blushing. "Well, I hope you'll love this one too," she said. "This coincidence. It has to do with Lucas."

"Lucas." He looked puzzled. "Lucas McFarlane?"

"Yes. I'll give you a hint," she said. "It's my name, too. McFarlane."

It was only now that it occurred to her, with a little jolt, that this might have been something he would have noticed when he first met Lucas—if he'd remembered her name from MacDowell.

It might even have been something he would have asked her about earlier this evening, she thought. If he'd remembered that.

"God, that is amazing!" he said.

She was silent, feeling suddenly unsure of what he might have recalled about her, what he might not. Finally she said, "And that's the least of it." She could hear the change in her own voice.

After a moment, he said, "Am I supposed to guess?" He tilted his head, a faint smile playing on his lips.

She smiled back. It's okay, she thought. It's going to be okay. She said, "No. You wouldn't be able to, I don't think." She lifted her shoulders, her hands. "It's that he's my stepson. Lucas is. My husband's son. By a first marriage."

"Jesus!" he said. His face was openly surprised.

"I know," she said. "We figured out the connection, that you were a writer of his, at Thanksgiving, actually, and it was exactly that surprising to me, too." She sipped at her whiskey. "I think *I* said 'Jesus,' too." She laughed, lightly.

"God!" He shook his head slowly. "Unbelievable!"

They sat in silence for a long moment. He grinned at her. "Well, I guess I'll be smiling at Lucas a lot more than I used to."

"He'll enjoy that, of course."

He was quiet again. Then he said, "But it's a bit embarrassing, really."

"Is it?"

"Isn't it?"

"Why would it be?" Annie asked.

"Well, what I imagine is that now, when I look at him, I'll be thinking of you."

"That wouldn't be so awful, would it?"

"No, not at all, not at all." He sipped at his beer again. Setting it down, he grinned at her. "God, some of those nights in your studio . . ." He shook his head. "Pretty damn memorable. All of them were, actually, those nights. It was . . . an amazing couple of weeks, wasn't it?" He leaned across the table toward her, his soft voice a kind of beckon to intimacy. "That was one residency I was sorry to see the end of."

Annie felt an almost physical recoil. He was thinking of someone else, obviously. The painter, perhaps.

And then it occurred to her: maybe not even the painter. Maybe one of any number of other people, other possibilities. As she had been: a possibility. A possibility that hadn't quite panned out, certainly not in the way the person he was remembering had.

She didn't know what to say. Her breath was coming short. He was watching her steadily, ready to smile again. "There was only one," she said quietly.

"One what?"

"Night," she said. "And actually it was an afternoon."

His face changed. Maybe it was coming back to him, the difference between the person he was sitting across from now, and whoever it was he'd spent all those memorable nights with.

"Hnn!" he said. "I . . . I didn't remember that."

"No," she said.

They sat in silence for a few long moments.

"Another brain fry, I guess," he said, and tried smiling at her.

"Yes," she said.

The waiter passed by just then, and she signaled him for the check, making an imaginary mark in the air.

"Hey, you don't need to . . ." He reached across the table to her.

"No, no, I do, I need to go. I actually . . . my cat is outside, and I ought to get him in. I was in such a rush to . . . to get to the reading, that I couldn't wait for him. The cat." Never had the truth sounded more like a lie, she thought.

"Well." They sat for a moment. He smiled at her again, a smile that was a lie, too. "Well, it *was* good to see you, Annie. A wonderful break for me from all the idle chatter of the tour."

"I can imagine."

He said a few other similar things, she did too, they managed it pretty well, and then the waiter set the folder with the check down, equidistant between them. They both reached for it, but Annie was quicker.

"Annie," he said sadly, "I'll take it."

"Oh, let me treat you," she said. She *should* pay for him, she thought. It would be like paying a tax on her vanity, on her foolishness. "It's the least I can do."

It was colder when she stepped outside, and some of the melt on the bricks seemed to have frozen, so that Annie found herself walking even more slowly and carefully than she had earlier.

He'd been apologetic about the mistake as they waited for her credit card, and she'd been politely, falsely reassuring. When she'd stood up to go, he tried to persuade her that they could start the conversation over. She doubted it, she said. And she did need to get back to the cat. "He's real," she said as she pulled on her coat. "And he'll be pissed."

Now, starting on her cautious way down Mount Auburn Street, she was thinking again that she was glad she'd paid. He'd taught her something tonight, taught her almost painlessly. Almost.

She'd thought she was memorable. How clear it was that she was not.

It wasn't a quality you possessed, she thought now. It was a quality other people endowed you with.

She felt small and foolish. Exposed.

She tried to tell herself that it didn't matter. She didn't even know Ian. He didn't know her.

Though she wondered what he *had* remembered of her. Something, anyway: he'd recognized her, after all. *Across a crowded room.* He'd been ready with her name.

But it struck her suddenly that he might not have remembered even that. Yes, probably he'd read it, read it on the Post-it Olympia had stuck on the cover of the book.

"Thank you, Olympia," she said aloud. She shook her head and laughed quickly, making her way down Mount Auburn Street.

She came to the bookstore. As she was passing its windows, she saw that it was busier than usual at this hour. Clearly, some of the audience from the reading had stayed on to move around the aisles, to stand among the shelves, browsing. She stopped outside, looking in.

And then she realized what it was, the detail that had bothered her when she entered the bookstore earlier tonight.

It was the chairs. The chairs were gone, the big, comfortable chairs Graham had loved so. The chairs where people sat and read through whole chapters of books they hadn't bought yet and perhaps had no intention of buying. The chairs, and so, of course, also the floor lamps that had sat next to them, with their shades glowing a welcoming deep orange in the evenings.

Their absence made the big room look more like a store, less like a library or a study in someone's home, and maybe that had been one of Sid and Olympia's reasons for getting rid of them; but she was overcome by a sense of loss as she turned to start her long walk home. She had sat in one of those chairs the first night she and Graham spent together, sat in it watching Graham behind the counter and pretending to read her book, *October Light*, while she waited for him to finish work so she could walk him home. She had read the same sentence over and over, and each time she lifted her eyes to look at Graham, he was always there, looking back at her.

The wait had seemed endless to her, but finally the lights blinked off and on several times, and the store began to empty out. She watched Graham talk to the last customers as he rang them up, watched him lock the door and turn the sign so it would say "Closed" to passersby, watched him turn off the lights and then come over to stand in front of her in the partial dark—the bluish light from the streetlamp reached in only at the front of the store.

"Don't get too comfortable," he said in his deep, rumbling voice. "You've got a promise to keep."

Now, making her way down the snowy streets, she was thinking of that other walk, their meandering, distracted walk down the summer sidewalks back to his apartment all those years ago.

She remembered how excited she'd been—almost dizzy with it: she kept bumping into him. He'd taken her hand, finally. Once they'd threaded through the nighttime crowd in Harvard Square (the jugglers, the people gathered around the street bands, some of them dancing), once they'd passed the tall brick fencing surrounding the dark of Harvard Yard and crossed Quincy Street into the emptier streets beyond, he had stopped and bent down to kiss her, gently, but searchingly.

"There," he said, standing straight again. "That's done."

Ash Street was treacherous, worse than Mount Auburn, the slippery shoveled pathways in front of the houses narrowed by the heaped-up snow on both sides. Sometimes there was no path at all, so that Annie had to climb over the crusted bank and then more or less *skid* down it on the outer side in order to walk in the street, watching for another cleared sidewalk to open up.

Most of the houses she passed were lighted inside. Here and there you could see someone, usually reading, sometimes watching television. In one case, a pair making music, he on the violin, she the piano. You could faintly hear its sweetness ringing out into the icy dark. Annie felt surprising tears rise in her eyes.

Now she came to Garden Street and turned left. The wider, civilized sidewalks here in front of the church and then the hotel were shoveled and salted, so for several blocks she could walk almost normally. She felt her body relax.

But when she crossed the street at the light and turned right into the relative darkness of Chauncey Street, her pace changed. She began to make her way more cautiously again down the icy sidewalks here.

32

ANNIE WAS IN a strange room as she came up from somewhere black. From nowhere—a deep, deep hole. She wasn't sure why she was here, or even where *here* was. There were voices from beyond a curtain, far away.

Someone came in and bent over her, looking curiously at her. Frowning. A woman. Annie didn't recognize her. Big nose. Iron-gray hair.

Now a pleasant, perhaps condescending, smile bloomed and changed the woman's face. "You're awake!" she said. Her voice was very cheerful, so Annie smiled back. "Yes," she said.

The woman set something down on Annie's bed and reached to smooth the covers over her.

"Much pain?" the woman asked.

Annie couldn't guess who this woman was or what she was asking about. Then she did feel it, yes, pain. Her arm. "No," she lied. "Not too much."

"Good. We'll try to keep it that way."

Bending over Annie, she began to talk. She was going to send Annie home with some medication, she said. She started to tell Annie details of when to take it, how often.

It was confusing. Annie was trying to write it down as the woman spoke.

After a moment the woman stopped, right in the middle of what she'd been saying. She was looking at Annie's hands, still moving. "What are you doing?" she asked. Her voice had changed, sharpened.

Annie felt ashamed. "Just trying to get it all down," she said. "There's so much."

The woman looked hard at Annie, and Annie too looked down at her own hands, her empty fingers bent around the pen that wasn't there. There was mild surprise at this. Actually, more in the way of bemusement than surprise.

When she spoke again, the woman's voice was different. Kinder. "Tell you what," she said. "I'm going to come back in a little bit. I want to let you rest for a while more. And then we'll call . . ." She looked down at the thing she was holding. A clipboard, it was. "We'll call Mrs. McFarlane, to let her know to come and get you," she said.

"Oh, no," Annie said. "It's *Mr.* McFarlane. It's Graham. My husband. He'll come and get me." This was the first thing Annie *knew*, and she felt an amazing welling up of pure relief: she remembered now who she was. And it was going to be all right. Because Graham would come. He would take her home.

The woman was silent for a moment. "Well, we'll figure it out," she said. She was speaking to Annie as if to a child. "For now, you just rest."

After the woman left, the light somehow grew dimmer in the alcove Annie seemed to be consigned to, so it wasn't hard to obey the woman. She closed her eyes, and she slept.

When she woke, she remembered it all.

Who she was, where she was, everything that had happened to her—and she wished she were no one again, waiting for Graham.

———

She'd fallen. On the way home from her drink with Ian, she'd fallen. She'd been carrying the book, Ian's book, in her left hand, so as she felt her feet leave the ground, she shot her right arm out, her free arm, to catch herself. But when the heel of her hand hit the ice, something in that arm gave way with a sharp, unforgiving pain, and then she was landing on her knees and her stomach. Her chin hit the icy sidewalk last, and her head was slammed upward—her head, which she'd been trying to hold up safely, out of danger, as she fell.

That was all of it, apparently.

She lay still for some moments on the ice, panting, feeling mostly relief—relief to be conscious, to be alive. Relief that it was over.

She became aware then of the pain, mostly in her arm, but also in her jaw, her chin. She ran her tongue over the inside of her upper lip and tasted blood, felt the dents her lower teeth had made in its surface as they were shoved upward into it.

When she rolled to the side to try to begin to stand, the astonishingly sharp pain in her arm stopped her.

She couldn't do this. She couldn't move.

But after a while—a minute maybe?—she tried again. This time she held her right arm pressed against her body with her left hand, held it as steadily as she could manage to while she lurched forward and up.

Her right knee was throbbing, burning, as she put her weight on it, as she stood, gingerly. "It's okay," she said aloud to herself. She didn't recognize her own voice. "It's okay. Just slowly, just slowly, just slowly, just slowly."

She tried a few steps. The knee was not too bad, she could walk. But the arm—it was broken. It had to be broken.

She could feel the warm blood on her chin now, her mouth tasted of it. Her head ached too, but she thought she could make it home. She had to let the cat in. *The real cat.* Then she'd figure out what she needed to do.

Every step on the remaining long blocks made the pain jolt through her arm. When she turned the corner onto Prentiss Street, she felt such relief she could have cried.

From the foot of the driveway, she could see Sam waiting under the light by the front door. When he saw her, he yowled his outrage over and over. Annie fumbled with her left hand into her purse for her keys, and then fumbled again to turn the key in the lock. Her right arm dangled, useless. The pain, which she couldn't have imagined could get worse, flashed with her slightest motion.

Inside, the idea of filling Sam's dish seemed impossible. Instead, she squatted and reached under the sink with her left hand for some of his dried food and tossed it across the kitchen floor.

Then she sat at the big table for maybe five minutes—or maybe ten, she couldn't have said. She let the tears rise and slide down her face—tears for the pain, for the terror of the moment of the fall, for her aloneness in all of this. When she'd finally calmed down, when she'd stopped crying, she went upstairs slowly and carefully, up to the landline telephone in Graham's study. Pressing her arm against the desk there, she used her left hand to call herself a cab to take her to the hospital.

"What does the other guy look like?" the cabdriver said, staring at her in the rearview mirror as she gingerly lowered herself into the back seat.

She had to wait two days, drugged nearly the whole time and with her arm in a sling, for the swelling to go down, for the orthopedic surgeon to fit her into his schedule. She watched television hour after hour, repeatedly nodding off and then waking to check the time, to see if she could take another oxycodone yet. On the third day, she came in for the surgery that would pin the pieces of her arm together.

———

In the car on the way home, she said to Frieda, "I forgot he was dead. Graham."

Frieda looked quickly over at her. "What do you mean?"

"I had some confusion, I guess. There are initials—P, O . . . post-operative . . . something or other." This is what the doctor had told her when he finally came by. It happened "not infrequently," he said, to the elderly after anesthesia—this confusion. He had warned her that she might have other episodes of it for a month or two, but said that it was a good sign that she'd recovered so quickly from this one, and that it was so minimal.

"Oh, yes," Frieda said now. She frowned and shook her head. "I don't remember the name either. It sounds like PTSD or something, but that's not it. Anyway, the doctor did tell me about it." She looked at Annie quickly. "You're not supposed to worry."

"I know," Annie said. After a moment had passed, she said, "I thought he was the one who would be coming to take me home—Graham—and I was so *glad*."

"Well, of course you were." Frieda reached over and touched Annie's arm.

After a minute, Annie said, "No. It was different from that. It was . . . more *important* than that."

She didn't know how to explain it to Frieda. Her gladness. It wasn't just that Graham was alive again. It was that she was too. *I loved him again*, she wanted to say. *I remembered that I loved him.*

Frieda stayed and had dinner with Annie. She'd brought over a soup she'd made, split pea with ham and dill in it, and she'd bought a loaf of dark rye bread at Formaggio to go with it.

While they ate, they talked about Annie's fall, about other family accidents. Lucas falling off a climbing structure in second grade and breaking his arm. Graham breaking his ankle trying to slide into third base at a bookstore game on the Common.

This was on account of Graham too, Annie felt—this ordinary, easy exchange with Frieda. The way he'd come back to her had made this possible.

Frieda had never broken anything. "Except, I suppose, my heart a few times."

"Oh well," Annie said. "We've all done that."

Frieda seemed to be waiting for her to go on, to discuss her broken heart.

Instead Annie talked about the night of her accident, the reading by Lucas's writer, Ian. Her quick drink with him afterward. She didn't mention his mistake, or her sense of shock, of humiliation. Or the relief, afterward, of escaping him. She told Frieda that she'd bought his book, but dropped it when she fell, something she hadn't realized until later. "So it's lying out there in the snow somewhere, I suppose."

"Oh, I can easily get you another," Frieda said.

She looked at Frieda, generous Frieda, her old friend. Her hair was even messier than usual, from the winter hat she'd been wearing. When they were leaving the recovery area, the nurse had said to them, "Are you guys sisters?" They must have looked puzzled, because she said, "Just, you know, you've got the same name." They looked at each other then, the tall Mrs. McFarlane, the short one, and they both laughed.

"No," Frieda had said. "No, but we might as well be."

Now Annie said to Frieda, "That's okay. I've got plenty to read."

Annie woke in the night. She'd been dreaming of Graham—so he'd come back to her in this way too.

She got up. Sam followed her into the bathroom, where he sat by the door watching her while she took some ibuprofen under the too-bright light, while she used the toilet. When she came out into the dark hall and turned toward her room again, he ran ahead of her and sprang onto the bed. She could hear his tail thumping slowly on the quilt as he waited for her.

She slid under the covers, easing him over with her body. He stood up, and then, as soon as she was still, he lay down again and settled himself against the rise of her hips under the covers. Slowly she felt his warmth radiate through the quilt. She reached over with her left hand and stroked him for a moment, feeling the way his body lifted slightly, the way it tensed in pleasure under her touch.

She was wide awake. She was trying to resurrect her dream, and couldn't. She just knew that Graham had been there, his enveloping, reassuring presence—and the same sense of joy she'd felt earlier in the day came to her again, a kind of peace descending on her. It was as though some part of her that had been missing had been returned.

She remembered so many things, things it seemed she'd forgotten. Things she must have willed herself to forget in her anger at him. The first time they'd made love—that wonderfully easy, slippery night when she'd walked him home from the bookstore. That he'd half carried, half danced her into his bedroom, his hand moving up under her skirt, his fingers finding her already, sliding into her already. That he'd gotten up hours later at a pause in things to go to the bathroom, and that on his return, he'd danced naked in the half-light of the room, his penis flopping as he leapt, his big body turning this way and that, as if he were offering it to her in this preposterous way. She remembered that she'd been embarrassed on his behalf at first, but then, slowly, amused, delighted. Later she'd thought that he was perhaps getting out ahead of the possibility of her finding him ridiculous by *being* ridiculous.

"Everybody loves a fat penis," he had said after he'd taken a deep theatrical bow and come back to bed. "Why not love the fat man who carries it around?"

Why not?

She *had* loved his fat penis, the way it filled her, how much she could feel it inside her. And she had loved him, the fat man—she had come to love even that about him—his bulk, his flesh. The touch of his beard, of his mouth on her body everywhere. How the talking in the dark—it didn't matter what about, just the passing of the words, the ideas, the jokes, back and forth—was part of all of it. She remembered his voice, whispering so as not to wake Sarah, but still somehow deep, rumbling. She remembered his laughing so hard once that he had to get out of bed and pace around the room to try to catch his breath.

All this, all this returned to her. Because of her fall. Because she'd gone to hear Ian read. Because of the chairs, the missing chairs that had made her think of Graham, made her remember that night with him.

Why had she gone to hear Ian, really?

Because of Graham. Because she'd still been angry at him—angry at him on account of Rosemary. Because, as she'd come to see, Ian—wanting the disturbance of Ian—had been, now just as much as when she was at MacDowell, a way of making up for something that had gone wrong between her and Graham.

She remembered again what she'd written to Gertie about Ian—so proudly. That nothing had happened. That he didn't matter, that it didn't matter.

But of course the truth was that she had wanted something to happen with him at MacDowell. She had wanted him. But not enough, apparently.

Had she been frightened? Was that it? Or was it just Graham, finally? Her sureness that in the end he was what she wanted.

Some of both, perhaps. In any case, she hadn't let it happen. They'd done that ridiculous thing instead. At the thought of it, she stirred uncomfortably and the cat once more had to readjust himself.

It seemed to her, lying there, that some of what she'd felt for Graham after the discovery of Rosemary was *envy*. Maybe partly because he had done it—fucked someone else—and she hadn't. But more, she thought, for his honest embrace of pleasure. Pleasure was who Graham was. It was his gift. It was the reason he'd said yes. As he almost always did.

"And me?" she thought, whispering it to herself. I said no, of course. But I didn't say no because of who I was, because I was the *moral being* that Graham wasn't. The reason I didn't do it was because I was scared, because Ian had scared me.

Not the person Ian was, no. She hadn't even known that person. She had understood that at the reading, she realized. She remembered now listening to him talk, hearing in what he said his bitterness— so separate from what was fine in the story he'd written.

No, Ian had scared her all those years ago because she was angry at Graham when she entered that dreamy time with him. Because her alienation from Graham had created the possibility of someone like Ian. And she had known somehow that sleeping with Ian would confirm that alienation, that distance from Graham, and she didn't want to do that. Because she loved him. She loved Graham.

She thought then of the uncomfortable sense of distance from Graham in the weeks just before he died. She had missed him in those weeks, she had wanted him back. She had been so happy when he'd suddenly seemed *himself* again, as she'd thought of it. When he toasted her beauty and Karen's, when he brought her flowers.

She had imagined that they would make love that night, that last night together, he had been so at ease through dinner, through the evening. When they left the rinsed dishes in the sink instead of cleaning up, she had been certain of it, even though she hadn't seen Graham taking his pill.

They'd gone upstairs. They undressed, they drifted separately back and forth to the bathroom to brush their teeth, to use the toilet. She had been aroused by his familiar nakedness, their nakedness together. He had touched her arm as they passed in the hallway once, and she had to catch her breath.

Finally they lay down together, and Graham turned off the light.

She reached over to him, started to move her hand over his furred chest and then down.

But he stopped her hand, he held it. "I'm so tired," he had said, and she could hear it, the exhaustion in his voice. "I just can't tonight. Can you forgive me?"

"I'll try," she said. She lay back down next to him. "*Big* effort, though."

They were quiet for a moment. He said, "I love you."

"I love you, too," she said into the dark.

"No," he said. "*I love you.* I always love you."

"Well, good. I know that."

"I *want* you to know that."

The window was open, and they heard one of the kids at the Caldwells' house calling out, asking if someone had locked the front door. They lay still for a while. Then Graham whispered, "God, I'm such a fat, sad, needy man. I need so much . . . stuff. From life."

After a moment, she said, "I thought you were a fat, *happy* man."

That's what she'd said. She'd made a joke of it, when he was trying to say something important to her.

Something about himself. Maybe even something about Rosemary. Yes, maybe he was beginning to try to explain Rosemary to her.

After a moment when neither of them said anything, when he was perhaps in some way hurt that she hadn't been able to hear him, to *listen*, he had rescued them. He said, "Fat? You think I'm fat?" And they laughed together.

There *was* so much stuff he needed, she thought now. She remembered his asking her to come and work in the bookstore once. It was during one of the periods in her life when she was lost, professionally. Lost and depressed. When she was renting herself out until something else came to her.

They were sitting in bed. Graham had been reading, and she had been pretending to read, but now her book was resting, opened, across her outstretched legs. She wasn't aware that he had stopped reading too, that he was watching her, until he began to speak, to make his suggestion, and she turned to look at him.

What had he said? *Have you ever thought of coming to work in the bookstore with me?* Something like that.

She hadn't been able to tell if he meant it. He was serious, but he might just have wanted to comfort her in some way.

She said no. She said it immediately, without even thinking about it. She said she knew he would devour her completely if she was his employee as well as his wife. Wasn't it enough that he had his cake? Why did he need to eat it too?

He had rescued them both then, too. "My cake! my cake!" he had cried, sliding over to embrace her, gobbling at her neck, her throat, opening her shirt to mouth her breasts.

What an impossible match they were! She could never have surrendered enough of herself to make it perfect for him. She sees that. And perhaps in some way that was part of what happened. That he needed too much, too much *stuff*, because of who he was. And that she couldn't give him enough, because of who she was.

He had understood that, it seems to her, and she hadn't.

And yet how open he was! How he kept coming at her with his love, with himself.

Her hand rests on the old cat, so warm, so alive.

She remembers what Sarah had said about her once long ago— that she was unreadable. But Graham had tried, always, to read her, to understand her. To keep her laughing, to keep her talking. The night he died, when they were talking in the shadowy kitchen, he had called her an open book. A book, open to him. She remembers that now too.

She whispers, "Reader, I married you."

Much later in the night, she senses the muffling of the house as the snow begins to fall, heavy and steady. She wakes once to the distant sound of the plow singing down Prentiss Street, and then goes back to sleep again.

In the early morning, in the strange gray half-light of the ongoing storm, she wakes again and gets up. The skylight in the bathroom is blank with snow and her face looks young in the gentle dusk the mirror offers. She goes downstairs. She feeds the cat. She makes her own coffee and sits at the big oval table drinking it, imagining Graham in this very spot, morning after morning, alone, as she slept on upstairs.

She remembers sitting here at the table the night John came over with his flowers, and her sudden conviction then, hearing his steps on the porch, that he was Graham, come back to her. She remembers too that after John left her alone that night, she had imagined how, in just that same way, she might wake up one day having dreamt Graham alive, and have to face her loss again. That this might happen over and over.

She watches the heavy flakes fall. They've bent the branches of the lilacs nearly to the ground, they've weighted the viburnum that Sarah and Lucas planted in memory of their father, they've covered the box shrubs that Karen disliked so much, they've made a circle of mysterious mounds out of the old chairs on the patio.

Looking out into this world, shrouded in the warm gray tones of an old photograph, full of the mystery of everything that's there but has been made invisible, she wants to record it, to make it last. She thinks for a moment of going upstairs to get her camera.

And then it comes to her, really for the first time since her fall, that she won't be able to take pictures, at least for a while.

That she will have to record all of this, remember it, on her own.

She feels it coming then, and she welcomes its return—the grief that seizes her.

About the Author

SUE MILLER is recognized internationally for her elegant and sharply realistic accounts of the contemporary family. Her books have been widely translated and published in twenty-two countries around the world. *The Good Mother* (1986), the first of her eleven novels, was an immediate bestseller (more than six months at the top of the *New York Times* charts). Subsequent novels include three Book-of-the-Month main selections: *Family Pictures* (a finalist for the National Book Critics Circle Award), *While I Was Gone* (an Oprah's Book Club selection), and *The Senator's Wife*. Her nonfiction book *The Story of My Father* was heralded by *BookPage* as a "beautiful, spare memoir about her relationship with her father during his illness and death from Alzheimer's disease." Her numerous honors include a Guggenheim and a Radcliffe Institute Fellowship. She is a committed advocate for the writer's engagement with society at large, having held a position on the board of PEN America. For four years she was chair of PEN New England, an active branch that worked with writing programs in local high schools and ran classes in prisons. She has taught fiction at, among others, Amherst, Tufts, Boston University, Smith, and MIT.